Bur

Robert Low is a Scottish journalist and historical novelist, with series based on the Vikings, and the early days of Scotland. He was also a war correspondent, reporting from Sarajevo, Romania, Kosovo, and Vietnam. He is now a full time fiction author.

Also by Robert Low

Brothers Of The Sands

Beasts Beyond The Wall
The Red Serpent
Beasts From The Dark

Border Reivers

A Dish of Spurs
Burning the Water
Shake Loose the Border

ROBERT LOW

BURNING THE WATER

CANELO

First published in the United Kingdom in 2020 by Canelo

This edition published in the United Kingdom in 2021 by

Canelo
31 Helen Road
Oxford OX2 0DF
United Kingdom

A CIP catalogue record for this book is available from the British Library.

Print ISBN 978 1 80032 223 3
Ebook ISBN 978 1 80032 090 1

Grateful acknowledgement is made to Derek Stewart and Julia Stewart for
supplying reenactment images used on the cover artwork.

Look for more great books at www.canelo.co

Printed and bound in Great Britain by Clays Ltd, Elcograf S.p.A.

Jack the lad Horner,
Crouched in his corner
Fingering a Christmas pie
Stuck in a thumb,
Pulled out a plum
And said 'Clever boy am I!'

Prologue

They went through three tapestry-hung salons hemmed with lines of bodyguard brilliant in Royal livery. There were birds somewhere in the high reaches of it; Henry Rae heard their wings whirring even as he was marvelling at the third salon, with its chair and canopy of rich embroidery. He should never have got so far – and certainly never expected to be ushered into the privy chamber beyond.

And out again. There was a flurry behind him and he half-turned into the sheened face of a rough-dressed man clutching a heavy box; behind him came two more, one carrying the largest pincers Rae had ever seen. In such a Royal sanctum they were as unlike the liveried servants and languid courtiers you would expect to find as a cow-pat is to a steak and ale pie. They looked at Henry Rae, embroidered and riotous with thread, as if he had dropped from the moon.

'Beg pardon, yer lordship,' the man said and knuckled his forehead as he was forced along by the scowls of the servants. The usher smiled apologetically, though Rae could see sweat on his forehead and the sight made him break out in sympathy.

'A mishap,' the usher muttered, then saw Rae's alarmed look and waved a hasty, placating hand.

'Nothing serious… His Majesty insisted on seeing you at once, Master Herald…'

They went on through doors and down corridors until they burst out into the tilt yard. Even so far away, the figure at the centre of the huddle could be heard roaring and the usher blanched.

Nearby, ostlers held a brace of caparisoned warhorses, partly under a huge contraption which Rae thought was a siege engine until he got closer, picking his way fastidiously over the churned, dung-slathered ground.

Then he saw that it was a lifting device and, dangling from the end of it, a figure in beautiful tournament plate armour turned slowly, the curses drifting and fading as he circled. A man held the removed helmet while others struggled to steady him; Rae saw the man with the wooden box start to fetch out tools, one after the other.

The hanging man turned and Rae saw the red, sweat-soaked face, the artificed auburn of beard pushing over the constriction of throat metal like the inside of a burst saddle, the eyes boar red and glowering. The king.

He knelt.

'Steady me, steady me, you bastard-born whelps.'

Men strained to stop the king turning. The man with the tools was a smith, Rae saw, already moving to one huge armoured leg. He banged it hard with a hammer and the king roared.

'Have a care, you dolt. You cunny-licking son of a whore, I'll rip your entrails out…'

'Can't get it offen, pardon Your Grace's indulgence, unless I bangs 'er 'ard.'

The king did not reply and the smith struck again, the bell-tone echoing round the yard. The king winced and said nothing and Henry Rae remembered the legendary leg, foul and festering and not allowed to heal by his physicians, who stated that the wound should be allowed to drain bad humours out. Every time it started to heal over, they'd cut it open, tie back the sides and fill the rawness with pellets of gold.

If anyone knows pain, Henry Rae thought, it is King Henry Tudor, Eighth of that name, God save and keep him…

'That man – is that the Berwick Herald? Is that Harry Ree, Sadler's man?'

Rae, jerked from his reverie, stepped forward and bowed, hoping his tremble did not show.

'It is, Your Majesty. Henry Rae, Berwick Pursuivant if it please Your Majesty, attached with Secretary of State Sadler while he is treasurer of the Earl of Hertford's army…'

'My army, you dolt – stop wittering. Give him the letter… the writ. Give him it.'

An unsmiling clerk handed Rae a fat package, bound and sealed with at least three great wax dangles. He had time to see it was marked for Sir Ralph Sadler, Secretary of State. It was also addressed to Sir Edward Seymour, Earl of Hertford and Warden of the Scottish Marches.

'That's the writ to extend my hand in the north. Have both of them read it with care,' Henry bawled. 'It tells them exactly what has to be done. Get you gone, man and tell them to read it with care… God's blood, you arse, what are you now doing?'

The smith was prising at the armoured knee joint, his efforts forcing the holding men to strain harder to keep the king from turning; the clerk stepped close to Rae, speaking fast and soft.

'You are dismissed, Sir Herald. Remove yourself soonest – he has discovered that an hour in armour has swole his bad leg so large it cannot be got out but by cutting off the plate. His Majesty is now in the worst of moods.'

Henry Rae backed away, bowed, turned and started to scurry off, thinking on how the king was supposed to be leading his army against France this year while the Earl of Hertford punished the Scots.

He could not see how the king could lead if he had to be winched on to a horse – if one could be found stout enough to carry him – and had to be cut out of his armour after an hour.

The bell sounds of the smith's hammer did not drown the roars, all the scurrying way back out of the tilt yard.

'Tell Hertford. Burn their homes. Raze their lives. Burn their ships. Burn their children and their wives and any who resist. Burn their damned dogs and sheep.'

The bell rang out like a knell and the king's roar followed it as a baleful echo.

'Tell the Earl, man. Burn them out. Burn everything, God curse them.'

Another knell and a fading tendril of hate from the false gold, hoarse-voiced Henry, King of England, chased Rae into a corridor.

'Burn the very water…'

One year later – Ancrum Moor, near Jedburgh

The stink was old and familiar, that iron pervade of spilled blood laced with dung and bile and the weft of men's fear. Fiskie was well used to it now, all the same, so that he barely snorted once and Batty had no trouble picking him over and round the great sprawl of corpses.

Knots of men had gathered, some silent, some jabbering nervously and all of them with the air of folk who no longer knew what to do. Batty recognised this, too – the aftermath of foulness, when men could not meet each other in the face for what they had done, nor never would manage the same in a looking glass.

There were some, all the same, whose hate made thin grim lines of their lips and the tightest stitch of them turned his face up as Batty approached. He was streaked with mud and worse, his gilded Nuremburg half-armour dinted with new scars, his slashed, puffed breeches and big overtopped boots scuffed and muddied. He nodded wordlessly to Batty, then stuck out a grimed hand with a leather bottle in it.

'The victors deserve a lick of *eau-de-vie*,' he growled, then glanced round at the carnage. 'The losers need it – but to the Devil with them.'

'Aye, aye, General,' Batty said, raised it in a toast, swigged a long time, then handed it back and glanced at the sour fruit swinging from the stunted tree.

'Your Grace,' the growler corrected, taking the flask and Batty acknowledged his error of protocol with a flap of his one hand; the Douglas Earl of Angus valued his station and lineage like a woman her new babe.

Though he was not nearly as innocent as one, Batty added to himself. It had taken the Earl long enough to find it, but he had had men scour the bare, bird-wheeping roll of the moor for a tree, since Eure, as commander of the English host, deserved no less. His second, Layton, they had drowned. The third Englishman everyone wanted to kill, George Bowes, had escaped.

'Remember Broomhoose,' Douglas had growled while Layton thrashed and burbled, spluttered and, after too long a time, died. Broomhoose, Batty recalled, had been a wee bastel fortress, a two-floored affair and one of the many burned out by the harrying English under Layton and Sir Ralph Eure the year before. An auld wummin of note had died in it, but why that place, above all the others, had to be remembered in particular was a mystery to Batty Coalhouse.

After all, the larger part of southern Scotland was a black desert. Jedburgh and Kelso were smouldering ruins, nearly a brace-hundred of other wee bastels and sundry dwellings scorched to the ground, four hundred folk slain, eight hundred more taken, ten thousand cattle, twelve thousand sheep – the list went on and on. Batty had heard it litanied out by the Earl of Angus, marvelling as usual at how wee rolls of paper could hold all this memory.

Batty could not read at all, but he saw between the lines for all that – the Douglas Earl of Angus was less bothered by his lists, or a wee noblewoman turned to ash in Broom House than the fact that Eure and Layton had pissed on the tombs of the Douglas while his estates burned.

That had brought the bitterest of rivals together – the Douglas Earl of Angus and the Regent of Scotland, the Earl of Arran – and took them here, to the wind-hissed moorland below Peniel Heugh and a victory over the English, marvellous as an eight-legged horse.

'You found a limb, then,' Batty said, nodding at the swinging figure and Douglas scoured up some spit, thought better of it and swallowed.

'We will cut him down soon and then send his head home.'

The men nearest him shifted uneasily at that and Batty thought the Earl would have trouble finding men with the belly left to take the head of Sir Ralph Eure, having to step through the slorach of badly-smouldering fire and mud to take his blackened feet and legs and lift him down. Still, it was none of his affair – he was interested in the living.

'Ye have prisoners, Your Grace,' he said and the Earl nodded, scowling, then hauled off his burgonet as if it suddenly weighed too much for his head; under it, his hair was plastered thinly to his scalp.

'There,' he said, pointing. 'They claim to be assured men who saw the light and came to our aid. I have my doubts of it.'

The men were hunched and trying not to look at anyone. They had been stripped of steel bonnet and weaponry, but kept their dung-coloured jacks, the pale mark of the X clear to see on the torn, stained quilting, wisps of stitching where they had torn off the red cross of the English when they saw which way the icy war wind was blowing. It left a pale shadow of itself, but since their counterparts wore a white X in the same place, it was as acceptable a way of changing sides as any and as old as the Border hills they rode over.

They were mainly Cessford Kers, the left-handed men from the Scots side of the Border. Among them were Nixons and Olivers, the latter arguing that they had been forced to it since Eure had 'taken their heidmen, Dandy, Rinyan and Patty, for hostage'. They had been united as 'assured men' enjoying pay and plunder from Fat Henry and his captains, under duress or not; they had become a lot less assured when they tasted powder and death on the wind-mourned moor at Ancrum.

None of them mattered to Batty; he saw the one man he wanted, the one in the stained, torn remains of a richer fabric – a tabard still coloured despite the slime and mud and worse. He had not removed it, of course, because a Herald's cote was better than armour.

'You,' Batty growled and the man looked up, his face streaked with filth and fear and misery. There was a moment when Henry Rae thought that, for all his Herald immunity, his time on earth was done and that was when he looked Batty Coalhouse in the face.

It was a harsh face, an undershot jaw curving up a scimitar beard of tow-coloured hair to meet the scowl of a lintel of brows coming down on a blade of pitted nose. Bog-water browned by weather and poor washing, marked and scored by age and bad usage that face, Rae thought. Yet the eyes were clear and grey as a storm-sea, even if they nestled above bruise-blue pouches.

'You are Berwick Pursuivant,' Batty said to him. 'If you want to escape the hemp, you had better tell all.'

'Who are you to say who escapes the hemp? A Herald cannot be harmed.'

The Earl stepped forward, truculent and with that boar-pig scowl all the Douglas had. From the one who fought with Bruce to this, Batty thought – but he had the measure of it.

'The man whose brace of guns gave you victory,' he replied shortly. 'Up there on the far slope of Palace Hill. We fired them until they turned too hot for safety, my good lord. Until one burst and killed two good men of mine.'

The Earl of Angus scrubbed his beard and then ran his hand over his sweated hair as if suddenly weary. It was true enough – this fat-bellied, one-armed *ingenieur* and his

8

brace of sakers had ravaged the Landsknecht and Spanish mercenaries as they rolled over the hill, all triumphant shouts and ribboned weaponry. Torn them to shreds with hot gusts of sharp metal and sent them running back the way they had come, slashed and stabbed and hacked by a vengeful pursuit of exultant Scots.

Batty Coalhouse was due more than a shivering, shit-legged fool in a fancy *cassack* – but while the Earl of Angus might escape censure for the killing of Eure and Layton, a Herald was a different stamp. No one would survive the killing of the Berwick Pursuivant.

'He is mine,' the Earl said, 'whether you care for it or not, Master Coalhouse. You may put him to the question if it be not too harsh – though it is a maze to me what he can tell you.'

But he already knew what Batty Coalhouse, master of the great gun, the slow match and the *granada*, wanted to know. It was what he always wanted to know – the where-abouts of one Maramaldo, who had done him some hurt years before. Cut his arm off, Douglas had heard, which was no surprise when you knew Maramaldo. There must be a long line of folk seeking redress of that mercenary captain, the Earl thought, for he is a blood-drenched chiel. Then he tried to ignore the swinging remains of Eure, an accusing dead stare in the corner of his eye.

He waved and Batty leaned on the high pommel of Fiskie and looked down at Rae.

'You carry messages, I jalouse,' he said. 'From court to court. Harry Ree – I have heard of you.'

Rae looked from him to the Earl and back again. Master Coalhouse was not a name he knew but for all this was a fat, one-armed man the look from him washed Henry Rae in a sluice of cold sweat.

'I do not know of you, Master Coalhouse. Yet His Grace the Earl has captured the baggage and I have been searched – there is nothing privy you do not know or cannot read.'

'Aye, indeed,' the Earl growled. 'We have read it. Put all to fire and sword. Man, woman and child without exception where any resistance is raised against you. I have seen your king's instructions to the Earl of Hertford, sir. Burn the very water, he was told. It is scorched into the hearts of all here. But if you have more, we would hear it.'

Rae had the grace to flush through his filth, but Batty merely scowled at the Earl.

'You have given him to me for this moment, have ye not, Your Grace?'

When the Earl nodded reluctantly, Batty turned back to Harry Rae.

'Then you are safe enow, Master Ree, if you have an answer to my next question and one I like. I cannae read.'

He paused and Rae waited.

'Maramaldo,' Batty said. Rae's eyebrows went up, for it was not what he had expected.

'What of him?'

'You ken of him?'

'Who does not. Him it was who did the deed at this Broom House…'

He tailed off, realising the spectre he had summoned up by the heads that turned to him, eyes feral.

'Aye,' Batty declared, soft and vicious. 'Captain General Fabrizio Maramaldo and his paid men. A byword for cruel, even in a land as abandoned by God as this. You ken where he is?'

Rae considered the question and saw the unconscious movement of Batty Coalhouse's sole hand towards the stump of his missing arm. A half-gesture, no more, but it told Rae all he needed about why Batty hunted the man and he narrowed his eyes thoughtfully.

Maramaldo had not been welcome in England, Rae remembered – the Pope had banned him from Christian armies years before, but King Henry thought that as good as a sealed letter of recommendation. Not against the French, mind you, for Maramaldo was too uncivil for them. But the Scots… well, the Scots deserved the likes of a Maramaldo and so he came north to join all the other Spanish, German and Italian mercenaries the king depended upon in the north.

Yet even here Maramaldo's cruelty had so sickened Sir Ralph Sadler that he'd sent him off on a false errand, escorting captured Scottish guns back to London. That was weeks before, Rae told Batty, spilling it like bile and as fast as he could get the words out. He will be in Newcastle now, or even York.

When the blade flashed, he yelped – but it was only Batty's big sword in his sole fist, slicing Rae's hands free.

'Run,' Batty advised, then he smiled and, looked at the slow-turning corpse of Sir Ralph Eure. There was a note pinned to his chest, but Batty did not need to read to know what it said; everyone had growled it to the captives they were gralloching.

Found guilty of Burning the Water.

As a message to Fat Henry it was as subtle as dropping your breeches and waggling your bare arse. Eure had been a disliked man since 1541, when he had started expelling Scots settled on the Northumberland side of the divide, handing their land and living to English folk – but, for all that, no one liked the blued face of him, nor could look for long at the blackened, blistered, burned feet and lower legs.

'Two gone,' Douglas growled, wiping his lips dry with the back of one stained hand as he watched Batty stare, 'and only Bowes to go. We almost had wee Georgie here – he is sleekit, that yin – but we will get him in the end.'

Some folk cheered, but it was half-hearted at best, from men too sickened by slaughter to be welcoming more of the same. There was fear in it, too, for this was the Douglas who had exercised his right of pit and gallows, the Law of hanging or drowning the guilty. It had been the Earl's boot on the neck of Layton that had driven that man's face into the muddy puddle serving as Pit and few were made cheered who looked on His Grace the Douglas now.

So it was an astonishment to everyone in that blood-soaked place of foul deeds, keening wind and dead, when Batty began to croon, tuneless as a sick crow as he urged Fiskie away.

'My love he built me a bonny bower, and clad it a' wi' a lilye flower. A brawer bower ye ne'er did see, than my true love he built for me.'

Chapter One

Berwick on the Tweed
Spring, 1545

He dreamed one of The Dreams. Not the one in Florence with Michelangelo. The one where Maramaldo cut off his arm. It was an old familiar, this dream, but this time Batty knew it for what it was.

There was the town, besieged by Maramaldo as he tried to be a *condotterie* of the first rank. There was the Red Tower which marked the gate of the place – Asti, a nothing walled town on the Tanaro, important only because Maramaldo wanted it.

Out there, under the gate, Batty's da lit the slow match on the *petard* he had been forced to arrange while Maramaldo pointedly paraded Batty and his ma as a warning not to fail. Faced with the inevitable, Batty's da had blown the charges, himself and half the tower out across the plain. There had been forethought revenge in it, all the same, cold and bitter as only the Kohlhases of Saxony could deliver it – triple the powder and the blast trained outwards, so that the debris whirled Maramaldo off his horse and his army off its kilter.

Batty had almost beaten Maramaldo to death with a ramrod in the aftermath, but folk had wrestled him down and, next day, a limping, bruised Maramaldo, pissing blood and smouldering with anger, had botched the work of chopping the offending arm from Batty.

This dream, however, had the wrong arm lashed and stretched for the farrier's axe and Batty could not understand why his right seemed fastened when it was his left that had been stretched for easier aim.

He woke, blinking from his own dream-shrieks into the smell of cooked leeks and foul straw. He took a moment to find out he was curled by a cold damp wall and that something furred and foul had nested the night in his mouth; his head thundered.

The smell of the leeks made his rank mouth water all the same and he scrambled round to see a man sitting at a rickety table eating with a spoon. It was a porray of leeks and the drips ran off his moustache when he grinned over at Batty.

'Aye. Aye – awake then? Yer head must be loupin'. Thirsty?'

All of which was true and Batty rolled over to take the proferred horn beaker of water, only to find his right arm shackled to the wall, which accounted for the strangeness of the dream. He looked at the man, who looked back at him and, grinning evilly, gave a shrug and drank from the cup himself.

'Now there's a shame,' he said insincerely and Batty knew he was not about to get up and bring him water, porray or anything else. He studied the man, from his broad, bearded face with its flat nose and sneer, down the shirt and jerkin to the breeches and boots. Not the best, but good clothes; the boots were for riding and Batty suspected that this was no cobbler or baker.

The fact that they were both in the same jail added weight to his assessment.

He lay back and thought about how he had ended here. He was fairly sure it was in Berwick and almost certain it was the Tolbooth prison, for he had come down to the town, an old haunt. He had fallen in with some old friends at the Brig Tavern and tried to lose the stink of powder and death for a little while.

It was, he admitted, unwise to have done so, for Berwick was English and, even though it was still open to Scots, Berwick was nervous. Ancrum Moor would be on all lips and those who fought in it on the winning side would be suspect and unwelcome.

Batty recalled playing Primero and losing, which fact he had not liked. He remembered, vaguely, announcing that he would take wagers on whether the notoriously crumbling walls of Berwick would fall down if he pissed on them. The gunners he had fallen in with agreed with cheers, for they lived in fear of the swaying towers they occupied crashing down if they ever fired off the ordnance mounted on them. The masons, having recently rebuilt the very part of the wall Batty was pissing on, saw it differently. The inevitable fight was bloody, tangled and noisy.

After that Batty could recall only a strange, translucent fog of *eau de vie* in quantity and, somewhere in it, a woman. He was sure there had been a woman...

'You are awake then.'

Batty craned round and saw the bland, chap-cheeked face of a Doorward peering through the grille on the iron-studded door. He knew the man, fought through the reek of his head for a name and came up with Cuthie. He said it and the man beamed and nodded as if he had been recognised by the king himself.

'The Sergeant said you might be,' he said. 'If not, I was to wake you – the Sheriff himself is hearing your case.'

Batty sucked that in and managed to extract the lees of something from it. That he was in the Tolbooth and not the garrison prison, the one known as the Hole In The Wall and reserved for those likely to hang. And of the Tolbooth cells, he was in the Fourpenny Ward – tuppence if shared. There was a Gentlemen's Commons across the way – a half-shilling a day – and the Deep for those with no money to pay their way. The Deep was mainly seepage from the drains.

So – Tolbooth comfort then. And Sergeant was a man he thought he knew well enough.

'Sergeant?' he queried. 'Would that be Red Rowan Charlton?'

Cuthie smiled and nodded.

'The same. Who says to bring you up and in presentable state.'

The door racked open and the Doorward stepped in, unshackled Batty from the wall and stepped back cautiously.

'The Sergeant also said it would be a pleasantry to himself if you cause no row, for it will only make matters worser.'

Batty levered himself up, brushed as much of the straw off him as he could reach with his one hand and looked at the man sitting at the table, now dipping bread into his porray.

'Bigod, you eat well in this lock-up,' Batty declared and Cuthie glanced almost apologetically from Batty to the man and back.

'If you have coin, you do,' he answered and the man grinned broadly, then waved expansively at the long-handled skillet of porray sitting in front of him.

'Eat. Help yersel' noo you have a hand for it... if you have the tuppence worth to pay, that is.'

Batty nodded thoughtfully, picked up the skillet, hawked deeply and spat in it, then emptied the contents on the man's head. There was a pause, a long moment of horror, where Cuthie's mouth started to form an O and the man sat, hunched up and dripping leeks and amazement.

Then, just as he bellowed, Batty backhanded the pot into his face with a dull clang; the man flew off his bench and into the wall, slid down and lolled; his breathing snored in and out of his broken nose, bubbling blood. Cuthie looked at Batty with utter horror.

Batty studied the copper skillet for a dent and smiled at the Doorward.

'No row,' he said, and tossed the skillet to one side. 'For the pleasantry of the Sergeant.'

'Christ in Heaven,' Cuthie said, looking back at the slumped figure as he followed Batty out of the cell, locking it firmly behind him. 'You have made a bad enemy there.'

'There are no good ones. Who is it?'

'Tam Wallis. One of the Wallis' of Twa Corbies. He did not get to be called Evil-Willit Tam because of his lamblike nature. In here for his ramstampit behaviour in the White Hoose tavern.'

Batty knew both man and kin by reputation only – it was a wise man who knew all those he was likely to have to end up hunting down – and merely shrugged, following Cuthie up the wind of steps and out into the Tolbooth entrance. Red Rowan waited, busy checking a fistful of papers and frowning as he laboriously formed the words.

'Was there trouble?' he asked, glancing up as the pair came in and Cuthie looked sourly at Batty, then shook his head.

'Tam Wallis spilled his breakfast,' he replied and Red Rowan, too busy to notice the exchange, merely nodded and smiled as if seeing Batty for the first time.

'Your case is up in a minute. The Sheriff is in a fair mood, so speak when you are spoken to and take your punishment.'

'For whit am I charged?' Batty demanded.

'Vagrancy, which is serious. Drunken and lewd behaviour which is the same.'

'You might have stayed your hand a little,' Batty replied, feeling his head thunder and Red Rowan grinned. His was not a pleasant face, having too much snub nose and a sanded look to it thanks to pale hair and lashes; he looked like a too-lean piglet.

'I did not strike you at all. I sent you *eau de vie* in quantity and Sweetlip Maggie Trotter and let nature exhaust an auld man and take its course. I plucked you, blissed as a babe, from herself's naked embrace all the way to the wee prison.'

That was nice of him and Batty said so, wondering what he owed.

'I had a whole angel in my pouch,' he said hopefully and Red Rowan laughed.

'The most of that went on a bad run at Primero,' he answered. 'The rest went on repairing your good graces with the Old Brig and some masons for damage done.'

Batty scowled. Eight whole shillings, gone like smoke.

'What paid for the drink and the woman, then? Am I in debt?'

Red Rowan shook his head, while folk moved round them like wraiths; the Tolbooth was busy of a Monday and Batty's was not the only sore head in it.

'Contingency fund,' he answered, laying one finger along his nose. 'Better than having you wreck more of the Old Brig and men's faces if I had tried to drag you.'

He leaned forward, serious as plague and whispering.

'And better yet than leave you to rant on about killing at Ancrum and your soul. Folk know you as Batty Coal-house, thief-taker and master gunner, lately with the army of the Scotch. Even those who believe you are vending yourself for King Henry's assurance are learning that menfolk they knew well are not coming home. The only reason you are not in chains, Batty, is because Sir Cuthbert is not inclined to follow the example of Carlisle. They have banned all Scotch from the market there.'

Batty acknowledged that with a half-ashamed admittance of wave. Sir Cuthbert Ratcliff was Captain of Berwick Castle and the only real power in the town now that the Marshall of Berwick, Gower, had been packed off to the Fleet in London following a dispute with the Warden of the English East March. Who was, Batty recalled sickeningly, none other than Sir William Eure, wrathful, plum-faced old da of the Ralph Eure Batty had seen swinging his scorched feet from a tree on Ancrum Moor.

Batty swallowed. He could easily have been in the Hole In The Wall, waiting a hemping and vowing to give up the drink. Again.

He did not explain that the soul mentioned had not been his, but a horse called The Saul, which had carried him for a wheen of years until shot out from under him by a moudiewart bastard called Geordie Bourne, on instructions from the Armstrong Laird in the Debatable Land. Not that the Armstrong Laird hated The Saul – it was Batty who had been the target.

The Saul had never recovered fully and had spent the last of his days at Powrieburn, where Batty had got Fiskie, his present mount. It was after Ancrum, already adding to the stains on his sleeping, that Batty had heard The Saul had died, kicking his feet up and rolling in the ecstasy of spring.

Mintie Henderson, mistress of Powrieburn, had been sorrowed and pleased to see him both at the same time, said he could bide longer – but Batty knew that Powrieburn wanted the powder-stained bloody memory of him gone and so he had politely accepted a night and then left, a little empty where The Saul had once been.

He had come down to Berwick, war or no war and tried to see if old faces and places would leach the sourness from him. That and drink a combination which, Batty reflected moodily, had merely added to his toll of troubles.

'Besides,' Red Rowan said, oblivious to all this turmoil in Batty's head, 'there are King's Men riding up and down the road atween here and Newcastle. Lobsters, no less and looking for ne'erdowells like yourself.'

'Lobsters?' Batty asked and Red Rowan nodded, frowning. Batty thought about it. Lobsters – those who wore Hertford's red livery – were hen's teeth north of Newcastle now and must be seeking someone in particular.

He said as much, but Red Rowan shook his head.

'If they are, they keep it close-mouthed,' he answered, then rubbed his beard with confusion. 'It seems to me they do not know what they seek, but will grab up every likely ragged-arse they come across and cart them south to be put to the Question by folk who do know.'

He stopped and looked Batty grimly in the eye.

'They want someone or something, Batty,' he declared. 'Just be sure it isnae you.'

Batty subsided thoughtfully and they waited, while wee legals muttered in knots and the Guild called-out men leaned on their halberds and failed to look like a Trained Band company, for all their fustian jacks and gilt latten sleeve chains. Some sign was given and Red Rowan stirred.

'That's us – follow on.'

He led, the Doorward brought up the rear and they moved up the Tolbooth steps to the next floor, all waxed wood and heraldic badges. The Sheriff was Sir Nicholas Strellie, according to the pompous announcement made by a staff-carrying official, sweating in the unseasonal heat.

There was an exchange of documents, a muttering between Sergeant and Sheriff, then Red Rowan stepped back and stood, silent and respectful, while the Sheriff studied, turned documents, turned them back.

Then he raised his hatchet of a face and peered at Batty over the bridge of his thick-rimmed eyeglasses.

'You are Bartram Coalhouse, of no fixed abode?'

'None in Berwick.'

'Guilty of the charge of vagrancy, then.'

Batty bristled at that and Red Rowan laid a quieting hand on his forearm, a gesture the sheriff noted with a scowl.

'I am not the vagrant,' Batty declared indignantly. 'I have coin.'

Then he thought about it and blinked at the lie.

'I can get coin. Besides, the Old Brig kens me well enough and I have bided there before this.'

Sir Nicholas studied, frowned, then peered at Batty over his precariously perched eyeglasses.

'The Old Brig,' he repeated flatly. 'This would be the place you ruined.'

'He has friends in high places ower the Border,' Red Rowan offered and the sheriff gave him back a glaucous eye.

'And low, I have no doubt. But his friends are all on the wrong side of the Border.'

The moment hung on a rusty nail of silence. The penalty for vagrancy was to have a hole put in one ear with a hot iron but the shaming mark of it was as much a pain as the branding.

'I can stand surety for him,' Red Rowan said and Batty breathed a little, blessed the man and then wondered what he would have to pay to rid himself of the debt.

The Sheriff considered it for a moment, then shrugged and pronounced.

'Jail.'

Batty heard Red Rowan sigh.

'Public lewdness,' the Sheriff went on, and the peering returned. 'With an unknown woman. In the street outside the Old Brig Tavern.'

'Aye, weel,' Batty said. 'I am certain the drab was too foxed to know where she was an' doubly certain I did not care. Drink had been taken by then.'

The stare intensified and then Sir Nicholas removed the eyeglasses.

'You do not much care for anything, legal or otherwise, I have heard. A thief-taker for money, I have heard, and more inclined to the dead than the alive in a posted Bill.'

'You have heard wrongwise,' Batty answered shortly, 'for there is no money in dead. Wardens who pay for those who foul served Bills like them alive, so they can hang them, all perjink and legal.'

The Sheriff glowered a moment.

'Lewdness and drunkenness – guilty. Fine and another ten-day.'

It was lenient – pillory in the stocks had been a possibility, but Sir Nicholas was no fool and knew the worth of Batty and the folk in 'high places'. Batty heard Red Rowan growl under his breath; the Sheriff spilled wax on a document, stuck his seal ring in and handed it off to a fat clerk, then waved Batty and Red Rowan away with a call of 'next'.

'If you believe for a minute that you will be sitting about my jail being served hand and foot and not paying a farthing for it,' Red Rowan muttered, taking Batty by the arm. He had more to say but stopped and stared at the length of blade in his face.

Beyond, men spilled into the room, armed and swift; a guard dropped his halberd with a clatter and put his hands in the air, while another gave a brief threatening flourish and was pistol-whipped to the ground by the long barrel of a caliver. A clerk screamed like a woman.

'Stay. Be doucelike.'

The voice was sharp and clear as a barking dog, the owner a barrel-shaped man in a cloak designed to hide his padded jack and his brace of big bollock daggers. He had a gimlet look to him and the half-dozen or so with him reeked of greased smoke and wickedness. The Sheriff glared at him.

'This is the Tolbooth. I am Sir Nicholas Strellie – are you mad?'

'I ken fine who you are and have heard you enough.'

The voice slashed through the room and Batty backed quietly to one side of Red Rowan, away from the crowd; he felt something dig him in the ribs and turned into the ragged-beard grin of a grime-faced man with a fistful of sword. He had a burgonet, a stained and slashed jack leaking wisps of wool padding from the old cuts and a backsword – the very image of every reiver Batty had ever seen. Batty waved in surrender and the man, seeing a fat one-armed old man, relaxed and lowered the blade.

'I am John Wallis of Twa Corbies,' said the barrel-shaped man and the Sheriff polished his eyeglasses furiously on the lace of one cuff; he clearly knew the name. Men bustled behind all their backs, tearing open kists and drawers.

Batty heard men crashing about below and thought about the Tolbooth prison and the man called Evil-Willit Tam Wallis. All broken nose and vengeance by now, he thought. Reeking of leek and about to be loosed…

'You have presided ower petitions regarding the ownership of my lands,' Wallis went on. 'The ones where Dacre of Lanercost claims his rights.'

'You have no deeds or registry,' the Sheriff said, replacing his eyeglasses on his nose. 'If you feel aggrieved, apply for redress…'

'We have,' Wallis interrupted. 'We have told you of deeds and registry, going back to the Flood and supposedly lodged safely in Edinburgh.'

'It appears there was a conflagration…' Sir Nicholas attempted and Wallis waved him silent; since the hand doing it was full of a long-muzzled dagg, the Sheriff did so promptly. Batty watched the grim of Wallis' face, the gaunt determination of it. It was, he realised, a face matched well with the body it was attached to, for the one was as grim as a wet gallows and the other was a solid wall for it to perch on.

'Aye,' Wallis agreed. 'There was a fire. Deeds and registry from the time afore the coming of Christ went up in smoke. But no' the Bastard Dacre's claimed writs. They survived, to be brought here for use in the upcoming case.'

Someone thrust paper at him and Wallis took it; sparks flew and were breathed into flame; Red Rowan stirred and Batty laid a quieting hand on his elbow, so that he glanced, took the hint and subsided.

Wallis put the flame to the papers, which crackled and smoked; wax seals melted and he dropped them to the polished wood floor. The Sheriff, alarmed, made to stamp them out and was backhanded casually to the ground, so that Red Rowan growled and started to spring forward, only to be hauled up short by Batty's iron grip.

'Help up His Lordship,' he declared blandly and Red Rowan found himself obeying. Wallis, unsmiling, looked at them with his apple-pip eyes and added more papers to the flames.

'There was a conflagration,' he declared. 'My Lord Thomas Dacre, the Bastard of Lanercost, has lost his claimed deeds and writs to Wallis lands, which did not survive.'

His men laughed like hunting dogs and the Sergeant bristled his own hackles.

'You will never get beyond the walls,' Red Rowan declared savagely, lifting the dazed Sheriff to his unsteady feet; there was blood on his mouth and beard and he blinked once or twice.

'My eyeglasses...'

They were smashed but it did not matter. Everyone, even him, could see the next part of the affair arrive like a charging bull. Evil-Willit Tam and a brace of others burst into the room, bringing Wallis' head round.

'Away lads,' he declared as his men began to spill back out of the doors. 'Fetch this Master Coalhouse. Take the Sheriff…'

Later it was a matter of sour wonder to Batty why he did it, but at the time it seemed as good a way of getting clear of the Evil Willit Tam and his leek-stained wrath – he whirled on the man behind him, kicked him hard on the knee and wrenched the blade from his surprised hand.

Then he stuck it in his teeth and jerked the Sheriff away, back towards the other door out of the court, the one that led up to the next floor. He then filled his hand with hilt again, cursing as the ragged blade-edge nicked the corner of his mouth. He kicked the hopping Wallis man who'd owned it on the other leg and watched him collapse, howling.

'Take the Sergeant,' he yelled to John Wallis, shoving Sir Nicholas behind him. 'He is better liked and can open any gate besides.'

The Sheriff stumbled, half-fell, then saw the chance Batty offered and scrambled up the winding steps, Batty shoving from behind as if pushing a fat beldame up a ladder. He was halfway when he heard the growl and saw the fresh-bruised face, the nose askew and still bloody. A shred of leek clung stubbornly to the nose blood on his beard.

'Hand him down,' Tam Wallis roared, 'or bigod I will come up an' skewer you.'

He had one of the guard's halberds, so it was no idle threat, Batty thought, even as he made his voice light and his manner easy.

'Come ahead. There is a length of steel with your name on it here. Ugly Fat Whoreson it is called.'

He shoved backwards, cursing the Sheriff to move his big arse; when resistance vanished, Batty went up a step or two, only to hear the Sheriff beating on the door and bellowing to be let in; those in the room above had barred it.

The halberd whicked like an adder tongue, then Tam came around the curve of stair, stabbing it in little movements. He had the reach and strength, but not the advantage of height and he knew it, stopped and frowned. Below him, smoke spilled in acrid billows and someone yelled his name.

'Your ma wants you,' Batty said, bringing a grin springing to Tam's face. He nodded.

'Mayhap we will get a chance to share a morning meal again sometime,' he said and backed away a little. Batty watched close and careful, so the hunch of shoulder and the tilt of head came as no surprise and he sighed, for he knew what was coming.

Tam spun and lurched forward, thrusting up. Batty stepped sideways, put one foot on the halberd as it shrieked metal on the step, then stamped with the other; the haft snapped like a bone and Tam fell forward, off-balanced by the ploy and gripping no more than splintered stick.

He fumbled and half-rolled, looked up and saw an unsmiling cliff of a face behind a solitary fistful of steel. The blade, when it sliced his neck, seemed cold as ice.

There was a moment of gurgling and blood and the Sheriff finally forced those inside to open the door; his swearing was a gilt-strip of bad cess on useless cowards everywhere.

Batty sat down on the top step, blowing a little and listening to Tam Wallis choke out his last, while the blood spread and spilled in thick rivulets, dripping step after step back down the stairs.

The Sheriff re-appeared, sweating, cursing and red-faced. The sight of Tam and all the blood silenced him to stare and heavy breathing; he stepped gingerly over the sluggish waterfall of gore and went off down the stairs, trailed by the coterie of clerks and servants scoured from the room.

Batty sat and looked at Tam Wallis, finally realised he was still gripping the gory blade and laid it down.

'Silly bugger,' he said to the dead man. 'Now I have the full cost of the Fourpenny Ward to bear and a purse full of wind.'

Below, he heard men stamping and roaring for the fire to be put out – well, it was sweaty and busy work but a good excuse against the more dangerous business of chasing the Wallis men through Berwick.

Batty knew the hue and cry would be raised sooner or later, but the men would be gone by then, out of gates shut far too slowly. He wondered if Red Rowan would be unharmed – and appreciated the service he had done, however forced, for the Sheriff of Berwick.

In the room at the Tolbooth top a meal was laid out for the Sheriff's luncheon; the man himself could be heard downstairs, roaring for his weapons and to have the fire out.

Left alone, Batty wandered into the room, sat in a carved, cushioned chair and helped himself to bread and meat and a fine Rhenish, wishing he had someone with him prepared to wager on how long it took to raise the hue and cry. Twenty minutes, give or take, Batty thought. He would put even money on it. You could be out the Briggate in ten.

Twenty-three minutes later, Red Rowan was back safely released, red-faced and bellowing for men and horses, a hot trod in pursuit of the villains who had dared to raid the Guild Tolbooth of Berwick in broad daylight. Who had double-dared to take him hostage for their getaway.

Batty ambled down to the door, chewing his way past the lolling goggle of Tam Wallis on the steps, the blistered, blackened floor, the guard moaning as he was treated for a gashed head. He chewed and swallowed idly, watching the Sheriff tripping over his lip and demanding for burning peat to be found and mounted on a lance, so that the trod would be all perjink and proper.

Batty almost choked on his mouthful. Burning peat in Berwick? As like to find a naked virgin with a bag of gold...

'I am Riding,' Red Rowan roared out to the curious who had gathered to gawp. 'I will do so alone save for garrison men, but if any wish to avenge this slur on the honour of the toon, they are welcome to join me.'

He saw Batty and scowled.

'Batty Coalhouse – you are the very man. Thief-taker and tracker. Get your weapons from inside and we will find you a nag.'

Batty shrugged and waved his handful of bread and meat.

'I am serving twenty days in the jail,' he reminded Red Rowan cheerfully. 'This Wallis is no matter of mine.'

Red Rowan did not reply, simply reined round, scowling like a black thundercloud as he clattered the horse dangerously fast on the cobbles, trailing men behind him.

The Sheriff watched them go, then turned to the Doorward who was now in charge of Berwick's law and order and only just realising it.

'Secure Master Coalhouse,' the Sheriff snapped. 'Return him to his cell. Since he has clearly enjoyed my luncheon, he will not need fed again for a day.'

Cuthie watched Sir Nicholas stamp off, then shrugged apologies to Batty.

'There is gratitude for you,' Batty said. 'I only sampled some meat and bread. And a glass or two.'

'Aye, aye,' Cuthie growled. 'Well done is ill served as they say – Red Rowan may think the same, since he stood surety for you and you would not ride with him.'

Batty had no answer to the truth of that but thought Cuthie more concerned about being left in charge than Red Rowan Riding without a Batty Coalhouse. He said so and saw the droop to Cuthie's shoulders.

'Still,' he added gently, 'you will not have to concern yourself long over keeping the peace in Berwick by yourself.'

'Why for?' Cuthie asked as they strolled back down the stairs, chased by trailing tendrils of char.

'Och, Red Rowan will be back in less than a day. He will not catch those Wallis men. Wynds and stairwells is more his style and the hills and moors are a mystery to him. I wager he will be back afore breakfast.'

'Away,' Cuthie exclaimed. 'He is fired for a trod is the Sergeant. He will not be back in a week.'

'A shilling says he is.'

'Done.'

Cuthie closed the deal and the door, though he was uneasy at where Batty would get a shilling – and at the sound of happy singing, pungent as the acrid smell of the smoke.

> 'There came a man, by middle day, who spied
> his sport and went away. And brought the king
> that very night, who brake my bower, and slew
> my knight.'

Berwick on the Tweed
Eight days later

There was sun on the sea to the east, dancing on it for the joy of shining and Batty wondered if it would turn its smile inland; over his head was a pewter and rain sky.

Fitting enough, Batty thought, for the mood in Berwick, which had not improved with the return of Sergeant Red Rowan Charlton and his muddy draggle of weary riders. If they ever had a burning peat on a lance point, it had long since got sodden-tired and fallen off. So had more than a few of the riders and all of them felt they had been out a week rather than a day and night.

Even winning a shilling from Cuthie was little compensation for Red Rowan's mood, for the Sergeant had put Batty to work while he served out his jail term, since he could not pay for the Fourpenny Ward; the shilling he took for 'the contingency fund'. The Sheriff made a great show of taking details he already knew, for the report he was writing into the 'untimely death of one Thomas Wallis' – but he was half-hearted and half-ashamed at best, because even he knew the death had been more than timely.

As Batty told him – a quim-hair longer in reach and Evil-Willit Tam would have stuck your own guard's halberd atween your lordship's hurdies.

Batty was clearly useless with a mop and broom, so he was put to fetching and carrying and Red Rowan had been snarling for seven days over the Wallis raid. Worse than a cuckold, Batty thought.

Each and every hour Batty would lug a wooden kit up the Tolbooth to the Sheriff's fine solar and lug the waste pot down again; each time he did it he stepped over the top stair, still crimson-tinged for all the scrubbing. If there was time and the Sheriff not in the Tolbooth, he would ignore the scathe of the Depute, a plump Guild man scribbling away in a corner, and stop to look out the least distorted panes of leaded glass at the sea.

The tower panes, on the other side, also provided a wavering view, this one of the long, cramped run of the wooden bridge, tumbled down to ruin and piling stumps by ice floes not long since. Which at least saved the Scots from coming to burn it, which was all-too frequent when English armies lost a battle. The first raid Scots did after such a victorious affray, Batty knew, was to come down to Berwick and fire the bridge and it was so established it was almost a tradition.

Not this time. The bridge would have been safe – if the ice had not smashed it – for the Scots were still stunned by their victory and unwilling to double the bet with the weak forces left. They also knew that Fat Henry still had troops around Berwick and more were arriving every day.

Not Maramaldo, all the same, for Batty scoured for word and found none; the Captain General and the ordnance he'd been taking south had vanished somewhere on the way and Batty had an idea what the lobsters searched for. He would have smiled if the thought of Maramaldo's Company of the Sable Rose, loose on the Cheviots with a brace of sakers, had not chilled him to the bowel.

Every day Batty took what chance he could with this marvellous all-round view, another part of which was down the Nungait. Today's riders were notables by the pennons and the arrogant way they scattered the throng, but they were not, as far as Batty could tell, anything to do with Maramaldo.

He watched them until he was snapped at by the Depute and told to take himself off. Even then he merely gave a withering glance and watched on until he was satisfied, before hefting the kit down the steps again.

He was spilling waste into the gutters, sluicing away the fishheads and dog shit when he saw Red Rowan come barrelling up the street, swathed in cloak and important hurry. The Sergeant spotted him and came up, his boar-eyes narrowed.

'How do you know the Musgraves of Bewcastle?'

Batty blinked at that and tried to think about answering the question while squinting to work out why it was asked. In the end, he did a rare thing and told the truth – he knew that the Musgraves of Bewcastle were at feud with the Grahams of anywhere and since he himself was a Graham, albeit a shame to the grayne and a by-blow besides, he supposed he was considered no friend.

'Mind you,' he added mildly, 'the Musgraves are at feud also with the Armstrongs, who are at odds with the Grahams. Mayhap a Musgrave accommodation has been reached with the Grahams.'

Red Rowan rubbed his rasp of cropped whiskers at this; the current relationships of Border graynes was confusing and ever-changing.

'Of course,' Batty added helpfully, 'I am considered an affront to the Grahams for various reasons, so that Name holds little regard for me. Mark you, Dickon Graham of Netherby owes me a favour yet.'

Red Rowan frowned and pondered for a minute; the rain started and Batty looked pointedly up at the sky, which stirred the Sergeant from his musing.

'Aye, well – Sir John Musgrave himself, no less, has just rode in and abides patiently at the Old Brig, having taken it over entire for his wheen of riders. He is asking for one Batty Graham, also known as Coalhouse, whom he knows is held at the Sheriff's pleasure.'

He eyed Batty with a jaundiced stare.

'He has paid your fines.'

So Batty was handed back his gear and weapons and escorted to the Old Brig. Escorted, for all he was supposedly now a free man, by a scowling Red Rowan who wanted to know everything that went on.

He and Batty stepped into the top room of the Old Brig, ducking the smoke-blackened beams of the finest room the tavern had to offer – it had a glass window in it. The light from it made everyone look as if they were underwater and, for all it was broad daylight outside, the place was dim as twilight, the folk in it half-shadows.

There were two besides himself and Rowan, Batty saw, his eyes sweeping the room with an old skill and his one hand politely just far enough from the axe-handled dagg thrust into his belt. It was not loaded or primed, but folk who did not know that might think before challenging it – besides, the axe head was a consideration in itself.

One of the men was perched close to the second, whether by old habit or deliberate pattern of protection – both, Batty decided, for the man he protected was clearly the one who mattered.

This one was slouched in a plush chair – the only one the Old Brig possessed – and made a deep growling sigh when he saw Batty, like some great cat circling and settling on a warm spot. Fifties, Batty thought, with enough hair and grooming to be considered handsome still, though the mouth was too thin-lipped. A large head and the body impressive, though it was hard to tell because of the cloak he had round his shoulders, which seemed to consist of half a pelt. The rain had spiked and darkened it so that he looked like a big-ruffed wolf.

Which is what he is, Batty decided. Mad Jack Musgrave, the Buzzard of Bewcastle.

He was aware of Red Rowan's scowl next to him – and that it was more curious than angry. This was reversed when the Buzzard turned a predatory stare on him.

'You. Out.'

Red Rowan's hackles went up at that, but he paused only a moment. The other man made a slight sound which might have been a laugh as the Sergeant turned back out the door, stiff with as much dignity as he could muster.

Musgrave shifted in his fine perse – black-purple, slashed to show the cramoisie underneath Batty saw. Black and crimson, like some prelate.

'Doff your hat.'

Batty raised a solitary eyebrow at that – then the hat. Musgrave grunted.

'Batty Coalhouse,' he said.

'It was me yesterday,' Batty answered. 'I am hoping it will be the morn's morn.'

'Less of your lip.'

This from the other man, a long streak of languid with a wee barbered fringe of beard and moustache, nervous fingers and bitten nails caressing the fancifully looped hilt of a thin sword. An *espada ropera*, Batty saw, a Spanish weapon for cut-and-thrust defence. For duellists.

'That is a fine hat,' Musgrave said and Batty glanced at his headgear and laid it on the table between them with a rueful grin. It was a plumed confection, that hat, and wind, weather and war had done much to reduce the look of the blue and white panache.

'Given out by Arran to his captains,' Musgrave went on. 'Albeit worn by someone more at home with a blue bonnet. Or a burgonet.'

He spoke as if words cost, spitting them out in fits and starts. Batty stayed silent, though he took in what he learned. The Earl of Arran, Regent of Scotland, was much given to plumes and sashes for his commanders, though he was unhappy to be anywhere near fighting. There he would start to panic and yell, wild brindled hair and beard flying, berating those around him like dogs the whole time – but give him politicking and he was a steady and sure hand.

Musgrave knew all this. Knew that Batty was captain to some of the Regent's hired French and Italian gunners and had been at Ancrum; despite himself, the sweat started to move like lice down Batty's backbone and round the curve of his belly.

'I paid your fine,' Musgrave went on and Batty acknowledged it with a flap of one hand.

'I will send the money round,' he declared loftily.

'You will send no coin,' Musgrave said coldly, 'for you have none. I tell you this because I offer you some – an Angel each seven-day for as long as I deem fit to need you.'

Batty squinted.

'For why?'

'For your skills,' Musgrave declared. 'Slow match, they call you, for the way putting you at any matter always results in explosion. Fyrebrande, for the same reason.'

He leaned forward a little.

'I am interested in the last name you have. Corbie. From the way a Billed man can run and jink and birl and think himself safe – until he turns and finds you waiting, like a corbie in a tree looking at a dying sheep.'

'I have sought out men with fouled Bills,' Batty admitted slowly. 'For Wardens,' he added pointedly. 'On both sides o' the divide.'

'You did not recently blow up an Armstrong fortalice in the Debateable on behalf of the Wardens,' Musgrave answered flatly, then offered a twist of thin grin. 'Though I am sure they were pleasantried of it.'

Batty had no answer to it, for the memories of that time, what was done and why were part of the reason for him drinking himself into the Tolbooth.

'You are a Scot, fair caught on the wrong side of the divide,' Musgrave declared. 'A known master of ordnance, so either buying or selling same, which is a hanging offence. Or spying, which...'

'Is a hanging offence,' Batty interrupted wearily. 'I tak' your point. You have offered carrot and whacked me with stick. What is it you wish?'

'I said to watch your lip,' the thin man declared and uncoiled like a striking snake. Batty did what he always did with snakes – he took it by the neck before it could get a fang out. The man gurgled and thrashed, appalled by the speed and the strength of that single arm.

The air was thick and coiling; the man writhed and Batty felt the throat-apple quiver like a trapped bird as he choked. Batty showed the man's purpling face a delight of yellowed teeth grin.

The slap started them all; Batty let the thin man go and he fell back, coughing, one hand at his throat and his face a bag of blood. His other hand was fumbling for a hilt when Musgrave slapped the table once more; Batty's hat shifted with the wind of it.

'Mind my plumes,' Batty offered mildly and waited while the hackles sank, slow and unhappy. Musgrave shifted.

'This is my associate,' he offered. 'Master Cadwaller Rutland, gentleman.'

Rutland was a court-rat, though Batty doubted he had the means or manners for Henry's own, or even the Scottish one. A much lesser light then – the neat little chain round his ravaged neck was a clue, a white enamelled and gold-ringed affectation terminating in a little ruby kine with a crowned collar. The red Dacre Bull.

The picture cleared, like the settling ripples of a pool. Mad Jack Musgrave of Bewcastle had been elevated to knighthood only recently, thanks to his joint leadership of the little Border reiver force which had scattered a Scots army at Solway Moss. That had caused King James to roll over and die of shame and all the country's present troubles.

The other commander had been Sir Thomas Dacre, a bastard sired of the Baron Dacre of Gilsland. Sir Thom had also been knighted by a grateful, exultant King Henry, so he and Mad Jack were joined at the helm and Mad Jack was known as his man. Enough nowadays to be known as the Bastard's Buzzard, though never to his face, Batty recalled.

Thomas Dacre of Lanercost and Musgrave of Bewcastle, a godless brace of bad cess; Batty found it strange that the Bastard's name should still be echoing in his head from the earlier events in the Tolbooth, but he put it from him as Musgrave started to tell him what he wanted.

'I need your tracking skills,' Musgrave said eventually, while Rutland tried to breathe quietly and failed. Batty merely nodded, for it was always best to keep a cliff of a face when your cards were poor, in life as in Primero.

'You led rebellion, I hear,' Musgrave said suddenly. 'In the Saxonies. Ower religion.'

He paused, as if expecting a reply and when none came, he scowled.

'Is it true?'

'That I led it, or that it was religion?'

'Both,' Musgrave spat back. 'And do not cozen me, else I will be the one seizing throats, Master Coalhouse. I will do it with a hemp rope, all the same.'

Batty thought about matters a bit longer, enough to rasp Musgrave, whom he now did not care for at all.

'I did not lead it, nor was it religious,' he answered. Not remotely – it was because a noble had taken Uncle Hans Kohlhase's finest horses as surety for a toll payment, promised on Hans' return. Then the noble kept them until forced to return them and when he did, they were foundered and useless.

'The Law favoured the noble,' Batty added wryly at the end of telling this, 'and my Uncle Hans did not accept the judgement.'

Musgrave nodded.

'There have been worse feuds over less,' he answered and there was only truth in that, as a Border man like him would know well.

'So you are not a godly man, then?' Musgrave said and Batty was frowning puzzled now. What is Mad Jack's great concern over my soul, he thought? Certainly there had been the Devil in what had been done by the Kohlhases afterwards, when they found themselves brigands.

Batty said as much and Musgrave nodded.

'In these Reformed times,' he said, 'it is always best to know who still holds to Confession and High Mass. Here in the north, we are less down on the affair.'

Is he telling me he is Catholic? Batty thought about it and decided it could be true; as Musgrave said – there were lots of folk in England's north who held to the Catholic religion and almost all Scotland still did. Still, the nobility who looked for Fat Henry's favour did not shout it aloud.

Musgrave looked sideways at Batty a little longer, then drew the fur collar of his cloak up a little, as if there was a chill breeze somewhere.

'I have a sister,' he said, 'who is a nun.'

He let that hang for a moment and Batty said nothing.

'She was coming north to me, to safety after her convent was… Reformed. Last I heard of her she was at York. That was two weeks ago and there has been nothing since.'

'Which route was she taking?'

Musgrave appraised Batty with an admiring eye; no hesitation, no sly hem and haw about what was needed so that the money got on the table first.

'Three carts and three trusted men of mine to drive them,' he said brusquely. 'Coming up to Kirknewton, then across to me.'

Long road for a shortcut, Batty thought, which is strange – Kirknewton is a bliddy awful place, whose very kirk is famous only because of the fallen flowers of Flodden buried there. Flodden field was a spit away and few travelled that road, for the memory was raw and the ghosts walked, so folk claimed.

'Three carts?' was all he said aloud.

Musgrave shifted slightly.

'She was bringing some of her… sisters,' he said shortly and Batty rocked a little at that. Bigod – a wheen of nuns, wheeling through a country which had given the least of its folk the right to scourge and dismember them. And worse. Small wonder Mad Jack is concerned about my religion, Batty thought. Less about my skin.

It was not an enterprise he cared for and said so. Besides, without word for so long, it was more than possible they were all already discovered. For delicacy, Batty did not add details on the inevitable outcome of that.

Musgrave was no fool, though and never winced at the possibilities.

'Find them, alive or… otherwise,' he answered piously. 'If it is possible, save my sister.'

Not the others if they get in the way was what was unsaid and Batty did not doubt Mad Jack would sacrifice a deal more for it. Everything, he thought, but the

Musgrave Name, recently raised to the nobility and more proud and dignified than other, more established families.

A single one-armed notorious such as Batty Coalhouse would cause little regard if he headed south to find some nuns and would be no loss if he was never heard from again, or caught with a parcel of wimple-wearers.

No one would believe tales of working on behalf of Jack Musgrave of Bewcastle even if they waited long enough to hear them afore setting my hurdies on fire, he thought.

Batty hoiked all this up aloud and used the name besides – the Bastard's Buzzard. He was baiting a fighting bear with a stick, he knew, so was surprised when Musgrave did not seem put out; in fact, he smiled, which made Batty's eyes narrow.

'Aye, right enough,' Mad Jack answered, 'You would know of bad cess names, mind you, having a wheen of your own. But you will do it, all the same.'

'I dinna think so, Sir Jack. I have little need of nuns and would not know God if he bussed me on either cheek.'

Musgrave's eyes narrowed.

'You need the coin, though. And you will hang if you don't.'

Batty squinted at him, then nodded.

'Aye, the coin would be a blessing, no doubt of it. Your carrot is good, but your stick is wormy. I have committed no crime in Berwick and if I have changed saltire for St George, it is all to the good of England, is it not? Who would not want *ingeniateur* Batty Coalhouse for their ordnance? Or as a wee pricker, scouting out the land ahead? You have proved that yourself.'

Musgrave brought his brows down – then laughed. It was not what Batty expected, nor what he wanted to hear, for it was the scrape of nail on the slate of his nerves.

'You are good, Master Coalhouse,' Musgrave declared fruitily and waved to Rutland, who rose unsteadily – Batty watched him warily – and went to the door. He called, his voice hoarse and had to do it twice before he was heard. Someone came up, clumping heavily on the steps and handed him a paper.

'I hear you play Primero well when sober,' Musgrave said while Rutland delivered it to his hand.

'No game is played well when drunk,' Batty muttered, anxious now about what was in the paper. Paper with writing on it never boded well when the Coalhouse name was somewhere included, he knew. A writ, mayhap, giving Musgrave the right of pit and gallows?

'Aye, well, Primero is a game of bluff when all is said and done,' Musgrave mused. 'You have played a fine hand here, I will avow you that. But now – knock or draw to mine, Batty.'

He laughed and held out the paper, so that Batty scowled.

'I do not read,' he declared. Musgrave smiled even more broadly and waved the paper at Batty until he took it.

'Find one you trust and who can. You will see it is a contract, all perjink and legal. It promises to pay you an agreed sum for the successful outcome of an enterprise on behalf of the Musgrave of Bewcastle.'

He paused and his stare was a gimlet on Batty's own.

'The other is the order, issued in Bewcastle placing Rafael Sabin, right-hand of Fabrizio Maramaldo, Captain

General of a company of mercenaries, in the jail there while awaiting trial for treason, brigandage and worse.'

He leaned forward, and the smile on him never crawled as high as his eyes.

'To avoid the hemp, Sabin will reveal to you the whereabouts of Maramaldo.'

Chapter Two

The wind was wicked and playful, picking up the quern-fine rain as it sifted down through a leering lout of sunlight and scattering it. If it was gold dust as it looked, Batty thought, we would all be richer than old King Croesus.

He rode with an itch on his back, an old feeling he had learned to trust – there was someone following him. Batty hoped that it was probably a Musgrave man, sent to watch and see what Batty did and where he went. Or it could have been the brace Red Rowan mentioned when he'd taken Musgrave's paper to him and got him to read it; it was exactly as Musgrave had said and Red Rowan, naturally enough, wanted to know the details, starting with the shine.

Batty told him – five pounds, English, which was now his set fee for most enterprises.

'And the enterprise?' asked Red Rowan. 'This Rafael Sabin who is held in Bewcastle gaol?'

He huffed and ruffed like a damp dog when Batty refused to tell him, then hitched up his belt and hooked his thumbs in it.

'I would take on the task of it,' he said, 'for only two things stink after a week – fish and an unwanted guest.

You have worn out your welcome in Berwick toon, Batty. Besides, men are seeking you.'

'Men?'

Red Rowan had taken a deal of satisfaction and time, revenge for Batty's refusal to allay his curiosity over Musgrave's task. Then he had admitted that at least two, possibly more, had been asking after Batty Coalhouse.

'I suspect Wallis men, looking for revenge for Tam,' he added and spread his hands. 'I have no proof of this, o' course, so cannot arrest either, for they have broken no law in Berwick.'

You would find one if you could be bothered, Batty thought viciously, but had taken the advice and left, wondering if Sabin would really reveal the whereabouts of Maramaldo. That was the true shining reward for this enterprise.

More to the point was how Sabin had come to be in shackles, a question Batty had put to the smiling Mad Jack.

'Caught rievin' nolt, no less, with a parcel of ribboned rogues,' Musgrave had replied. 'We hanged them and kept him.'

Rafael Sabin's name had sent a feeling through Batty from crown to heel, a chill so cold it was fired. He remembered Sabin, a face as grim as plague atop a body thin as a spiderleg as he watched Maramaldo wield the axe on Batty's arm, his sallow face showing only curiosity, his dark hair, which always looked wet, dagged to his cheeks. Twenty years ago at least, he recalled and was made aware of his own age and fat by it.

'He recalls you,' Musgrave had said, 'and feels remorse. He did not care for what was done to you then.'

Did nothing, all the same, Batty thought now, hunching up under the rain and wondering what he'd have done if the positions had been reversed. Then he thought about the rogues Musgrave had hanged – four of them, Mad Jack declared and called them Landsknechts because that was what Border folk called all the paid men of armies.

They were not all Germans, Batty knew. They were Maramaldo's men, from the Italies, the Dutchies, Spain and elsewhere, who wore their wealth in ragged and stained finery, parti-coloured and paned. They draped themselves in geegaws and amulets, festooned themselves with ribbons, rings and chains and ear bobs in gold and gems, all of it negotiable and usually gambled away.

Batty knew them well, the memory almost an ache. Yet Rafael Sabin was now Chancellor of the Sable Rose, the right hand of Maramaldo and the man with the power to negotiate and agree *condotta* – contracts – with employers. What was the likes of him doing stealing shitty-arsed cattle from Bewcastle?

It meant that the Company of the Sable Rose was somewhere close to Bewcastle and a thousand and more folk, with all their carted lives and beasts, would need a deal of feeding. Even so – and even allowing for Sabin's nature as he remembered it – Batty could not think that the Chancellor of the Sable Rose would be out on the *herschip* like some eager youngster.

It was a nagging thought, but the man at his back worried Batty more. It will be yon Rutland, he thought, with no more skill at tracking than a blind slewhound with no nose. He hoped that was so and that it wasn't the Wallis men he was feeling like heat on his shoulderblades, for he was riding like an arrow straight into their Cheviot hills and brooded on the rotted luck of that.

Still, if it was Rutland then he would not last long, for the Wallis would get him. If he was lucky, he would turn up days later, only stripped naked and robbed even if his assailants learned who he was and who his Master. Probably because of it. Rutland was no man for the moor and hill, as awkward and vulnerable as an egg on a busy path.

The Wallis had no fear of Musgrave riders, or even the great Dacre himself, for this was a country where a hundred riders could be got in half-a-day if even the least of Names sent out word. If you were a Nixon, or a Charlton or an Armstrong, you could have a thousand swarming the Cheviots and at least half would have a Scots lilt to their talk. The Wallis Name was not great, but they had others at their back who might dare to bait the Dacre Bull.

Men will fight for drink, coin or quim, Batty thought, but they will exert themselves for the grayne for free.

He rode on through a land of brightening whin and gorse, the colours shrieking to the damp blue sky that winter was done with – and that was strange in a land where spring did not mean much to snow and wind.

He picked his way on to a drover road and then on south and west, towards the loom of the Cheviots, the sun sweating him and the warm rain sluicing it off again.

Towards dark, when sun lowered like a fat red hen on roosting eggs and the cold crept out with weasel teeth, he came up on Langton. It was a spill of cruck houses and a tower ruined by war then further wrecked by folk pilfering the last stones for sheep pens and barmkins. They looked at him with suspicion and appraisal, seeing a fat old man with one arm offering them a flash of coin for a place at their fire and a lick of their pot.

The heidman weighed up the possibilities and also saw the padded jack under the big wrap of cloak and the burgonet under the blue bonnet, the former pulled on to offer protection from the rain as well as the impression that there was no war hat beneath. He saw the worn hilt of a backsword, a brace of daggs in saddle holsters, another pair shoved through the belt and one of them with the butt converted into an axe. He saw a tribe of knives and knew they were for throwing, thought he spotted the hilt of a vicious bollock dagger down one boot.

At which point he revised his opinion on what was helpless and easily robbed in favour of biting the offered coin and making a place by the fire. He would have presented not only his smoke-blackened howf but his wife and daughters, too if Batty had offered as much coin again.

Batty saw to Fiskie's comfort under a rickety lean-to while the elder of the heidman's boys looked at the tattered dyke and the gate with a dubious eye and an accent thick as pease brose.

'Eer hobby cud loup yett,' he said and Batty assured him that Fiskie was not likely to jump the gate. Then he followed the boy back to the howf and hunkered round a pit fire, the smoke eddying up into the rafters and out through the straw, though a deal of it was blown back by the rain-wind outside and hazed the inside with reek.

The heidman was a long streak of dourness, his wife a once-pretty girl worn to a nub of womanhood by poor food, lost babes and work, yet she had a ready smile even if she had few teeth left to make it winsome.

Most of the smile was because they were eating Batty's decent food, rations of salt meat and cheese all but free of spoil and better fare by far than the heidman and his wife usually enjoyed; it had been a wet summer the year before and a hard winter, so even folk who grew hardy oats rather than the wheat of farmers further south were notching in their waists.

Batty accepted their porray of roots and poor hope and watched them fall on his bread, good wheat with only a salting of bone meal and sawdust. They savoured the last of his cheese, hard and pale with hardly a mould on it and only a couple of weary worms falling out at a tap; Batty watched them crawl round the wood platter as if looking for relatives while the fire popped and smoked and, outside, the wind argued with the rain. The heidman and his wife gobbled the lot and beamed.

This is better lodgings than on many a ride, Batty thought; yet the comfort of it was denied him, driven out by a persistent uneasiness, like unseen eyes from distant hills. Outside somewhere, the Watcher still lurked, Batty was sure of it. Less sure than ever that it was Rutland, who had seemed ill-skilled for such a task as riding into the wilds and avoiding all trouble. Someone more skilled then, Batty thought as he chewed. Bigod, Coalhouse, you have tumbled in a bear pit.

He pulled out his flask and swallowed, became aware of the eyes on him and sighed, facered by his own stupid mistake. Then he had to watch as the heidman's throat bobbed like a mad bird and only stopped when his wife snatched the flask from him and sucked it like a bairn on the teat. He listened to them spit either love or hate at each other and thought of Maramaldo and the first time he had seen Rafael Sabin.

He had been 16 and had learned his trade in eight years sweating at the elbow of his da, a Kohlhase from Saxony. Both of them were cared for by Batty's ma, Bella Graham of Netherby, tupped by his da practically in her own bed and so the disgrace of her Name.

The year before Batty's sixteenth saint's day, Maramaldo's troop had served the Pope against the French, but the fight at Marignano had ended all hope of the Holy League winning and Maramaldo knew when to quit a burning building.

So the next year saw them with Charles of Egmond, lending support to The Black Gang From Arum and fighting in Frisia. The Arumer Zwarte Hoop were led by Big Peter and, like him, they were all peasant farmers annoyed with the Hapsburgs. They were good farmers, but poor fighters in the end – Big Peter's best success came when he went to sea and sank a score or more of ships.

Before the year was out, Maramaldo changed sides and started to hunt out the almost-defeated Black Gang he had once run with. It had been a hard snow, so foraging had taken Maramaldo's troop a long way from their winter camp; besides, men were out after loot as much as food, because fighting peasant farmers was not lucrative.

In smaller and smaller groups they used savagery and surprise to scatter the herds of villagers they came on – but the cattle were not always cowed.

Batty did not even recall the name of the place, but remembered coming up on it with five others, led by Sabin; even then Sabin was Maramaldo's favourite and Batty should not even have been out, save that all men were needed for foraging and Batty was no green sapling who knew next to nothing bar working big guns. He had grown up in a rough camp of hard men and knew which end of a knife to point at a rival.

They came to find the men they had sent earlier, another handful who had vanished into the drifting snow like wraiths and had not returned.

'Found drink and women,' Sabin declared moodily when Maramaldo sent him in pursuit – but he went and Batty went as well, with instructions from his da to bring back this or that and 'a little something for your ma'.

Batty remembered the smell at first, like a forge where hot iron has been just quenched. He had smelled it before, but not as strong and did not need Sabin's warning hand to stop, crouch and fetch out his backsword. It was blood, lots of it and not yet so frozen it would not reek.

They found their missing men not long after, throat cut and belly slit in a grue of their own bloody slush. The snow whirled, making Batty blink, sending everyone into an instinctive huddle; the charge when it came was better resisted as a result, though Sabin took the brunt of it.

The fighter who did it was big and bearded and howling. He wore the tattered remains of looted war gear but mustered only a pitchfork. Once he had been part of the Zwarte Hoop but this was either his old home or he been left behind in this vill through sickness – for all that, he wielded the fork like a half-pike and drove it hard into Sabin's thigh, sending the man over, screaming.

Others followed him, desperate and ill-armed but looming like shadows out of the snow-wind so that they seemed a host of hard charging men like themselves. Batty remembered the farmer-warrior, tearing his pitchfork free and looking for another man to fight, searching the snow. It was because I was wee, Batty recalled, that he didnae see me until I drove the steel into his belly, a fingerlength below the navel.

The backsword had not been all that sharp, for Batty had neglected the weapon and such close-quarter blows before this had been affairs of fists and boots – when it spilled over into drawn blades, there were always bigger men to intervene and cuff lugholes.

But the whole length of the sword had slid in, easy as pushing, until Batty had felt it grate and knew it to be man's backbone. There had been a moment of disbelief from the big man and then a frantic jerking, like a gaffed fish, so that the sword had sprung free of Batty's hand, flying up to throw off a little spray of rubies into the snow.

Sabin, howling and cursing, had levered himself up and then fell on the tumbled Zwarte Hoop man with a bollock knife, stabbing and stabbing until he was bloody to the elbow.

Batty had found himself sitting, shivering and colder than the slush under his arse or the flakes on his cheeks warranted, while the hard men of Sabin's foragers recovered and scattered the Zwarte Hoop's last army.

This man was the first he had ever knowingly killed. Certainly the first one he had ever shoved a bar of metal into and Batty sat a long time looking, until he knew every pore and hair on his face, the splash of blood on one cheek, the eyes blank as a saint's statue. Sabin's shrieking vengeance had left the rest of the man tattered and sodden with blood.

Perhaps he had come home looking for peace, Batty thought later, or just stumbled on the place as a refuge. Either way, he'd led the folk in defence of what little they had, for there was no rival mercenary band here, just one weary Zwarte Hoop fighter and a lot of villagers.

Growling, the men had gathered up what villagers had not fled, then fell to looting what they could carry.

'Go back,' Sabin had declared thickly to the others. 'I will join you presently.'

No one was fooled, or cared, so they went a little way and then dumped their loads and hunkered, waiting for him to finish exacting revenge. When the cold started to bite, the Frenchman, Loreq, began a vote which left Batty, unsurprisingly, with the task of going back to see if Sabin was faring well.

'For that leg was bad hurt,' Loreq argued. 'Perhaps he has fallen and needs help.'

In which case, Batty thought sullenly as he plootered all the way back to the village, they should all have gone to help, for what could I do with a weight such as Sabin if he couldn't walk?

Sabin was walking well enough, though he had tied one of his fancy ribbons round his upper thigh to staunch the bleed. Batty came up in time to see him slide his dagger round the neck of a woman while those still left alive struggled in the other ribbons he had used to bind them. Sabin had already blinded the woman by slow degrees and was now killing her the same way; two men were already dead and a girl was groaning, still alive for all her throat was slit and the blood was everywhere.

Sabin turned his head when Batty came up, his eyes feral and his mouth wet. Batty, cold as old iron, took his still bloody backsword and thrust it into the moaning girl; he heard a shriek and knew it was the mother, struggling to free herself.

He stepped forward and did the same to the one Sabin held. When he felt the thrust and the slackness in his hands, Sabin flung the body away and rounded on Batty, gore dripping from both hands and his eyes gone wild and unfocused.

Batty had backed away and Sabin, limping so hard he was dragging the leg, followed him in a fury, but was unable to catch the nimbler boy. When they were alone in the whirling snow, Batty stopped, his sword up and his mouth dry; his legs shook as Sabin lurched towards him.

The cold and effort had brought some life back to the eyes, though and Sabin was clearly sapped of real strength so that he stopped, eyed the sword and breathed like a mated bull.

'You come between me and my blade again, Balthie,' he had said, then ran out of breath. He did not need the rest of the warning; Batty had stood to one side and let Sabin drag himself past, for he would not put his back to the man and had not done since. Even on the day he had been strapped down for Maramaldo to maim, when he had turned his head so his ma would not see his terror and found Sabin instead, blank as stone, his eyes black and small as apple pips.

He blinked back to the fire, and heard the mewling of cats – then realised that it was the woman, crooning songs to the flames; his flask was empty and the man grimed his way to the side of his wife and started to paw her. Batty could stand the reek and the rasping singing no more, got up and lurched out of the smokey howf into the rain-washed night.

There were faint corpse-candle lights, wriggling worms of pallid comfort marking where the rest of these tallow folk lurked; Batty decided to go and talk to Fiskie. Better that than more of the reeking shelter and the scrape on his nerves either of singing or sweaty coupling.

He did not like this feeling and had tried to make himself believe that it was the same old scrape, the heightened senses that had served him so well in the past. But he knew it was a lie. There was something else, like a wind bringing the scream of something far in the distance.

Chapter Three

Near the bastel house of Akeld
A day later

The water in the burn frothed and surged, leaping its way over stones as shocked by the assault as all the creatures who had made their home along the banks. Fiskie splashed across what was normally a sluggish ripple and the water gurgled up over Batty's boot soles, while the horse protested at the sudden slap on his hot belly.

It had rained all night, but the land steamed under the assault of the sun, while birds ripped their throats out with joy from every budding tree that dripped on the rolling swell of green and yellow. Yet the nights were frosted and sudden chill gusts swept up and over ridges, strong enough to tear away the new buds.

This morning, the heat had gone leprous on the smell from the huddle of trees and it hit Batty's battered nose with a shock of familiar chill and old horror. It spilled memories into him, entire maps of hamlets and vills with their charred timbers and blackened bodies.

He stopped on the rise above the burn and leaned his elbow on the pommel to study the place a little better, squinting through the haze at the trees. Yet it was only when the horse in them moved that the picture sprang into view, like a deer shifting in a dappled glade.

The beast was a pack pony, the hefty saddle slipped beneath it so that it walked awkwardly as if heavily pregnant. Nearby was a cart, only partly visible – it was the wheel pointing to the sky that made Batty grunt softly, for it reminded him of the breaking wheel that had ruined Hans Kohlhase from his life.

That and the smell, pungent and richly sickening; Fiskie blew out indignantly when it trailed into his flaring nostrils and Batty patted him soothingly, narrow-squinting to see if there was danger here before he moved down.

There was a long moment of waiting, sweating silent, while a blackbird sang for a note or two, then whirred away. Batty nudged Fiskie and they went down to the line of trees.

The pony raised its head and whicked softly, hoping for someone to sort out the mess of its loading saddle, so that Batty had no trouble dismounting and moving to it, speaking soft and walking slow.

The saddle was a solid wooden affair, ripped free of what had been loaded on it and he unlatched it and let it fall; the pack pony stepped free of it and shook rain off like a dog.

The cart was upended, but the contents here had been long plundered, too, save for a scatter of lanterns which still had oil in them. The bottom of the cart was split apart, the planks wrenched free and the only chest left with content in it spilled it to the still soft ground out of a splintered secret panel – a black stain trampled in the mud, laced with soiled white like dead doves.

A nun's habit and wimples, wrenched from a hiding place and which none of the raiders would want. Batty hunkered on his toes and looked at the ground, the tangled churn of footprints too confused for him to make sense of numbers. Enough, all the same, to deal with the poor woman who had owned the habit and had hidden it carefully away.

They had stripped her plain dress from her and no doubt done things where death was a blessing from her God. Nearby was a man, untouched save by small beasts and birds – he had been dead at the start, Batty surmised, shot by a big war-arrow which someone had carefully removed; the broken shaft lay nearby, but the point had been dug out for reuse.

Batty studied the shaft, saw the waxed thread and the good feathering. A longbow arrow made by someone prudent, who knew the value of a barbed arrowhead. A prized longbow archer, then, with a hump of muscle on one shoulder from hauling on the big warbow to send a four-ounce arrow four hundred ells and more. With a swagger from being paid more than anyone else and allowed more leeway – Chester men could still kill a Welshman on sight, by law.

No Chester men here, though and few English at all, but just as skilled. Descendants of those who fought for Hawkwood in Italy – mercenaries like himself, Batty thought. Who knew the value of everything, including the cheap coin of human life.

At last, he forced himself to look at the stinking-black parody of what had once been human. They had torn wood from the cart and oil from the lamps to burn her beaten, bound, violated body but last night's rain had contrived to save part of her – a blue-white arm, a leg to the hip, a last raggled wisp of greyed hair from the charcoal scalp.

The rest was twisted the way fire always wrenches the shrinking sinews, making the agony clear as lambent flame and the body a parody of a Barbary ape; the grin was one Batty knew all too well and there was no humour in it at all.

He spat the stink of it from his mouth and levered himself up thinking that he had found the missing nuns. Thinking that he might well have found Musgrave's sister. He did not need to think on who had done this, for he knew already.

Not Border thieves but Reformers, all hot for God and scorching out Catholics in the north. He felt them, the unseen presence of them coiling like some insidious adder, looking for any excuse for outrage.

He mounted stiffly and rode on towards the bastel house, which he knew was no steading but a fortalice of the Dacres, usually filled like a bad barracks with men in his pay and long since taken over by Wallis riders.

Not now, though. Batty stopped below the crest of a ridge, dismounted and hirpled through the rough tussocks and gorse to the shade of a gnarled tree where he hunkered down and listened to the hills.

The sun burned him, for all that the short day was wet, and his leg hurt where he had been tumbled into a deep dene on Tinnis by a shot from Geordie Bourne. The same one which had killed The Saul, though it had taken the beast a year at least to die from it.

I thought I would die from it, Batty remembered, while laid at the foot of a brace-hundred drop with men scouring for me.

He shook it from him and all the other memories that surfaced and rolled over to leer at him; the Armstrong men whose arms he had chopped off – all left ones like his own and the answer to a dead horse's head message from the Laird of the Armstrongs. The Armstrong powder mill blasting Hell into the Debatable. No Toes Will Elliot slung in a cage from the roof of a fortalice only a little larger than the one he now peered at.

The bastel was a tall, two-floored tower whose steep-pitched roof and crow-gables gave some indication of how thick the walls and slates were. A crow perched on the top of the wrenched-open door, there was a dog kennel but no hound and the whole place was blind-window empty, cracked like an egg.

Batty did not think it was blown out of all life – there was the faintest blue of smoke, but the folk inside were keeping quiet. He wiped the sheened sweat from his face as the flies and midgies hummed and whined, driven off in the next minute by the sudden puff of a cooling breeze which still had rain in it.

There was another tower beyond Akeld, an older and taller affair from the time of the Wallace and the Bruce, though the stones had fallen in here and there, or been removed for building Akeld's barmkin wall. The top, uneven as a ragged old tooth, was crowned with a lattice of wood; a look-out post built out of one of the old floors and as good a corbie nest as you would find.

It was clear there was someone perched in it and the entrance, once a doorway whose stout studded wood was long gone, was blocked by two upended carts in a V that was too neat to be an accident.

Batty lay in a patch of damp, peering through the winter-sere fronds of a bracken clump; there was new green in it and a small spider moved purposefully, spinning and drawing out silk for a web. Peasies skimmed; a cushie-doo mourned in the trees.

And a man stood beyond, bare-arsed and pissing in a high arc towards the battered stone tower.

His breeks dangled at his knees and he had laid aside a long-barrelled musket to unbreech himself for the act – though the slow match was upward, out of the damp, Batty saw and still glowed like a fevered eye.

He had a friend with him and dressed like himself, though standing hipshot and arrogant, leaning on a longbow and laughing. No more than sixteen, Batty thought, taking in the look of the pair.

Gesses and lederwams and tellebarrets with tall feathers. Puffed and slashed and parti-coloured, they were as foreign here as papingoes in a rookery, Batty thought, though they have more than just a vicious shriek to them. There were sumptuary laws that prohibited just about everything these men wore – but it would be a brave beadle who called them to account for it.

One of them shouted out and Batty knew the tongue, though he did not speak more than a few words of it. He had heard it often before – a Slav way of speaking which brought back the camps he had been in, the stink and the chatter, the swagger and gaud of men and women like these.

They dress like Landsknechte, Batty thought, because everyone apes those German fighters who themselves want to dress and strut like the best soldiers around – the Swiss. But this pair were neither Swiss nor German but *stradioti* from the Balkans and he knew that they would rub shoulders with Albanese, Levantines, *genours* from Spain as well as Germans and Italians.

He knew the like well enough and thought about who their Captain might be for a long time while the spider industriously spun and scuttled. It might be Thomas Buas of Argos, he thought, who had served Fat Henry at Calais. Or Theodore Luchisi, or Antonio Stesinos; Fat Henry had used all of those *capitanos* for his wars with the French.

Batty had not heard that any were here in the north of England, all the same. Only one Captain General was known to be here and he blinked away the bads cess of it even as he wryly congratulated himself on his own skills. Bigod, he thought, not only have I found the lost nuns – I have found the men who burned at least one of them.

Not Reformers after all – worse than that. Men who did not care for anything that did not shine. I do not need Sabin, Batty thought bitterly. I have stumbled on Maramaldo all myself alone.

He stared at the spider and saw only a blur while his mind whirled. I am like a wee dug chasing a running stallion, he thought bitterly, with no good idea of what will happen if I sink my auld teeth into its galloping hurdies.

He watched the pair sourly, saw the one with the longbow decide to outdo the exploits of the other by moving closer, then fumbling down his breeches and baring his arse. Batty held his breath; if anyone had as much as a good sharp rock, the bare-arsed fool would end up bloody and possibly dead.

There was a sharp bang and a fount of white smoke from the top of the tower; the two lads whirled away and the one with his ribboned hose and breeks dangling round his knees fell over and rolled away.

There was a pause, then the pair laughed, one hauling the other up while he – shakily, Batty thought – covered himself. Batty could not believe that the shooter had missed; even allowing for poor eyesight and bad powder, the youths were scarce twenty feet from the tower, clapping each other on the back, slapping their thighs and laughing.

Like rabbits cornered by a terrier, Batty thought, the defenders are frozen with fear. He had seen it before and worse – men who would rather kill themselves than die in battle, though it was incomprehensible to Batty that an armed man would do such a thing in preference to fighting.

Yet he had long since learned that there was no fathoming the fear in man nor beast – even the two lads, still capering, were wisely wary as they jeered and cat-called.

That annoyed Batty, all the same, for pissing and waving your bared hurdies at folk who were laired up and had little chance left was cruel as pulling the legs off one side of a spider, just to see it run in frantic circles. He looked at the insect, busy spinning away as the lads laughed again; there was a second bang and a white plume of feathered smoke and the lads scattered, not laughing now.

Then they realised they were unhurt and whoever had shot had missed again and went back to howling and jeering. The time between the shots was too quick for reloading, so there was more than one decent firework in the tower, but Batty shook his head at such poor shooting. Still, he had the idea that the folk behind the carts in the tower had just a little bit of dignity left, squeezed almost out by terror and it angered him that these callous lads had no respect for it.

Think themselves hard men, he mused. Think themselves all swagger and front-of-the-queue. Something moved at the corner of his vision and he squinted at the man who had come out of the bastel house. Drawn by the noise, he mused, watching the man shake his head with disgust and vanish again. Batty wondered how many more there were – then he slid out one of his little knives and felt the balance of it on his palm as he measured distance.

A long throw and, once done, it would set Batty to the dance of it as sure as leading a maid to the ring by one hand. One hand is all I have, he thought and then grinned. Yet it is all I have needed so far...

He rose a little, feeling the pain in his knees. He paused, poised and threw, watched the sun-silvered whirl of it, like a spinning wheel of light.

The lad who owned the gun jerked sideways and fell full length in the steaming grass without so much as a yelp. For a moment, the other carried on jeering and laughing – even pointing at his fallen friend and slapping his thigh with amusement at what he thought was a simple, careless fall.

A wee bit foxed with drink, Batty thought, which is helpful.

The boy stopped laughing in another second, stared for a lot longer, then fell to his knees and started to shake his friend. Now he discovers the knife, which has taken his friend in the neck, Batty thought. As good a throw as I ever did... aye, there. He has the way of it now.

The boy looked up and round, at the tower and then about him, holding the knife which he had drawn from his friend's neck. He sprang back from the body as if it was on fire and fumbled at his bow, which was as big as he was and needed someone bigger and stronger to do it justice.

Still, even a slight lad could stick you with a fletch, Batty thought and flattened himself in the damp grass for a bit, then risked a peek; the lad had stuffed the knife in his belt and was crouched, the bow smarted and nocked with a long arrow, though he turned in an uncertain half circle. For a moment, Batty contemplated a second knife, but had to admit that he had been more than lucky with the first throw. If that had been a hand of cards at Primero, he thought, I would be sweeping a deal of coin into my bonnet, held by a willing woman.

He also knew that, if he had been down there, he would have been yelling his lungs out to let the others know that a snake was in the henhouse – but not at sixteen. At sixteen I would have been as rank silly as this boy, Batty thought, putting personal dignity above sense. He will not yell for help; he will try and avenge his friend and restore his affronted pride at having been caught in such an ambuscade.

Now was the time Batty was for wriggling back and away, but even as he did so he caught the first glimpse of someone beyond the carts, a face pushing out of the shadows. Even allowing for Batty's eyesight, which he was forced to admit was not as fine as it had once been, it was not pretty and not young that face, but it was undoubtedly a woman. She seemed to stare directly at him, as if straight into his eyes – then she was gone.

Batty slithered back down the slight slope, but the face stayed with him even as he made his mind up that he had done all he could. These were the nuns and at least one of them was alive, with perhaps a wagon driver, maybe two. They had a brace of engines with them – calivers by the sound – but could not hit a bull's arse at barrel length and were pinned by men who knew the trade of siege.

Maramaldo's men, no less, Batty was sure of it, and the two *fantoosh* lads were the least of them, given the task of watching in the rain because they were young and at the mercy of grimmer veterans. Batty did not want to discover how many grimmer veterans there were in the bastel house.

Batty had paid for some precious time for the victims, but the hot-damp and the midgies were starting in to irritate and he had, he thought, done all he logically could, for there was no way he could save them. Only a fool would try and Bella Graham of Netherby did not raise her wee Batty to be a fool.

He hummed to himself as he worked out that it was best to let matters take their course and tell Musgrave his sister was fell murdered and that Maramaldo had done it.

'He slew my knight, to me so dear; he slew my knight and poined his gear,' he sang under his breath. Let Musgrave hang Sabin, he thought and I will watch with as little on my face as he had on his when Maramaldo took my arm…

Inside I will be dancing, he admitted and hummed on: *'My servants all for life did flee – and left me in extremitie.'*

Straightening stiffly, he started to limp off to find Fiskie. The slither of noise made him turn and he found himself staring into the equally astonished eyes of the lad with the longbow.

Chapter Four

In the tower at Akeld
Not long after

Sister Faith prayed, as she had been doing for two hours or more, turning the ring round and round her wedding finger, feeling the smooth wear on the indentations and the crucifix. It had been given to her by her mother, afraid of the year and the apocalypse promised in Revelations – 'half-time after the time', which was seen as referring to *Anno Domini* 1500.

She remembered it vividly, for she had turned thirteen on the day the Archbishop had died and her mother and two brothers had turned up just as all the nuns and novitiates turned out in the rain to see old John Morton carried off to a crypt in Canterbury's cathedral.

Her mother and two younger brothers had looked so cold, standing outside the convent of the Priory of St Sepulchre while the Benedictine nuns tried to look pious and failed. A deal of that had to do with the carved arch over the Archbishop's effigy – the angels and cardinal caps were fine, but the fat barrels with MOR on them made straight faces difficult, even if the Archbishop's family thought it a dignified play on his name – MOR-tuns.

In contrast to everyone's shiver, she remembered, she had felt warm and at peace for all her thin novitiate clothing, for she had known, on that day, that God was real. He lived. It had been that simple for her and the peace it brought had been total and encompassing.

Now, in this place of sick heat and damp, after all the years between – even after God, it seemed, had abandoned the Sisters to the destruction of Henry Tudor – that conviction was with her still.

Yet she was deeply troubled for the others who lay and sweated and groaned in the fetid dark of the tower and she rubbed the ring round and round, the crucifix on it up and down, as she always did when she needed a special prayer answered.

Not for me, she argued, for I am ready to join You, my Lord. For the others. And she bowed her head and repeated the prayers once more. There were only two, so they did not take long.

The first was for Sister Benedict, who had not made it to the safety of the tower. Sister Faith had watched the cart roll away, the staggering horses lashed by Si Wood until two arrows had brought one beast down and the cart to a tangled halt.

She had seen Si felled by a youngster in ribboned finery and was sure it was the same one who continually bared his nethers so that the defenders in the tower would fire off what little powder and shot they had. Sister Faith was more concerned that one or both of those ungodly youths would finally work out that they were unharmed because the nuns they had trapped would not kill anyone, but fired into the air instead.

Sister Benedict was gone and Sister Faith knew it, though she had not told the others; Sister Benedict had been one of their only two hopes and the others had visions of her and poor Si Wood hurrying towards

Bewcastle and Sister Benedict's brother, a powerful lord in the area who would bring righteous wrath on the heads of their tormentors.

The second hope was for Sister Mary and Leckie, who had gone off in the opposite direction – that had been Sister Faith's idea, for it gave everyone a chance and had allowed the remaining sisters and carts to reach the tower. She was not so sure that Sister Benedict's sacrifice had allowed Sister Mary and Leckie to reach Wooler, all the same.

Sister Faith did not want to destroy this hope, so her prayer was silent, spilling from behind tight lips and squeezed eyelids. She had an idea that these men, so unlike any soldiery she had seen, were foreign and mercenary, likely to visit Hell on their captives and somehow in the pay of Thomas Horner – but still her contract with God would not allow her to pray for Sister Benedict's quick death.

Instead, she asked the Saviour to accept Sister Benedict's soul and to comfort her in her hour of need, while beseeching Him to speed Sister Mary on her way. She spoke under her breath the same way she had once spoken aloud to her mother, before she had gone to be a nun. She had been troubled then, too.

Her mother had understood, as she had always done and Sister Faith smiled at the memory. Dead and gone these many years, yet the drift of her ma's face was still sharp and bright when Sister Faith remembered and she repeated the words her mother had said to her then.

'Ne'er mind where you are now, or the world, or anything in it. If Jesus has called, then let Him hold you and comfort you as I have done. If He is coming for you, then run to Him. Turn away, let go of all else and run to Him.'

Now Sister Faith wept, not with grief but in farewell, for Sister Benedict, the other nuns in her care – even her mother and this life, which she thought would end soon.

After a time, she smiled through the tears and straightened her small body. She felt the lack of habit and wimple – a homespun dress and cloak and kerch was not the same. She turned the ring, that old, familiar gesture, then composed herself and offered her second prayer.

'Jesus, I have never asked for a thing for myself, not ever. Yet You Yourself have said that if you ask it shall be given. I am willing to die, Lord, if it is Your will, which encompasses us all around and...'

The words failed her, faltered and stopped. She gripped the cross until it bit the palm; the wind seemed suddenly more chill and she shuddered.

'Dear Saviour Jesus,' she said, raising her head to the dark and the dank, hidden stones, 'send a Deliverer to save the others from this evil.'

And she thought of the man she had seen, the one who had thrown something that had felled one of the boys. Killed him, she thought and wondered at that. Yet St Michael carried a sword and it was not just for show, but to smite the enemies of God.

Sister Faith wondered and then prayed a third time, for the soul of this unknown man.

Five miles away
At the same time…

Batty woke with a yelp, launched upright straight from a dream and blinking into the shredded remains of it, the sweat slick on him.

The nun, on fire in the rubble of Florence.

It was an old dream which had returned to him during the business with Mintie Henderson at Powrieburn and had lurked around the edges of his sleep ever since. It was not always the same, even though it had once been a reality.

During the siege of Florence in '30, Batty and Simoni, the one the world knew as Michaelangelo, had struggled to keep the fortifications intact and had discovered the enemy had tunnelled in under a convent.

So Batty had blown it up at the crucial moment when the enemy broke through. Blown it to flames and rubble and millwheeling dead – and the nun, screaming and on fire.

Michaelangelo had dragged Batty away and the nun had been left to shriek and burn, so that Batty was never sure, afterwards, whether he would have helped her or not. Michaelangelo was more assured about it.

'If you had, you would have ruined your one good hand in all the world,' he had told Batty later, head to head in the flickering dim of the Inn of Ropes. It was true horror to Michaelangelo, that lost limb, for his hands were his life, as he said often. He shuddered sometimes when he looked at Batty, reaching out to touch the stump with a gesture of wonder and revulsion, for it was his biggest fear.

'I could not sculpt,' he would say then. 'I could paint still, with only one hand and no matter which, but it would not be the same. There is no *terribiltà* in paint.'

And all the time he would work away with his red chalk, bleeding genius over the back of plans of the fortifications while folk lurched in and out and the noise whirled like flying rubble.

Batty remembered that Simoni seemed immune to it, the frantic couplings – women did not seem to interest him at all – and the mad dancing and music of those living with the imminence of death.

Yet he sketched them, his quick, grimed, broken-nailed fingers moving like spider legs, catching the frozen moment of a wild laugh, an exposed chest, a flung hand, then tossed the half-finished affair away. By the end of a night, there would be a blizzard of scrawled, crushed paper, like muddied snow, all round the chair he slept in, head fallen into his pillowed arms on the scarred table.

The men liked him, Batty remembered, because he did not much care for company at all, but yet sat with them and they felt honoured by it; for all his fame and title, he was as filthy and uncouth as they were and they loved him for that, as they loved the way he could make their likeness on paper.

'This siege will last as long as the wine,' he told them and they agreed and started in to drinking it faster than ever, so that he laughed, his mouth like an open drain in his big ugly face.

'There is too much *algarde* in this inn,' he would shout, suddenly and for no reason and people would cheer. Then he would list all the names of wine, in alphabetical order – *antioche, blanc, charrie, chaudel, clary*, right through to

vernage and, finally, roared out by the others as the chorus
– *VIN.*

Batty blinked the memories away and wiped the sweat
from his face, grateful for the catlick of wind which lipped
its way through the tangle of whin and gorse he was laired
in. His leg hurt and had gone stiff; he cursed the boy and
his bow.

The stun of surprise had lasted an eyeblink, but the boy
got to business first – youth, Batty thought bitterly, over
the moss of age. He had drawn and shot, but the first was
half-hearted – barely back to the chest, never mind the ear
– and his aim poor; Batty had felt the blow on his lower
leg and was shoved off-balance by it, falling on his back
with his arms and legs waving like a beetle.

The boy should have followed it up by dropping the
bow, hauling out a knife and pouncing, but he was young
and had not learned enough; he hauled out another arrow
and started in to nocking it.

He was still doing it when Batty pointed the dagg at
him and pulled the trigger. The boy yelped, dropped the
bow and covered up with his hands, as if it would shield
him from the hefty ball of lead.

He did not need to, all the same; the dagg's wheel
whirred and sparked and nothing happened. For a
moment, there was stillness, while Batty stared in shock at
the misfired wheel-lock and the youth crouched, scarcely
believing his reprieve.

There was a long moment of staring as the ball, freed
from the charred wad, rolled casually out of the dagg's
long barrel and plunked at their feet. Then the youth
whimpered and dived for the sword at his waist. Batty
cursed and flung the dagg – the axe-handled one. The
trick had worked before and the axe blade had sliced into

a head as if it was a blown egg – but this time the whole engine of it clattered into the chest and face of the boy, flinging him backwards.

He was half-stunned and Batty gave him no chance to use even the half wit he had; he scrauchled across to him like a scuttling crab, bollock knife out of his boot and buried once in the neck, to cut off any screams that might bring others, then once, twice, three times more in the paunch, sickening-hard punches until there was only kicking and gurgling.

Only then did Batty roll away, stifling his own moans at the burn in his left calf, breathing hard like a galloped stot. He lay for a time with the wind, until he had enough breath and too much pain, then grunted upright and examined his leg.

The arrow had missed bone and had just enough power in it to go through the flesh of his calf, so that he sawed off the shaft with the gory bollock dagger and drew both ends out. He let the blood flow a little, then packed clean rainwashed moss in it and bound it with a ribbon or two from the lad's finery.

The lad was still, his face turned up and marbled eyes staring at God. It was an old-young face, still barely able to beard up but crow-footed round the eyes, which were bruised and pouched, the nose already fretted with little blood-veins and pits. The mouth snarled yellow teeth and the lips had pox sores on them.

Batty knew the face well – all the Maramaldo men had it. Satan made in the image of a fallen angel, leering above the silken finery of a houri in a Turkish brothel.

He searched the lad and found his own throwing knife, a pearl drop pin he liked and some coin, all of which he took along with the axe-handled dagg, giving it a look as if it was a dog which had failed him. Then he hirpled up on to Fiskie and rode away, arguing that he could make for Wooler and that this was no place for him now; for all he knew the bastel house was stuffed with Maramaldo men who, sooner or later, would find the two boys they'd set to watch the tower.

They would work out that both had been stabbed and wonder about the folk in the tower; he had a grim laugh to himself at the thought of them considering whether the nuns they had trapped were quite as innocent as they seemed.

Unless they were all callow as the boys he had killed, they could not miss the spoor of it, all the same, nor fail to track Fiskie.

That was before the pain in his leg set in with the coming of early night. The clouds shrouded moon and stars, which stopped him riding entirely, blinded by dark. Barely able to slither off Fiskie's back, he had crawled into a shelter of bushes and crouched in his cloak, wondering if he had put enough distance between him and danger so that he could wait until daylight, get his bearings and then ride hard.

The Lord is my herd, nae want sal fa' me.

It came to him from the silted memories stirred up from the bottom of his soul by the dream of the burning nun – whose face, Batty suddenly realised, was neither the original, nor Mintie's which he had once imposed on the image. It was the one briefly glimpsed when he'd left Akeld. The old woman in the tower.

Na! tho' I gang thro' the dead-mirk-dail; e'en thar, sal I dread nae skaithin.

Remembrance of the prayer came from Alesius, that silly wee cant from Edinburgh whose real name was Sandy

Kane. Every gown who spouted Latin was for changing their name, Batty remembered, to something higher and mightier – Sandy was one of the fawning hangers-on round Schwartzerde, the German who called himself Melancthon, and Batty had met them all once in Saxony.

The pack of them, in turn, spent their time denouncing the cult of saints and arguing about whether they were really eating Christ at the Last Supper. That's when they were not wriggling like belly-up pups round Luther and trying to hump his leg with ecstasy whenever he pronounced on something.

Sandy Kane was hot for Scottish bishops to read the Bible in 'the mither tongue' and composed great pontificating blasts condemning the prohibitions against it – but could no more understand it than he could some *mahout* from the Indies.

So Batty had taken great delight in reciting the Lord's Prayer to Sandy whenever he could – *he waukens my wa'-gaen saul; he weises me roun, for his ain name's sake, intil right roddins*. That had even set Luther giggling.

The leg ached and Batty grunted. He wanted to touch it but knew he would not be reassured with the swell and the sicky seep of blood through his makeshift bandage. He gritted his worn teeth and forced himself up, growling like a bear with the stabs of pain as he hobbled to Fiskie, who looked at him with a reproving, jaundiced eye.

'Well might you chastise me,' Batty murmured, hauling himself into the damp saddle, 'but I will be punished for neglecting you, by and by.'

He patted the neck of the horse and even managed a soft laugh as he turned away, seeking the dim way to Wooler.

'*Ye hae drookit my heid wi' oyle; my bicker is fu' an' skailin.*'

77

Chapter Five

In the tower at Akeld
Dawn the next day...

Cornelius was small, old and wizened as lizard skin. He wore a Moorish *cheche*, a winding of black cloth which covered his head and looped across his face as a veil, but he was not a Moor nor anything like one.

He had baggy breeches and a shirt over which he wore a robe which he fondly believed made him look academic and alchemikal, though Klett thought the ragged, stained garment summed up the man for what he was – a slovenly fraud.

'We should leave this place,' Cornelius declared portentously. 'It is ripe with the fevers.'

Klett saw Cadette, Ponce, Jacob and others nodding and looked moodily at Cornelius, who saw the scowl and felt a stab of fear that he had gone too far.

'I have *cinquefoil* for it, of course,' he added hastily, 'which resists poisons with the virtues of its leaves, numbering the totemic five.'

Klett simply stared. He was thinking that he would like to dispose of Cornelius, who was not a decent Alamain, or Fleming despite the name. He was from Spain, but not even a decent dago; he was a *marrano*, a Jew who had converted, out of fear, to Christianity. He was also

Maramaldo's favourite, an alchemist and astrologer and a skilled notary. Notaries were what drove the likes of the Company of the Sable Rose for they were the ones who legalled out the *condotta* – even if Maramaldo would break such an agreement in an eyeblink if it suited him, he valued them as providing status and dignitas to what otherwise, he claimed, would be a band of murderous apes.

Cornelius' name, Klett knew, had been taken from Heinrich Cornelius Von Nettesheim, the magician from Cologne everyone had called Agrippa. The little *marrano* swore he had been apprentice to this magician and had knowledge from the vanished Fourth Book of *De Occulta Philosophia*. Since no one had ever known or seen of such a fourth book in that trilogy, it was hard to gainsay him.

Klett was stuck with him and knew the man was there as much to spy and report for Maramaldo as he was ostensibly to offer advice and divination. His advice, as ever, was to abandon the current enterprise.

Klett knew the *marrano* was right and that Maramaldo would be furious at what Klett had done. An angry Maramaldo was not A Good Matter, for Klett had seen the bloody results of flayed pulp and did not want to be next on that list. Only success would rescue him now.

All of this, to Cornelius, was simply a long, agate stare which withered his resolve; he blanched.

'Or vervin,' he offered weakly, 'cut from the third joint if the fever be tertian. The fourth if it be in quartane...'

'Quartane fevers did not kill Johannes, nor Locan,' Klett said eventually. 'Blades did. I do not think our nuns have become expert knife-throwers overnight, nor that the one man left to them is an assassin of note. Especially if I shot him, as I believe.'

Cornelius bobbed his head and spread his arms in apology.

'I merely advise that this matter is prolonged...'

'We should be done with the business,' Cadette interrupted, his square face sour beneath a plumed confection of hat, the brim trimmed with lace.

'If you had not gone off burning nuns,' Klett replied mildly, 'and stopped the others carts as you were supposed to...'

He broke off and smiled winter into Cadette's glare until the man dropped his eyes and muttered.

The tension was broken by the arrival of Horner, dressed in sober finery; beside the popinjays of Klett's company he looked a drab sparrow.

Here, Klett thought bitterly, is the architect of our woe, the man who came with a tale so slathered in rich reward that it was impossible to ignore – a cartload of nuns and a trio of useless men carrying a hidden treasure so valuable Maramaldo could not pass it up.

Now two of my men are dead, Klett thought, and all these hardened warriors are frustrated by those same nuns, locked up in a crumbling tower and well armed – as they had been for two days. If it was left much longer, Maramaldo would be here and Klett's task for him unfulfilled. The Captain General would not be happy at that.

Unless the matter was done with and the treasure unveiled. If there was treasure... Klett looked sour at Horner as he came up.

'Well?'

'Tracks of a horse, heading off towards Wooler. It seems we have a cuckoo in our nest.'

Horner's tones were clipped, though he was a lot less haughty than he had been when he'd arrived in this place. A lot less clean, too, Klett noted with a cold comfort.

Horner had been hot to rush the place on arrival. Klett, fresh from scouring four Wallis defenders from the bastel of Akeld, had looked at him with a jaundiced eye and pointed out the lurker on the tower top.

'Armed, no doubt,' he'd pointed out. 'So the first hero will fall, for certain.'

He'd left the words hanging there for Horner to chew on, sitting on his too-fine beast and watching smoke spilling greasily up out of the tower.

'Trying to signal for aid,' he had bellowed and started his fine horse prancing.

Sow's arse. Klett smile had been iced but polite.

'I think not, Master Horner,' he had answered, as if gentling an excitable bairn. 'They are starting a fire for their own ends – who is there to come to their aid in a God-forsaken hole such as this?'

'The filthy devils who own Akeld,' Horner had answered, scowling, 'but not before we have those nuns.'

Klett had frowned at that; Horner seemed to know more than he was telling and Klett already had the uncomfortable notion that Maramaldo had not told him the entire weft of the plan. Capture some nuns and carts, he had been told and make a deal of noise around Akeld; Klett did not know the reason for any of it and that ruffled him.

He had lost the thread of that when Horner highstepped his horse towards the crumble of tower, his slim sword raised and trying to look the very picture of Mars, exhorting Klett's men to rush the place. It might have worked too, for he had good seat and was only slightly foolish with the ruined droop of his wet hat-plume, but the man on the tower ended his mummery.

There had been a bang and a spout of smoke from the ruined crenellations and the fine horse shrieked, then went into a mad frenzy of bucking and throwing; the very first one pitched Horner up in the air and down in the mud.

For a moment there had been confusion, all splash and ripple, Klett saw, with no order. Mercenaries of Maramaldo, hardened veterans my sorry arse – no more sense than a barnyard of chooks he'd thought then and subsequent events had not improved his opinion.

Klett knew he had been given these, the least trained and youngest, because Maramaldo could spare them and Klett did not like the thought that he was as expendable.

Horner's fancy stot, keening with pain, had finally staggered, coughed and fallen with a shriek that was altogether too much like a child for comfort.

'I fear he has done for your fine mount,' Klett had offered and was genuinely sorrowed for the animal, even as he fought to keep his face straight at what had happened to its owner.

Horner, slathered with mud and fury, had looked aghast at the dying, screaming horse, then up at all the riders round him, one by one, as if bewildered. For a long while no one had moved – then Jacob, the least ribboned fool of the pack, stepped forward, placed his caliver muzzle on the blood-frothed head of the horse and fired.

The great gout of flame and noise jerked everyone alive, it seemed – save for the horse. Klett remembered that Jacob had stepped out of the smoke, blowing on his slow match and offered Horner a scathing look for not performing the act himself. Then he had looked at Klett, the broad, flat, bearded face giving no more away than a shuttered window; Klett had known then that none of these men would rush the tower.

Horner, wiping himself down, had managed a wan smile, though it never reached his eyes. He had looked at the horse, then the clenched crouch of Klett's company and picked his hat out of the mud.

'Meinherr Klett,' he had said. 'Oblige me by removing that offence.'

Klett remembered that he had not liked to be treated like some servant, nor appreciated this pressure put upon his skills. Yet he could not refuse it easily and had swung out of his saddle while everyone watched with interest and the *marrano* Cornelius scuttled up with a tall, leather-covered edifice.

The great leather cover came off and what most had taken to be a lance was unveiled as a long hackbut gun. Even those who had seen it before, whistled with admiration and Horner saw Klett smile, the first time this had happened.

'That is a fine thing to see,' Horner had admitted, then stopped speaking entirely, for the affair was not a matchlock as he had thought, but a wheel-lock. Horner, who had only heard of Klett's marvellous engine, had never seen such a thing in his life and said so.

'It is made by my father and brothers,' Klett had answered, with pride.

It was longer by a foot than a tall man, the octagonal barrel decorated with filed and cut cannelures, ornamented with engravings. There was a strange ornamental saw-blade hook halfway along it but Horner had watched as Klett unscrewed it and put it carefully in a pouch.

'What do you think of my Wall Gun, Master Horner?'

'Is that what it is?' Horner had declared, seeing what the hook was for – bracing the monster on a wall or beam. It meant the kick of it was fearsome and he shook his head.

'For shooting at artillery batteries,' Klett added.

'If you can hit anything,' Horner had remarked mildly, then eyed the tower and the small figure darting about on it. The German had moved his weapon closer, making sure he was out of range of the shooter's own weapon, which meant a long shot for any gun – no caliver could make it and few hackbuts, none with any chance of hitting.

Cornelius had then brought a second leather bag and Klett unpacked a contraption of hooped wood and spokes – a small two-wheeled carriage. The barrel hook had been removed, Horner had seen, to facilitate the fitting of the gun to the hoop on the carriage.

He had marvelled as Klett loaded the great weapon – the ball was a quarter-pound if it was an ounce, he thought – then fixed the entire affair to the little hooped carriage using trunnions built into the barrel.

That will bring the kick of it down a deal, Horner thought, but still…

There had been another bang and fountain of smoke from the tower, but it was clear it was more in hope than expectation; Klett had lain down behind his weapon on the least muddy patch of grass, legs splayed and toes turned outwards. He'd dug his feet into the soft turf a few times and padded his shoulder before snugging the butt to it.

Horner had watched with narrowed eyes – the gun was not held under the arm, then, but up at the shoulder, for better steadiness and sighting. There had been a flicker of movement up on the tower roof, then the familiar whirr and spark, the blast of noise and a fountain of smoke.

When it cleared, Horner had seen that Klett's feet had scored an inch or two of rut.

'High and to the left,' Klett had declared and Horner had spotted the fresh, bright scar on the old stone – Christ, if that even passes near you, it will whip off a limb, he'd thought. Or your head – if it doesn't break the shooter's ankles.

After a long reload, the second blast from Klett's gun had blown a deal of stone chips everywhere. The third shot had seemed to miss entirely – then a figure rose up on the tower, shrieked and fell away; men had cheered.

'Well done Meinheer Klett,' Horner had said, but the German had merely nodded, then indicated his men as he started to pack up the weapon.

'They still will not rush it,' he had said flatly. 'Even nuns can shoot.'

So matters had remained since, for no one wanted to risk it and the decision to let thirst and fear corrode the resolve of mere nuns had seemed sensible at the time. The youngest lads, Johannes and Locan, had been left to watch, irritating everyone with their capering; each bang of the defender's guns let Klett knew that the nuns were tough as old chooks and not about to give in easily.

Now Johannes and Locan were stabbed to death and there was a mysterious third party at this fayre, which had gone on too long already; Klett did not like it and said so. He was surprised when Horner seemed unworried.

'This new arrival may be a messenger I am expecting,' he declared and Klett bridled at this revelation of secrets kept from him. He demanded answers, but Horner only shrugged. Klett had had enough.

'If your messenger announces his presence by murdering two of my lads,' he growled, 'then he had better be quick in delivering it. Quicker than the kinch of rope round his neck.'

'It seems unlikely,' Horner admitted, 'but mayhap your lads surprised him and gave him no choice. Of course, he may have killed no one and we are conflating the events. I would prefer anyone you find to be alive and brought to me.'

'I have few men for such a luxury,' Klett spat back. 'Two fewer than this morning.'

'Then do not sit here, all louche and goggling. Rush the tower,' Horner rasped.

'More will die so if we rush in,' Klett answered. 'Captain General Maramaldo will need a deal of golden balm to soothe his rage at losing so many to this enterprise.'

'You have already lost two men,' Horner pointed out. 'If you had stormed the place at the start...'

'Do not presume to tell me my business,' Klett answered coldly.

'Someone must,' Horner replied, flushing from chin to hair roots. 'I am a gentleman and will not be spoken to like some servitor by the captain of a company afraid of a handful of nuns.'

Klett did not like Horner, nor his frequent snide hints that he was party to plans and decisions made by the Captain General himself. He had even suggested that the Company's contract was, in part, with himself; Klett had dismissed that, of course, but his unease at being kept in the dark did not make him diplomatic with this puffed popinjay.

'You are, if your claim is true, nothing at all,' he spat back. 'Former steward to the former Abbot of Glastonbury, who was hung and drawn for treason in 1539.'

Horner fell silent and gnawed his nails for a bit.

'True enough,' he admitted. 'but he died without revealing where the treasure of Glastonbury was hid. I know. It is here, with those nuns.'

'So you told Maramaldo,' muttered Klett. 'Here, with those armed nuns, you said. And now someone else knows of it.'

Horner leaned forward, his eyes all glitter and gimlet.

'Then hunt him down,' he said. 'And take the tower. I have spent too long on this enterprise to be thwarted at the last.'

He paused and then delivered the cut he knew would wound Klett to the quick.

'There are greater events at play than you know, Mein-heer Klett.'

Not far away…

The lark was too astonished at the noise and could only hover, but Batty was not watching her as he sang, he was watching the buzzard.

'*He slew my knight, to me so dear; He slew my knight, and poined his gear,*' he crooned, while the lark fluttered indignation at the noise and the buzzard sat in a gnarled tree for a contemplative moment. When it launched off its branch down into the grass, Batty knew what he would find; his tune became rank.

'*My servants all for life did flee, and left me in extremitie…*'

The singing ended when he came on the bodies, the buzzard flapping off in interrupted disgust while the early, gorged ravens could only hop and waddle, too full to fly. They stood a little way off, wings outstretched and beaks open, hissing bad cess at Batty.

87

The man had been spread-eagled and staked out through his palms, but not before his privates had been cut off and stuffed in his mouth. His eyelids, nose and ears had been sliced off, an eye gouged out with a stick and he had been used as a target for archers or spearmen. Maybe even lances, Batty thought as he hunkered and tried to keep the spit in his mouth; he looked round then, not wanting to find prickers riding up on him.

But this was not the work of Border horse, he thought. This is the work of mercenaries hardened in rape and plundering – Maramaldo men, who wanted answers to questions from this man and had taken a good hour to kill their victim. The slit belly had been all business – looking for swallowed coin and trinkets – the sliced eyelids and other parts had all been to inflict horror and pain enough to force information out.

But the target practice had been all fun; Batty thought of the boy with the longbow and spat the memory of him into the grass.

They had taken even longer with the woman – another nun, Batty saw. The ravens had been an unkindness to what the mercenaries left and Batty covered the thing with her torn, plain dress, stripped from her right at the start. Rape had only been the beginning of her terror and pain.

He sat back on his heels and swilled spit round his gums to try and rinse the foul out of his mouth while he wondered what they had been wanting to know. He found the inevitable black robes, ripped from their hiding place and flung away as worthless; he covered the corpse with them.

No place for me, this, Batty thought levering himself up and squinting up at the weak sun. Lowering, he thought, though I can be in Wooler vill before it goes, providing I take no time for anything else. Like burying folk.

Then he thought of the nun under her black robe and the one he had found burned and the one whose eyes and face thrust out of his mind's darkest recess to stare him in the conscience. He cursed.

It will be the nuns in it, Batty thought, bringing up the memory of the one in Florence whom I might have saved if Michaelangelo had not dragged me away. Or I had let drag me away…

'*I sewed his sheet, making my mane; I watched the corpse, myself alane,*' Batty sang as he levered himself up and swung Fiskie's head round. '*I watched his body, night and day; no living creature came that way.*'

The lark gave up in disgust and whirred into the moor while Batty rode back the way he had come, hunching into a new fall of rain.

Even closer…

His arse burned from too long in the saddle and the insides of his thighs were chafed because he had not dried out properly after the last rain. He could have done so, but the ragged peasants in the mean cruck house he had sheltered in had taken offence and he had thought it wiser to quit.

After taking all his money, Rutland noted bitterly, which was more than enough to compensate for the rogering of their filthy daughter, who'd had the temerity to ask for more and then set up an outcry when properly dismissed like the peasant she was.

Rutland hated this; the hills and moors were no place for him and he wished for Bewcastle at least. He wished for Edinburgh, in truth and dreamed of London as some faraway Camelot…

But here he was, following Mad Jack's instructions and tracking like some native of the Indies – though the truth was that he had no idea about tracking at all and was moving in the general direction the peasant scum had told him. Before they threw him out.

He would have given up long since, but the burn of his throat was with him still and would be until he revenged it. Find the German soldiery or Master Horner, he had been instructed. Give the message by mouth, for nothing was written for folk who may not have had the skill of reading it anyway. Return.

Cadwaller Rutland did not like being a fetching dog, but he was also canny enough to know that he had little choice, was clinging on to the office of gentleman by a cunny-hair. So he had followed everyone's instructions – including the filthy peasant scum's directions – right to a dead nun and a cart driver.

He wondered if the man was Batty and, after a long time of trying not to be sick and waving away flies, got enough of a look to see two arms. Rutland was not disappointed – he had a score to settle with that one-armed fud, but he would have to wait his turn in the queue.

He dwelt lovingly on that all the long way over the rolling Cheviot hills, peering and squinting to try and find some semblance of a trail that looked more than a faint sheep-track, but could not tell one scuff from another. Near Akeld, he had been told, but was none the wise for that, though he kept scanning for signs of a dwelling. Any dwelling; his arse hurt and his back ached and he wanted hot food, strong drink and a decent sleep.

He was so intent on it that he did not realise there were men coming up on him until one seized the bridle of his horse.

Startled, Rutland jerked and his horse reared, spilling him from the saddle with a thump. He heard men laugh mockingly and struggled up, fighting for breath, to see three of them, sitting on rough-coated nags.

They were strange, bedecked with ribbons and a cut of clothing that Rutland knew instinctively was foreign and particular. Mercenaries; he fumbled out his sword and struck the proper pose.

'I warn you,' he said and a man laughed. He was hard-eyed and scarred down one cheek and did not seem facered by Cadwaller Rutland, duellist.

'Any little throwing knives left?' asked another in execrable French and Rutland, bewildered, had no reply to this.

'What do you think, Cadette?' the man asked and the scarred one shrugged, then jerked his chin at Rutland.

'Take him.'

The others dismounted and Rutland backed off a little way, watching; the two men unlimbered big practical backswords and eyed him warily.

'Wait,' he said. 'I have come...'

One of them lunged and blades clanged. There was a flurry and the man reeled backwards cursing and holding his wrist where Rutland's rapier had pinked him. Rutland smiled; he did not know what language the man was spitting oaths in, but he knew fear and pain when he heard it.

'Look,' he said patiently. 'Take me to your captain. There are matters he needs to know.'

The other one hesitated and Cadette looked disgusted at him, then hawked and spat meaningfully.

'In the name of Christ,' he said, shaking his head with disgust. Rutland whipped the rapier back and forth with little hissing sounds.

'It would be better for you to do as you are bid,' he declared, arrogant and annoyed now. 'Take me to your captain. Before someone else is hurt.'

'I think not,' Cadette said flatly, hauled the dagg out of his belt. He blew on the slow match wound round his wrist, touched off the one on the dagg, pointed and fired. All the while Rutland watched, astounded.

It hissed at the pan for a bit, so that Rutland had time to be shocked out of his silence, time to say 'no' exactly twice and put up his free hand, palm out, as if to block the effects. Then the great bang sent a lump of shot ripping through him, hurling him backwards out of the fountain of smoke, rolling him over and over; horses squealed and Rutland's mount bolted.

Cadette pinched out the slow match and stuffed the pistol back in his belt.

'Fetch back his horse,' he ordered one of the men, 'and load him up. Klett will want to see his cuckoo. Alive would have been preferred, but only that Horner one cared for that. Dead will do.'

Not long after…

The ravens were getting sorely tired of Batty Coalhouse and wearily flapped off in disgust as he came up, cat-cautious and with his one fist loaded with axe-handled dagg.

He had taken a circled route back to where he had started, to where the burned nun lay and was halfway round the curve of it when the shot wafted faintly out of the late afternoon twilight. It made him rein in and sit for a while, thinking it over while the rain sifted down and Fiskie blew out displeasure in soft snorts of disgust.

In the end, Batty cut across to where he thought the sound had come from, though he was thinking that it was foolish all the time he was doing it. When he came on the churned earth and the blood that had so interested the ravens he spent a long time watching, until he was sure only the ravens, himself and his horse were alive in the place.

Someone was shot, probably dead, by three or four men who came on him over a crest – the earth and all the blood told Batty that much, but who had done what to whom remained a mystery, as did the reason they had carted off the body. Still alive, after all that had leaked from him? Then the sun leered bloodily off some glitter in a fern patch.

Batty found the culprit and picked it up. Fell off when he was hoisted on to a horse, he thought to himself. Dead or alive, probably the former but it was no matter – they would take him back to the others at Akeld and consider that they had found the killer of their two men. Which, Batty thought, is useful to me.

He tossed the little ruby bull in the palm of his hand before stuffing it inside his jack. Poor wee Cadwaller Rutland, he thought, dead in my stead and so has served me a good turn, though he will never know it.

Why the likes of Rutland had been sent out bothered him for a while – a wee court-rat like that, useless as hen shite on a pump handle out in the Border wilds? Sent on a particular task by Mad Jack – it was hardly likely to be about tracking me, Batty thought. Wee Rutland could not find his hurdies with both arms, let alone follow me across the Cheviot wild – so where was he riding?

But there were more pressing worries and he lost the thought somewhere along the whin and gorse, had it pushed out by the face of the nun in the tower. It would not leave him alone and the more he worried at it, the more it became impossible to put down.

Batty rode on into the blood-egg tremble of sunset and reached the burned nun by last light; the packhorse was still there, cropping grass unconcerned and came up, glad to meet another of his kind and exchanging nuzzles with Fiskie.

The nun had not improved any and the birds and beasts had not helped, so it took Batty all his time to force himself to the task, trying to be quiet because he was so close to where he did not want to be.

He managed the nun on to the re-saddled packhorse and fastened her there with pack-straps until she lolled, grim, blackened and stiffly grinning. It was awkward work one-handed and the packhorse did not care for it much, so it was dark by the time he had finished. In the end, though, the packhorse turned out to be such a docile beast that Batty felt bad about what had to be done. But now that he had made his mind up, he wanted it done swiftly; he was too close to the bastel house and the tower to linger long fastening a dead nun on to a horse.

'Swef,' he crooned softly to the beast, splashing the lamp oil over the wizened scorch on its back. 'I am right sair sorry for this, for you dinna deserve it. But needs must...'

He had worked it out in his head on the way to here, a simple plan, or so he thought, because simple plans were always best. In and out, he thought. Grab the nun and away, easy as begging.

Because, he argued with himself, it might be Mad Jack's sister in there and, if it is not, she will be proof to Mad Jack back in Bewcastle that his sister is dead. Then he wondered if this grinning scorch of nun was, in fact, the sister and made a note not to tell this part of the tale to the Bastard's Buzzard. Five pounds English, he thought to himself, was never earned harder than this.

He sparked his firestarter, each flare seeming as large as a cartwheel. He blew it into flame, made it bigger, then thrust it at the nun.

There was a moment when nothing happened, then a soft sighing sound sent flames racing; the packhorse whinnied anxiously and Batty whipped out his sword and pricked it viciously.

'Away wi' ye,' he growled and the packhorse, astonished, pained and afraid set off at a fast lick, up over the ridge and down the other side; the flames streamed from the nun like a cloak. Like the one in Florence, Batty thought and scrambled up on to Fiskie.

'Ride, my bonny,' he said and Fiskie took off like a rat heading for a drain.

Batty heard the cries through the rush of wind and the soft drum of Fiskie's unshod hooves; mercenaries are as hagged as any auld beldames, Batty thought with a flush of satisfied triumph, hung about wi' wee medallions against this, or charms for that. A burning nun on a flaming horse coming at them out of the dark, after what they had done earlier, will send them running like chooks.

The next second he was hanging grimly on as Fiskie veered, too late to avoid hitting a man unseen in the dark. One meaty shoulder of the horse sent him flying with a shriek, but it was all Batty could do to hang on; on the other side he saw that the burning nun had been bucked off by the frantic packhorse, whose mane and tail had caught alight.

The black finger of the stone tower loomed and Batty hauled Fiskie up in a skid of damp earth, then hurled himself off. He landed badly on the wounded leg and felt it give way with such a shriek of agony that he did not have to bellow himself, though he did anyway.

He crashed a shoulder into the carts, called out that he was a friend and started to haul himself up and in – only to fall and roll to the feet of a shadow woman whose caliver was pointed straight at him and whose eyes were gimlet.

'Freen',' he croaked, then saw the face more clearly as he blinked sweat and pain out of his eyes. The same face that had shoved itself out of the dark earlier to haunt him.

'Get ready,' he gasped, trying to lever himself up. 'We are leaving...'

The leg buckled and lanced agony through him; he found himself on his knees, supported by the nun, who wiped his forehead as if he was a bairn.

'I do not believe we are going anywhere,' she said and Batty bewildered and blinking, suddenly saw more faces behind her, thrusting out of the dim to peer curiously at him. One wizened mouth opened in a gummed smile under bright blue eyes set in a rutted field of wrinkles.

'Ah kin coup ma lundies,' it said and Batty groaned with the bad cess of it. Then the pain rolled over him like red billows and drowned his senses entirely.

Chapter Six

In the tower at Akeld
Sometime later…

'Ah kin coup ma lundies.'

The ingenuous blue eyes were smiling and the paleness of her wrinkled face told how she had spent a lifetime cloistered. Batty struggled to come to terms with what had happened and where he was.

The tower. Not one nun but a whole parcel of them – even with the best intent, Fiskie could not carry them all.

Fiskie… he started to struggle up but the dull ache in his leg made him gasp and the nun's blue eyes clouded with a child's sorrow. The pale hands were brisk and efficient, all the same and made him comfortable with strength and ease. Then the gummed smile returned.

'Ah kin mak' a whole whirlimagig.'

'Aye?' Batty answered, unable to think of anything better. Then another figure wraithed out of the dappled dim and patted the first nun on the shoulder.

'Well done, Sister Hope.'

'He kens noo that ah kin coup ma lundies.'

'It is a time since you were able to do that for real, Sister,' the other nun chided gently and Sister Hope sighed and vanished. The first nun looked at Batty, her face as familiar to him now as his mother's.

'Sister Hope is old, but remembers when she was a child. I think couping her lundies was the one thing she missed most about becoming a nun. It means...'

'Turning cartwheels,' Batty growled, struggling up as best he could. 'I ken fine what it means, mistress, though I am surprised to hear a good Fife lilt on a nun from as far south as yourselves.'

'We are all God's children,' the nun replied. 'I am Sister Faith.'

Batty told her his name and noted that only Charity was missing. The nun frowned a little.

'She in the tower top with a caliver. Sister Charity has many skills, one of them the art of loading such engines.'

As if to prove it, there was a loud bang from above, followed by shouts and a few jeers.

'The skill she is missing is hitting,' Batty replied, struggling up to his knees and feeling his head swim.

'She is shooting into the air,' Sister Faith declared firmly. 'None of us will kill.'

That accounts for it then, Batty thought and wanted to tell Sister Faith that she had almost run the course of her misdirection, since the two boys had last been seen a scant twenty feet from this laired convent, and closing. Before he had killed them.

But the noise made him drag out his axe-handled dagg; the maddened horse had set fire to something else, whose leaping flames seared the night and made crazed caperers of the shapes running back and forth. One stood still and bawled order at them and Batty could feel the man's rage like the heat from the flames; the horse fell and rolled in a screaming shower of sparks and flame. An arrow, Batty thought... then a huge red blossom bloomed, ugly as a leprous lily; the great boom of it shook the tower and rattled Batty's teeth.

Powder, bigod. Batty was exultant – the horse had not been felled, but had fallen, after charging into their powder store. He felt a pang about the packhorse and started to scramble up, thinking of Fiskie.

A dark shape loomed and Batty cursed as Fiskie squealed in the dark; he heard him running.

'No,' said the nun and it was neither order nor request, just a statement on what Batty was about to do. He fired at the dark shape, the whirling sparks from the wheel and great gout of flame blowing all night-sight away. The acrid, unseen smoke brought tears and coughing, but Batty still heard Sister Faith hoarsely asking forgiveness for him; it felt awkward and uncomfortable.

Fiskie. The horse was gone, galloped into the night, with his two holstered daggs, ammunition, food, water, skillet – everything save what he wore.

He was cursing himself, the horse, the night and all in it when he felt the movement. He dropped one dagg, whipped out another and swung round... to find Sister Faith staring back down the long muzzle at him.

There was a long moment, then Sister Faith sighed.

'That is what they do, such machines,' she said.

'What?' Batty asked, carefully securing the pistol.

'They put fear in you,' she answered, then cocked her head. 'God did not send you to kill.'

'God did not send me at all, goodwife,' he answered. 'I just came.'

And wish now I had not, for I came to sweep up one nun and gallop off and now I have three and the horse is gone besides. He squinted at where the scattered flames were dying, beaten out by shouting men. Christ,

99

if I had known all this aforehand, I would have ridden on to Wooler.

'No, you would not,' said Sister Faith and Batty jerked round to look at her. She had a face that had been no great beauty when young, but had a swan serenity, where you knew everything was working away furiously underneath, but it never showed. She had brown-spotted hands folded neatly in her lap – and wore a wedding ring, which surprised Batty.

'Whit?' he managed, after a long moment of staring.

'You were thinking that you would have ridden on if you'd known what lay here in the tower,' she said, then stared into his face.

'You would have come anyway,' she added.

'Christ's Wounds,' Batty answered with a poor laugh that sounded shaky even to him. 'That's a skill that will get you burned, mistress.'

'Sister,' she corrected, 'and do not blaspheme.'

'And that's a title will get you burned twice,' Batty said. Sister Faith smiled, then glanced out to where the flames were sizzling and dying.

'Burned like her? Who was it?' she asked softly.

Batty was busy in his head, working out what he had on him – a peck of coin, a brace of daggs, a bandolier of apostles slung round him, a backsword and a selection of knives – so he had told her about the other one he had found before realising he might have sweetened it a little.

When he snapped his lips shut and looked at the nun, she bowed her head for a moment and Batty heard her prayers, saw her turn the ring round and round. Finally, she looked him in the eye again.

'Do not mention this,' she begged. 'The others will lose heart.'

'Aye, aye,' Batty answered, flustered enough to be harsher still. 'Best not tell them we are trapped and helpless – what brought you this way? Bewcastle is a long wheen o' miles from this place.'

'Sister Benedict told us we were bound for Kirknewton, where we would find help organised by her brother, the Lord of Bewcastle,' the nun said, then sighed and crossed herself. 'She was trying to get there when they caught her.'

Batty grunted. Kirknewton? Well, it was supposedly Reformed, but the place was a huddle of wee cruck houses and the church, no more. Notable, he recalled, for being where men were buried in the aftermath of Flodden field.

It has more ghouls than living folk, Batty thought and is closer to Berwick than Bewcastle – he squinted at why Mad Jack would have done this and could not come up with any reason that made sense. There was another, more pressing problem…

'What's your plan, then? Sister.'

'You are,' she answered and rose up to walk towards him.

'Watch…' he warned, alarmed as she put herself in full view of the outside and took the few steps to kneel by his leg and smiled.

'If the Lord wants me to die,' she said, fishing out a candle and a small knife, 'then I will die. But I won't die afraid.'

She stuck the candle on a stone, rose up again and seemed to disappear, then materialised again with a flicker of flaming light. Batty worked out that she had gone down steps; there was an undercroft to the tower.

She lit the candle then looked at him.

'Drop your breeks,' she said and, for a moment, Batty hesitated and had back a long, slow smile which made him flush. He stood feeling all the unseen guns and arrows on his back, shed the breeks and lay down as she ordered.

A thought struck him as he watched her heat the knife in the candle flame.

'How many Sisters are you?'

'Myself,' she answered, 'Sister Hope whom you have met. Sister Charity on the roof as I said. And our last driver, Trumpet, who is dying.'

She told him the rest; Trumpet Baillie was the ex-soldier who had driven one of the carts, who had manned the caliver and the tower at the start and had been shot by some sort of large gun or small cannon.

'It went through the stone,' she said, calling softly to Sister Hope to hold the candle for her while she worked. 'Through stone, Master Coalhouse and blew a lot of it and worse into his face. He is dying slowly and blind in the undercroft.'

She looked critically at the knife and Batty felt his throat go dry.

'Ah kin mak' the whirlimagig,' Sister Hope declared, smiling gums at him. Sister Faith looked fondly at her.

'She is no longer afraid,' she said and Batty watching the knife and trying not to think about it, wondered aloud what had changed.

'You are here,' Sister Faith answered, 'called by prayer.'

'Ach, listen wummin...' Batty began, but the knife descended and the pain slammed him, from where the blade touched to the crown of his head and blew all the light out.

The rain hissed like snakes and the bastel house was blued with smoke from a fire of damp wood and a chimney badly cleared from the scumfishing that had emptied it of Wallis men in the first place. It reeked of old char.

In the dark dank of the undercroft, Cornelius raised his head and wiped his bloody hands on a rag; his shadow danced madly on the wall as the tallow guttered.

'He is gone.'

Klett grunted and it seemed to Horner that he did not care much, but he was wrong; Klett felt the death of Ponce keenly, but not because he had known the man for a length. In this business, he thought, it is sensible not to become attached, for life can go pleasantly along on its way in plunder and whores and then – bang. Your fine friend is blown into Hell.

No, the death of Ponce was one more added to the tally he would have to present to Maramaldo and he felt that sharply enough, though he would not show it. There was another, Martello the Italian, nursing a shoulder which had been put out of joint when he was struck by a running horse. But Ponce had been with Maramaldo a long time.

'The ball cut too many vitals,' Cornelius added.

'Shot from close range,' Jacob added morosely, 'as he was about to enter the tower. Those nuns are skilled.'

Klett glanced sourly at him.

'No nun did this,' he growled and then stirred the other corpse with his toe, so that Rutland's head lolled. 'Nor is this our cuckoo. At least, not the one who killed our boys with throwing knives.'

Jacob had no answer to that, nor did Cadette, who kept as far back in the shadows as he could; they both knew that the man they had lugged in had no throwing knives on him and hands as soft as kneaded pastry, save where a sword hilt had raised some callous on his right palm.

He was – had been – a wee gentleman gamecock, though what he was doing out on the wilds of the Cheviot was another matter. A Wallis, Klett thought, starting to poke a neb into what had happened around Akeld. The thought of what they would do when they found out – or found the bodies of their kin, the original occupants – was one which raised a panic Klett fought to control. Yet again, he could not understand his orders to remain here.

Maramaldo on one hand, the Wallis on the other... they had to finish this now, swiftly and regardless of cost, for it was clear there was another cuckoo and this one had gained entrance to the tower. A Borders man if his unshod nag of a horse was anything to go by and a fighter judging by the pistols in the saddle holsters and the gear in bags.

It did not help that Horner, still hugging secrets to himself, was black-browed over Rutland's death.

'He was my messenger,' he told Klett bitterly. 'I saw him before. I warned you of him. Of not killing him...'

'How are we to know this?' Klett spat back, equally vicious. 'You *think* he is your messenger, but he may well be working with the other one, the one who is now in the tower.'

Horner's dismissive wave only fuelled Klett's raging suspicion that there were matters being kept from him by this papingo, whose involvement in matters was more than simply a treasure.

The only matter they shared, it seemed, was the thought that where there was a brace of new cuckoos...

'Twice reason to be done with this business,' Klett declared. 'Before first light, rain or no, we will be at the place.'

He glared pointedly at Horner.

'If you have matters to say, best say them now, for once we are broken in, the ram is through the gate.'

Even Horner understood the term; no quarter would be given to the occupants. He disagreed with a vehement shake of his head.

'Alive, your Captain General commanded. Alive, Meinheer Klett.'

Klett did not reply, simply stared at the dark and the faint smudge of the tower through the lisping rain, as if willing it to crumble with his eyes.

Inside, Batty woke and found a new face looking at him. It was younger than the others, but reduced by dark and flickering candle to planes and shadows, so that the eyes were drown-dead pits and the cheeks seemed shrunk into blackness. This skull stretched into a smile, brief as a blown candleflame – then she drew a black veil across it, leaving only her eyes like pits.

'I am Sister Charity. Would you like water?'

He nodded and she handed him a horn beaker, turning to speak over her shoulder as he drank.

'Sister Faith – he is awake.'

The old nun came up as he finished and handed the beaker back.

'There is more,' Sister Charity said. 'Water is what we have most.'

The rain ran down the inside walls like the soft patter of playful cats and Batty realised he was in the sheltered spot, under the overhang of latticed wood that formed part of the watch platform of the ruined-tooth tower. His leg ached and he moved it gingerly.

'What have you done to me?' he growled at Sister Faith.

'It was filthy,' she replied. 'I cut the flesh away, cleaned it out and bound it with some healing herbs, a simple prayer and clean linen.'

Batty was silent, drinking the water and wishing it was *eau de vie* while he thought about Sister Faith, who prayed vehemently over the deaths of those who wanted to kill her and could cut his leg up as if she gutted fish for the pot.

The other one watched him, even when he returned her stare; he did not do it often, for her eyes were fierce affairs that she shook at him like a fist with every glance. He did not try to match it, but remembered where she should be.

'Who is looking out from the tower?' he demanded and watched the Sister blink annoyance.

'No one. You can see nothing for dark and rain, so it would be a pointless exercise in getting wet. Besides, Trumpet needs my help now that you do not.'

And she was gone, leaving Sister Faith smiling at Batty's face.

'Yes,' she said. 'She is boldinit for a nun is she not?'

Batty was not growing any less disconcerted by the seeming ease this woman had in reading his face for thoughts, but admitted it with a wry smile.

'She was not always a nun, of course,' Sister Faith went on. 'She came late to the embrace of God, unlike myself and Sister Hope, who came to it young.'

She broke off and laughed softly.

'While we could still coup our lundies,' she added and Batty moaned.

'No more o' that – each time it is said I suffer pain and loss of sense.'

There was silence for a time, broken only by the sound of rain and, eventually, by the chick-chick-chick of someone striking flint to tinder. There was no shower of sparks, so Batty assumed it came from below.

'What was she, then?'

Sister Faith looked at him for a moment, then followed the train of his thought.

'A whore,' she said flatly and watched Batty's eyebrows shoot into his airline. 'From the Spanish Netherlands. They called her La Tormenta.'

Batty stared and Sister Charity came up in time to hear the end of it and, to Batty's surprise, she winked.

'I could suck a curl into the toes of your shoes,' she said and Sister Faith touched her arm chidingly, though her smile robbed it of sting and Batty was left reeling, his mind like a whirl of blown leaves.

Then the glare snapped him back to the flickering flames and the hunched form of Sister Hope, rattling skillet and pot.

'In the name of Christ douse that!' he bellowed and started to struggle up until the pain lanced him. 'It will show you up like a shadow-puppet, to be shot.'

'Do not blaspheme with the Lord's name,' Sister Faith declared severely. 'Besides – we need a fire here, to cook food for the children. It makes the undercroft too reeky if we light it there.'

Batty fought with the sense of it for a moment, until the full import smacked him like a hand back and forth on both cheeks.

'Children?' he asked weakly.

There were five – three girls, an older boy and a chubby-limbed crawler with the solemn stare of a cat. All of them save him perched on a cloth-covered chest like mice on a ledge and looked warily at Batty when he came down into the candled undercroft.

'Joan, Margaret and Alice,' Sister Faith said and the girls stared until the nun clapped her hands at their rudeness; they rose and bobbed wobbling curtseys.

'The babby is Stephen,' Sister Faith went on, 'and this is Daniel.'

Daniel was older, on the cusp of double years and scowling suspicious through the grime of his face while Sister Faith stood behind him, hands on his bony shoulders. All of them were thin, Batty noted. And one of the girls coughed because of the damp.

'Children,' Sister Faith said, 'this is Master Coalhouse, summoned like the Archangel Michael, by God and prayer, to take you to safety.'

It was the Latin way she said it, that '*michaelangelo*' that snapped Batty's head back. That and the surety of what she said, which she laid on him like some dank smothering cloak.

'I was not summoned by God,' Batty answered weakly. 'I just came.'

But the solemn eyes watched him, itching his back all the way up into the tower proper.

'Bairns,' Batty said as he limped back up the worn steps behind Sister Faith, half-bent to scuttle to the fire. He leached its comfort and warmth even as he wished for an end to the cooking and the damned thing to be put out. The rain may do it anyway, he thought, listening to it sizzle and spit from the rogue drops that came through the ruined roof.

There was a distant crack that brought Batty's head up, though he could not see the flare. He heard the ball strike the top of the tower and whine off; one of the girls gave a whimpering cry.

'We could not leave them behind, for they are orphans all. We are the last nuns of St Margaret's almshouses,' Sister Faith sighed. 'Part of the See of Glastonbury and forgotten when that place suffered dissolution from Master Cromwell.'

She signed the cross and shook her head. Another crack, this one ending in a loud slap against the stonework. Batty knew there was no one up there, but the shooting was nag all the same, which was the purpose.

'God salve Cromwell's sins,' she added, 'for what Thomas did to England and Glastonbury. Him and the king both.'

That talk will get your head on a gatehouse spike, Batty thought grimly, then remembered where they were and almost laughed. Sister Hope gathered up a small kettle and went off down the steps with it.

'It took five years,' Sister Faith went on, 'but then we were remembered. Thomas Horner remembered us.'

The way she said the name made Batty look up to meet her cool stare and gimlet eyes. Oho, he thought, now comes the reason why the likes of Maramaldo's men are hunting down some nuns and weans in the wild of the Cheviot.

She read it in him in that disconcerting way she did, but already he was growing used to it and it did not rasp as it had at first.

'Cromwell wanted Glastonbury,' Sister Faith said slowly, composing her hands in her lap and twisting the wedding band. 'He wanted it the same way he wanted all the other holdings of the Church, to swell the coffers of the king.'

'And drop a wee bitty into his own purse,' Batty added laconically. 'I have heard of the man. If Christ walked among us again, Thomas Cromwell would have deceived him anew.'

'God be praised,' Sister Faith said, 'and for all your blasphemy, you are right. Cromwell was a grasping man, who did poorly by the Abbot of Glastonbury.'

'I have no doubt of it,' Batty said. 'When Cromwell wished for something, he would keep at it until folk gave into him.'

'Abbot Richard did not,' Sister Faith said firmly and then sighed and made a fresh crucifix in the air. 'Though it was the end of him.'

Batty was silent for a moment, wondering how the Abbot of such a powerful place such as Glastonbury could have been brought to his end. Finally, he had to ask.

'A Christmas pie,' Sister Faith answered which was so far from what Batty had considered that he was left lost and blinking into Sister Faith's enigmatic little smile.

'You know of Christmas pies?' she asked and Batty frowned his way through what he thought he knew. Rich gifts atween prelates, he knew. Packed full of arrogance and nonsense as well as the richest meats and finest spices – saffron, which was worth its own weight in the gold used to gild the pastry, for example. Monstrous large affairs, too, with some even containing live birds cunningly placed at the last, so that they flew out when it was cut.

Sister Faith nodded sadly.

'Just so. Given upwards, from abbot to bishop, bishop to archbishop, archbishop to... king. Fawning gifts to show the riches of the monasteries and abbeys that sent them. Now the Christmas pie is seen as the very mark of idolatrous corruption.'

She shifted slightly; below there was soft singing; Sister Hope, hardly less of a child in her mind than her charges, was perfect for the task of keeping them from fear. Batty remembered, with a sharp twist in his gut, how Sister Hope's own fear had supposedly been driven out because of the arrival of the saviour, Batty Coalhouse.

'Abbot Whiting knew of Cromwell's attempts to loot Glastonbury and in 1538 he thought to subvert him by sending a Christmas pie direct to the king. It was a fine affair, a rich savoury – but the meat of it was not venison but twenty carefully wrapped scrolls of vellum, each one a deed for a manor belonging to Glastonbury. It was to be payment for exemption from the Act of 1536.'

'Blackmeal,' Batty declared and nodded, for he was a Borders man at bottom and none better than they knew the concept of paying those with power to keep them away from your door. Sister Faith sighed.

'The time for such exemptions had passed,' she said, 'though few knew it. Swept away in a rising tide – Thomas Horner, the Abbot's steward, knew it and was a strong swimmer. Few knew that, either.

'The pie went in the care of Master Horner,' Sister Faith went on, 'that rank-faced treacherer, who delivered it to Lord Great Chamberlain Cromwell instead. His reward was a plum picked from that pie – Mells Manor, which he now dwells in. The others stayed with

Cromwell, who saw the riches of Glastonbury not only in treasure and relics, but in valuable holdings.'

Batty could work out the rest – the Abbot would be put to the question and had probably died of it. Sister Faith confirmed it.

'Cromwell sent his commissioners to find fault,' she said. 'It was not hard for them. Layton, Pollard and Moyle – those names will be remembered for eternity, if not by those of Glastonbury, then by God. It took them two years after every other holy place had been ransacked, but Glastonbury fell and Abbot Whiting went to the Tower and died there – executed for treason, they said. But I know he died being put to the Question.'

'Aye, well,' Batty said, easing his leg a little. 'Cromwell himself was brought low the next year and himself executed for treason, so all's well that ends ill, as they say.'

Sister Faith nodded.

'God's punishment,' she said simply, 'which two at least of those commissioners also suffered – Pollard died in 1542 and Richard Layton died last year in Ghent, having pawned plate belonging to the Chapter at York to fund his foul life. Moyles waits to face his God with his deeds, but has fallen from favour and no longer pursues the treasures of Glastonbury. Some they had, but the best were gone – including the rest of the manor rolls and deeds. All spirited away in secret.'

The skin on Batty's arms was creeping now as he listened to the soft lilt of the nun's voice.

'Cromwell's death put an end to it – or so we at St Margaret's thought. New fleas bred, as they will, fighting for royal favour. The Earl of Oxford was elevated to Cromwell's seat – and his records. Lord Wriothesley became Lord Chancellor and anxious to make his mark, so Thomas Horner went to this one with Glastonbury's tale. The Lord Chancellor saw the advantage in it and set Thom squinting and peering.'

She broke off and stared bleakly at the dark.

'No doubt the taste of that plum had a lingering sweetness that made Jack The Lad Horner want more of the same.'

She lifted her head and looked squarely, almost defiantly, at Batty.

'He ciphered it out in the end, where the Abbot had sent the treasure – but the last nuns of St Margaret's almshouses, former leper hospice and sometime orphanage – the least of Glastonbury's possessions – quit the place a fortnight before he got there.'

She stopped, then crossed herself and kissed the rosary ring.

'God forgive me for the sin of pride in thinking myself clever to have persuaded my Sisters to Horner's imminence. Sister Benedict was sure we would be safe in the north, in her brother's care. Not me, O Lord, but thine Hand...'

Pointing them north to Bewcastle, Batty thought, the hair on his arms bristled as boar, led by a Sister whose brother in Bewcastle was Catholic enough in the unReformed north to appreciate the worth of relics from Glastonbury. Not to mention a wheen of manors in Somerset.

Did Mad Jack know what his sister brought him? Was that the main interest? And why send them so far off course – was that to keep them at arm's length and secreted from any tainting of Dacre or Bewcastle? Batty whirled it round and round but could make no firmness out of it and gave up when his head hurt.

'We took the children,' Sister Faith went on, 'but Thomas Horner does not care for us or them. He looks to stick more fingers in this Christmas pie.'

She stopped for a moment and, when she continued, her voice was all henbane and aloes.

'There is a special pit in Hell for Master Jack the Lad Horner.'

'You have the treasure of Glastonbury in your keeping,' Batty said dully, remembering the chest on which the children had perched. 'Here, in this place.'

He felt the crushing weight of it all and his leg ached so much he had to sit and did not need an answer from her to know the truth.

'Christ's Bones, wummin,' he said wearily.

'Mind your tongue, Master Coalhouse,' Sister Faith answered sharply.

Batty had nothing left to say, simply gave her a look halfway between an ox waiting for the last hammer and admiration for her certainty that Batty Coalhouse was the way out of their doom.

The dark split with another crack but this was aimed at the base of the tower and the smack and whine of it was louder. Batty wanted to tell her the truth of it all and how, at last, he had been dealt the worst of hands by God, but the nun who had been a whore came up from below, wiping her hands on a cloth and looking grim.

'Old Trumpet has gone to God,' Sister Charity said and she and Sister Faith fell to their knees and started praying.

Batty listened, dulled almost to oblivion, while the soft words pattered out like the rain; beyond, the dark seemed blacker now that the fires had been put out and he wondered where Fiskie had gone.

Not that it mattered. Three nuns and five bairns were not going to ride out clinging to Fiskie, never mind the chest they would want to take with them.

Nor would these *routiers* be bluffed for long – Batty wondered when Maramaldo would come, for come he would. If there was serious plunder in it, Fabrizio Maramaldo would not leave the matter to underlings. He was on his way, sure as birds laid eggs.

And here is me, laired up like a silly wee levret. Batty Coalhouse who has dogged him like a slewhound these last years – Maramaldo will take delight in that, for sure…

He blinked and shook himself, hauled out the last two daggs and fell into the familiar, awkward routine of loading and priming them with one hand and his stump. In the dim, he did it mostly by feel.

The ones outside would want to present their Captain General with the prize before he got here, so men would come before dawn, he thought, when life is lowest and dark is most; he knew well enough the way mercenaries went at the work. Since the nuns would not shoot straight, he thought, then Mrs Coalhouse's unlucky bairn must, even if he stands so poorly in the sight of God.

You can only play the cards you are dealt, he thought, in life as in Primero.

Chapter Seven

In the tower at Akeld
The second day...

They took some persuading, but in the end the Sisters agreed that Trumpet could neither lay dead in the undercroft with the children, nor take up space above.

'We can hardly bury him,' Sister Faith pointed out and Batty had to admit that.

'We can put him out of the tower,' he said, 'but not just by rolling him out the door, where he will be as close as ever. The stink will waft in with every breeze. Do you have rope in that cunning wee chest below?'

Sister Faith looked at him then, head cocked to one side as if to query his belief that they would last as long as it took for Trumpet to start smelling bad. Or perhaps she thought it was part of his cunning escape plan.

Or that he simply wanted a look in that chest, he thought in the end. That would be it.

There was rope, which materialised from nowhere Batty could see, so Trumpet was lashed and manhandled up the rickety ladder to the tower top, a sweating affair. Sister Faith and Charity pushed from below, Batty and Sister Hope pulled from above, and the rope was securely fastened to the lattice work on the tower top in case they should lose grip and allow it to plunge all the way down the ladder.

Finally, panting with the effort, Batty heaved Trumpet up on to the rickety platform on the tower top, then to the ragged stone edge. At which point the leg fired pain through him and he sat down heavily with a curse. Sister Hope came to him, concern in her childlike gaze, while Sister Faith called up from below to ask if he was hurting.

'I am sun and shiny watter,' Batty lied, then turned to Sister Hope. 'Shove him ower, Sister, there's a good quine.'

He sat back, feeling the rain-wind wash the sweat from his face. He was soaked inside and out and the padded jack weighed all the more for it. Drag you down like a big stone, a wet jack, he said to himself. Like the last of the Kohlhase at the Elbe at Wittenberg, on the day the band had been moving out, trying to avoid the troops of the Elector after having been camped too long nearby; Saxony was no longer safe for the Kohlhase name.

They were delayed because Hans Kohlhase and his right-hand, Georg Nagelschmidt, had been trying to deal with Luther, who held a lot of power then and had a problem of his own, Batty recalled. The good Doctor had acquired a stoked hatred of Jews and Hans had put it about that he and the rest of the Kohlhase brigands had been warring against all the Jews in Saxony, who had been led by the foulest of them all, the ignoble Von Zaschwitz, secret gaberdined moneylender and horse thief.

Well, Batty thought, after all we had done already a lie like that was hardly here nor there – even the band's physicker, the Venetian Jew Loppe Bassano, had laughed out of his big, bearded face.

But Luther had wanted to believe it and it was as good an excuse as any to meet Hans, Georg and Batty in his farm, where the big-breasted ex-nun he had married ran matters with iron efficiency. Batty had not been keen on it, all the same, since Luther did not just have a downer on Jews, but had ranted about rebels not that long since – *nothing can be more poisonous, hurtful, or devilish than a rebel. For baptism does not make men free in body and property, but in soul; and the gospel does not make goods common.*

There was more of the same, yet Luther was a smiling avuncular old sot, built like a dancing bear Batty had seen at a fair once. He had welcomed them warmly, his fleshy smile plastered on a brosy face with a large forehead and hair sticking out from around his ears like sheep wool.

He limped from the last of an attack of gout, but drank wine with relish and congratulated them on their work against *the Devil's people*, but it was all fakery. It took three fat bottles and a good hour to reveal, at least to Batty, that his biggest dislike of the Jews was how they would not be swayed by his personal efforts and eloquence to convert.

It was an outrage of pride in a man who claimed to be humble, but that was the cast of Martin Luther, Batty thought. He was in the middle of writing a hymn on the Lord's Prayer and fulminating about making war on the Turk – but there was a copy of the Mussulman's Bible, the Qu'ran, which was well-thumbed.

Hypocrisy was the least of Luther's faults but it was the one the Kohlhase band had come to deal with and Luther spilled out the meat of it indignantly, as if none of it was his fault. The gist of it was that one of Luther's patrons, Philip, Landgrave of Hesse – and a man who had been hunting the Kohlhase band like a bad-tempered Spanish Inquisitor – had wanted to marry one of his wife's own waiting women. He did not want rid of his wife, mark you, who was unconcerned about this arrangement.

The Landgrave had thought this new Reformed-to-Protestant religion, which allowed priests to marry openly, could be persuaded to other liberal practices. So he had gone to Luther and his cronies, citing the polygamy of the ancient Biblical patriarchs and an alarmed Luther, silly old fawning sod that he was, had advised the Landgrave to forget all that and just marry the woman in secret.

Which he did – with Luther and his cronies as guests and even witnesses.

'Scarcely secret,' Hans had pointed out and Luther had given him a hard look, then collapsed like the windy old bag he was.

Of course it had not been a secret and when it came out it was roundly condemned by everyone – especially the Elector of Saxony. John Frederick was a slit-eyed whoremonger with a great bush of beard and the manners of a boar, but he was also Luther's patron. The entire Protestant League he and others had made at Schmalkald a decade or so ago now encompassed almost all of north Germany, throwing out Catholics, thumbing their nebs at the Pope and holding Luther up as the figurehead of righteous religion.

The Landgrave, of course, was now desperate, wanted help and was threatening to make public the good Doctor's part, which would put a considerable tarnish on Luther and League both.

'So you wish him removed,' Hans had said coldly and Luther, huffing and hemming, had not quite admitted it but made it clear. The coin he handed over made it clearer still – if a band of notorious brigands attacked the Landgrave and killed him in the process, it was only one more act of horror to add to the pile heaped on them like faggots.

Afterwards, Georg had been full of the joy of spring and the promise of at least hot food and wine when they reached the next village along the Elbe.

'We shall wave a coin or two,' he exclaimed so everyone could hear it, 'and they will bow and bring out their willing daughters.'

It was a good attempt at raising morale, for the last months had not been good for Hans Kohlhase and his war against Saxony; yet Luther's scheme was too much like turning the Kohlhase Band into hired slaughterers rather than righteous revengers and there were a few who said so.

Not that it mattered, because Luther's cronies, Melancthon and Bucer, had clearly put Luther up to killing the Landgrave, but were not around to keep him to it. The bastard Doctor thought about it only long enough to realise that he was biting the Elector's feeding hand. He no doubt hummed a few pious lines of '*Fater unser*' to absolve him of any sin – then ran off and alerted the Landgrave to his imminent assassination.

If he ever wondered how Luther had come by the information, the Landgrave never bothered to ask and the dazzling possibility of appeasing the Elector with the heads of the notorious Kohlhase pack buried the thought of it forever. The delight of wine and women and hot food had hardly left Georg's mouth before the bolts and arrows flew and the Langrave's ambush burst on them. It had hardly been a fight at all, for everyone had fled for the river.

The smart ones got out of their gambesons and jacks – Batty, with his one hand, had long since settled on a frontfastener, with three easy buckles and had that off with a skilled twist or two. He was kicking off his boots when the wet-mouthed shriekers came down on him and he went into the water, throwing off ironmongery as he went.

He had made it. Others sank like stones. Mortensson, the Swede, with his back-laced quilting, Svart Juan the Spaniard with his pointed and embroidered jack, Derk Kohlhase with his ankle-length Irish maille coat.

They all washed up later, rolling in the shallows like half-ashamed returning prodigals, to be stripped to the wounded curdle and left for the chewers and peckers to remove the last cloth of them, the flesh itself. No one would know of the marvellous creation of God that had been Mortensson, with his righteous Christian wrath against injustice, or the darkly-handsome Juan's astounding hatred of people who ill-treated horses, or the maiden-winning smile of adventurous Derk, youngest of the Kohlhase.

Gone, if they were lucky, into a marked hole in Christian ground, or else just bones scattered to oblivion – which was better than being taken alive, as Hans and Georg had been. To be then braided into the turning spokes of a breaking wheel in a cobbled street and left to slowly spin and rot in a Berlin street.

All gone except for me, Batty recalled, who had hauled himself out the far side, in a soaked serk and one sodden boot. Thirty-nine years old, as poor and almost as naked as the day I was born.

He heard Sister Hope grunt, the slither of the body going over and sank down in the lee of the damp stones feeling the ache of his leg. The same one he'd strapped a dagger to, inside his last sloshing boot that day, he remembered. He had wanted to go back to Luther and unstitch the paunch of him, but matters were too dangerous even then and he had concentrated on using it to get himself away to safety and return himself to fortune.

Sister Hope's face thrust a grin at him and he came back to the present and started to lever himself up, then caught the soft, subtle creak of sound, saw the rope taut and thrumming. He groaned.

'I meant for you to untie him, Sister, afore you rolled him off the edge...'

Sister Hope looked uncertain and then on the point of tears, so Batty patted her shoulder soothingly and considered the problem of Trumpet, now hanging and swinging gently from the tower. He hefted the rope – too much weight to haul it back up, even if all of them tried. He could cut it, but he had wanted to keep that rope, in the vague, distant hope that it might be used as it was now – to dangle off the tower like a lifeline.

Save that whoever had the desperate strength to try it at the very extremity, would now have to scramble down the length of a dead man to reach the tower's foot.

Batty sat down and laid his head back against the wooden poles of the tower platform, feeling the rain on his face. Soft as kisses, like the day he had lain hidden and watched Luther lumbering about his garden. The day he had clenched and unclenched his one hand on the knife for a long time before choosing life and safety over the sure death he would have if he ran in and gave the good Doctor Martin Luther some Kohlhase vengeance.

Luther was alive still, Batty had heard, though sick and bad-tempered as a mangy old bear, growling sermons against the Jews from every pulpit he could climb in. He was spared, Batty thought wryly, for some higher purpose – to be elevated to the Right Hand of God probably.

While I will elevate no higher than this poxed tower.

He heard a hiccup of sobbing and then soothing voices; it would be Sister Hope, bubbling snot and tears like a bairn scolded by the Big Bad Man in the tower because she had made a mistake. Batty sighed at the bad cess of it all – trapped with three Sisters, five bairns and certain to be at the mercy of Maramaldo, the man he had spent most of his life hunting like a tiger.

Some tiger me, Batty thought, whose snarls can only make daft nuns weep.

Then, as he morosely struggled to get back to his feet, he heard Sister Hope's querulous voice through the last sniffs.

'Was he not wonderful to come?' she said. 'A sainted man to risk his life for children.'

'I would not enrol him in the canon of saints just yet. We have no idea why he came at all.'

Practical, with an edge to it and a hint of accent – that would be Sister Charity, the Spanish nun from the Netherlands, the former whore who had not forgotten the iniquities of men.

'I dinna jalouse why else he would come? Did God not send him, Sister Faith?'

Batty could almost see Sister Faith pausing in her twisting of that wedding ring to pat comfort into Sister Hope.

'He came out of prayer,' she declared firmly, 'and we must not cast off God's gift.'

'He came for what is in that chest,' Sister Charity persisted and Batty thought about matters for a time after they had fallen silent. He thought about how ill-named the Spanish whore-turned-nun was. And he thought about Sister Faith's certainty that he had come in answer to prayer – brought by God to be the Archangel Michael, he thought. Michaelangelo, same name as the man who had prevented me from saving a nun once – or, at the least, provided the excuse for me not to save her.

He felt the skin pucker on his neck and arms at the strangeness of that... before shaking the mystery away from him; he made loud noises to alert the Sisters as he came down the ladder.

There was only Sister Faith left, sitting by the last embers of the stamped-out fire, no more than a shadow in shadows as Batty levered himself down beside her. Below, he heard soft singing as one of the Sisters lullabied the bairns to sleep. Hope, it would be, Batty thought and then laughed softly at his next thought; Charity was too cold for that.

Batty was hungry, but had already worked out that food was scarce and kept for the weans. Water they had, if only what they licked off the stones, but none of it would matter when the men came for them all.

'I thought you all named yourself efter saints,' Batty said when the dark silence grew too black and long. 'Even male ones, I am told.'

'We three were so named,' Sister Faith declared, 'but took these names when we left St Margaret's. After the three Christian martyrs buried on the Aurelian Way.'

'So there were truly three such saints, then?'

Sister Faith nodded. 'Sisters, too – Pistis, Elpis and Agape, which is Greek for Faith, Hope and Charity. Their mother was also martyred. Her name was Sophia, which means Wisdom.'

'I suspect more tale than history in that,' Batty rumbled back and Sister Faith smiled.

'Mayhap. But there was another Sister Faith, from Aquitaine in the time of the Romans. She was persecuted and martyred for refusing to make pagan sacrifices, even under torture with a red-hot brazier.'

Batty watched her twist the wedding band and saw the iron in her. Bigod, here was one who would thrust her very face into such a brazier if it glorified God, he thought. The problem with such folk is that they tend to haul other's people's less eager nebs into the flames as well.

'How do you get to be a saint, then?' he asked. 'For it seems you elect yourself – or someone else – to such a role. Whether they wish it or not.'

His bitterness made it clear he was referring to himself and Sister Faith's insistence that he was the Archangel Michael. She pursed her lips.

'God disposes,' she replied.

'I am mightily lacking in flaming sword,' he spat back, 'and even had I such you would be hagging at my back not to cut or burn anyone.'

'There are many swords and many ways to use them. Even swords that do not look like such.'

'Many Michaelangelos as well,' Batty replied with a sigh. 'You would probably be as well with the one I knew.'

And he told her of Florence and the burning nun, not knowing why but spilling it from him like vomit.

'He was right, mark you,' he said at the end of it, 'though it had more to do with me burning my last hand putting her out. Losing the use of his hands was the worst thing Michaelangelo Buonarotti could think on. He did not care for much else.'

'You like him, all the same,' she declared and Batty admitted it.

'We knew him simply as Simoni. He was one of us, but better than any,' he replied. 'In the short time Florence became a Republic, they reinstated an old custom, the

Signoria. It meant electing folk drawn from good families every brace of months. Nine were chosen and had to deliberate together for the good of the city, though they were not stipended for it. They got two servants in green livery, a cook and a jester, a fancy silver and plumed helmet and a crimson cloak lined with ermine.'

Batty laughed softly, smeared with memories.

'They elected Simoni. First time he turned up looking like that we laughed until we fell over. Giobbo Minuto choked and had to be thumped back to life. Simoni never wore it again, or turned up with his entourage of green men.'

Batty stirred and eased his aching leg.

'Yet he made us feel finer than we were. Made pictures of us as if we were important folk who could commission such, folk like the Pope himself. He was patron to Michaelangelo, then as now – though your Holy Father stood on the opposite side of the siege then. Until Simoni, the only likenesses made of most of us were the *pitture infame*. You know of these?'

He felt her shake her head in the dark.

'Stuck up on walls in Florence,' Batty went on, 'and left to fade and blister. Limnings of malefactors and outlaws. Like me. Like those out there.'

'I thought they were men-at-arms,' Sister Faith replied wryly. 'Knights of chivalric intent.'

'Aye, you may dream of it. Them, too, who still care. Oh, they have laws and contracts and notaries and rules, none of which are worth a bawbee when it comes to the bit.'

Batty hawked up some spit, thought better of it and swallowed.

'Maramaldo is their Captain General, a proud title, as is the one he covets – *condottiere*. So called because he is the one who agrees the *condotta*, the contract. That details such matters as payment – in florins, *che considerato il mercato che qua è*, which is Italian for 'considering the way the market is'. There are agreements on those recruits paid on reaching barracks, on *paghe morte*, the money collected per month for men who are dead or missing but still kept on the Rolls. On this and that and the other.'

'Italian, all of it, because that is the bearpit of war thanks to all the witless stushies of the cities there – though the Germanies are growing hotter by the day and France will flame when Fat Henry crosses the Channel. Or England, if France crosses the other way. Mind you, no one who wants a good fight need stir a heel-length from a door in the north, for war is headed back this way, sure as chooks lay eggs.'

'The world is at the end of days,' he added morosely. 'God and all his saints are asleep and have left it to the likes of Maramaldo.'

'You are one of them, then?'

It slashed into Batty, lanced to the very quick of him so that he winced with it.

'Aye and no. I was once with Maramaldo and serve yet as a hired soldier, but no one is like Fabrizio Maramaldo.'

He leaned forward a little.

'D'you ken what '*condottiere*' means, Sister?' he asked, hoarse with loathing for them, for himself, for the hand God had dealt him to show how lowly his standing was in Heaven.

'A person who agrees contracts,' she answered primly. 'You have just said so.'

He chuckled bitterly.

'It means dealer,' he replied. 'You can be a *condottiere di scarpe* and merchant decent footwear. Or you can be a *condottiere d'armi* and merchant death under arms.'

He eased his shoulders a little and finished with one dagg, squinting down the barrel into the night.

'To be known as a *condottierie d'armi* is what all Captain Generals wish,' he went on. 'That and the trappings of a noble birth most do not have. None of us paid-for soldiers are noble knights, nor anything near it and, of the worst of us, Maramaldo stands head and shoulders from the crowd.'

He looked at her resolved, determined face, all creased like a linen sheet and wanted to let her know the truth, even as it sickened him to tell her.

'Even the Pope will not permit Maramaldo in any Christian army, which is why he is here, with the Reforming Henry Tudor,' he told her. 'Once he is done here, there are a wheen of Reforming Catholics and outright Lutheran protestors in the Germanies, for they are as damned by the Holy Father as Beezel-bub.

'Fat Henry Tudor pays the coin but even he will not contract Maramaldo directly, leaving that to his commander of the north, the Earl of Hertford. This is because Maramaldo is too much of a Satan to inflict on the civilised French, enemies or no, but the Scots are imps of Hell anyway, so they do not matter.'

He had her gaze now, fixed her with one of his own as if driving the words into her like nails on a cross.

'Burn everything. Burn even the water was what Fat Henry told his men to do to the Scots and if anyone is capable of that, it is Maramaldo, who believes that fire is to war as mustard is to sausage.

'In the morning, afore it is proper light,' he added bleakly, 'such a *condottiere d'armi* will come to our door to sell us death. Maramaldo and the most of his men are not here... yet... but still we hold poor cards, Sister and will be asked to knock or draw. You must tell me what you wish me to do. For myself, I will fight.'

There was silence for a long moment, then he felt and heard her rise stiffly, saw the wink of gold from that wedding band as she smoothed her habit.

'It is my belief,' she said sadly, 'that if you stood with one foot in Paradise, Master Coalhouse, you would remove it to fight.'

'Better to fight and fall than live without hope,' Batty answered sharply and she nodded slowly back at him.

'There is always hope when God is involved,' she said, 'but it is also my belief that Master Horner is not in control out there and any promises made by him are nothing, while those made by the men who have already tortured and killed our Sisters are even less. I will load the calivers and pray for the souls of those who attack us. I will not kill anyone and I suspect my Sisters in Christ feel the same.'

She left him in the dark and fumbled her way to the stairs and down to the poor gutter of tallow to find Sister Charity had already loaded the calivers and sat with one across her knee. She had replaced her face veil so that only her eyes showed, glittering with a fevered light that told Sister Faith her disease had flared. For a moment, Sister Faith wondered if Sister Charity was as resolved against killing as she once had been. Then Sister Hope stirred and made her smile; the children slept around Sister Hope, who whimpered in her own sleep like a pup.

Sister Faith sat in the last glamour of the butter glow and thought about the man upstairs, who had come in answer to her prayer. He was an ugly man – the ugliest man she had ever seen – scarred and hard and had already killed two men he had admitted to and more, she was sure, he had not. He swore. He drank. He gambled. He showed no religious feeling at all.

In the end, the questions thundering in her had no answer and she bowed her head, took the ring in her fingers and twisted it.

'Dear God. Your wisdom encompasses us all around. I thank You for Your blessings and guidance. You sent this man to save the others, the children and I only wonder... how should I trust him?'

She heard no answers as she stared at her pale hands, only a soft, tuneless singing from above, like a hymn for poor, dead Trumpet.

> *'I sewed his sheet, making my mane; I watched the corpse, myself alane; I watched his body, night and day. No living creature came that way.'*

–

They came before dawn, in a rush like a wind over the moor. The first sign of it was a night-owl whisk of arrows at the entrance, one of which shunked into the wood of the carts, two more sailing over Batty's head to clatter and splinter on the far wall.

Then the figures came lurching out of the dark, silent save for grunting as they stormed the carts and began tearing them aside. Great dark figures they were, so that Batty's first shot, a thunderous blast of flame, pitched one away and blew away all night vision.

His second dagg was out and in his hand when a desperate figure, reeking heat and fear, hurled himself in a rushing shriek at Batty, scrambling over the carts like a mad spider. Batty backhanded him with the long barrel, pointed and shot at a second figure he saw bursting through the barrier; the wheel whirred and sparked, but nothing happened.

Cursing, Batty flipped it to grasp the barrel, then chopped viciously on the man he had already backhanded – he had kept the axe-handled dagg second for this purpose – and the man shrieked as it hacked into his thrown-up forearm.

Batty cut and slashed, seeing the man he had failed to shoot stumble down the steps to the undercroft, where the bairns were shrill as bleating sheep with screams. There was a bang and flash from down there and the man flew backwards to loll on the top step, snoring in bubbling gasps through a faceful of blood.

The man Batty had been hacking died with a last whimper just as another shadow fought over the splintered carts and came on, all snarl and rage. He slammed into Batty, who grunted with the effort of it, flailed with his elbow but couldn't get a decent swing. A hand raked his head, the nails digging for his eyes and he roared, kicked, squirmed, trying to get his good arm working.

He heard another bang and a pained yelp, managed to get his arm under the crushing weight of the panting thrashing man and heaved; they stumbled apart like exhausted dancers and there was a moment of staring, a moment of white eyes and sweat-gleam in the dark.

Short, Batty noted. A wee man. And in that eyeblink, he was back when he was young and had both arms, when his da was growling instruction at him 'for the learning in it'. Batty knew even then to listen closely and learn fast, for Maramaldo's camp was a hard university for laddies.

'Never,' his da had ordered vehemently, 'pick a fight with a short man.'

The short man grunted and Batty blinked out of the reverie. My da never explained what you do if a wee man picks a fight with you, he thought bitterly and launched himself, swinging the axe-handled dagg and snarling like a pit dog. The wee man met him with a blade of his own; sparks flew and they locked, sweated and spat and struggled for a moment, then broke apart, panting.

Somewhere over the squealing bairns, a voice started to bellow and the man jerked, though he did not turn his head.

'Batty Coalhouse,' he said and Batty felt a wash of weariness – he knows of me, he thought.

Bugger.

'My name is Klett,' the stocky man said and half turned his head as the bellow came again, followed by a blowing horn.

'Have we danced afore this?' Batty asked, not eager to close for another bout yet wondering how the man knew him – wondering, too, why the name was familiar; he heard someone coming up the steps and Klett did too, for he backed off, trying to watch Batty and the way into the undercroft at the same time. When his back hit the splintered remains of the carts, he stopped.

'We have not,' Klett panted, 'but I know you well. I have hunted you a long time, Coalhouse. Since the wedding feast.'

The world fell away from Batty's belly then, but a hunting-horn farted out a long, rasp of note and this time Klett jerked like a gaffed fish; a long barrel poked, wavering, up the top step where the snoring man lay and

Batty managed a feral grin as Klett saw it and the nun behind it.

'Your ma is calling you,' he said as the horn sounded again and Klett heaved suddenly, lifting himself backwards on to the cart and rolling away. As if contrived, a shower of arrows spattered in, two hitting the carts and a brace more lancing past Batty, close enough to make him curse.

Batty saw one hit the man on the step so that he gave one last, sudden snort and died. Another was low enough to make the nun – Sister Charity, he saw – bob down into cover.

Batty himself hunkered down on the slathered flags of the tower, but it was reflex, for all his mind was filled only with the memory of the wedding feast of Von Zachwitz, the noble who had robbed Hans Kohlhase of his horses. It rose like a body from a marsh, bloated with horror – the Kohlhases had invaded the celebrations, captured the very noble who had caused all the problems for Hans and then…

Watched bride and groom die. Batty almost spoke it aloud, sick with remembering. You stuffed the groom's mouth with powder charges and lit them, the voice in his head accused.

The bride, though – that was inspired. A chaplet of sausage charges, the slow match cut with Batty's consumate skill to last just long enough for the bride to see her groom die before her own head blew up.

A nice, pretty woman – until the charge went off. Respected woman, too, from a family who once made furniture and clocks then found fortune in using their staghorn and ebenist art, their skills with cogwheels and lever locks, to make guns.

The family had become rich enough to elevate a daughter to the nobility, providing a dowry Von Zachwitz needed in return for the heraldry they craved.

Batty bowed his head under the weight of it all, remembering the names embroidered into the wedding table linen.

Von Zachwitz and Klett.

Chapter Eight

Her life was a tallow flame in a wet wind, every ragged draw of breath into her only serving to make folk wince, each exhale leaking like the blood they could not staunch.

The bairns were orphans, used to hardship even if they had shrieked a bit with the bangs and the flashing, but now their hard eyes were melting as Sister Hope failed to beat the arrow. It had come down in that perfect curve all missiles have, as designed by God when he made the world; this one arced down the steps and took one of His own nuns low in the back, cracking her ribs open like a pry-bar on an old bird nest. She had been protecting the youngest of the bairns with her body, gathering her chicks into her rough wool dress like a Scotch Dumpy.

Sister Faith prayed and wiped, Sister Charity probed and cut, but only the shaft was loosened out; the great barbed head could not be removed and Batty had known it from the moment he had seen her.

He let them bind her up all the same with no word of the pointlessness of that, while he scrambled to haul the dead out, awkwardly crouched so he would not be the next one to take a longbow shaft. The man Batty had hacked with the dagg was easiest to lever up and roll over the remains of the cart barrier, but Batty needed help with the one on the stairs because he had half-armour all the way down his thighs, segmented like a brace of lobster tails.

Not that it had done him any good, for the shot which killed him had fretted his face into a bloody parody of the Italian cutwork lace which decorated his cuffs; his last snoring breaths had been through a nose and mouth blasted to ruin. Batty wondered what the caliver had been loaded with and Sister Charity, after signing the cross on the man, told him it had been her rosary beads.

'Unstrung. I used half-a-dozen, for I had no shot left and they were only wee,' she added and, because of the veil, Batty could only see her eyes, which were full of pain.

She is sore sorry for having done it, he marvelled and never considers what he would have done to her if she had not. But he said nothing and sat patiently while she murmured prayers at the face ruined to shreds by a slew of hard wee prayers; Batty sat silently and took in the fluted breastplate and the segmented tassets, the roped edges and lace and ribbons.

Ten florins in that armour, Batty thought. About a year's food and drink and made special for him, not plundered. A Lance Captain, for sure.

Then they tumbled him out and Batty thought that the man called Klett was mired up to his armpits, for Maramaldo would not be pleased to learn that three nuns and one-armed Batty Coalhouse had contrived to kill so many hard veterans, never mind a Captain who commanded a Lance of thirty men.

Maramaldo would know by now, of course, for it was his trumpeters blowing and bellowing for the attack to be called off and Klett had known it even as he had gone back over the carts and away.

Sister Charity crouched and watched while Batty went into the undercroft, reeking of smoke and flame and blood. Sister Faith was praying while Sister Hope heaved wheezes in and out, the children sitting at opposite sides of her like brave sentries.

All save the oldest, the boy called Daniel, who stood like a shadow, his small arms folded across his thin chest as if he hugged himself; when Batty came down he looked up as if staring at a mountain or a distant horizon, then turned to look the same blankness at Sister Faith when he heard her intone: 'Father in Heaven, bless us this day.'

'Ah kin coup ma lundies.'

Batty jerked free of memory, shivered with it. Her blue eyes were bright and open and Sister Hope sighed out that proud boast with her last breath, gone to the sunlit meadows of her youth, turning cartwheels and careless of showing her legs, or her unbound hair. Her wizened monkey face had a smile on it that defied the cracks and lines to somehow make her look like a blissful girl.

'Our Father,' Sister Faith murmured. The air braided in Batty's throat and he had to look away from that face. He thought about the woman with the hand of her boy; though she had clung tight and never let go, Our Father had plucked the boy away anyway.

'She is beautiful.'

Her voice brought him round to look, seeing the calm assurance of her eyes.

'Sister Hope,' she prompted. 'She looks beautiful and at peace. God be praised.'

'Things have looked better,' Batty grunted. 'It seems your God picked the wrong man, which is no surprise to me. I cannot save you, your Sisters or the bairns.'

'My God?' she replied quietly. 'Our God. Yours too.'

She sat and folded her hands in her lap, twisting that wedding band – no, Batty suddenly realised, not a wedding band. A rosary ring. Which, he supposed, was a wedding band of sorts if you were a nun, married to Christ.

'You were chosen by God to rescue these children. Sister Charity, too, perhaps.'

Not herself, Batty noticed. Not placed anywhere in that.

'I do not know why God chose you, Master Coalhouse,' she went on, 'but the fact remains that He did, which makes you the most fortunate of men. Few are so picked by the Almighty.'

'Do not lay this on me, woman,' Batty growled back, stung to anger. 'I came here out of stupidity, thinking there was only you to spirit away. Even then I considered the matter foolhardy at best, but had come to look for the nun who is related to the Musgraves, or proof of her death.'

He subsided, glowering and waved his one grimy hand as if to dismiss the entire affair.

'You were the proof.'

She said nothing and then went to help the children wash Sister Hope and prepare her for a burial that was more wish than surety. Batty sat, hunched and cold and hungry and emptier than a banker's heart.

'I am not chosen,' he muttered.

—

138

He sat on a faded chair of yellow satin plush wrapped in a boatcloak and furs so that only his face showed. It was like the chair, that face – same colour, greasy, tattered and stained with old pollution.

If you had not known Captain General Fabrizio Maramaldo before this, Klett thought, you would know all you needed to know just by looking at that face. The flickering shadows in the undercroft of Akeld's bastel did little to help.

Horner would have agreed if he and Klett had dared do more than breathe beside each other. Poxed, Horner saw. From the sores on his lips to the sweat on his tow-coloured brow, Maramaldo is bad poxed and perhaps dying of it.

Yet the glitter from those pouched eyes had more than just fever in them and the rake of them across his face almost made Horner blanch.

'Five men,' he said, the Neapolitan accent thick as clots. 'Five men are dead. One of them is Giovanni Cadette, a Lance-Captain of skill.'

No one spoke and the eyes raked round. Cornelius hovered nearby with a napkin and a bowl filled with something; Klett doubted if Maramaldo would drink the brew, even if it had the balm of poppies in it, for the Captain General had not pissed for five days and his bladder must be like a football.

'It was a simple enough task.'

The eyes were settled on Horner like blowflies but the words were directed at Klett, who squinted, bemused. He looked sideways at Horner, who was smirking and, gradually, the truth hit him and fought with the disbelief all over the field of his face.

'I sent you Master Horner,' Maramaldo declared. 'With a plan. All you had to do was capture some nuns and bairns and a trinity of useless men.'

'They were careless...' Horner began.

'When I desire you to speak I will say so. Until then stay silent.'

Horner stayed silent and Klett cleared his throat.

'I was not party to your plans, Captain General,' he said bitterly.

'And this accounts for your failure... how?' Maramaldo spat back, then winced. There was silence for a moment.

'Nuns,' Maramaldo murmured as if savouring the gravy of the word. The eyes seemed to grow colder. 'Who have killed five and are still not taken from their tower after — how long have you been here, Klett?'

'Five days.'

'Indeed. Five days. Five dead. No treasure. You have even contrived to kill one Master Rutland, who is known to me and was expected.'

'He came to find me, with information...' Horner interrupted, then fell silent as Maramaldo scorched him with glare.

'From my employer?'

'I am sure of it,' Horner replied and Klett, bewildered, suddenly realised that Maramaldo had less interest in the treasure. What he was interested in was now a mystery to Klett — as was why Horner was involved; his focus had seemed to be all on the treasure.

'This Rutland came with messages. Unwritten. Assurances that our plan proceeds apace,' Horner went on, bobbing his head while Klett fought his wild thoughts, his head flickering like a flame in a high wind.

'Is that certain?'

Horner's head threatened to bob off the stalk of his neck.

'You would wager your life on it,' Maramaldo said eventually and Horner nodded.

'Indeed I would. The Lord Chancellor...'

'That was not a question, Master Horner of the office of the Lord Chancellor.'

There was a longer silence, broken only by ragged breathing in the thick air.

'Balthie Kohlhase,' Maramaldo said suddenly and Klett simply nodded, trying hard not to raise his eyebrows at what he heard in Maramaldo's voice. Was that... fear?

'Why is he in the tower?' Maramaldo asked. 'Why is he here, in this place, at this time?'

Klett heard the suspicion and wondered at that, wondered also at Horner's quick interjection. He had marvelled at the presence of Balthie Kohlhase, whose name had dogged his heels like a black hound all through his life it seemed. He had lied, all the same, about hunting him for that was the task of his two brothers; now that he had found what they had failed to, Klett would present Balthie Kohlhase's death like a triumph.

'His arrival is unfortunate, but nothing has strayed so far from the plan that it cannot be rectified,' Horner said primly. 'However, we must move more swiftly. The Lord Chancellor wishes this matter resolved to his satisfaction and without delay. We do not have much time.'

Maramaldo grunted and shifted slightly, though it was painful to watch him.

'When it is proper light, we will see if Balthie can be persuaded to recognise his folly. If he does not, we will blow him and his nuns out of that place and quickly, too.'

'The treasure...' Horner bleated, then faded under the renewed gaze. 'It is fragile. Not so much gold and silver. And other matters. The Lord Chancellor...'

'Will take his chance,' Maramaldo said. 'As I said, we do not have time left for niceties.'

'I was promised the nuns,' Horner muttered sullenly. 'I took assurance...'

'Contracts have been agreed,' Maramaldo admitted, his voice a slap. 'They will be adhered to, among gentlemen.'

A spasm of pain rippled him in the chair and he waved one hand, a weak flap of dismissal while the other flicked at Cornelius to offer his brew.

'We will see whether Balthie values nuns or sense,' he said hoarsely, then turned to Horner. 'Then we will all get what we desire, either way.'

'What the Lord Chancellor desires...'

Maramaldo's dark stare was a fierce glitter on both men and Horner went quiet so quickly Klett swore he heard the man's teeth click.

'In the morning,' Maramaldo said to Klett, 'you will reason Balthie and his nuns out of the tower. If not, you will blow him out by the afternoon.'

'The guns are not up yet...' Klett answered, sullen that he still had no clear idea of what his master was doing and that he had been so clearly left out of the planning of it.

'Until they are you may delight us with your marvellous contrivance,' Maramaldo replied blissfully. 'That wall gun. And Master Horner...'

Horner, who had been looking at Klett's sullen discomfiture, jerked round to face the stare. It was colder than he'd ever thought possible, glassed as a sucking sea.

'I am not contracted by the Lord Chancellor. If you wave that man and his wishes at me again, I will hang you up by a rod through your heels and flay you alive.'

—

The morning was all lark song and savoury with smells. Torn grass and turned earth mingled with woodsmoke and hot pottage, while voices hummed like bees; somewhere down by the river came the steady rhythm of axe on wood.

Cutting wood for fires and ruining that windbreak, Batty thought. Akeld will have a breeze up its nethers once Maramaldo's men have gone.

Which would not be in a hurry, he saw. There were a brace-hundred of them, with horses and pack-mules but this was but an imp of the Great Satan that was Maramaldo's loftily named Company of the Sable Rose.

Somewhere over the horizon would be a few hundred more, shifting slowly and steadily in this direction, with pikes, muskets, bows, horse, bairns and beldames, sway-hipped gauds, notaries, secretaries, carts, tents and all the panoply of a great company.

And a brace of stolen sakers, Batty remembered.

He stood on the tower top, behind the largest segment of the rotten tooth stump of it, which left only his head exposed to the men trailing up to stand beneath with a square of white linen on a pole. For all that, Batty felt an itch on his back at the thought of the men circled behind him; he did not trust Maramaldo, even with a parley flag.

The man himself came up, carried on a chair of yellow plush by four men on outrigger poles. Batty marvelled at that – the great Maramaldo, reduced to an invalid carriage.

Then he saw the yellow face and narrowed his eyes at that. This was not the Fabrizio Maramaldo he remembered, wielding a farrier's axe with one hand and his face a richer, different colour entirely.

'Kohlhase.'

The one who called out was Klett, the man he had fought. There was another with him, pouter-pigeon puffed with self-importance and Batty thought this was the one the nuns had spoken of, the one called Horner.

The one who mattered was struggled up to join them by sweating men at each corner of the great oak seat lashed to poles. He was smothered in a huge green cloak festooned with madder ribbons and trimmed with a fur made rattier by the rain.

'Careful you cunny-licking scabs,' he spat, but it was a gusting puff of the bellow Batty had remembered; the men gentled the affair to rest, then stood back to wipe the sweat and rain from them, shuffling uncertainly.

They were achingly familiar to Batty and as unlike the men from the Borders as monkeys to mice. They had *pluderehosen* and *venetians*, pansied slops in all colours save decent, the material rich and thick and pulled through the slashes so far it dropped almost to their knees.

They had silks and ribbons, geegaws and favours, were parti-coloured here and there and as gaudy as parrots; Batty remembered himself when he was part of it and felt a spasm of old ache, quickly gone.

Then he saw the only sparrow in the bunch, a fussing little man in a strange gown and turban, nodding like a bird and with eyeglasses on a loop round his neck. He was thin as a stork and carried a battered leather satchel – a book, Batty saw. One of Maramaldo's clever wee men, he thought, who can read and scratch out the Latin for agreements. A soothsayer, he added to himself, seeing the symbols on the man's robe; he remembered Maramaldo had a weakness for alchemists and fortune-tellers. Not that you would need one to predict the future of the great Captain General these days; one look at his gaunt yellow face would do.

Klett's voice jerked him from the reverie.

'Your dagg is very fine,' he said. 'By Hofer from Ferlach in Carinthia.'

'Is it?' Batty answered. 'You saw a lot in the dark – but it was right in your face most of the time and hard to miss, I will admit.'

Then he humped up his good shoulder in a lopsided shrug.

'I had it from a stinking-pyntled moudiewart back-shooter called Clem Henharrow, so I would not know anything about its true origin.'

Klett nodded thoughtfully.

'It is well made – the axe is in the handle where others I have seen place it on the muzzle, which is not so good.'

'Because it fouls up?' Batty hazarded and Klett laughed.

'Perhaps you might clot it with all manner of foulness, Master Coalhouse,' he answered softly, 'but the true reason is that folk use it for more prosaic purpose – cutting wood and the like; the blows knock the barrel out of true.'

'Ah well – you would be the expert in guns, Master Klett. I am hearing you have a singular one of your own.'

Klett nodded.

'I do. I am instructed to blow you off that tower with it if you do not come out, you and your nuns all.'

'And weans,' Batty answered, then added into Klett's bewilderment: 'Five bairns. Did you not realise there were bairns here as well?'

Klett's quick, bewildered glance at Maramaldo then Horner showed some bitterness – if he had known, it was a recent revelation, Batty thought. Horner was blank-faced as dressed stone.

'Oho,' he called out mockingly. 'Master Horner omitted to mention there were bairns, did he? That would be because you would have to slay them when it came to the bit, Klett. Think you could do that?'

'Send them out,' Horner interrupted. 'And see.'

'What do you call it?' Batty asked, then nodded into Klett's bewilderment. 'The name. Of your gun.'

'*Doppelhaken*,' Klett replied shortly.

'A double hackbut,' Batty translated. 'My, but it is a fearsome engine. Must weigh a bitty and kick like a bad-tempered mule.'

Klett lifted his face from the work and rested cold eyes on Batty's own.

'Enough. Come out of the tower or you will see it in action, just before...'

'Ach, weesht,' Batty interrupted. 'Let the man who matters speak – besides, it has been a long time since I have heard the voice of Fabrizio Maramaldo and from what I see now, it is diminished a great deal.'

Maramaldo's face was straw and whey, the sweat on it out like fat pearl drops. His cheeks had always been pouched as a squirrel, but now they were sagging though the veins on them were intricate as brocade needlework. The little beard he had always affected as long as Batty had known him was cropped and shaved to a parody that only enhanced the cracked lips; there were sores on them, Batty saw and his thinning hair was plastered damply to his skull.

His voice, however, was firm enough.

'Furca and fossa,' he said. 'March treason.'

Furca and fossa – the pit and the gallows, which was high justice dispensed by hanging where it was possible, or drowning where it was not. Batty remembered Layton, face pressed into a shallow puddle with the Douglas boot on his neck. Eure had only escaped the same when someone had found a gnarled tree, only high enough by being on a slope.

'Aye, aye,' he answered admiringly. 'You have learned a bitty in the time you have been in the Borders, Fabrizio. But there is no March treason here – you are the riders come here to spoil. Besides, you have no writ.'

'Ah, but I have the rope,' Maramaldo countered, 'and your strange decoration proves that your tower is a suitable spot for hanging. Besides, there is a stream in spate which will serve as drowning pit.'

'Him?' Batty offered back, peering down at the blackening swing of Trumpet Baillie. 'He heard you were coming to address us and could not stand the thought of listening to your poxed voice, Fabrizio.'

There was no anger at all in the answer, only a measured weariness, as if the whole business of Batty Coalhouse was tiresome and trivial. Or it might be the illness, Batty thought, though he was aware that his reasons for believing the first was because it echoed what was in himself; he was done up over the business of Maramaldo, no doubt of it.

'Come out, Balthie. Hand over this treasure, the nuns, the *kinder* and all. You are netted like a thrush and there is no escape. You have two hours.'

By which time his guns will be up, Batty thought. Certainly Klett will have assembled his *Doppelhaken* and be ready to shoot; he thought of Trumpet's face then and shivered.

'Aye, aye,' he replied as lightly as he could. 'You were never a good hunter I suspect, for the first rule of catching a bird is to make sure the net has gone over.'

Maramaldo was already slumped and being carried off, so Batty was not even sure he had heard his last sally. Just as well, Batty thought, for it was not very good.

Then, just as he started to turn away, he caught sight of Horner and was sure, with a lightning-strike of certainty and for no reason he could justify, that the man knew Batty would be here. If not in the tower, then Akeld.

He went slowly down the ladder from the tower, nagged by the revelation, stunned by it. Horner had known. Maramaldo had not expected me, for all his intimation that he had hunted Batty like a thrush; Maramaldo had never hunted in his life, unless you counted guddling in the entrails of those he had gutted, convinced they had swallowed their riches.

He turned it over and over until he became aware of Sister Charity, crouched with her caliver, determined and solid. Sister Faith stopped praying when Batty came off the last rung and simply looked at him.

Bigod, he thought, if I have the right of it, then Horner was not surprised to find me here. If so, then he was told it by someone close to Mad Jack – mayhap Rutland spilled all he knew before he died?

He sank down in the lee of the carts, feeling hunger growl through his belly and rob him of any chance of ciphering it out. No food, little water, less shot, little powder – this is a poor hand. If it was Primero, he thought, you would throw it down on the table with a dismissive curse and accept the loss.

Not here, though. Here the loss was sharper than vanishing coin.

Still, Maramaldo's appearance gave hope, Batty thought. Here is me chasing the *condotterie* of old, the bellowing, roaring fell cruel Captain General Maramaldo. The man who took my da, my arm and my ma from me without so much as a blink, for the relief of his own anger and to stamp his command back on demoralised men.

Now, after two decades hunting the beast, I have got up with a mangy lion, a pox-sick man who cannot stand straight. He, in turn, has known he was pursued by a young Hercules, Balthazar Kohlhase and has only managed to diminish that by a limb until now, when he sees the reality is a fat old man with one arm.

We are each of us pursuing phantoms, Batty thought bitterly, and wasting our lives on it.

Chapter Nine

In the tower at Akeld
Night of the second day...

The distant crack was a whip across their nerves; Batty saw the wince in Sister Charity even before the ball struck the ruin of carts, blasting splinters, tearing through to thunder against the back wall of the tower, which seemed to shake.

Batty brushed a few slivers off his jack as if it was lint on a fine embroidered doublet, but the gesture barely raised a smile on Sister Charity's face.

'It will be too dark to shoot soon,' Batty said. 'Besides – his shoulder must be rawer than a wormy dog's arse by now. Beggin' your pardon, Sister.'

They were huddled in the lee of stone near the entrance, for Klett had started on the tower top, then realised no one was daft enough to be up on it and concentrated on plunking a relentless hail of fat ball-shot at the entrance, both over and through the carts, which were now mainly kindling.

'You would be better below,' Batty said, but Sister Charity shook her head; the veil was loose and Batty now saw the reason for it – she was poxed and it had showed in an unhealthy waxen sheen and lumpen face. Small wonder she had given up her auld life, Batty thought, to become a nun. Less wonder that she ended up serving in some piss-poor almshouses – no decent convent would have her.

She read it in his face and managed a slight smile.

'The Spanish call it the Dutch Curse, the Hollanders say it is the Spanish Pox. The French say it is the English Disease and the English call it the French Plague.'

She paused, her red-rimmed eyes brimming with more than fever.

'They all have it, no matter who began it. The truth is, of course, that it is God's way of showing how the sin of Lust punishes itself.'

Batty had nothing he could say that would not be scowling, so he kept quiet. He was no stranger to a woman's poxed face and the memory of a particular one soured him into looking away. She misread the gesture and shifted the veil back into place.

'I will stay. You go below – Sister Faith will appreciate the company and if they rush us, you are better placed there.'

He thought about it for an eyeblink; Klett had been shooting for some time and was almost certainly held to it, though Batty could not understand Maramaldo's reasoning; there should have been blood and fire long before now, with the realisation that neither Batty, nor nuns, nor bairns were coming freely out. All this bang and crash could not fail to bring the Wallis out, full of vengeance and sharp steel.

If Maramaldo had not finished the business here, it was because he would not – or could not. Batty wondered, for a glorious, gooseflesh moment, if the Captain General had died. Then he dismissed it; not only was God not that good at dealing such a winning card to a poor hand like this, but the signs were against it. If the Captain General was dead, there would be more nerves and unease within the ranks of his men.

No, he thought, not dead. Ill, mayhap, with some favoured captain in charge and holding to Maramaldo's last command – shoot them out of the tower. If the Captain General did not recover by the time the sakers came up and found light to shoot, that would be what would be used.

It came to him that Maramaldo might want nuns and Batty alive, to bargain with Mad Jack for the release of his favoured lieutenant, Rafael Sabin.

He told Sister Faith this in the undercroft, conscious of the bairns listening with their too-round eyes and pale, wan faces. She did not speak for a time and Batty felt ashamed that he had somehow failed her and her God – then anger at her for having made him feel this way.

'There is another small hope,' he offered and saw the cock of her head. It was so slight he was now wishing he had never mentioned it at all, but ploughed the stony furrow of it anyway.

'A kennel with no wee dog,' he said. None of the hard mercenary men were Borders bred or had been here long enough to know the way of it, Batty was sure, so they would have missed it. Maramaldo might, too, because he was not at his best in his thinking.

'The first thing anyone does, if they have help they can rely on,' Batty explained, 'is release the hound before barring the bastel door and yett. A wee bitty wool in the collar, coloured to show who is come unbidden to their door, knotted for numbers. The beast will run where it has been trained.'

'Where?'

Batty shrugged. The nearest Wallis stronghold – Twa Corbies was most likely – but he doubted if there had been a colour to mark the likes of Maramaldo's men and the knots would be too few now.

'But the Wallis are watching and gathering,' he added. Little help to Batty Coalhouse, who had slain one of their number on a stair in Berwick's Town Hall – but he did not mention that.

Eventually, Sister Faith shook her head and Batty admired the iron in her that would not let her give into the slender fantasy of it.

'If the Wallis are coming at all, they will wait until they have sufficient force,' she said. 'Which will be too late for us.'

She beckoned the children off the chest and into her embrace. They had to step over the linen-wrapped corpse of Sister Hope to do it.

'I know you are tired and afeared,' she said to them carefully, 'but there are a few things you need to learn about God, so you must listen closely.'

She turned to Batty, who was just realising that the shooting had stopped and was uneasy about what it meant.

'We will baptise them anew, conduct Holy Communion and Extreme Unction,' she declared and Batty turned as a figure slithered down the steps in time to hear this. Sister Charity looked outraged, her eyes burning behind the veil.

'We are not priests,' she declared. 'We can baptise, but only a priest can perform the other rites. It is sacrilege.'

'I do not believe God would suffer his little ones to be denied the peace and love of the Sacraments simply because we are not priests. But I know your doubts, Sister and if you believe it wrong, do not participate. If there is a sin in it, let it be mine alone.'

She moved to the chest and opened it; despite himself, Batty peered in and, even prepared for a lack of glittering gold, jewels and coin, he was disappointed.

He was, in fact, bewildered by what he saw. A flat slate stone, a beaded bracelet – a rosary, he guessed – and a rosary ring like the one Sister Faith wore. There was a pewter cup and a dented plate, a book which was not like any Bible Batty had seen before, then a deal of cloth in various sizes, some of which seemed to be robes.

After that came a leather tube like a fat, long quiver and, finally, a small package of wrapped silk.

No coin. No gold ornaments. No jewelled copes or mitres.

Sister Charity laid things out and, at the end of it, Sister Faith laid a hand on her arm.

'I love you Sister and am as sorry as you are that you are here. Thank you for your strength, which is strongest to me next to God's Own.'

They embraced and Batty felt like an unwanted onlooker as he turned away and moved back up to the tower. Behind he heard them start to pray and then realised that what had been drawn from the chest was everything a priest would need.

The pewter cup and plate were chalice and paten, the innocuous book a missal. There was, he now realised, stole and maniple, altar cloth and vestments. The treasure of Glastonbury, he thought and gave a wry laugh; bigod neither Jack the Lad Horner nor Maramaldo would be pleased to find the truth.

Nor was he pleased himself, for it made a complete mockery of what he had done, what he had risked. He was now aware that he had failed the nuns, the bairns and even, in a strange way he could not reconcile, the Abbey of Glastonbury and the burning nun in Florence. Probably even God. Galloping in like some barrel-bellied, single-armed ancient knight, he thought, to sweep away nuns, five bairns and a chest of secret geegaws for a Catholic priest.

Silly auld fool.

He hunched into himself and thought on how poor his cards were. Then again, he thought, it is only God taking his long overdue justice for all that had been done by Batty Coalhouse, a justice that should have been taken after the wedding feast of Von Zachwitz and his Klett bride. After he had left the nun to burn in Florence. Or any number of other terrors he had tried to board up inside his head.

Mayhap helping Mintie Henderson of Powrieburn would add a tip towards balance. Helping save the baby Queen of Scots should add a feather. In the end, he thought it unlikely to weigh much in his favour; there had been too much grim death dealt out for the approval of angels.

He wondered at this moment, all the same, for he had expected some sign or gesture that this was the end for Batty Coalhouse. All men do, he recognised, as if the world does not just go on without them and so must tremble and crack at the imminence of their passing.

Yet there was nothing, not in the wind, no fire in the sky nor blood in the water. Not so much as ripple on his neck to warn that Batty was leaving for the welcome darkness of the lost worlds, the unlit pastures, the undiscovered glades.

'You are almost done.'

He jerked and then scowled at her.

'Bigod, Sister Faith, you have an unhealthy and unnatural way of coming in on my very thoughts.'

She smiled benignly.

'You are not hard to fathom, Master Coalhouse,' she answered. 'You are almost done, as I say, for all the sins you have thought secured from thought are bursting free. Will you be baptised in the name of God?'

'Will it get me dealt an ace?' he responded with some of the old fire and she smiled softly and shook her head.

'Then I will play these cards,' he answered, 'in life as in Primero.'

'Will you help us bring up the body of Sister Hope?'

He levered himself up, grunting and fought the swaddled corpse up the steps until lay on the tower floor. He had thought the Sisters wanted her body rolled out of the entrance like the rest and was squinting into the dark, wary of Klett still lurking there.

'You are a brave man,' Sister Faith said and that snapped his head round, as did the soft touch on his grimed, calloused hand. Her own was lizard-skin warm, the fingers curled gently into his and he was struck dumb and breathless by the touch, so strange to him these days. She saw it and smiled sadly.

'Have you so little contact left with anyone, Master Coalhouse? Have you never loved, neither God nor girl?'

Batty had no answer to it, though he was full of them, choked with old feelings of comfort and love, so fleeting and long ago in his life that it seemed it had scarcely brushed him at all. Yet the bond never slips, he thought, it stretches and flexes like a stream of honey.

In that maddening, familiar way she seemed to read it right out of his face.

'I can understand now why God esteems you, even if you and He have a deal to work out between you before you are ready to meet Him, face to face.'

She placed the leather container at his feet and then handed him the silk-wrapped package, as big as his one good hand; it felt hard and round in his fingers.

'These are the treasures of Glastonbury, Master Coalhouse' she said. 'and I am sure still that God sent you to save them. As sure as I am that His Hand is over us when we go out.'

Batty heard the last and had suspected as much for some time. Still the reality of it made him suck in a harsh breath.

'Bigod, Sister,' he growled hoarsely, 'you saw what they did to the others. To women… nuns…'

She smiled up at him.

'Sometimes it is far easier to die, Master Coalhouse, than it is to live. You know this already, of course.'

He had no answer to it, simply stood and held the mysterious package, the leather cylinder at his feet, while the eldest boy came up from below with a torch and the two nuns hefted up the body of Sister Faith.

Then, preceded by the bobbing light and chanting prayers, they all stumbled out of the tower and into the shouts and stir.

He stood for a long time alone in the dark, feeling the wobble in his legs and the sick, sad loss of everything.

–

The bastel house of Akeld was fetid with reek and sickness – Sister Charity knew it at once and glanced across at Sister Faith, but her head was bowed and she murmured prayers, turning her rosary ring, while the children huddled close round her and stared at the hard-eyed men.

The hardest turned his granite on the Sisters, then the children, then Klett and, finally, Horner.

'This Balthie is still inside, you say?'

Horner nodded. 'As are the Glastonbury riches.'

The man scrubbed his draggled chin and squinted at Klett.

'Get him out,' he ordered and Klett kept the scowl from his face; Jacob Juup was Maramaldo's favoured right-hand next to Sabin and would carry out the last orders given to him by his commander. Thick as dogshit in the neck of a flask, Klett sneered to himself – but he simply nodded and went off.

Jacob Juup considered the nuns and the bairns; get them out, Maramaldo had said and seize the treasure. He had not said what to do with them, though Juup could guess – but guessing Maramaldo's thoughts was not safe so Juup fell back on orders.

'Stick these in the corner,' he began, but then Maramaldo woke up and felt his pain, began a bellow for Cornelius that ended in a weak whimper.

'Your Master is ill?'

It was the veiled nun; Juup looked at her down his considerable nose.

'If you have prayers…'

'Who is that there?'

Maramaldo was a whisper of his old self, but even that was vicious, so Juup told him and then ushered them forward. He saw them look at each other and was surprised to hear a soft laugh from the veiled nun.

'Pray for me,' Maramaldo growled. 'Light candles and pray, for I am cursed with ill humours…'

'You have an ague,' the veiled nun said coldly. 'A light fever that comes and goes. You have pains in the funda-ment, too harsh to permit riding. On your palms you have scab, slight enough to be mistook for cold-chaps or bad callous, so that you wear gloves, for it hurts to grip without them. On the shaft of your pintle you have a callous which was a sore long since. Mayhap two. They do not hurt, but when the fever is on you they putrify.'

There was silence.

'Have you lain with any poor soul when the pustule was putrid?' she demanded. 'I hope not for her sake – you are poxed.'

The air went still for a moment, then started to coil; Juup held his breath as Maramaldo cleared his throat.

'Half and more of the Company are afflicted. It is the way of matters.'

'How long since you passed water?'

There was a pause, then a voice answered from the dark.

'Five days.'

Cornelius shoved into the light and the other nun signed the cross at the sight of him; he grinned back. The veiled nun simply removed her veil and Cornelius recoiled – now it was the nun's turn to smile.

'He will die if left much longer with piss choking him,' she said simply and nodded to the cup Cornelius clutched. 'Your foul muck will seal the pain but will not cure him of that. I can cure him. I can make him piss.'

'Listen to me, Jesuit,' Cornelius huffed. 'I have a potion distilled from herbs taught to me by Agrippa himself, a Magister Magi whom you will not even have heard of. Mixed with quicksilver and given incantations from the fourth book, it is a sovereign remedy for the blood, for quicksilver is the First Matter and the herbs come from the high passes of the Alps, where the mountaineers enjoy clear skin and a lack of sanguine humours because of these plants…'

'Pish,' Sister Charity said mildly. 'Harum-scarum, hocus pocus. There is no cure for the pox and he will die of it, by and by. As will I. I can make him pass water, all the same – can you do that?'

Maramaldo struggled and folk lifted him upright, the pain of that scouring his face with harsh lines; his glare silenced the spluttering Cornelius.

'How?' he demanded and she told him. His face went from yellow to cream and every other man around him shifted subtly with the revelation of it.

'Will it work?' Maramaldo hoarsed out and the nun cocked an eyebrow.

'Look at me,' she commanded. 'Who better to know the way of it?'

Maramaldo looked for a long time, then turned to Juup.

'If she kills me,' he ordered, 'slay her, her companion and all the children.'

Then he looked at Sister Charity, who was searching the straw in the stalls.

'If you succeed, I will spare your lives,' he said and he heard the other nun's dry laugh.

'I am Sister Faith,' she said, 'and God, not you, will spare us.'

Sister Charity laid a hand on Sister Faith's shoulder and patted it. Then she looked at Juup.

'I will need two strong men to hold him upright. Off the ground, with only his toes touching. They must not let him go. Take an empty knife scabbard and let him bite on it.'

Juup licked dry lips and nodded, picked two men.

'You must be still,' Sister Charity said to Maramaldo as they hoisted him up. 'No matter what, you must not wriggle. Master Juup – a rope on each ankle and strong men to keep them slightly apart. Do not let him kick or jerk.'

Two more men obeyed Juup, looking uneasy at it, especially when Sister Charity demanded Maramaldo be stripped of breeches and underclothes. He grunted when they unlaced his points and whimpered when they started to draw off his trunk hose – crimson and paned so that the yellow silk lining gushed out like pus from a wound.

He hung there, belly hanging down and distended further than usual, sheened with a slick unhealthiness. Sister Charity took the cleanest straw she could find and tested it for rigidity; those men who saw it brought the crotch of their own legs together slightly.

'You have left it go too long,' she chided and Maramaldo licked his pustuled lips, his voice hoarse as crows.

'Do it, woman. Just do it, in the name of God.'

Sister Charity looked at the men each in turn and they nodded their readiness; She held the leather scabbard out and Maramaldo took it like a dog a bone and, quick as an adder, Sister Charity reached out and took Maramaldo's prick, shrunk to the size of a pea. She stretched it with one hand, then skinned the head free; Maramaldo's brows went up and his eyes widened.

Juup felt his legs close involuntarily when the straw went in; Maramaldo gave a muffled grunt deep in his throat.

Sister Charity was slow and steady, but Maramaldo's cheeks blew in and out as he clenched on the leather, accompanied by the boar-like grunts; everyone save him watched with fascination as the slender straw rod vanished.

Like a twig up a chicken neck, Horner marvelled and then the straw rod reached the end – everyone saw it by the jerk and sudden stillness that froze Maramaldo. There was a satisfied little grunt from Sister Charity, then she started the straw on the way out. Maramaldo began to whimper expectantly and started to arch, so that the men on his ankles gripped harder.

There was a moment, just before the straw came out, when everyone saw the seepage, followed by a spatter of darkness that might have been blood. Then the straw came out and with it an evil-smelling flow of what looked uncomfortably like the lees in every ale cup men had looked in. The men holding his ankles almost leaped away from it, but they were not needed now, for Maramaldo held himself splay-legged and emptied like a burst dam.

There was a fresh spurt, almost as dark as the first. Then another and finally a steady gush, growing ever paler and reeking like vinegar; Maramaldo, who had been panting out little pig squeals, started into grunting relief like a bear on a scratching post. Sister Charity sniffed the straw and frowned, then turned to Cornelius.

'You have seen?'

The astrologer nodded, wide-eyed.

'Good. You may have to do this in the future. Find a rod in that alchemikal litter you hoard – gold or silver and thin as this straw. Wear gloves.'

And she tossed the straw to one side and grinned at the utter horror on the little magician's face.

Maramaldo, sloe-eyed with relief, stirred a little and finally looked straight at Juup.

'Kohlhase?'

They were inside the tower. Klett was wary and hackled as a wet cat fresh from the bag, but there was no one beyond the carts, nor down in the undercroft. Men lugged up the chest while others watched and Klett eyed the ladder that led upwards.

'Zerdig,' he ordered and jerked his chin at it. Zerdig scowled, then moved reluctantly to it, his backsword raised as if to poke the darkness above.

Up in the tower, Batty listened to them struggle with the chest and grinned. Little good may that do you, he thought, unless you like priestly vestments, or the chest itself. Which was a fine affair, he had realised, lined with silk and covered with ponyhair to keep weather out.

He heard the ladder creak, saw the dark shape and pointed the dagg. The whirring wheel and sparks were warning enough and the man cursed and hurled himself away before the thing went off with a blinding flash and a gout of smoke.

'I have another,' Batty called out, though he did not add that it was as empty as the first, for he had no shot left at all and only a handful of Sister Charity's rosary beads, which he would now load.

There was a pause, muttering voices raised in argument, then a voice which Batty recognised as Klett's.

'Come down. Your nuns and *kinder* have gone and we have the treasure. In the morning we will shoot you from there with the sakers.'

'How many shots?' Batty demanded.

'What?'

'How many shots, d'you think? To get me blown out of this perch. Two? Three? More?'

'As many as it takes,' Klett replied, his voice annoyed now.

'I wager you cannae do it in less than six,' Batty replied. 'You are the nearest offering to a gun-layer they have, I warrant, and you are unable to hit a bull's arse with a swung shovel. How is your shoulder, Master Klett?'

Batty almost felt the answering scowl through the darkness. Aching, for sure, he thought.

'We will see,' Klett replied. 'Zerdig, stand sentry at the door. Make sure Meinheer Kohlhase remains in his little nest until we blow him away.'

Batty heard them go, risked a squint into the dark over the side of the tower and thought he saw them; he heard them, for sure, cursing and stumbling under the weight of the chest and he laughed.

He sat with his back to the stones, looked at the shadowy shape of the leather cylinder and thought he had an idea on the contents – lots of tight-wrapped scroll deeds to manors all over Somerset. I am a rich man, he thought wryly, for whoever possesses these possesses the legal right to ownership – well, providing he has enough style to pass as a gentleman.

The silk package was another affair entirely and it took him a time of peering at the contents in the dim to work out what they were. Even then he was not sure – a round wooden bowl and, nested inside it, two small phials carefully mounted in filigreed gold cases and stoppered with wax and seals. He had no idea what they were – though the bowl was of some use, for it had started to rain and he put it out to catch some.

Then he drank, gratefully, while he considered his position. The watchtower was simply a fretwork of lashed poles on the uneven rotted tooth remains of the stone tower. There was a rough-planked floor with the trapdoor in it, hinged to swing up and battened with a fat wooden latch; there was a similar one on the underside.

The only other item of note was a winch made from wood and clearly used once to haul the timbers up the outside of the tower. This was where he and Sister Hope had lashed the rope for safety while they hauled Trumpet up; it stretched out into the dark and creaked softly when the lisping rain-wind shifted his lashed corpse.

When Batty risked a quick lean and peer, he saw the guard below and to the right, as close under the lee of the tower without actually being in the entrance, for he feared putting himself in the dark and whoever might come down into it with a loaded firearm.

Batty hunkered down and endured the rain, might even have dozed until a snap of sound brought his head up. Another followed, with shouts and a mournful lowing.

Cracked whips and wet miserable oxen, the cries of equally dripping and exhausted men; Batty knew those sounds as he knew his own breathing – the guns were coming up, hauled out of their Cheviot hidey-hole under the lash of Maramaldo's will.

I was wrong, Batty thought, squinting at the still-dark sky, the rain pebbling his face. If I stay here longer, I will be elevated higher than this tower, but only as long as it takes for me to crash to the ground again, in bloody bits.

–

She watched Horner watching the chest and gnawing his nails while the fire and sconces bloodied his face. Apt, Sister Faith thought, for a man more fitted for Hell would be hard to find, even in this place.

The stone house of Akeld was worse up the under-croft ladder than down, for this was where the original occupants had been scumfished out. Sister Faith had not known the term, but Juup told her it was the name they had in these parts for what Germans called 'rauchwerfen'. That was a joke, he explained patiently, since the German word for kicking someone out was 'rauswerfen' and the word for 'smoke' was 'rauch'...

Yes, Sister Faith understood, but Juup seemed sullen about her lack of laughing and went back to sitting, scowling down his hawk nose at the sleeping Maramaldo as if her lack of humour was all his fault.

Smoking them out, whatever you called it, had black-ened and reeked the entire top floor of Akeld with a damp char and the children had found portions of it and contrived to get it on them, as children will do.

Men came and went with seeming purpose; one or two muttered to Juup and every time it happened, the man they called Cornelius raised his head from the book he pored over endlessly, muttering to himself. Once or twice he caught the eye of Sister Faith and looked away.

Sister Charity sat with the children, hands in her neat lap, veiled and silent as an icon; Horner had tried to speak to her and failed, falling silent under the intensity of her gaze.

Sister Faith watched him and knew he could not resist it longer – there, she was right...

Horner got up and moved to the chest, had a hand on it when Juup opened one seemingly sleeping eye.

'Step away or lose it at the wrist.'

Horner jerked as if pricked and stumbled back a pace, then rounded on the bush-bearded German.

'At least open it,' he burst out. 'See if the treasure lies within. They may have left it in the tower...'

'In which case it will be there still,' Juup replied blandly, 'for the Captain General to order recovered when he wakes and looks in the chest.'

Horner twitched and fumed, then rounded on Sister Faith.

'Is it in the tower? Is it? What have you done with it, you bitch-tick...'

'That is no way to talk to Christ's brides,' Juup said, which amazed the Sisters as much as Horner; Juup saw it and raised a lazy eyebrow.

'What? You think all Hollanders are Lutheran?'

'In my experience, such religious feeling does not sit well in such a band as this,' Sister Charity replied and Juup laughed.

'Ach, ja, you would know, little Sister, for you did not get poxed at Matins or Compline, I think. But you would be wrong. We have cut, gouged, burned and stabbed believers all over the Italies, the Germanies, France – everywhere. Catholics, Lutherans, Jews, people who follow God, those who follow the Devil or the infidel god of the Saracens, which is the same thing. Or even worse – those who do not believe in any god at all.'

He shifted slightly and stretched.

'We have stabled horses in monasteries, pissed in fonts, burned mosques and sacked churches. All with religious feeling, Sister.'

'Do you believe in nothing?' Sister Faith asked quietly.

'Coin,' Cornelius interrupted before Juup could speak and the Captain acknowledged it, with an added frown at having been interrupted.

'Florins, guilders, thaler, batzen, kreutzer, shillings,' Cornelius went on. 'A Mass of coin, as it were.'

Juup and he both laughed.

'And you?' Sister Faith asked, turning to Cornelius. 'Do you believe in Lord Jesus Christ – or is it Simon Magus?'

Cornelius blinked, but did not seem shamed or outfaced. He shrugged.

'Do not discount the magi, Sister. They had power before Christ came to the earth. Besides – pick an army. Any one you care to. You will find they all fight with God on their side, which at least makes sure He wins.'

Juup grinned as the Sisters crossed themselves.

'You may not know God in full,' Sister Faith answered him, 'but He knows you, magus.'

'None of which answers the question which my Lord Chancellor will insist on knowing – where is the treasure from Glastonbury?'

Horner loomed over Sister Faith who looked briefly up at him, then bowed her head and prayed, turning her ring round and round her finger. Horner hovered on the edge of striking her, but was aware of Juup's mocking look and eventually subsided. He glowered at the Captain.

'Remember why I am here,' he said and Juup's smile broadened.

'Remind the Captain General when he wakes,' he replied. 'I am sure he will listen carefully to your complaints, Meinheer Horner.'

Horner's eyes slitted.

'I will be sure to ask him before he learns that you have failed to extract this fat, one-armed old man from the tower, Captain Juup. Again.'

He went back to gnawing his nails, wondering if he had scored a palpable hit on the Hollander, for that badger-bearded stolid face gave nothing away. Yet everyone knew that the lack of a Balthie in suitable chains would put them all at risk when Maramaldo woke up.

Like the treasure, he consoled himself moodily, Batty Coalhouse is not leaving in any hurry.

-

Batty had determined on leaving in a hurry. While it was still dark and before folk found out that the chest was as empty as balls after a night in a brothel.

He had worked out the way of it and moved swiftly once he had, wrapping bowl and phials up and stuffing them inside his jack, looping the cylinder round his back like a quiver.

Then he leaned over, quiet and careful and took the rope in his one good hand; Trumpet trembled. You can only play the hand you are dealt, Batty thought, in life as in Primero. At least I have one good hand left.

He clenched it round the rope and hauled it up a little way, then heaved it sideways, then back; slowly, like a fat pendulum, Trumpet started to swing.

Below, Zerdig huddled in the lee of the tower, afraid to go into the dark of it for fear of the one-armed man coming down the ladder, unseen and unheard, to fire off that axe-handled dagg.

So he hunched up and got wet and cursed Klett for it, knowing the Lance-Captain did not like him and sure that he was not about to be sent any relief and would be here all night. At least here he would be safe – it was unlikely that a fat, one-armed man would come down the outside of the tower, after all. Not even down that rope with a dead man at the end of it.

The rain spattered him with heavier drops and a wind hissed. From the corner of his eye, he saw something black against the night, moving like a swift shadow. An owl, he thought, though it was large and he peered anxiously; this land was full of *gespenster* and the people in it were hardly better than trolls.

He had hunched himself back into his shoulders and misery when something made him turn his head... in time to see the grave-wrapped dead come howling down on him out of the night. He never had time even to cry out.

Batty let the last of the rope go on the inward swing, heard the crack and thump of it and made for the ladder like a rat out of a drain. He half fell down, had his bollock knife out even before he scrambled over the last splinter of the carts and out the door.

The corpse swung and turned, bumping the old stones of the tower, but Trumpet's last blast had struck the guard hard and he lay moaning, his face bloody and his breath bubbling in and out of his nose; Batty knelt to him and peered into the unfocused glass of his eyes.

'Never play Primero,' he said sorrowfully, 'for you have no luck at all.' He slit the man's throat. Then he looked at the swaddled, tumbled corpse.

'God keep you, Trumpet. Blaw a blast at the Lord if you see Him, as a reminder that I am supposedly on His good work here.'

Then he went into the dark, limping on his bad leg and rolling like a sailor, out past the finger of tower, with the lights of fires all around.

There was noise in the night – singing, loud talk, the zing of a beggar's lyre – and Batty turned slowly in a circle, letting his eyes search the dark. He wanted a horse; he wanted Fiskie and all his gear, but thought that too much of a risk while the vague, gnawing thought came at him again, the one he'd had ever since Sister Faith had started in about him being chosen.

If he died here, on this muddy, rainwashed ground, it would be as if nothing had happened with his life at all. No one would remark on it bar those he owed money and if the nuns and weans recalled him at all, he fancied it would be brief, for they would be rubbed out of the picture soon enough. God is like Michaelangelo, he thought, with spit and a thumb on the chalk of our lives.

He shook it from him. The nuns had stood here. He had stood here and was standing yet and he heard her speak as if she was next to him, twisting her rosary ring.

'God came to this valley, Master Coalhouse. He came and He touched us all, sent you to us. Mayhap... just mayhap... you are not who you believe yourself to be.'

'She's as banging daft as a yett on a windy day,' Batty muttered. 'I am me myself and not one thing more. I am not chosen.'

Then he gathered himself a little, felt a sudden lightness; he was out in the night and the wet, with as good a chance of escape as any. He looked at the flickering lights, picked the least dense and took a deep breath.

Set a stout heart to a steep brae, he said to himself and moved off.

They were eating and talking, flickering shadows back and forth against the flames and he realised the fires were fewer here because they were larger with more men gathered round them; the blood started to pound in his temples as he saw he had walked into a pack of them. Right in, like a raw orb fallen from nest to viper pit.

Someone belched and others laughed; they were close enough to poke with a stick and Batty hunched himself, trying to make his shape nothing much and certainly not one arm less.

Then he ploughed forward, walking slow and trying not to limp too much, his flat bonnet pulled low. Heads looked up and someone spoke a challenge; Batty waved his one good hand.

'*Unter der Fuchtel stehen.*'

There were good-natured jeers and catcalls trailing him as he stumbled on and Batty kept going, relentless as a millwheel in a race until, eventually, he grew light-headed and realised he had stopped breathing.

He sucked in air then and glanced back at the shadowy shapes, who were paying him no more concern than the dark.

Unter der Fuchtel stehen. 'Standing under the stick,' was the term used for punishment detail – you had annoyed some commander who was entitled to beat you with a stick, or give you some shit to shovel. Sending someone off on some pointless errand beyond the warm assurance of fire and guard was typical and excited only ribaldry from folk glad it wasn't them.

Batty blew out his cheeks and shook rain off, remembering all the times he had shared such a fire with the same sort of men.

Then he turned his back on them and plootered on into the night.

Chapter Ten

Later, out on the Cheviot hills...

He stumbled and hirpled until his hips and knees struck something hard and he fell over it, with time only to think 'dyke' before he tumbled to the far side and lay there, looking at the lightening sky and the face of a curious sheep.

There were many curious sheep, penned in the hip-height barmkin wall with a spreading tree at the centre of it for shade and shelter; Batty crawled through the droppings to it, put his grateful back to the gnarl and lay, blinking at the dawn and wondering if he had done enough.

He was sure he had not, that he would have to be up and away as best he could through the rain and moor, once it was light enough to work out the way down to Wooler. If he could reach that place...

The sheep cropped and stared at the fat one-armed man nodding towards oblivion.

–

He woke from a dream of Bella Yelland, with a yelp that sent the sheep licking his face away with a plaintive mewling. The rain had stopped, but the tree dripped and

174

it was now full light, eldritch with clouds so thick the only way you could tell where the sun lay was by the milk-glare being brighter in one spot than elsewhere. There was a silence so immense you could hear a snail breathe.

He was facered by the dream and lay, aching and cold, thinking on Bella and the summer they had gone from scampering bairns to coupling like frantic stoats. Ned and Batty's da had been friends, gunners in the service of Maramaldo and, even then, Ned had been more interested in drink than war.

Batty and Bella had scarce gained fluff hair on chin and quim, but discovered the whole business of copulation and were so rigorous in the learning that they frequently could not stand up without trembling.

Then Ned had spoken out against Maramaldo, though drink had more to do with the courage in it that any lion heart. He and Bella had then left in a hurry and, the night before she did, Bella and Batty had sworn blood oaths to be united, to never forget, to be as one once again.

The next year a big flaxen-haired Dutch girl ran away from her parents and her farm to join the Company of the Sable Rose and Batty's memories of Bella grew misted as breath on a mirror when faced with her pink and white breasts.

The next time he had seen Bella had been at Bologna a decade and more ago when the Emperor Charles was being crowned; Captain General Ferrante Gonzaga, seeking to impress his lifelong master, was hiring every man he could find to make his contribution to the coronation procession magnificent.

Batty had come down with what was left of his own small Company, for easy money and no fighting. He had been 30, one-armed and gaunt with hatred, and didn't even realise Bella was in the same camp, staring at this one-armed man and roaring orders and curses at Ned Yelland's gun crews. Bellow Yelland, they all called her but never to her frown of face.

When she had spotted Batty, she lost her scowl in an alchemy that transformed it into the sunniest of smiles, cracking her chap cheeks and showing as much gap as teeth.

Batty had been shocked at the sight of her, for her face seemed to have swollen in places and sunk in others, was as homely as a suet bun and nothing like the fey beauty he had swived years before. He knew why, of course, because Calvin's wife had told him of it – she's been poxed caring for the Goodwife, who had been poxed by Calvin himself.

At the time Batty had stared at Bella until her quiet smile and bird-tilt look had made him realise how much he had also changed; he shifted sideways, as if to hide the missing arm and she laughed.

'Have you been sent to recover the tub of Orkney butter we stole when we left Maramaldo for the second time?' she demanded. Orkney butter was a mix of oil of olive, wax and sheep tallow, an expensive and highly-prized way of proofing gun barrels against rust; Maramaldo would flay such a thief for the loss of a single pat of it, never mind a tub. But Batty was more facered by the knowledge that Ned and Bella had rejoined the Company of the Sable Rose.

She admitted it with a light shrug.

'After he took your arm,' she said and had looked at Ned, lurching about and getting in everyone's way; it was clear to Batty who ran the gunners now, clearer still that his own da's death would have left a vacancy the Yellands had not been slow to fill.

She saw it all in his face and her gaze was defiant.

'Well?' she said. 'Are you here to claim Maramaldo's due?'

'When I catch Maramaldo up,' he retorted, 'I will ask him if he misses it still.'

She shook her head then and gave a soft, gentle laugh.

'I had heard you were chasing some Saxon noble over horses,' she replied. 'Now I find you are chasing Maramaldo for the loss of your arm.'

She smiled sadly.

'Next time we meet, I trust you will be less busy.'

'Next time we meet,' he had said sullenly, 'I trust you will not be back with Maramaldo. Again.'

Her face had grown even sadder then and Batty felt ashamed of his sourness, so that he managed to chase enough of it away for a grin. Then she kissed him, no more than a flick of the end of her nose on his cheek if he was honest, and stepped back a little.

'It was my idea to join Maramaldo,' she said, 'for Ned is too sodden to run matters these days. It was for a season only and I had my reasons.'

She paused, then leaned forward a little.

'Never be minding about Maramaldo, all the same. Old sins will end old sins.'

He started suddenly, realised he had drifted off again and was now more afeared than ever of his dreams – Bella Yelland, sprung up like a villain in a mummer's play, haunting his dreams with strangeness. He had not thought of her in years and was troubled by the idea that Sister Faith had the right of it – he was all but done and the great lake of black sin he had dammed up deep inside him was leaking at the seams.

Then a hand clamped his shoulder like a horse bite, hauling him up to his feet and the lancing agony of his leg. Bewildered, he stared at the bearded faces, the tilted bonnets and jacks and gauntlets of a crowd of men, one of whom had him gripped tight.

'It is him right enough,' boomed one. 'The one-armed bastard moudiewart from the Berwick Tolbooth. The one who slew Tam on the stairs.'

'Are you certain, Anthone? He was seen in the tower at Akeld wi' yon nuns. I would not care to hemp wrangwise here.'

The one called Anthone shook Batty like a terrier with a rat.

'I am certaintied of it, Chilman. This is the man who slew your sister's man, nuns or not.'

Batty, fighting for sense, realised these were not Maramaldo's men but the Wallis riders. He wanted to tell them of Akeld, but a hand closed on his throat and squeezed breath and words out of him. The face behind it was slit-eyed with hate and triumph; this will be Anthone, Batty thought as his world narrowed to the stare of an angry man.

'Aye, gasp, you wee fat murderer. Once the hemp goes round, you will choke harder.'

'Hold, hold,' cried another voice and Batty almost wailed with relief when the hand was removed; he sucked in rasping breaths and blessed God for his reprieve.

'Fetch Mags,' the voice called. 'She will want to see justice done on her man's murderer.'

Batty cursed then and would have waved a fist at the sky if his arm had not been held fast. You may be the font of all life, Batty thought savagely, but, God, you are a vicious bastard in the everyday of folk…

There were five men; Batty would not have missed them if he had been in his right mind and was bitter about that as much as anything. Three went back through the sheep and the ones called Chilman and Anthone dragged Batty under the tree. Dazed, he stood there while they looped a rope up over a branch and scattered the sheep from around them.

They had slip-noosed it as far as Batty's head, as far as touching his brow with the rasp of it, when Batty finally found his force.

He lashed out a kick which took Chilman in the shin and sent him hopping and roaring. Anthone, one hand on the rope and the other grasping Batty's good arm, was whirled sideways by a tremendous strength and sent flying over the barmkin wall.

Freed, Batty started to run, stepped on to the injured leg and felt it buckle under him with a fiery shriek of protest; he fell and rolled through the sheep, hearing the curses of the three men who had gone out over the barmkin wall.

'In the name of Christ's Wounds, Chilman – can you not hang on to a fat auld man wi' the yin arm…?'

Someone fell on Batty's back as he struggled up; a hand came round his mouth to try and get to the neck and Batty found a finger close to his teeth and bit, snarling. He felt it go clean through, felt the horrible moment of the sever in his mouth and spat it into the face of Anthone, while Chilman bounded away, holding his hand and screaming 'my finger, my finger'; the sheep bawled and milled.

The others came roaring up, ploughing through the protesting sheep, with one shouting angrily at the others to stop mollycoddling the old bastard and get a rope round him. Is he your bliddy sweetheart that you treat him so kindly?

Batty wanted this one more than the others and thrashed and bellowed his way upright, first to his screaming knees, then his unsteady legs, with men hanging off him like hounds fastened to a bayed stag.

A grip on his wrist slicked away; men cursed and one howled as Batty kissed him with a forehead. Another took a roundhouse whack from Batty's fist and then they piled on him like a football ruck.

Anthone had the noose round Batty's neck and was snarling triumph, hauling hard so that the old-blood darkness closed in on either side of Batty's sight like a narrowing tunnel. He heard a voice shout out 'Ware – its Mickle Jock.' For a moment he thought he heard a rumble, then a crack and, finally, the world gave up on him.

The bastel house of Akeld
The next morning...

It was a Scotch morning according to Sister Charity and Sister Faith had no reason to doubt her accuracy – the mist sat tight on the hills and flowed down into the valley like a burn in spate. Everything dripped.

'Pestilential country.'

Juup was hunched up under a hooded cloak and Horner stood next to him; Sister Faith was aware that Juup was here to make sure Klett was kept alive as long as possible and so they were at odds on that. Horner was here because he would not let Sister Faith beyond reach of his hand now that he knew the Glastonbury riches were not in the chest.

Sister Faith prayed for Klett's quick death and God's mercy on him, her knees aching in the damp as the man swung above her from a trio of lashed poles. He was upside down and leaking what was left of his life into a watery pool and had screamed a long time, from the moment a sullen Maramaldo, weaving still when he stood, had consecrated him to flaying for the sin of letting Batty Coalhouse escape. Poxed, possibly to death in the long term, the short-term Maramaldo was still a sink of viciousness.

'It was Zerdig,' Klett had shrieked, but Zerdig was dead and so Klett, as Maramaldo had pointed out, had to take responsibility.

'As will you, when you stand before God to explain what your own men have done at your command,' Sister Faith said sternly, which had made Maramaldo scowl. He needed Sister Charity and her skills, which Sister Faith knew; it would keep them and the children alive, despite Horner.

That one leaned forward as she knelt, watching what was left of Klett drip his life to a close. The man who had taken the skin off Klett was a big, stolid-faced Saxon and the camp's best butcher when left to his own; Sister Faith was sure she would not eat of any meat tonight.

'Sister,' said Horner quietly. 'I respect and understand you. I understand also how you feel about the late Abbot, but that is long past and gone. Now is now and the Lord Chancellor wishes the Glastonbury treasure. The king wishes it. How can you think to oppose those wills?'

Sister Faith prayed and let him wheedle. She knew he wanted the deeds and would pull more plums out before he gave them to the Lord Chancellor, who would hand what was left after his own plundering to King Henry.

Henry would not care so much for deeds – he wanted the other riches, the real treasure of Glastonbury...

Horner stopped after a while, when Maramaldo rode up. Back in the saddle, he noted, even if he fidgets. Fit and well enough to realise the mess everyone was in, but Horner did not say any of that.

'Has she spoken?' Maramaldo demanded and Juup shook his head; after a short pause, Horner did likewise. Maramaldo grinned.

'Well, the plan proceeds, Master Horner, whether your fabled treasure is in it or no. In a little while, we shall have a small war and then all will be resolved.'

'War plans seldom last longer than the moment they are begun,' Horner answered and Maramaldo drew himself up in the saddle, a moment spoiled by the drip on his nose.

'You are the expert on war here, Master Horner?'

Horner said nothing for a moment, acknowledging his lack. Then he slid a stiletto into the ribs of Maramaldo's preen.

'I do not have my part of the contract,' he said. 'Thus the Lord Chancellor does not have his due and so neither does my king, who will not look kindly on someone who let slip the Glastonbury riches. This puts your own reward at risk.'

Maramaldo wiped drops from the brim of his helmet with one gauntleted hand.

'Let me worry about your king,' he growled. 'The grace of your Gross Henry will be assured by others, not you. I am still curious as to why Balthie Kohlhase is here and am sure you have knowledge of it; be grateful for that, Master Horner, for otherwise you would be discovering how Master Klett feels.'

'Felt, Your Honour.'

Faces turned to the wet mourn of Juup, who looked damply back at them.

'He is dead,' he explained to Maramaldo, who saw the etched blanch of Horner's face from the corner of one pouched eye. That one's life dangled by the thinnest hair, for Musgrave had insisted that he be removed together with the nuns, for reasons which had not concerned Maramaldo until now. Yet he needed the nuns and was sure Horner knew why Balthie Kohlhase had arrived into the middle of this; he wanted that knowledge before he killed the man.

I wonder, he mused, if Master Horner can feel the breath of the Devil on his neck.

The wind tendrilled to his own and made him shiver, so that he touched an amulet of St Gregory for reassurance. Then, with a grunt, the Captain General shook himself, reined round and moved away, bawling orders to set his army in order.

Somewhere in the Cheviot hills
At the same time…

There were voices, a smell of woodsmoke and a rain-sodden breeze. He knew he lay on a bracken bed and was covered with rough wool, so he thought there was a shelter, open at least on one side to the elements.

Batty did not open his eyes, for he heard movement and did not want to let anyone know he was awake. Instead, he examined himself with closed eyes and little movements, starting with the leg he knew well as a dull ember of ache from knee to ankle, with a hot centre where the arrow had gone in.

The other leg muttered a reply to it, but that was an old injury from when he was tumbled off The Saul at least a year since by Geordie Bourne's shot and sent whirling down a long drop. He had scarted all down one side, he recalled, but the opposite one ached now – boots and fists, Batty thought as he remembered the recent fight.

His forehead hurt and he remembered why; the bastard-born whelp who had bruised it had his nose broken, for sure, he thought with savage triumph. Yet he ached as if a horse had been ridden back and forth on him – or men had kicked and beaten him. Both were equally likely, he thought, for God clearly thinks I am worthy of punishment, whether I am an archangel or no.

There was a soft clunking of pewter and tin – pannikins and plates, Batty thought. Then something rapped loudly, paused and did it again.

'Away in,' growled a voice close by and Batty knew it for a woman. There was a clatter – a door opening, which made this no three-sided shelter – and there were more voices, the shrillest and loudest from another woman.

'There he is – the murderer of my man. And you cosset him like a bairn, Trottie Wallis. Hand him up to me, as my rights demand…'

'Divven you yell at me, Mags,' came the growling reply. 'Your rights? You had them only when you were wed on to a Wallis man. Now you are a no better than a Robson again and have no rights unless we Wallis hand them to you.'

'You rank auld besom,' spat Mags viciously. 'I will have the murderer of my lovin' man or else…'

'Or else what, you sow?'

Good for you, beldame, Batty thought to himself.

'Lovin' man,' Trottie went on scornfully. 'This is me you speak with, Mags Robson. Me who handed you balm for the bruising and powders and paints to cover your shame of being thumped by your lovin' man, Tam Wallis.'

There was silence and Trottie growled on like a pit dog.

'He didnae get the name Evil-Willit for playin' the lute an' bringin' you posies, Mags Robson.'

'He was still fell murdered in the Tolbooth at Berwick...'

A man's voice this and Trottie went for the throat of it at once.

'Fell murdered? I heard he had been killed for his foolishness in pursuing a personal quarrel when everyone else was fleein' the place. Killed, I might add, by this fat single-armed auld man here, so he was scarcely skilled and thus no loss.'

'Aye, well – there was a quarrel. Tam was assaulted in the gaol...'

'Pish and fiddle,' Trottie spat. 'I know you are sweet on Mags, Leckie Wallis, and will stick your big boots under her bed when suitable time has passed, but divven come tellin' me of Tam Wallis' finer traits to cozen your way with her. He was my kin, mind, and I know him well. It comes as little surprise to me to find that this lovin' man o' Mags Robson was in Berwick gaol in the first place for beatin' a wee unlucky hoor half to death.'

'Bigod, Trottie Wallis, you are rank midden with little shame nor pity...'

'Ach, be silent Mags. In my own home I may speak as I please. Take your hate elsewhere...'

'I will have my due,' shrieked Mags. 'And have others who agree...'

'Aye aye – who might they be?'

The new voice was familiar, a quiet rasp that ground out a silence at once.

'Headman Robson?' the steady voice added. 'I think not. Away, Mags. Tam Wallis died and we will kist him up with due ceremony and a deal of lies aboot his bravery and finer qualities. But I will decide if his slayer is to be hemped, not you nor any of those foolish enough to stand with you.'

Batty could almost see them shift and slither off, muttering. He almost cheered.

'Is he well?'

Batty stopped breathing a little as Mags clattered cooking pots again; she clearly gave some affirming sign, for the voice grew closer.

'When can he speak?'

'Ach, bless Your Honour, he can speak now for he has been awake and listening the whole time.'

Batty sighed and opened his eyes, blinking back to the world. He was in a cruck house whose one window was unshuttered to let the rain-wind blow out the peatfire reek. There were tools and baskets on hooks, a creel for tarn fishing and bunches of grasses and herbs, pungent with last summer.

Faces, too, a brace of them. One was the bearded bluff Batty remembered on the barrel-body of John Wallis, Headman of the Wallis in these parts and, if he wanted to give himself the graces of it, the Laird of Twa Corbies.

The other was a woman, long gone from beauty into crabbed old age and greasy grey hair straggling round cheeks as knobbed and cracked as last year's apples. Her eyes were black as little jet beads, never resting one place on Batty's own face, but moving restlessly, as if seeking some way in past his eyes to search his soul.

'You will be Trottie,' Batty grunted. 'My thanks – it seems I owe you my life and care. Was it you got me oot from under the lads who wanted me hemped?'

'It was not,' Trottie answered sharply. 'You owe Mickle Jock for that.'

'Aye, well, I will shake his hand with the one I have left when I see him.'

John Wallis laughed and perched himself on a three-legged stool, the better to be at Batty's eye level.

'You will wait awhiles,' he said. 'Mickle Jock is Trottie's ram, who finally ran out of patience with all those causing his ewes distress and upset. He ran at them – caught Anthone a right clankie-o. He may have broke a bone or two there.'

Batty recalled the milling sheep; in a pen, with nowhere to run, they would have panicked and anyone who knew the beasts was well aware that they were not docile all the time and could be roused to a fair rage if it came to the bit.

'Weel,' he said to Trottie. 'Nudge him a sweet tumshie in his feed. Have one for yerself…'

'Divven try and charm me, hinney.'

Her voice was cold and sent Batty's eyebrows up with surprise.

'I am a Cheviot Wallis,' she went on, 'and from the time I could make my own water I have been taught to hate you and your kind, all the blue bonnets from across the Border. I was told it is a fine thing to cut the throats of you – and if it hadn't been for the upset to my sheep, I would have done so.'

John Wallis saw Batty's look and laughed, then laid a hand on Trottie's arm.

'Away, Trottie – you are a soft as fresh sheepshite when it comes to wee lost souls, be they litter runts or injured auld men with but one arm. And speak true now – there is as much bad cess against Mags as Christian charity in this.'

Trottie huffed and clattered pots but did not deny it; smiling, John Wallis looked at Batty.

'I recall you from the Tolbooth,' he said levelly and Batty agreed that it had been him and that he remembered John Wallis well enough.

'Your wee bonfire o' the Dacre deeds was no doubt fine,' Batty added carefully, 'but I believe there are copies.'

Wallis sighed and nodded.

'Wee lawyers will ruin us all,' he answered. 'It was a gesture, hopeful of letting the Dacres know our mind on the matter, to make it clear that even if the rights to Twa Corbies and more are stamped with wee lawyer seals, it will be on parchment only – they will need an army to serve their writ. What is the business of them nuns?'

The last took Batty by surprise and he moved a little, trying not to wince.

'Caught up in matters,' he said, which was no lie but still stepping lightly round the truth. 'They came to Akeld in time to find your Wallis men suffering at the hands o' mercenaries from across the water.'

'I had heard,' Wallis answered grimly. 'Five good men ill-used and hung.'

'A wee hound told you,' Batty said and Wallis nodded, considering Batty carefully now.

'You saw that? Well, why would you not – you are a Borders man, a hot trod ride all on your own, I have heard. What brought you here?'

He was sharp, Batty realised, firing off his arrowed little questions at the end of some seemingly empty witter.

'Bewcastle sent me,' he answered, judging truth was best here. 'One of the nuns was sister to Mad Jack himself and he wanted her found from her overdue. I did not expect Maramaldo and his men.'

'Well, I would not concern yourself overmuch,' Wallis answered. 'Them paid-men are set for a slap sooner rather than later.'

'They have guns,' Batty pointed out. 'A brace of sakers, no less.'

Wallis smiled some winter at Batty and levered himself up.

'Guns,' he said scornfully. 'Big slow useless engines, deadly only if you run straight at them.'

'Like Ancrum,' Batty responded, irritated, then wished he had not hauled out that spectre by the scruff of the neck. Wallis said nothing and Batty wondered if the man knew who had commanded the ruinous Scots guns at Ancrum. Probably not, he realised in the next breath, because I would not be treated so kindly.

'Can he ride?'

'In the morn,' Trottie answered without missing a beat. 'A wee bit rest and some o' old Trottie's best care will see him in the saddle by then.'

Wallis nodded, turned and left while Batty struggled a bit more upright, wincing at the pain in his leg; he realised it had been rebound with fresh cloths. Trottie grinned gum at him.

'It had been dressed nice,' she said, 'by a nun, no doubt, complete with clean water and long prayers.'

When Batty nodded, she cackled at the suspicion in his eyes and capered in a little circle, which made him sit back a bit. She cackled the more and made the sign of the horns at him.

'How do I ken this? Witchery, think you?' she demanded. 'Mother Shipton's eldest bairn mayhap?'

She laughed again at Batty's look.

'Silly bugger – the cloth binding you was wimple linen and we have been spierin' you and yon parcel o' Christ-brides for a three-day at least.

'Well, cow piss cleans better and the De'il has his saving eye on you,' she added.

Christ's Blood, Batty thought, it was bad enough when a nun told me I was chosen by God. Now this hedge-witch tells me I am Auld Nick's favourite imp. It was better, he thought bitterly, when I was plain Batty Coal-house, of no fixed abode in Heaven, Earth or Hell.

Still, the thought reminded him of Sister Faith's last charges and he looked round for his gear; Trottie produced it in flourishes, right down to the wrapped silk bowl and the phials – but this last she handed back with a frown.

'That's no poison or love potion you have in them wee jugs,' she declared and made the horn-sign again. 'Yet there is power in it.'

Batty took the leather container beside him and nodded cautiously to her, feeling weariness descend on him.

'Thanks for you care. I have nothin' to give but advice and it is this – nivver leave these hills, beldame. They will bind you in iron chains and burn you at the stake.'

Her cracked-bell laugh followed him as he ducked under the lintel of sleep and fell through the door to oblivion.

–

He walked in a street and thought it might be Berlin save that it was free of horse-apples and ruts. He wasn't certain where he was in the end, for it had houses he thought he recognised from Strasbourg and even Rome; at one point he passed what he was certain was Giovanni Acuto's tomb and that was in the Santa Maria del Fiore in Florence.

He could not stop to find out, no matter how hard he tried, and realised he was flanked on both sides by tall men in the livery of Maurice of Saxony, all sweeping moustaches and halberds; his arms were bound with smooth rope and each liveried man-at-arms had a grip like an iron band on one shoulder.

They walked in silence for what seemed a long time, down this endless street where people walked, looking amazingly fresh, the women with immaculate dresses and the men with pressed doublets and shoes that looked new.

Then he heard a slow, repeated creaking, like a door opening endlessly and, gradually, a speck on the street's eldritch stretch grew and grew into the breaking wheel. A burning nun stood by it, her eyes embered; the creaking was her turning it with flaming hands.

Now he heard noise behind him and craned to see a crowd, fifty or sixty and growing, led by a dark, saturnine man he knew well. Ahead, a masked man in a stained butcher's apron bounced a hammer meaningfully in one palm and, next to him, a bride with a chaplet of flowers and a bloody grin stretched out her hand to take his.

He fought, but was propelled inexorably towards the turning wheel and the hand of the Klett bride, leading him to where his limbs would be broken and braided into the spokes.

'Prepare to meet thy God. His approach; so dreadful is the sight that what can man do, man who is but rottenness and a worm, when even the Cherubim themselves must veil their faces in very terror?'

He turned to the speaker and knew it would be Cauvin, had listened to that grate all the way from Strasbourg to Geneva, had seen the tics and twists of that bearded mouth daily for weeks.

'Jehan,' he called out. 'How is the Madame Cauvin?'

Jehan Cauvin smiled, that self-assured, self-involved smile.

'Gone, Balthie,' he declared. 'Gone to her destiny, as decreed by a loving God. Though I never experienced the slightest hindrance. She was never troublesome to me throughout the entire course of her illness.'

'I am sure she died without fashing,' he answered wryly. 'Same as she lived. Ach, Jehan, you may know God well, but you are a misery to women.'

Cauvin nodded, smiling, to where the Klett bride waited, a strange wind blowing her hair like the flames of the nun turning the breaking wheel.

'You would know the misery of women, Balthie.'

He heard the nun laugh, a harsh gargle of sound. Ach, he thought, astounded. I did not know nuns could laugh…

–

He woke, eyes wide open and coughing up smoke in his throat. From the nun… then he realised it was the fire, swirling a cat-tail flick from the damp wind blowing through the open shutters.

It was morning on the moor, with a spanking wind from the west and the peesies blown ragged with the clouds as they played will-o'-the-wisp with sunlight. He could see it all through the open shuttered winter and could feel the warm, a leprous heat thanks to the rain. There should still be white on the grass to shiver early lambs and snow caps on the high tops; even the season is whirlimagig, Batty thought and then lay back, trying to blink the images away.

By God, he thought to himself shakily, one o' these nights yon nun will get me. Yet the Klett bride was new; he had never dreamed her before and as for Cauvin...

He remembered the man, young and intense, dark-bearded and full of himself. The Saint-Madeleine church had packed him off from Strasbourg to Geneva, with a couple of carts and his wife, Idelette and he had not wanted to go. Batty had been hired as much to make sure of it as to protect him on the way and had been offered the task because, it turned out, Madame Cauvin knew Bella Yelland.

Poor Idelette Cauvin, Batty thought, struggling with pregnancy and the knowledge that her bairn would almost certainly die as soon as it was born. Bleak with the knowledge that the man who spent his time rehearsing sermons – twice on Sabbaths, three times during the week – had certainly poxed her. In between muttering about the Genevans, whom he hated, the Jesuits whom he hated and someone called Servetus, whom he hated, Jean Cauvin spent a deal of time in hot, darkened *auberge* rooms starving and sweating himself as a precursor to drinking concoctions of *lignum vitae* mixed in sack.

Once he even had a physicker giver him an enema of the stuff, which Batty knew the Spanish called *guayaco*. If the dagos were any measure of efficacy, Batty thought, then any philtre made from yon fancy tree from the Americas was of little use.

In the end, Cauvin was pale and wasted and still poxed. All he got out of the experience was a new hatred, of physickers above everyone else. Should hate become a measure of piety, Batty thought, feeling the sweat on him, then Jehan Cauvin, whom folk now lauded as God's anointed John Calvin, will be a wee saint. If Protestants are allowed such.

Batty found out then that it was Bella who had persuaded Ned to return to the good grace of Maramaldo and still fought to understand that.

'Here.'

He came out of his dream-shreds into the wrinkled malfeasance of Trottie's face as she thrust a horn beaker of something hot at him; he looked at it suspiciously.

'Anis, wolfsbane – the one that isn't venomous – centaury, fox clote, vervain,' she intoned. 'All good for wounds and bruises. White willow to kill the pain – and some chervil against the bad dreams. Sweetened with a wee taste of honey – the brew, that is. Nothin' will sweeten dreams as hagged as yours, Batty Coalhouse.'

Bigod, you have the right of that, Batty thought, sipping cautiously; it was not entirely bad, so he drank it down, then crawled unsteadily up and buckled himself back to his old life.

Trottie watched, tucking a grey straggle under her grey lace cap.

'You are all but done,' she said and it was so much an echo of Sister Faith that Batty jerked; Trottie grinned gum at him.

'With the beaker,' she added and held out a grimy hand for it, grinning when Wallis called from outside for Batty to fetch himself. Batty thought the grin sly, but was reassured to see she made no more witchy moves, which were unsettling.

Eventually, he nodded pleasantly to her and thanked her for her hospitality, then hirpled through the door – and stopped short. He had expected a pen, sheep – Mickle

Jock with a scowl between his horns even – and a few armed riders. What he got stunned him.

There were men right enough, but no wee handful; you could not see the sheep pen for them, long hundreds of mounted and ranked riders, all lanced and armoured for war. John Wallis grinned down at Batty as a scowling Chilman, nursing his gnawed hand, brought forward a horse.

'A thousand here. Some hundred more at Twa Corbies,' John Wallis declared and waved one expansive hand. 'Behold the power of the Wallis, the Robson and Charlton and Dodds and all else who owe us the hand of friendship.'

He leaned on the pommel of his saddle.

'Yet there are King's men gathering in numbers and meeting with Musgrave. Around Wooler, or so I hear and the place is busy as a Truce Day meeting.

'But I don't fear them, nor your wee band of ribboned mummers, guns or not, for I have these at my back. Now mount – I would hear of nuns from Glastonbury and why the King has sent an army into the Cheviots.'

Chapter Eleven

Eglingham Hall, a day's march south of Wooler
At the same time...

'D'ye know how to fish, young Lord?'

The young Lord Ogle eyed Musgrave warily, wondering if he was being patronised; since he had come into the lordship recently it seemed to him that everyone was anxious to give him advice and that most of it was patronising when it wasn't self-serving. Sometimes both.

'What has this to do with our expedition?' he asked sourly and Jack Musgrave kept his smile, even as he thought what a sow's arse the boy was.

But the boy had a slew of relations clustering jealously round him, all called Oswin or Cuthbert it seemed, and his late da, the bold Baron Ogle, had managed to get himself slain at Ancrum and leave the estates to a callow eighteen-year-old. The Ogles were stout supporters of King Henry on the eastern Border and Musgrave needed their good grace.

'It has everything, your lordship,' he managed, staring round the faces; they were all the same, that Ogle stamp of sharp chin, wire-thin lips and the sort of eyes which were considered large and handsome when young and turned every middle-aged face to frog.

'I have thrown a line in a decent trout pool,' Cuthbert Ogle offered and Musgrave gave him a brief look, then ignored him; Cuthbert was a mere clerk, for all the family name and had contrived to get himself captured at Ancrum. He had brought the old Baron's body back for burial at Bothal and considered himself to be the new Lord Ogle's most trusted advisor.

'No doubt, Master Ogle,' he said. 'Following the ways of your betters is laudable in one of lesser birth.'

Cuthbert fumed and seemed on the point of spitting bile in reply – but this was Mad Jack Musgrave, the Bastard's Buzzard of Bewcastle and he did not have the belly for it. Musgrave seemed almost disappointed when he did not, but the young Lord Ogle noted Cuthbert's disorder with some satisfaction, for he was tired of the man's endless, obsequious advice.

'The true mark of lordship,' Musgrave continued airily, 'is the ability to adapt the ways of those who have no finer breeding – yet avoid compromising station or honour.'

He paused and nodded to the man next to him.

'Master Sabin is without breeding,' he went on and smiled. 'He will, I know, forgive me for mentioning it, but let is also be said that such a lack of bloodline does not detract from his many skills.'

Master Sabin's face was as blank as a new wall, even under the weight of all the stare now turned on it; he did not as much as blink his olive-pip eyes, nor take them from Musgrave's face. Framed by the iced wings of his hair, his own face seemed something badly carved from old oak.

'Master Sabin,' Musgrave continued, 'knows how to extract a bothersome pike from a decent trout pool. It does not involve tedious hours of hook, line and coaxing and some would say it does the art of fishing little favour.'

They were all watching Sabin, but were disappointed to see nothing at all. Not a flicker on that bog-water brown face with the grooved lines at the corner of his mouth, which the neat-trimmed iron beard did not quite hide. Not so much as a slight toss of a head cossetted in a fine, brimmed cap of cramoisie which, on the hanging knives of his long white hair, looked like a drop of blood on snow.

There was silence for a long moment, though the gap in conversation was mercifully covered by the neigh and clamour of the camp which surrounded the half-built house at Eglingham.

There were skeins of red-liveried men in it, all brought by the Ogle master of Eglingham – better known as Captain Luke Ogle from the Earl of Hertford's army and commanding a Company of Hertford's own liveried Band. They had been lent to Musgrave for this one important purpose.

Which seemed to be fishing as far as the young Lord Ogle could make out. He sighed, eventually, when he saw nothing more would be forthcoming without a new question. So he asked it, gritting his teeth at the benevolent uncle smile from Musgrave, a man he was starting to detest worse than Cuthbert.

'You rid yourself of a troublesome pike at night, young Lord,' Musgrave declared. 'Taking a torch and a boat if need be. You pass the former over the top of the pool, which then makes everything clear, right to the bottom where fish sleep. Yes, they do, gentlemen. Pike included. If you wake them, they swim to the light. If they do not, they remain still. Mazed, you see? Either way, they can be easily netted and removed.'

He looked round triumphantly.

'That is what we are doing here. Master Sabin is Chancellor of the Company of the Sable Rose of Captain General Fabrizio Maramaldo and has agreed a contract which makes that well-known company the torch.'

'We know their burning qualities – saw it at Akeld, to the Wallis. That was part of the contract?'

That was Captain Luke Ogle, wearing Hertford's red coat livery to match his face, it seemed. Choleric, Musgrave thought, over the outrages perpetrated at Akeld. Or that he has been taken from the Scotch wars and sent here to be commanded by me. Or perhaps because we are encamped round his half-built new house at Eglingham, ruining what gardens he has been trying to create.

'The necessary flame in the torch,' Musgrave answered eventually, with a slight dismissive wave. 'When the Wallis rise up from the bottom of their pool to investigate, Captain General Maramaldo will occupy their attention until we, like a net, scoop them all up.'

He paused and beamed.

'Thus ending another Catholic rebellion in the north, to the happiness of my Lord Hertford and the king.'

'Catholic rebellion?' Luke Ogle said flatly. 'A brace of nuns and the Wallis? And you sent by the Dacre from the West March to see it ended? Still, I can see why Dacre would mislike the Wallis – did they not burn the Bastard of Lanercost's land claims on the Wallis in Berwick?'

'Lord Dacre of Lanercost,' Musgrave replied pointedly and everyone heard the iron creep into his voice. 'is not involved in this. No Dacre is. The proof of Catholic involvement came from the office of the Lord Chancellor himself, by way of one of his trusted commissioners, Thomas Horner. Nuns from Glastonbury, no less, travelled to the north to spread sedition. D'you think my Lord

Hertford would have sent you under my command with his own men if he did not think this had the possibility of becoming a second Pilgrimage of Grace, Captain?'

Mention of that event, less than eight years ago, clicked teeth shut; the popular uprising in the north against Fat Henry's dissolution of Catholic monasteries had been quelled viciously and black heads and haunches still decorated gatehouse spikes from Carlisle to York.

Luke Ogle was enough of a Captain to know when to push an attack and when to retire; he merely blinked like a soporific owl, then turned to his kin and master, the young Lord Ogle.

'My Lord, I will see to the troops. When do we march?'

'When I say,' interrupted Musgrave and no one missed the steel clash of his tone. 'We are a day from Akeld and, when Captain General Maramaldo sends word that he is firmly engaged, then we shall move in on the mazed Wallis men, smash them to ruin and spoil their famed tower of Twa Corbies.'

The captain straightened while Lord Ogle tried to find words to express his outrage, but politely. Finally, the captain bowed to his fish-mouthed lord and nodded sourly to Musgrave and Sabin.

'Remember Broomhouse,' he said in a low voice, turned on his heel and left Musgrave fuming in his wake.

'By God,' he managed eventually and everyone heard the shake in his voice, though no one was fooled that it was anything other than anger under tight rein. 'Yon officer needs a lesson in protocol.'

'There has been a sufficiency of lessons,' the young Lord Ogle declared suddenly, rising from his seat and gathering up a fine short-cloak. 'Fishing being the least of them.'

He nodded curtly to Musgrave and went out, trailed by the swarm of relations. Last to leave was Cuthbert, who smirked at Musgrave.

'I think you have annoyed the Baron Ogle, my lord,' he declared.

'How is that working out for you?' Musgrave replied, bland as secret venom. 'The thinking.'

Cuthbert frowned, scowled and scuttled; Sabin laughed.

'Broomhouse,' he said flatly. 'Why do folk constantly carp about that place?'

Musgrave noted the twist of grin, the dismissive attitude and remembered that it was Maramaldo who had done the deed, though Lord Eure had taken the blame, since it was his overall command. Eure had paid the price for it, of course – hung on a tree by the vengeful Scots after Ancrum. He mentioned it, almost idly, to Sabin.

'So I understand,' Sabin replied in his clipped, tainted English. 'It was not Maramaldo himself, you understand, it was me. Which is why I am curious – we burned many other places as well as this Broomhouse.'

Musgrave poured wine to cover his momentary lapse of concentration; he had not realised Sabin had had a personal hand in the matter, but it did not surprise him. The man presented himself as the perjink Chancellor of a mercenary company – the person trusted by his Captain General to negotiate the details of contracts and to be a conduit to the men of the Company – but he was an old mercenary, Musgrave thought, marinaded in sin and blood.

'Broomhouse Tower,' he said, then paused. 'Do you even recall it, Master Sabin?'

Again the shrug. 'Not more than another. Screams and smoke.'

Aye, Musgrave thought. Just so. Smoke from the fire you set, screams from the auld woman who burned alive in it. No ordinary old woman but the much respected and noble Lady of Hume, matriarch of the entire Hume Name, on both sides of the divide.

Sabin shook his head when Musgrave told him this.

'So I have been told. Now I know this and I know less than before – one old rebel *frau* is hardly here nor there in such affairs.'

'Aye, well, it may yet come to hag you,' Musgrave answered curtly. 'Yet – no matter. I need word from your Captain General on how matters progress. There are some two thousand men at Twa Corbies. Wallis, Charlton, Robson and others. If your Company is to survive, they will need rescued.'

'You think the Sable Rose cannot beat a rabble of dog-riders?'

Musgrave shot daggers back at Sabin's wry, amused look.

'You have never fought Border riders, Master Sabin. I would not underestimate them if I were you. Nor would I end up in their clutches if they know it was you burned Broomhouse. They will hand you to the Humes, who will deal harshly with you over it.'

'There is little risk of that – your plan runs true, Lord Musgrave.' Sabin replied with an acknowledging bow and Musgrave sipped his wine.

Yes, it ran true enough and he thanked God for the arrival of Thomas Horner, pompous little tick with his writ from the Lord Chancellor. All but accused me of being in league with Catholic recanters and worse, he recalled, because he had found out that the nun leading the group he sought was my sister. Thought to find her at Bewcastle, all snug and at Compline.

Well, he was put right on that, Musgrave thought. My sister, whom I had not seen since I was six and meant less to me than the horse I ride. My sister bringing her dangerous un-Reformed cant to my door, threatening everything I have built so far...

Yet there had been opportunity in it for a man charged with bringing the Wallis to heel for daring to trample on the dignity of the Dacres.

All it took was a message directing her and her runaway nuns through the Wallis country and the dispatching of Rutland to find Maramaldo, who sent his Chancellor, Sabin. When he arrived, a contract was signed and Horner sent off with it; Sabin, of course, remained as a 'guest', but he was an experienced Chancellor and it was not the first time he had been a hostage.

In return for service against the Wallis, Maramaldo got what he desired most – back into the good graces of King Henry and out of the pestilential damp north. Back to France and plunder, with the addition of the two sakers they had been ordered to escort south.

Musgrave did not know whether Maramaldo had taken himself into the Cheviot with two stolen guns and the intent to ignore his orders, but he had certainly thought better of it. And now Hertford and Henry both would welcome the previously-detested Maramaldo like the Prodigal if he came wrapped in the aura of having helped forestall another Catholic revolt in the north.

Horner, for his part, would wait to get whatever the nuns were carrying, what the Lord Chancellor sought. The truth, Musgrave mused, was that the Lord Chancellor would get a good portion of the treasure, whatever it was, to sweeten the news of Thomas Horner's untimely death. Battlefields were dangerous places, a great loss to the office of the Lord Chancellor, so sorry, my condolences...

He had to go, to keep the secret of Musgrave's sister. The nuns would die for the same reason, them and the bairns – Sabin had laughed aloud when Musgrave had put this to him, without revealing the why. Not that it mattered to Sabin, who was interested only in the 'how much?'

'*Grussgott*,' he said mockingly, when a sum was agreed. 'A commissioner of the Chancellory, two nuns and five *kinder* – yet you people declare the like of me too fell cruel for civilised folk.'

Musgrave did not like the tone then and was no better disposed to it now. Yet he turned the bright coin of his plan over and over in his mind, noting the nick and shavings in the immaculate of it. Rutland was one and Musgrave was annoyed at that, not because of the loss of the wee papingo, whose talents had been limited, but because of the stupidity in it caused by Maramaldo's mistrust of his own Captains.

A mistrust not misplaced, Musgrave noted, since Sabin had added his own codicil to the contract, a private arrangement that Maramaldo did not know of – Batty Coalhouse.

Musgrave had heard the cracked bell of Sabin's voice when he said the name. There was longing in it, the same as a wolf looking on a lone sheep, but there was also a tinge of fear.

Musgrave foresaw a quarrel brewing between Sabin and his master, but that was no matter to him, provided it did not hinder his own ambitions – rid the Cheviot of the stain of Wallis, secure the Dacre of Lanercost rights and bask in the glory of that Border house.

It had been easy enough to steer Batty Coalhouse towards Akeld and all the one-armed bastard-born had to do was wander into the trap and be caught; yet he had escaped – Sabin had had word of it that very morning. Still, if Coalhouse was with the Wallis, then he would be scooped up in the same net as the rest of those troublesome fishes, as Musgrave had pointed out to the scowling Sabin.

So all was still well and he was cheered by it as he went over his little speech to the young Ogle, preening himself with the way he had put the youth in his place.

Then it came to him, sudden as a gaff, that the term used for this way of fishing had a new and darker meaning these days, because it brought black blood to the eye and vengeance to the hand on both sides.

Burning the water.

Akeld
At the same time…

She saw them moving suddenly, with a fluid purpose not seen before. It took her notice because it seemed to transmute the clay she had seen into a tarnished glimmer of gold.

The one called Holy Cross had been simply another beribboned ugly draped in geegaws and medallions, the face under the broadbrimmed cap ruined by a red scar from hairline to jaw, nicking the nose on the run down and another from cheek to cheek – the Holy Cross which gave him his by-name.

Now he and the tall, lanky Spaniard they called Marillo, the blond Portuguese albino they called Nevar, the Fleming known as Witt – all the men who had growled and spat at each other round the fire – were transformed.

Sister Faith saw them kissing their amulets and dressing for war, looking at one another and knocking helmets together, or slapping hands like some deal had been made and she realised that what she had taken for growling animosity round the fire had been the opposite – the affection of wolves.

They were skilled, honed fighters who put their trust in one another and so, she saw, would not be easily defeated. And though they snarled slyly behind his back, they would follow the orders of the clanking, half-armoured likes of Juup, the Captain who ordered them into a huge square centred on the bastel house.

In the middle of the brimming maggot movement of it all sat Maramaldo, armoured and helmeted, plumed and perched on a white horse, so that all could see him and, she saw, take comfort from that. Sister Faith's heart fluttered then, for it seemed such a power that nothing could overturn.

Save God.

She saw Daniel, stick-thin and sitting with Holy Cross, watching while he buckled and strapped – helping him now and then and getting a friendly clap on one shoulder. The other children huddled round Sister Faith, who watched from the bastel's thin, high window as the scarred man told Daniel how to keep blades and armour from rusting.

'Cut of all the legs off a goat from the knee down,' he explained in his thick accent, 'soak them in smoke for a day and keep them for twenty after that. Crack the marrow from them and grease your blades and they will stay bright even when wet.'

'He is lost to us, I think.'

The voice came from Sister Charity and Sister Faith knew she spoke of Daniel, knew her colleague was right – the mercenaries called him 'Suckling', in the same way they had given by-names to each other and that name, Sister Faith realised sadly, was more to him now than the one he had been baptised with in the sight of God.

Daniel would not come away with them when they were freed and, if forced, would run back to be with these glorious folk who promised more than a lifetime of huddling servitude in the Church – the one, Sister Faith remembered, that Horner called, scathingly: 'that foul republic of wooden sandals'.

She and the others would be freed, Sister Faith knew, for Maramaldo had said as much the night before, coming to them out of the darkness like a wraith.

'Tomorrow,' he had announced, breathing slow and heavy in the flicking tallow, 'there will be a fight here, though you should be safe inside the house, for these dog riders are no match for the likes of us.'

'I have heard they beat a Scotch army only recently,' Sister Faith responded, 'with no help from anyone else.'

Maramaldo dismissed it with a wave and a grin.

'A Scotch rabble,' he corrected, 'ill-led and straggled out on a march. Dog-riding prickers like these can do well under such circumstances.'

He paused and encompassed the room, the Cheviots and possibly the world with another wave.

'These people are secret fighters,' he went on. 'They use their wits, ride by moonlight for a little plunder and they are the finest secret fighters in the world, no doubt of it. But their weakness is the love of their own places. Who would want this land? It is cold, wet, with nothing on it at all and good only for grazing. Yet they will abandon their secret Riding and come out, all plumage and boasts, to be shot down by my archers at the hint that one of their mean towers is threatened.'

Sister Faith had seen the archers, hump-shouldered and strong, chaffering with the pikemen, whom they considered a lesser breed. Already Daniel was testing his puny strength on Holy Cross's powerful longbow and being congratulated for moving the string an eyebrow hair.

'Besides,' Maramaldo added, mistaking her thoughtful silence for fear, 'plans are laid which makes their ruin assured.'

'More slaughter – what is worth this affront to God?' she asked and Maramaldo laughed, harsh as rooks.

'Our Lord will forgive,' he answered. 'An eye for an eye, tooth for tooth saith the Scriptures – though I only came to read them recently, now that Holy Books are no longer solely in Latin.'

Sister Faith crossed herself against such impiety and Maramaldo laughed.

'You are a good woman,' he said to her surprise, 'but have been cloistered too long. The world is not as you have made it, Sister.'

'I know what the world is made of,' she replied, stung. 'It is made of more folk seeking God's redemption than it is of folk like you. God grant you peace, Captain General.'

Maramaldo made the sign of the cross and laughed.

'God grant you release from alms,' he replied. 'You see? I greet you as you greet me – both of us would starve if our prayers were answered.'

'Do you believe that for true, Captain General?' she answered and he frowned.

'Of course. Listen – if Plato stood up and called: "follow me and discuss Forms which cannot be seen" at the same time as Caesar clapped a hand to his swordhilt and yelled: "follow me and conquer Gaul" who would have the biggest crowd?'

He smiled – almost sadly, it seemed to Sister Faith and answered the question himself.

'A man would be shamed to follow Plato.'

'And if it was not Plato,' Sister Faith replied, looking him in his pouched, ravaged face. 'If it was Our Lord Jesus Himself, who called out: 'follow me and find a place in Heaven'?'

Maramaldo acknowledged the sally with a slight flap of one hand.

'You may find it hard to believe, but there was a time, woman, when I hadn't given a blow to anyone. And not just when I had bare legs and toddled. I was a peaceful youth – but the wolf goes after lambs and the marten chases chickens, so that state did not last for long, not in my small corner of God's world. The only way to stop lawless trash is to become a Law. Yea, though I walk through the Valley of the Shadow of Death, I will fear no evil, Sister. For I am more fearful than anything in that valley.'

She had no answer; beyond, she heard the men round the fires singing:

Maramaldo takes good care of us
Beer and spirits he shares with us
Music for our leisure,

Pretty girls for our pleasure
With our beer and our wine,
Sable Rose men, we're so fine.

'Tomorrow,' Maramaldo repeated, 'we shall fight and we shall win. Afterwards you and the children – those who wish it – will go free. I suspect my current employer will want you dead, so I would run hard and fast. Charity will remain with me.'

Sister Faith had known it all, since the revelation that she was a piece in a larger plot and that Sister Benedict had been betrayed by her own brother. Still, the saying of it made her heart weep and her eyes turn to where Sister Charity sat in the dark. Just Charity. Not Sister Charity...

'Once a nun, always a nun,' Sister Charity had said later. 'Even if I am not wearing a wimple.'

Now she stood behind Sister Faith and the children wearing a hodden grey dress and a simple kerchief round her head and cheeks, though she had contrived a cloth veil across her face.

'He keeps us as surety against Lord Musgrave of Bewcastle,' she said and her voice was bitter. 'Aye, him who is brother to our departed Sister in Christ and his own sister in kin. He has used her and us for his own ends. Captain General Maramaldo does not care for that.'

Sister Faith heard the tone and the terms and cocked her head a little.

'You speak as if this Maramaldo cared for us,' she said and felt ashamed at the prim in her voice. Sister Charity might have smiled or scowled; only she knew behind the veil.

'His nights with me are not what you might think,' she replied flatly. 'He is as bad poxed as myself, for all he looks so fine. It will take him in a different way – with me it will show in my face, all the sins of God's punishment for the world to see. On his, little at all – but his mind is rotted and will grow worse and worse. He will die, mad and screaming. Some of his men know it too – that Cornelius for one – and wait for the moment when he is clearly too mad to follow.'

Sister Faith could only stare, mute as a swan.

'He wakes at night,' Sister Charity added and Sister Faith heard some sorrow in her voice now. 'He calls out a name – Bella. Then he curses her. I fancy it was this one poxed him, though I cannot know any more surely than he can himself. Yet he believes it – and that she lay with him deliberately to do it.'

Sister Faith bowed her head and turned her rosary ring. Outside, the banners snapped and cracked and men fought with horses made restive by a rising wind.

It was morning and the Company of the Sable Rose dressed for war.

Twa Corbies
At the same time...

The wind was rising, a freshing breeze that drove off the stink, save when it swirled it to Batty's nose, a rank smell made up of too many horses and men in close proximity for too long. If they stay here another five-day, Batty thought, sickness will rake its way through Twa Corbies.

The place reeked with life now, all the same – thousands of horses and men, all chaffering one another. Somewhere, a man cranked a rosined wheel and men danced to the hurdy-gurdy lilt; beyond them, more men milled in a brutal game of football.

Above it all loomed Twa Corbies, four stories of solid stone topped with gable ends on which stood the weathered lumps that gave the place its name, blackened with old smoke and age. Once they had been carved eagles, but time and legend had turned them into a brace of ravens, giant versions of the ones which swooped and harshed round the tower.

John Wallis reined his big stot to a halt in the middle of this foam of men and turned, beaming his triumph at Batty.

'What say you now, Master Coalhouse? Do the Cheviot men have the match for this Maramaldo?'

It had been the recurring theme all the way here – and the reason I am not wearing a wee rope collar, Batty realised. John Wallis needs reassuring that he can take on hard mercenaries from the Germanies, Landsknechts as he has heard and with all the fear and trembling associated with that name. He needs someone who knows them well.

'Aye, mayhap,' Batty mused, stroking his raggled beard. 'If you catch him on the march. If not – keep away from the front of his brace o' sakers.'

'You will advise me on it – we move out soon. Willie, leave off with that hound.'

The last was directed at a boy struggling to put a collar on a big, shaggy wolfhound and having little luck, since the dog had its arse firmly planted on the turf and was trying to drag itself by the front paws.

'I want him beside me when I ride, da.'

The face was a sullen mirror of John Wallis, who was as unimpressed by it as he was by the dog.

'To what end, Will? Your fierce wardog may kill one o' those Germans if he dies laughing at it trying to scrape the worm–itch from its hinter–end, but that is the only way it will happen. Take the collar away and the beast down to Dog–Anthone to be physicked.'

He watched briefly as the boy did as he was told, then turned and shrugged apology.

'Bairns,' he declared, then signalled Batty to dismount.

'War is no place for them,' Batty said and John Wallis scowled uneasily.

'A truth his mother reminds me off daily. Divven you start also.'

They shouldered through the greetings of the crowd of men, who saw that the Master of Twa Corbies had arrived and sensed the imminence of Ride; Batty heard them as he climbed up and into the hall of the place.

'Tarset and Tyne,' they yelled. 'Wallis men.'

The cries echoed and bounced, leaped like fire from head to head as the Names roared out their presence to God – Robson, Charlton, Milburn and Potts.

Hume, Hume, Hume. Remember Broomhoose…

They sent their hatred galloping off ahead of them and Batty felt the chill suck at his bowels; the last place he wanted to be was facing Maramaldo's cannon across a muddy Cheviot hillside surrounded by Border horsemen. English or Scots, all the Humes were fired to madness by mention of Broomhouse – and all those who stood as friends to them were also lit by it.

Besides, there was a nag at him, as if the world was a Michaelangelo drawing with part of it smeared by his big spade thumb. He knew the missing piece was vital, but he could not see it clearly.

They moved into a vaulted area – the kitchen, Batty saw, which would be the warmest place – where John Wallis scattered folk from the fire and sat down heavily, sticking out his booted feet until the heat smoked water from them.

'Bigod,' he sighed, 'this time last week I was mopping sweat from my brow and waving away midgies.'

'Cheviot weather,' Batty agreed and those who knew you could get four seasons in a day in these hills, grinned a little. Not many, Batty saw – and the woman who banged down a pewter mug of slopping ale had a scowl fit to sour gilt; a joint turned on a spit, filling the place with delicious smells and Batty with an ache of hunger, but no one offered him any.

'So – you slew Tam and there are folk here who would still hemp you for it,' John Wallis declared, signalling for food to be brought to himself. Batty heard the growls, saw the harsh, lumpen faces round him, dark with hate.

'Fair fight,' he offered back and tried a smile, though it died of neglect a minute later. 'An old man with the one arm defeats a bonny fighter o' the Wallis on the stairs of the Berwick Tolbooth – well, I can see why this would facer his kin.'

'Some would say such a fight could not have been fair for the very reasons you say,' John Wallis went on, picking meat with his fingers and blowing it cool; Batty's mouth watered and, suddenly, the events of the last few days washed over him. He felt weary and stretched thin – so thin that he jumped when he felt the nudge on his knee.

It was the wolfhound nuzzling him and looking hopefully at the plate near John Wallis; Batty scratched it gently behind one ear and it laid a delighted muzzle on his knee.

'Well, at least the hound likes you,' someone said and there was harsh laughter. Batty shifted.

'It is a fine judge. As are you, John Wallis. If you wanted to hemp me you would have let yon men accomplish it – especially since one of them will now need a fresh finger to pick his scabs with.'

Someone laughed at that, though it was choked off.

'You have not kinched my neck because you need me for something else.'

John Wallis cocked a considering eyebrow and Batty was regretting his moment of flared temper, became conscious of the leather cylinder still slung round his shoulders as John Wallis looked at it – but before anyone could speak, a small storm burst on them.

'Diamant, Diamant. There you are, you bugger – come away.'

John Wallis' son – Willie, Batty recalled – grabbed the hound by the neck ruff and started hauling it, though he made little headway. Then he stopped and looked anxiously at his da.

'It got away from me,' he said. 'You made me take the collar off and the leash with it,' he added bitterly.

'Here,' Batty said, reaching out and plucking a morsel off John Wallis' plate. 'Dangle this and he will follow you, meek as a lamb.'

Willie looked, nodded, then went off, holding the meat as high as he could while the dog padded after. No one spoke until John Wallis shoved his plate at Batty.

'Since you have fouled it with your fingers, you had best eat the remainder,' he growled. 'Pass him the salt.'

Suddenly, the hall filled with mutter and business and Batty could not speak for the racing of his heart; he had been offered meat and salt and so accepted as a guest by

Twa Corbies. No harm would come to him now – he heard a familiar cackle of laughter and turned into the wizen of Trottie's face, wondering at how she had come along, unseen, with the other riders.

'The De'il looks after his own,' she said and John Wallis, mild as new milk, waved her away. He watched Batty as he ate, allowing him a few mouthfuls which Batty tried to chew a little and not gulp like the starving man he felt.

'You have supped – will you drink? I have beer and wine and sack. Some Dutch brandywine, gunpowder proved.'

Batty hesitated, caught between desire and another promise to purge himself of his old life. Bliddy nuns, he thought bitterly, have hagged me with God Himself…

John Wallis sent his eyebrows into his hairline when no answer came.

'I had heard you were well versed in the ways of war and no stranger to drink. What is your preference?'

Batty gave in and sighed.

'I am not fashed regarding strong drink and have one proviso only – that it has not been previously swallowed.'

Beaming, John Wallis summoned a black bottle from someone and poured. It was the brandywine, tested for strength by having some black powder poured into the liquor and the contents lit. If the powder also ignited after the brandywine was consumed, it was a good distillation and Batty knew from the eyewatering smell that it would be. They swallowed, grimaced and grinned.

'So,' John Wallis said eventually. 'How will this Maramaldo fight?'

Chapter Twelve

Later, at Akeld...

Maramaldo would fight like the Devil. Batty said as much, though he pointed out that it was not the question John Wallis should be asking – and then told him what it should be, straight out into his scowl.

Why would Maramaldo fight?

'He fights for pay,' Batty added helpfully while John Wallis stroked his beard and frowned under his dripping burgonet. 'So who is paying him to come to Akeld?'

The Dacre. It was not a difficult tally to add up and when the news of it went round, the howls went up an octave. Tarset and Tyne. Hume. Remember Broomhoose.

The wind caught the shouts and tore them from mouths, leaping on over the hills like a joyous dog, new-released. The trees were old to the way of it and already all bowing away from the domination of a filthy east wind which was growing in viciousness.

'We'll have weather,' said Chilman, squinting at the lead sky. Then he grinned through his mad beard at Batty, who agreed soberly and then nodded at the sight of the man's rag-bound hand, too bulky with wraps to fit in a gauntlet.

'Sorry for your loss,' he said and Chilman's grin widened.

'Och, dinna fash. It is a rare tale to tell round the inn at Wooler – how Batty Coalhouse and me fought, tooth and claw until he toothed and I lost the claw.'

He laughed and reined away, became one more figure in a jack of plates, big boots to the thigh and a combed burgonet. Like all the others he had a man-and-a-half long Border lance, which they called a stave, slung round one arm by a hoop of leather to let him free both hands. At his waist he had a belt with a bollock dagger on one side and a basket-hilted blade on the other and his horse held the dangle of a latchbow, a targe and a leather cylinder of bolts.

He was no different from the hundreds of others, now moving silent on shoeless horses, so well used to making sure no bridle jingled nor scabbard rattled that they did it in broad daylight among an army of men.

Batty was aware of his lack – he had his dagg still, but it was loaded with his last charge of rosary beads and he suspected he would not be offered fresh powder and shot. He had his backsword and six wee throwing knives, plus a stiletto down his boot, so he was not toothless, but he rode a gift-horse he did not know at all and had John Wallis and his picked men round him, to make sure he did not take it into his mind to gallop off.

John Wallis had shown interest in the cylinder, but had not pressed the point when Batty had told him it belonged to the nuns and held 'wee writings from their auld monastery'.

'God did not dispose well on their behalf,' he noted wryly, 'to have ridden them into the path of red war in the Cheviots.'

Batty had thought then what he thought now – that it was no accident or hand of God which had placed

Maramaldo and nuns at Akeld, though he could not work out the why yet. Mad Jack was in it, all the same, he was sure of that – Dacre would use him to keep his good name out of matters – but Batty could not understand why Mad Jack would contract Maramaldo to hunt out the sister he had sent Batty to rescue.

He found out when he came over the rise and looked down on Akeld, while the wind wheeped and sucked and danced. It tore at mane and hair and beards, whipping through the moor, snapping the banners of Maramaldo's Company, drawn up round Akeld's bastel.

They had Companies of pike circled in *schiltron*, with stirrup-drawn crossbows safely protecting them. Longbow archers, too, Batty saw, and some matchlock muskets – and the two sakers occupying one side.

'The banners,' Batty pointed out and the entire of it fell into place, like squinting at one of Michaelangelo's drawings in the bad tallow light of an inn until you finally realised that the face was your own.

'What of them?' demanded John Wallis, while his Border horse careened off right and left, whooping and shouting. Batty told him.

There was the Company's banner, white silk with a splendid black rose on it and the old ache of that made Batty blink. He could not see the words underneath the rose clearly, but he knew them by heart – Jay Lay Emprins.

'It means "I Have Undertaken",' Batty told John Wallis, though he did not add that 'empreigne' also meant 'to make pregnant'. The joke was that the banner also read 'I Have Fucked You'.

There was also a blue and white banner, big as a bedsheet, the colours split diagonally. That one belonged to Zurich and came from the Zwingli forces at Kappel when they went up against the other Swiss cantons and lost. The fancy one, Batty told them, the one split into arrowheads of red, white, blue and gold, was the *Jehova-sonne*, with its golden rayed sun in the centre and a symbol which was the name of God in Hebrew.

'Protestant flags,' Batty explained, 'displayed when Maramaldo fights for that cause against Catholics. He has another, a golden one with a silver cross that belonged to the Duke of Ferrera that he flies when he fights Lutherans. You will not see that one anywhere today.'

John Wallis looked and frowned and still did not understand.

'You are a Catholic rebellion,' Batty explained grimly, 'and those wee nuns, innocent wee wimples that they are, are proof of it. Maramaldo is out to get himself back into the good graces of Fat Henry Tudor by putting down a Catholic revolt. And Dacre gets his revenge on you.'

The Wallis scowl went deeper by a notch.

'He claims us as Jesuits? God, the lie in it.'

He banged a fist on his knee, making the horse shift nervously.

'He has not won a bliddy thing,' he growled, 'and he will recant his claims on us when I stick steel in his dancing-master beard – I thought you said this was Dacre revenge for the Tolbooth?'

It was and Batty told him as much; disguised as something else and using men who flew no Dacre scallop-banners or Red Bulls to tie him in directly with the deed. Wallis shook drips from the brim of his burgonet and swore at the perfidy of it.

There was a thump, as if a giant smith had slammed a hammer into the moorland; they felt the tremble of it right up through the horses, which shied and squealed.

Something whirred overhead like a mad bird, hit a copse and splintered through it for a long way. Bar shot, Batty recognised – two balls joined by a short length of bar-iron and the whole capable of ripping entire ranks to ruin.

He told John Wallis, who blanched at the sight of the cracked trees, the trunks white as broken bone.

'Keep away from the front of those guns,' Batty advised. 'Look – they have a plank platform to let them roll easier but are not fascined or gabioned – not bulwarked so that their movement to right or left is limited. He can swing them if he wants, though they are monstrous heavy to move swiftly. Thirty degrees – any further will recoil one into the other...'

His words were whipped away by the gusting rise of wind and Diamant capered round the legs of Will Wallis' already fractious nag, so that he fought to hold it and his da looked sourly at him.

Will Wallis, Batty thought. What a burden is in that name for a wee lad – I swear bairns weep at the moment of birth because they know what their parents will foist on them with baptism.

The Names fought like moonlit riders, knots of them attached by kin and old ties darting forward with yells and screams – Tarset and Tyne. Hume. Robson. A-Dodd, to me.

Batty saw Trottie, dancing on her thin ankles and waving her arms in what might have been spell or simple excitement, screaming: 'Get to them. Divven give them fortune this day. Slay them German money-sojers.'

The German money-sojers were unfazed at first – the long pike-spears kept the riders at bay, as they were designed to, but the killing part of the Sable Rose was less than effective, thanks to the wind.

It caught the crossbow bolts and hurled them sideways. When the prized longbow men launched their hissing volleys, the wind scattered them like chooks.

The Border Riders rode up and stabbed, retired, came back in little flocks and flurries, shot off pistols if they had them and latchbows when they hadn't, so that men started tumbling beneath the proud Sable Rose banners; the Wallis men cheered.

Twa Corbies might win it after all, Batty thought, if this wind keeps up and there is no shortage of powder, shot or bolts.

Something smacked his helmet and he jerked, thinking it a spent missile. Will's nag went into a mad frenzy of buck and kick, so that the boy flew off and, just as his father reined round to go to his aid, he cursed and flapped one hand, struck by something on the gauntlet.

Then the missiles streaked in – hail, Batty noted with amazement. Large as chicken eggs...

The war stopped. Horses bucked and bolted, men yelled and ran. The pikemen hunched up and dropped their long spears to shield their heads as the hail pelted down on them like the wrath of God.

Batty fought with his own horse, hanging grimly on as it squealed and tried to bolt, circling only because Batty held it on a tight right rein; he wondered how long it would be before the beast remembered to buck.

It never did, for the stinging barrage slackened to a wash of ice-water, a torrential downpour that closed the world to something seen through a dark glass. Weather. In the name of Christ, this is weather indeed even for the Cheviots. Batty fought the horse to a trembling standstill and suddenly found Chilman at his knee, waving his filthily-bandaged hand.

'Yon guns…'

Batty stared uncomprehendingly for a moment, then realised what Chilman was saying – the sakers would be sluiced to ruin, the slow matches out and the powder no doubt drenched to a black slorach.

'Have you pins?'

It was a shrewd question roared out above the hissing bellow of water from a man who knew a good gunner always carried such – the spikes for hammering into the touch holes of guns, thus rendering them useless. It was the final act a gunner could do when his weapons were in danger of being overrun and Batty's last trio of spikes were in three bands on the bandolier not occupied by apostle charges.

His one hand was too full of reins to reach for them, an instinctive gesture – but his face was as much of a betrayal and Chilman nodded, his beard scattering droplets and his grin gapped as a badly-copsed wood.

'Aye, Headman John thought as much – come with me.'

Cursing, Batty forced the uneasy horse in the wake of Chilman's own, the rain battering down like an emptied pail. Grey shapes loomed; more Wallis men and John Wallis in the centre of them, his beard dripping.

'Ride for them engines, boys,' he roared, spitting water with every syllable. 'Ride with Batty here, who will drive a stake into each black heart o' them.'

Tarset and Tyne. Wallis men… the roars went up and temporarily drowned the mad-snake hiss of the rain. Batty met John Wallis' steady gaze with a miserable one of his own which told the Laird of Twa Corbies all he needed to know; he grinned back into Batty's bad-cess glower.

'Away, Batty,' he bellowed and slapped his backsword down on the horse's rump – with an outraged squeal and a whip of wet mane into Batty's face the beast was off. There was nothing left but to hang on and pray to a God Batty was convinced now hated him personally.

–

Maramaldo felt the horse go out from under him as it turned and twisted, set to trembling by the battering of hail and so nervous now that it skittered at shadows and flicks seen at the corner of an eye.

One such set it dancing sideways on the treacherous mud. All four hooves scrabbled frantically for grip, scouring up ruts, there was a moment of whirling and a thump that drove most of the air from him, then Maramaldo rolled in a welter of filth and wet.

He had just enough time to think himself lucky for having spilled free of stirrup and tangle when he crashed into something solid and the rest of the air whoofed out of him.

He was gone from the world for only a moment or two, blinked back into the sheeting, blinding rain and the realisation that he was hard up against a great circle of wood and iron. Wheel, he thought, half dazed. A wheel on one of the sakers...

The horse was gone – treacherous lump, Maramaldo thought, for all it cost. I shall feed it to the Company...

There was a thump and a spray of watery mud; Maramaldo looked up and into the grim drip of a familiar face, melted with age and the distortion of water.

Balthie Kohlhase.

–

Batty came off the horse awkwardly when it lumbered almost on to the guns; he landed badly, stumbled on to the shriek of bad leg and fell heavily on the wooden deck, where he lay for a moment with the rain in his eyes.

Then he levered himself up with a grunt. The bastard horse was gone, he thought. Fiskie would have bided like the good beast he was, but the borrowed one had simply sauntered off.

There was fighting all round, for he could hear it like a muffled brawl through the rain hiss. This is no place for Mistress Kohlhase's wee lad, he thought and started to move to where he thought the guns lay, shuffling through the grey sheet of water; sooner this was done, sooner he could be away from the middle of Maramaldo's army. The thought of that brought more shiver than the cold rain.

He fell over a bucket and cursed, but when he began to lever himself back up his one good hand closed on a shaft and he found himself looking at a mallet, a great wooden affair with dented caps of iron. Used to hammer free the locks that kept the wheels fixed – fourteen hundred pounds of recoiling cannon is not something you want rolling about – it was now just litter.

The gunners had fled, leaving buckets, wad-screws, spongers, rammers and a *botefoux*, the fuse match in it soaked to ruin. Batty moved to the gun as through a waterfall, laid the mallet at his feet and fished in the drench of his apostles until he produced the spike, four inches of iron nail. He worried the sharp end of the spike into the touch hole, fetched up the mallet and banged it hard; he had to hit it six or seven times and the last one was a poor stroke, bending the final third of nail sideways.

Good enough, Batty thought exultantly. Pick that out, ye moudiewart bastards...

He reached the second gun, colliding with the front of the long barrel and just as he thought of dropping the mallet and fumbling for another spike, something lunged out of the grey mist and made him rear back; the length of backsword meant for his face rasped over the ornate muzzle, followed by the hand and the desperate snarl of face behind it.

Batty gave the face the mallet with all the force his arm could muster; there was a spurt of blood and teeth and the man vanished, shrieking. Beyond him, though, Batty heard cursing and clashing; the fight was closing in on the guns as Maramaldo's men recovered themselves.

A horse cantered out, squealed and veered away trailing reins Batty tried in vain to grab, dropping the mallet to do so. Cursing, he fumbled out the spike, slithered up the rainwashed length of the gun and found the touch hole. He worried the spike in and then had to go back for the mallet.

When he found it, men were careering madly around, wraiths in the grey mist of rain; Batty ducked under the muzzle, to put the gun between him and this new fighting. He moved up the length of it again, listening to the rasping breathing, the curses and wild, wet chopping sounds.

He stumbled over a foot and thumped heavily on his bad leg, which made him curse and shoulder his length into the wheel – a good, dished wheel, he noted. Not perpendicular, which warped out of true with the weight and the forces expressed on it, but this was a Scots gun taken as plunder and stolen by Maramaldo. The Scots bought in good guns, well carriaged – though, unless they had a Batty Coalhouse, they served them badly...

All of it went racing through Batty's head in the time it took his eyes to travel up the fine leather of the long boot he had tripped over, up to the spreading, soaked breeks with their extravagant panes to the gilded half-armour, all fluted and roped up to the lace collar. The face above it, yellow as clotted cream, smiled a twist of grin at him.

'Ill met, Balthie. It seems you have taken pains to hunt me out – well here I am. Though you will find me no easy mark.'

Which had more truth than lie in it, as Batty saw; Maramaldo had a length of steel in one fist, but he seemed dazed and unable to rise. Batty raised the mallet.

Here was his hated enemy, the focus of all his bad cess for as long as he could remember. The stump of his arm seemed suddenly to be on fire.

Chapter Thirteen

Later, at Akeld…

Who did?

It was what Sister Faith asked when Batty came to say his farewells and was such an echo of that moment when he had stood in front of Maramaldo, hammer in hand that he had to shake his head at the way she could read his mind.

He had stood for what seemed a long time with the rain pouring off him, staring into the drenched face of his hated enemy – then he had raised the hammer and whacked it down. Once. Twice. Three. Four. Five.

Each one had made Maramaldo twitch and driven the spike deep into the fuse hole. Then there had been shouts – here he is. Rescue…

Batty had let the hammer drop from his sodden fingers and Maramaldo's surprise betrayed itself only by the merest twitch of a wet brow.

'If you did not arrange for me to be here,' Batty said to the slumped Captain General as shapes loomed out of the grey, snarling and vengeful. They lumbered up, paused and piled on him.

'Who did?'

The bellow had the last of its air driven out by kicks and punches; Batty's last coherent moment before the white sear of agony blossomed round him, was Maramaldo's voice.

'Alive. You cunny-licking bitch-ticks – alive.'

Who do *you* think did?

Maramaldo had asked that when Batty arrived back in a world of pain struggling up from where he lay. He grunted with the hurt that caused him and looked at Maramaldo, sitting opposite in dry and splendid clothes.

'Someone treacherous,' he muttered and touched a swollen lip. 'This is bursted. You might have said "alive and unharmed".'

'Consider yourself Dame Fortune's favourite,' Maramaldo said coldly, 'that there was at least "alive" in what I said.'

'I might have bashed in what little brains you possess,' Batty reminded him, feeling a twinge in his sole elbow that spoke of a kick. He still wore his soaked clothes, too, and looked sourly at the dried and preening Maramaldo.

'You have hunted me long and hard,' Maramaldo replied, 'so it was a mystery to me why you did not – save that you would have my length of blade in your paunch.'

'Aye, aye,' Batty answered wearily, 'we would have ruined each other's day, sure enough – but the true reason is discovered at the last. Neither of us sought the other here. Someone else brought that about, for their own ends.'

Despite himself, the cold made Batty shiver and Maramaldo shifted slightly to pluck up a cloak, which he flung casually; Batty wrapped it round him, dextrous with one hand so that Maramaldo smiled wryly.

'You are clever with that one wing,' he declared. 'I did you a favour, it seems.'

'Pray it is never returned,' Batty answered sourly, then glanced at the cloak, which was a virulent green with red trim. 'Unlike this cloak, which will keep me warm but is too loud to sleep in.'

'You never had taste or style,' Maramaldo answered, rising and spreading his arms. 'What d'ye think, then – every inch Mars, is it not?'

Black boots to the knee, with golden spurs fitted with small bells that tinkled when he walked. Fat breeks the colour of dried blood, paned to spill a white silk lining in gouts like gushes of water. A doublet to match, ribboned at the shoulders and over it a breastplate of fluted steel, gilded and ornamented with cherubs and fruit. A broad-brimmed hat with a soaring panache of frothing white plumage.

'You look like a whoremaster with his head stuck up an egret's arse.'

Maramaldo beamed. 'The very look the Sable Rose demands… come. There is someone you need to meet.'

They had walked out together, as unlikely a pairing as wolf and dog and so ill-dressed they would have been stoned in any Edinburgh wynd. Here, no one noted it and only acknowledged them at all because one was the Captain General.

In the yard, the sun steamed a mist from the drench of Biblical weather which was now a distant memory. Insects whined and buzzed, smoking round Maramaldo's carrying chair which was occupied by a slumped figure; closer to, Batty saw it was Horner and marvelled at the man's temerity. Then he saw it was not Horner's choice and that he would have quit the throne if his hands had not been nailed to the armrests by Batty's remaining spikes.

Maramaldo stopped and looked at the slumped figure, then reached out one gauntleted hand to take Horner by the hair and raise his head up. The face, Batty thought, looked like a bag of blood left a day too long; the blood-stains on the armrests were still new and bright.

'He did not resist very long,' Maramaldo declared. 'Told all he knew before the first spike had gone all the way through. I did the other, just to show illness does not temper me mild.'

Batty was chilled by the cold viciousness of it, but then thought he had been too long apart from the man and had forgotten much. Maramaldo saw it and turned a mirthless smile on Batty.

'Of course, I could not leave him half-fastened, so we spiked his other hand. I beat his face for the pleasure in it; I do not care for Master Horner of Mells.'

He paused and stared hard at Batty.

'We are the same, you and I,' he declared and Batty wished he could muster a counter to it.

'Yet we are opposites,' Maramaldo went on. 'Fire and water. Earth and air...'

'Sane and mad,' Batty almost muttered aloud, but did not. Maramaldo gave up searching for another example.

'We are both... lacking. You an arm, me a heart, some would say.'

'A soul.'

This Batty could not keep behind his lips and Maramaldo frowned, then shrugged.

'So your wee nun says. The one hot for Christ, not the poxed one.'

It was the first intimation Batty had that the Sisters were alive and he felt strangely raised by it.

'No matter the missing part, it separates us both from good company.' Maramaldo declared. 'So we share that, at least.'

He shook Horner's bloody head to make the man moan – and wake him, Batty saw.

'I took a *condotta* from this Musgrave fellow,' Maramaldo went on. 'We were to bait the local trolls, this Wallis tribe, let them to gather and be the anvil to a hammer of King's Men.'

Batty had worked this much out and saw, from the easy way men moved around him, that the fighting was long done. Poor John Wallis, he thought, trapped by Musgrave and Dacre cunning; it doesn't pay to bait the Red Bull.

'The details were arranged by Rafael,' Maramaldo went on and then jerked hard on Horner's hair, making the man whine and spit through his broken lips. 'And this one. Rafael remained, as is proper, to ensure the details.'

Rafael remained as hostage, Batty corrected silently. A normal arrangement.

'Horner brought my copy of the *condotta*, all Latined. Cornelius read it and it was as agreed – in return for service for a certain period la-la-la-la the Company of the Sable Rose would be paid la-la-la-la-la and guaranteed of the good grace of His Majesty King Henry, to be included in his army bound for France.'

'Aye,' Batty agreed. 'There is better shine to be had in France.'

'Best of all in Saxony,' Maramaldo answered, 'which is the new cockpit of war after the Italies. But France will do for now.'

He jerked again and Horner groaned.

'No mention of Batty Coalhouse in it,' Maramaldo went on, cold and vicious as a north wind. 'Not in the copy I had. But Musgrave had another, it seems, which Master Horner knew of. One with a name in it – yours, Balthie.'

This time the jerk was savage, the gauntleted fingers twisted hard into the hair, so that Horner whimpered.

'A private arrangement,' Maramaldo went on. 'Who did it? Eh, Horner. Who did it?'

Batty knew the answer before Horner whimpered it out in a puff of bloody froth.

'Sabin.'

Maramaldo let the head drop, wiped the gauntlet on one of Horner's shoulders.

'There you have it,' he answered bitterly. 'Treachery from one's own chancellor.'

'Hardly that,' Batty replied wryly. 'Rafael Sabin would scarcely think you so set against such an addendum.'

Maramaldo's face was a white chill that Batty was hard put to stare into.

'My decision to make. Not his. Not ever his.'

Aye, he was right in that, Batty thought. When your wee right hand begins to handsel deals on his own, it means he considers his master lacking. In a company of mercenaries, that is not to be tolerated.

'Rafael must hate you in handfuls to have risked this,' Maramaldo said softly, which thought had only just occurred to Batty, too; the cold sweat slithered the length of him.

'He follows his master's lead like a fawning wee dog,' Batty said, hearing the croak of it from his dry throat. Maramaldo shifted from one foot the other and suddenly seemed weary.

'I do not hate you, Balthie,' he answered, 'though continually hearing of your desire to track me down is a

233

scrape. You might consider why you never did, Meinheer – I was not in hiding.'

Batty did not like to dwell on why he had always seemed to miss Maramaldo, no matter how he tried. Like the burning nun, he thought, I can always be diverted by seeming good sense.

Maramaldo shifted his weight a little – his bladder is bothering him again, Batty thought.

'You were nothing to me, though the business of your limb was… messy,' he said, as if was discussing coppicing a tree. 'Done in anger and not a little pain – you beat me with a ramrod if you recall.'

'Almost to death,' Batty admitted. 'I am sorry for the "almost" in it.'

Maramaldo's smile was twisted and humourless.

'You see? The same, you and I.'

He hitched the weight of the fancy half-armour and sighed.

'The *condotta* forces me to remain until this new tower – what is it called? Two Crows? Yes, that. It is to be reduced. Since my guns will have to be drilled out of your spikes, this will take some time and I am not pleased. I wish to be gone from this pestilential country.'

'The feeling is mutual, I am sure – but Musgrave will hold you to your *condotta*.'

Maramaldo nodded.

'Then you must find a way to end it,' he declared. 'I will not risk the good grace of King Henry or the promised fees at this late stage, so someone must call this business off. You know these people, this country.'

I was wondering why I was still in the world, Batty thought. They sat at a scarred table torn out of Akeld and littered with a spread of papers and maps, old cups and cracked glasses, the harrigles of a meal and spilled red wine. The usual remains of a conference of captains, which had turned as ever to Primero and wagering; the sight brought a sharp pang of remembrance. What had become of the old crew? LeBois, Desaix, Blymmedes the Greek... only Sabin and Maramaldo seemed to be left of the ones Batty recalled sitting at just such a table, cheating furiously at cards.

Gone to the gusty breath of guns or the violation of blade or the silent, secret disease. Now new and younger men ordered Maramaldo's company – and that was part of his problem, Batty realised.

It was clear that whatever war had been waged was now done with, though the bulk of the Sable Rose was not here but moved to Twa Corbies, all save the guns. They sat morosely silent while men moved round them and hammers clanged, picking away at Batty's spikes.

They sat opposite one another, Batty and the man who had taken his arm and Sister Faith asked, later, why Maramaldo had not killed him out of hand. Was he not the fell cruel mercenary commander, anathemised by the Holy Father?

That, Batty told her, was exactly why Maramaldo let me live. He had worried the same matter himself like a dog with a dug-up bone and only came firmly to the meat of it when Maramaldo looked at him over that littered, scarred table and said:

'The *condotta* Rafael made is rotted. Rafael has betrayed me.'

There it was, though the truth in it was that Maramaldo was rotted, poxed, without cure. He would live for years yet, each one marked by the decline of his acumen, crumbling bit by bit to the ruin of the Company.

Maramaldo knew it, feared it, feared the young, hard men he led watching and waiting. These were not Desaix, Blymmedes and the like, who had come with the young Maramaldo and knew him as well as any. These new captains only knew Maramaldo by reputation and when that started to tarnish...

Maramaldo now saw the beginnings of it with Rafael, his trusted lieutenant who was starting to add secret codicils to agreements. It was a step from there to ousting the Captain General.

Such things were normal enough, Batty recalled. The Company could vote one commander out and another in if they thought the new one could make a better fist of matters. The Companies themselves changed and split and reformed – Maramaldo's had had many guises, the Sable Rose being only the newest; that black rose flag had once been a golden purse, potent symbol of the Company of Fortune and when Batty had been working guns for Maramaldo, he had done so in the Compagnie di Vendetta – the Company of Revenge.

All led by Maramaldo, who could feel his iron grip slipping and whose mind was poxed enough to smoke up more fears than there were.

There would be others involved, of course, captains Rafael had subverted to vote Maramaldo out, so Maramaldo needed success. He needed Musgrave's coin to sugar men back to his side. He needed a new *condotta* with King Henry, transporting the Company and the guns it had stolen, no questions asked, back to the other side of the Channel – that contract would not, Batty was sure, be arranged by Rafael Sabin.

But the biggest reason for Batty's survival was that he was home, in the Border lands. He had kin here and even if Maramaldo was not exactly sure of how welcome Batty was in any of their houses, the kin-ties of the Borders was something he already knew well enough – a brace thousand and more Wallis men had turned out to fight him over a handful of stones and a waste of moorland. That had shocked him and Batty belonged to the Grahams, a more powerful Name than Wallis.

Killing Batty would cause a feud Maramaldo did not care for; bad enough he had fired the country with a simple burning at Broomhouse without adding to the flames of it.

After all, this was Maramaldo, trailing a funereal cloak of outrage behind him – rapine, arson, violent conduct, adultery, incest, parricide, uxoricide, sacrilege and heresy. In his home town of Naples they waited to hang him on the gloriously-worded charge of: '*trattando ignominiosamente le vergeni e le matron a guise di meretrici e di schiave vilmente vendute*'.

Which was only the least of it, Batty thought – Naples was not the only city where Maramaldo had 'treated virgins and married women ignominiously, as if they were prostitutes and slaves to be basely sold'.

Maramaldo did not want any new stain showing up the old and soiling his chances of joining Fat Henry's army, so he would slaughter no nuns or weans for Musgrave and certainly no Batty Coalhouse for Rafael Sabin.

It came to Batty, as he sat at the scarred table idly turning over discarded Primero hands, that there was as much admiration as hatred in his consideration of Maramaldo. He might dress like a brothel pimp, insist he had been knighted personally by the Pope and strut as the very font of chivalry – yet *Dux pertissimus* was a title Maramaldo also revelled in and that had been fairly earned – Most Experienced Commander. *Dux cautissimus* was another – Most Prudent Commander and he valued that even more, for employers liked their paid Captain Generals to be more Fabius The Delayer than Alexander The Great.

Most of which was unsaid between them and all of it understood. Maramaldo turned and waved, bringing a gilded clank of soldiery up carrying a familiar cylinder of leather, scuffed and battered now.

'I make a *condotta* with you, Balthie,' he declared, grinning. 'This rich payment and the freedom of your nun and children – just the one nun, Balthie, for the other I will keep. In return you will find a way to end the *condotta* with Musgrave which does not involve me breaking my bond.'

Batty eyed the cylinder sourly. No gift to return that which was stolen, he thought. Especially since the likes of Maramaldo could make no claim on such holdings as those wee parchment Rolls represented – bad enough that some Scotch Lord might, let alone a foreign blackguard such as the Captain General.

He said nothing, all the same though he knew Maramaldo read his face well enough.

'I also return your weapons and personal possessions. Your horse, saddlery and accoutrements. You have one hour to arrange yourself and appraise the nun of matters and a ten-day to achieve all – she will, of course remain. Every good *condotta* requires assurance.'

'And Rafael?'

Maramaldo's eyes went a colour that had no name and which Batty did not care for.

'He remains with Musgrave, for the moment. Perhaps he suspects I know of his treachery – *nessuno me lo ficca in culo!*'

He recovered, breathing hard.

'Horner will live,' he went on, 'for the Spanish whore-nun is skilled enough with physicking and I do not want him dead. I shall free him back to his Lord Chancellor once we are safely gone from this place, for this Musgrave fellow wants no survivors inclined to link him to the nuns he betrayed here. One his own kin, I believe.'

He glanced slyly at Batty.

'Musgrave thinks they are all already dead – nuns, *kinder* and Master Horner. This will become truth if you fail. I will risk the wrath of another Broomhouse over it, you must believe me, Balthie.'

'I might just take these Deeds and run,' Batty pointed out and saw Maramaldo's slow smile; he flushed. He knows I will not and voicing it aloud shows I have no plans for it. Aye, push down on my shoulders God, Batty thought bitterly. See if they are wide and strong enough to bear this.

Bliddy Sister Faith…

She was all perjink and proper in the upper floor of Akeld, hands folded in her lap and the bairns gathered round her skirts – all save the eldest boy, Daniel, Batty saw. He did not ask where he was, but told her what had happened and waited until she had finished a prayer for Horner. Jack The Lad Horner will need it, Batty thought, as well as Sister Charity's skills.

Who did it?

It was the first of the many questions she asked, quiet and calm, twisting away at her rosary ring. He told her the name and why Rafael Sabin did it. He held out the silk-wrapped container with the phials, returned by Maramaldo who did not comment on them, even if he knew what they were. Batty was not surprised since he scarcely understood what they were himself, only that Sister Faith valued them highly.

But she was a mad old biddy who looked quietly at what he offered and then shook her head.

'God gave them into your hand to keep safe,' she declared. 'It is not safe yet to release them to me.'

Batty wanted to throw them at her, shouting that he clearly recalled her shoving them at him in the dark and marching out to the dubious mercy of Maramaldo. So God had not given them at all…

Yet here they all were, mercied by Maramaldo, a man whose murder of arch-enemy Ferruci in Italy fifteen years before was now spawning the term *maramaldesco to describe* someone so fell cruel he would keep stabbing a dead man.

Perhaps there was God in it after all, Batty thought and then hoped He would remain in it, for Maramaldo's personal Devil would drive him to carry out his threat against Sister Faith and the bairns if all else failed. There was a limit to Maramaldo's good sense and temper and the pox ate it daily.

'What will you do, Master Coalhouse?'

It was asked with no more emphasis than if she wanted to know how many cards he wanted at Primero and Batty had no true answer to it.

'Ride,' he said and she heard him do it, leaving a faint sound of singing behind him like a waft of incense.

> 'As I was walking all alane,
> I heard twa corbies makin a mane;

The tane unto the ither say,
Whar sall we gang and dine the-day?'

A few miles away, at Twa Corbies...

They watched the figure caper along the crenelated roof, scrambling up the slick steep-pitched slates now and then to get higher. They listened to the wild singing and Lord Ogle leaned on his ornate stick and cocked an eyebrow.

'It is my fervent wish the old beldame tumbles down.'

Musgrave agreed, for the old beldame was giving the men collywobbles with what some thought were hurled spells; Maramaldo's hard-eyed paid-men were the worst, creeping around making crosses or clutching amulets with both hands. He was tempted to give the order to shoot her down, but that would not sit well with men determined on no hint of Broomhouse.

'In ahint yon auld fail dyke,
I wot there lies a new slain knight;
And nane do ken that he lies there,
But his hawk, his hound and his lady fair.'

'What is she chanting?' Sabin asked, frowning and Musgrave told him – some local verses concerning murder. No spell at all, he added, though it would be a benison on all of them if Sabin would dispose of her and the entire place.

'My Captain General says no,' Sabin replied, nodding in the direction of the stolid-faced captain called Juup. 'He has sent his emissary to tell me this.'

Something in Sabin's voice made Musgrave look at him. They stood in a knot of men, mostly Ogles, who were listlessly pointing out the salient defences of Twa Corbies. Most were agreed it was a hard place to crack open, for all the long hundreds of men they had surrounding the place, for they had no idea how to shell the defenders out without causing more Broomhouse outrage, which was the one matter they were all fervently agreed upon not doing.

'Even if they are Catholics,' Luke Ogle kept saying sarcastically, shooting glances at Musgrave each time he did so. Musgrave took Sabin by one elbow and steered him out of earshot of the others.

'Is there a problem regarding the Captain General?'

There was, but Sabin was not about to admit it. There were five captains missing from the men clustered round Twa Corbies and all were well known to Sabin – were, in fact, the ones he had gathered to his Cause. Rafael did not believe in coincidence.

He was making dismissive sounds and gestures when a rider appeared, jouncing like a badly-packed sack on a donkey, his legs bare, knobbed and unhealthily white, a robe hauled up to let him ride; Sabin knew the robed figure of Cornelius at once and felt a lurch that felled him to silence. Cornelius was another he had been working on.

Cornelius slid off the horse, buckled at the knees for a moment, then gathered himself and scurried towards Sabin, who saw the whey face and its unhealthy sheen of sweat; the lurch dropped his bowels away.

'Meinheer Cornelius,' Musgrave began and then stopped, astonished, as Cornelius ignored him and stared goggle-eyed at Sabin.

'Tannhauser,' he said hoarsely. 'Jacob. Ruggiero, Langlands and Louis Limousin. He has them all.'

Musgrave saw Sabin's face seem to stretch and set, so that the cheeks grew white over the bones beneath.

'He was not sure of me – though he will be now.'

Aha, thought Musgrave. Master Sabin has overreached himself and Maramaldo has clipped his wings. Interesting...

Then it grew more interesting still.

'Horner and the nuns are alive,' Cornelius went on, striding back to the horse and dragging a book from a bag fastened to the saddle. 'Coalhouse, too.'

'The nuns and Horner, you say?' Musgrave demanded and Cornelius spared him a brief glance, long enough to appraise and then ignore.

'Coalhouse – is he there, with Maramaldo?'

Sabin's voice was an edge that cut through Musgrave's outraged demands for his question to be answered.

'No,' Cornelius replied, clutching the book to him. 'Maramaldo let him go. Some errand – failure will mean the death of the nuns, Horner and those execrable children.'

'Errand?' demanded Musgrave and, at last, had an answer from the cream-faced little man.

'North. No idea what. He rode out an hour ago and he no sooner had than Maramaldo started rounding folk up. My God, Rafael, what he is doing to them... I knew I would be next, so I came here.'

Sabin could imagine, though he did not want to. He felt a hand on him and looked down to see Cornelius plucking at his doublet, face wide-eyed and pleading.

'Rafael – what do we do? We must flee – you must save me. You got me into this...'

Rafael stepped back, letting Cornelius stumble. He looked at Musgrave.

'Take your men,' Musgrave said, seeing the possibilities at once. 'Stop Coalhouse – do what you will with him. If you do, the others die and all is served.'

'Give me some more men.'

'For a one-armed man on his own?'

Musgrave's voice was a harsh scald and he waved a dismissive hand as he did so.

'None other than your paid-men – there must be no involvement of the Musgrave nor Dacre in this or, God forbid, King Henry. You have a sufficiency of your own.'

A dozen, Sabin thought bitterly. It would be enough, provided Balthie did not fall in with any of his kin on the way. Besides, it was the only way – if Batty returned to the shelter of Maramaldo there was no possibility of getting to him, or of Musgrave getting rid of his own problems.

He nodded and turned away, leaving Cornelius floundering in his wake.

Musgrave felt the eyes on him and turned to see all the Ogles looking at him. Ogling him, he suddenly thought with a dangerous urge to giggle. Instead, he nodded and smiled, bland as new milk and moved back to their company.

'Problems, my lord?' Luke Ogle asked with vicious hope. Musgrave smiled even more widely.

'I was hoping to persuade Master Cornelius to perform some magicals of his own on yon woman,' he declared and watched people cross themselves piously, shooting glances at the scuttling figure.

'Burn her on the roof, no doubt,' the young Lord Ogle answered thoughtfully and folk blanched at the idea of a burning woman on a Border roof until the lord realised what he had said and started to flush and bluster.

'A simple gag would suffice,' Musgrave offered and folk laughed uneasily as Trottie danced on the roof and jeered down at the men unable to get in, though there was only her, two men, a dog called Diamant and a boy called Will Wallis inside.

> *'Ye'll sit on his white hause-bane,*
> *And I'll pike oot his bonny blue een;*
> *Wi ae lock o his gowden hair*
> *We'll theek oor nest whan it grows bare.'*

Chapter Fourteen

Later, at Kirknewton near Akeld...

In the time it took him to murmur the entire song, Batty could see the solid block of the kirk tower and the huddle of cruck houses gathered on it like chicks round a hen. There was a fringing of fret-leafed oak and some men working sheep whistled up their dogs and vanished, leaving the ewes to jostle in the bracken before returning to a meander of grazing.

A mere Scots mile and a bit from Akeld, Batty thought, so they would have heard the noise of it – mayhap some of Maramaldo's men rode out on a forage and they are wary of more.

He looked around, not anxious to encounter any, but the haar was rolling in to drown the light; Fiskie stirred and muttered.

Batty patted him, glad to be reunited with a beast he had not hoped to see again. Almost as glad to find his gear, though one dagg was missing and he was woefully lacking in powder and shot. He nudged Fiskie on down the track, seeing the ruts deepen, following it round to where it became fringed with wet-black drystane dyke; by the time he had reached this point, the haar had thickened and rolled in like a blanket of wet linen. He shivered.

'Mony a one for him makes mane,' Batty crooned softly, peering this way and that. 'But nane sall ken whar he is gane…'

> *'Oer his white banes, whan they are bare.*
> *The wind sall blaw for evermair.'*

The voice was deep and resonant, coming right out of the milk-mist and seeming so close that Batty cursed and jerked the rein so that Fiskie snorted. A figure loomed, formed from shadow into a tall man with a face like a benign slewdog and a long black garment which Batty recognised as vestments.

The wee minister of St Paulinus's kirk, Batty thought, hearing his heart banging.

'A goodly song that,' the vicar declared, 'and apt since it is called Twa Corbies, at least hereabouts. Who are ye?'

'Who asks?'

'The vicar of St Paulinus's kirk – and the man told by running sheep-men that raiders from the war around Akeld and Twa Corbies are coming down on us. Yet I see a horde greatly diminished to a drookit auld man with a single arm.'

'Batty Coalhouse is the name under all this drip,' Batty answered. 'Your sheep-men echo the itch down my backbone, so I am supposing your raiding horde will be here presently – I would gather what flock you have into yon stout-walled kirk and bar the door.'

The cleric squinted a little and the nodded.

'I did not think you came to adore our adoring Magi,' he replied, 'fine carving though it is – the Magi have belted plaids, no less, did you know that? Will you light down from yon stot and take shelter? You look peaked to me.'

Batty felt peaked, but there was no question of stepping down and taking shelter, though he thanked the vicar, who glanced at the sky.

'And God said let the waters of Heaven be gathered unto one place,' he intoned and then grinned wryly, a graveyard of teeth that echoed the tombstones around him. 'As it says in my good Myles Coverdale book, though it omits to say that the Lord let said waters be gathered all in *this* place.'

'There was hail,' Batty remembered and felt silly for saying it; he felt light-headed and fey, so he shook himself like a dog and nudged Fiskie on.

Peaked, he thought. Aye, I am peaked... and he sneezed. He almost brought Fiskie to a halt with the shock of it. A sneeze. Well, it might equally be a bad humour brought on by rain, a herald of snotters and sweating – or it might be the start of an all-too-short visit of the Death. He tried to feel for swellings in his armpits but could not be sure.

Not that it mattered, he thought dully, since the sheep-men have confirmed what I feared – I am followed. It will be Sabin, for certes, out to prevent me...

From what? The question hung and swung, leering at his poor pretensions of being Galahad. What in the name of Christ am I supposed to do to halt a war?

And the word popped into his head as if placed – blackmeal.

He felt the strap of the scuffed, battered leather cylinder like a brand and mulled it over. Dacre might be persuaded to leash Musgrave for some richer manors in England. Might be dazzled by it to offer more, even…

Lanercost, then and Thomas the Bastard; the wool in his head fluffed up even as he turned Fiskie to what he thought was west, with a drift of south in it. There was a time when he left the world and came back to it, swaying in the saddle and confused about time and place, when Fiskie stopped.

Batty had a few moments of dragging at his shredded thoughts before he realised the mist had lifted just in time to stop Fiskie at the bank of a slow-flowing stream. Too wide to jump and, if Fiskie was anything to go by, too deep to ford.

'Aye, aye,' he soothed, patting the beast's mane. Everything dripped and he was soaked through – shivering, too, he noted. He had a long moment of squint and consider before he concluded he was headed north and east and that this might well be the Till, a branch of the Tweed. North of where he wanted to be and he cursed: left to his own, Fiskie was headed to the only home he had known, which was Powrieburn across the border.

'Tweed said to Till
'What gars ye rin sae still?'
Says Till to Tweed,
'Though ye rin wi' speed
And I rin slaw
Whar ye droon yin man
I droon twa…'

He found himself giggling at the old rhyme and caught himself, though he took a long time about controlling the tremble. Ague, he thought, for sure. And sneezed. Then he turned south, hoping he could stay awake.

The moor stretched, tawny and green and glistening in the watery new sunlight, as if there never had been hail or the sort of rain that presaged the Flood. A wind sighed, but it was colder than a witch's tit and set Batty shivering again. His chest felt tight and pained. He coughed up a gob and spat it free of him.

He moved in and out of the world, finally emerging into a bone-chill wind as Fiskie plodded stolidly up a hill, right across a spring-ploughed field. It was only after a moment of head-wobbling deliberation that Batty worked out it must be Branxton Hill. The cairn on it was confirmation, for it was not all made from stone – some of those smooth, round white shapes were the skulls of those who had died thirty-odd years ago.

Flodden. Bigod, Fiskie had turned his head the wrong way again and Batty felt the sudden wash of weary defeat. I will never reach Lanercost, he thought, but wander in circles until this plague kills me.

The shivering was not all wind, Batty realised, nor even because of imagined wraiths – but he was not surprised when the ghosts turned up a little later. He was almost pleasantried to see them, or so he told himself, if they were all old friends come to escort him quietly to be Judged. His breathing rasped and each one hurt a little more than the last, so he might well be about to stand in front of the Maker.

Aye, fine for you, who had a life.

Francesco Azerbi was gloomy as he walked alongside the horse, in the same scuffed and cracked high boots and patched breeks he had worn on the day he'd died. Landriano, Batty recalled, in '29, when the Spanish Duke of Terranova whipped Count St Pol's Frenchies.

We won, he remembered, but Cecco, silly bastard, saw the ball bounce and roll from what must have been the last roundshot fired from Frenchie guns. He went for it as if it was a football match – the look on his face when his leg vanished in a spray of blood and bone was priceless.

Yet I wept for him, Batty recalled, the last time I ever did for anyone. He was my last best friend…

I owed you money – besides, your tears were nearly all relief that you still had both legs.

I had no arm, mind you, Batty reminded him and then noted that Cecco was walking fine enough now.

A phantom leg for a phantom.

It was a poor jest under the circumstances and Batty said as much, wondering why Cecco had come to haunt him in the first place. I was your last best friend…

Not the last. Simoni has that honour.

And there he was, striding along with his spade beard and his hands full of paper and charcoal, sketching even as he walked.

Dead then, Batty said and then could not be sure, for Michaelangelo looked the same as he had when they fought for Florence. Even the big horse-tooth smile was the same.

You should have come with me, Batty. I would have made a statue of you. In gold.

No David me, Batty told him. Besides, I thought yon Cellini was the goldsmith.

He did it with gentle malice, for he knew Michaelangelo hated Cellini, his nearest rival in sculpture.

Pervert! Soddomitaccio! He could not even have a woman the normal way. He stole the gems from the Holy Father's tiara!

And off he went into a long litany of Cellini's faults, a liquid rill of Italian, just as he had in the inn in Florence the night before he had warned Batty he was leaving. His voice trailed after him long after he had gone and the wind blew, eldritch cold and full of old possibilities.

It hissed at what might have happened if he had gone to Rome and sought Michaelangelo out after all. It whispered wonders about what kind of Batty might have been if Cecco had lived and their friendship gone on. Would he have then, sick at heart, switched sides for four florins a thirty-day to fight in the last bastion of the League of Cognac, the doomed Republic of Florence?

If not, he would never have met Michaelangelo. Or a burning nun.

The shivering wracked him and he fought to control it, fought to crush the 'what ifs'. You don't do that Batty, he heard himself say aloud. You play the hand you are dealt, in life as in Primero...

Nor do you let phantasms rent your head like an empty room.

The thick Borders accent made him turn, head heavy as a twenty-pound shot so that he could feel it wobble on his neck as watched his mother step carefully round a scatter of horse dung, arms clasped round her to hold the shawl he remembered, the one da had got off a *stradiot* who swore it had belonged to his own mother. Black and fringed, with a swirl of red flowers and firebirds – Muscovite, his da had insisted.

I never had anything as braw, save memories of hame. Better things tae keep in your heid than ghosts, Balthazar.

You loved your Graham home, Batty remembered. Even though they hated you for going off with a lad from the Germanies.

Och, that was just family. You think ye ken them, Balthie, but you dinna.

Widdershins with that, ma, he mocked – you think you ken me, but you dinna.

She laid a hand on his knee, standing by Fiskie's head and looking up at him from beyond the grave with that old, familiar look that ripped the heart from him.

Every wee lad thinks his ma disnae understaun' him. Silly wee Balthie...

Silly wee Balthie, he echoed dully. Who watched her step round the horse dung and then turn to look over her shoulder, her face the grey-blue it was when he found her on the morning she died. Of fever folk said, but it was more than that, with a husband dead and a son maimed.

Did you enjoy the wedding?

And he knew she would be there, the Klett bride with her fizzing chaplet of sausage charges, the slow match burning down and her smile flaring out from underneath it.

She tilted sideways – not just her head, but all of her. Swung sideways at the same time as something struck Batty on the shoulder and the side of his head. He smelled freshly crushed dung and had time to think that he had fallen off Fiskie and where there was dung there was horse and where there was a horse there was...

–

Bella is stiff and trembling. Batty thought he knew her until recently, thought he had seen all of her, stripped naked, splashing

*in secret pools in the hills, or lying in the grass chewing a straw
and waiting, sloe-eyed, for him to scramble free of his breeks.*

*That suited her wildness. The last time they had fucked had
been in a rich man's house, abandoned in haste so that everything
was left, from drapery to heavy, dark furniture and even carpets
from Arabia.*

*In the rich red candlelight, in that setting, her wildness had
become something else, at odds with it all. It unsettled Batty as
her mood does now. He tries to tell her it is war, that it is foolish
to grow attached... but then realises what he says and has to
clamp shut on saying more.*

*I will kill him, she says to him, sitting and hugging her knees.
One day and in the worst way possible...*

*Things change, places merge and flow. Maramaldo rides his
horse, the one he had at Asti, the one whose legs were torn out
from beneath it by the whirling statue of St Secundus, blown from
the Red Tower of Asti by Batty's da. Maybe a leg was whicked
off by part of da, Batty thinks, watching the horse, waiting for
the moment.*

*Instead, Maramaldo leans down and leers at him. We are the
same, you and I, but different. Unwanted in decent company...*

*And the burning nun who is Sister Faith holds out a hissing
chaplet of sausage charges which, for all Batty tries to avoid
taking, somehow ends up in his one good hand, with the slow
match down to the glowing nub.*

*The explosion is strangely soft and slow, an expanding bloom
of white light...*

–

The white light blurred and took shapes, took sound. A
voice and a face, though it took him a long moment of
fighting with the fog in his head to match both to memory

and circumstance. He found the face, a long mourn of bad road with a beard fixed on one end and a balding fringe on the other. In between was a single eye bright as a jewelled toad; the other was a puckered ruin of scar tissue, usually hidden under a black cloth bound round his head.

'Stucley Taylor,' he mumbled and had back a grin and a nod.

'Well, at least you know me and are no longer talking with ghosts and angels called Michael,' Stucley answered. 'Your fever has broke at last.'

Batty became aware of the truckle bed he lay in, walls, a ceiling. There was a half-shuttered window and a peg on the back of a stout door held a grey cloak and a hat with a ratty feather. He lay under a warm blanket and seemed to be wearing no more than a sark.

'Alnwick,' Stucley declared and Batty let that seep into him and bubble up alarm.

'Alnwick?'

Stucley nodded.

'Where you are. We found you out on the Flodden moor — bliddy Fortune favours you in life as it does Primero, Batty Coalhouse, for we were only there at my insistence. Left to the troop I led, we'd have turned back an hour before.'

Flodden to Alnwick. Fevered...

'How long since?' he demanded and felt Stucley steady his panic with a firm hand on one shoulder.

'Easy. You are breathing easier, but do not have the legs for springing up yet. Four days is the answer.'

He paused and frowned, shaking his head.

'You are a tough one-winged old crow,' he went on, 'for I have seen the ague you had on others and they mostly died of it. They were not recovered in four days.'

Four days. Sabin... where was he? And what was happening round Twa Corbies after so long?

Stucley patted him as if soothing a nervous horse or a sick dog, then told him why he was out on the moor at all with a band of Riders.

There was no Warden here since Dacre had fallen from favour and the function of it had been taken by the Warden of the East March, Sir William Eure.

'But he died at Ancrum,' Stucley declared bitterly and Batty recalled that Stucley, ex-gunner and now Land Sergeant at Alnwick, had been a loyal retainer of Eure. He did not think Stucley knew that it was Batty and his guns who had ruined Sir William's day at Ancrum and vowed not to mention it. Nor of watching the man, swinging and burned at the hands of The Douglas and his men.

Stucley, left with the mess caused by Eure's death, was trying to keep the reins of Law tight in the Marches in the midst of a whirl of too much war and too few spare men. When he heard tales of plunder and March Riders around Twa Corbies he rode out with all the men he had – six – to see for himself.

Batty did not need to hear the rest, could guess it. Discovering not a dozen or even a hundred but thousands involved in a siege round Twa Corbies, Stucley wisely scuttled back into Alnwick, taking with him the fortunately discovered Batty.

'Now you can tell me the truth of matters,' he declared, fixing Batty with his one good eye. 'I know you Batty Coalhouse and it is no happenstance to find you in the middle o' all this.'

Batty told him, flat out as a slapped hand on a table.

'I can halt matters if I can get to the Bastard Dacre at Lanercost,' he ended. 'Though Sabin will be closing in and probably waiting for me beyond the walls of Alnwick.'

Stucley stroked his beard for a long time and then shook his head.

'God's Wounds, if a man is known by his enemies, then you are the best-known in England and Scotland both. D'you think ye can sail up to the likes of a Dacre, even a wee yin such as the Bastard in Lanercost, with a hail-fellow-well-met? And what will you do to persuade him to put a halt to whatever is going on?'

Batty had no answer to that, but saw that his possessions were all neat and perjinkly hung in a corner of the room – the battered cylinder of Deeds with it. He saw, too, the little wooden bowl and the vials on a table.

Stucley gave up waiting for an answer.

'I shall send you some broth to put life back in your legs,' he declared, 'but now that I ken what is happening round Twa Corbies, I will have to report it.'

That would be foolish and Batty said so, pointing out that Dacre and Musgrave had contrived to make matters look like a new Catholic rebellion in the north.

'Besides,' Batty finished. 'Who will you report it to? There is neither Warden of East nor Middle Marches.'

Stucley muttered into his beard for a moment or two and then was forced to admit the truth of it.

'Gower would be favoured for the post,' he admitted, 'save that Sir William disliked him and his last act was to have him sent south to answer charges. He is in the Fleet Prison and unlikely to be Warden of anything.'

Gower had been Marshal of Berwick, Batty recalled. Poor wee Red Rowan, he thought, who is having more and more thrust on his shoulders for less and less pay.

'That will be why the great and good are gathering,' Stucley went on. 'Grey of Wilton, Sir William's son Henry, Wharton and the Bull Dacre himself, brother to the Bastard Dacre at Lanercost They will be elbowing and offering favours for consideration of the Warden posts.'

It took a moment to sink through the last mist of Batty's brain.

'Wait. Bull Dacre is here? In Alnwick?'

'Never likely!' Stucley replied with a snort. 'He is at Norham, though, which his da was Captain of at one point. In 1522, I think. It's held presently by Richard Bowes, kin to Sir Robert, the engineer who surveyed it last year.'

He paused, bleared by memories of his former occupation.

'They are filling it full of *contramures* and *peterera*,' he muttered. 'Slings and murderers, Batty, all modern and loading at the breech. Bull Dacre came out of his own hold at Naworth at the request of the King himself to oversee the works.'

Once a gunner, Batty thought and then felt weary and despairing; the Bull Dacre at Norham wasn't the one he needed – or mayhap, he thought suddenly, it is. He is the head of the Dacre Name, called Bull because the banner of the Dacres he flies is a red bull. Only he is allowed to do that.

The Bull Dacre was also as fiercely protective of his Name as a cat with kits; he would not want his bastard brother in Lanercost spoiling his chances of being made a Warden of the March. Perhaps he might be persuaded to throw his weight against his brother – and Norham was a mere a lick and a spit away.

Batty blessed the uncanny luck which had felled him on the moor just long enough to be guided to it. He felt a tingle at the thought – Fiskie, too, had stubbornly resisted heading towards Lanercost.

Christ's Blood, he thought as he shook himself free of the moment, yon Sister Faith will have me canting on my knees if she keeps up her 'chosen by God' babble.

'Aye, well, perhaps he will see me when I am well enough,' Batty declared blandly and closed his eyes against the suspicion pouring from Stucley. Eventually, after a long time, he heard the man leave; when he opened his eyes, he was alone.

He creaked his way upright and had to sit on the edge of the truckle for a long time until the world settled, looking at his knobbed knees sticking from under the sark. Not his own garment, he noted, which was hooked up behind the door and still damp.

Hardly St Michael with flaming sword, he thought bitterly. I can barely sit upright.

By the time the broth arrived and he had allowed himself to be tutted at by a chap-cheeked woman called Greta, he had graduated to standing upright, though he permitted himself to be chivvied back to bed.

He found a flask from Stucley and blessed the man for it – good brandywine and, even if it was confiscated and cost Stucley nothing, the thought was a decent gesture. He drank it from his new bowl and sat, examining the vials over and over, poking them with a grimy finger.

Clay, with firm waxed stoppers and writing all over in the Latin – he knew the shape of the letters, even if he could not read it. There were crosses, too, so it was not some Devil's work inside, but it made no sense and he tucked them away, finished the drink and secreted the bowl away, too.

Well, he thought, belching barley and feeling sleep settle on him, I will have to try Norham. There will be a way in, through moat and *contremures*, inner and outer wards. Avoiding slings and murderers. One that doesn't involve swinging like a Barbary ape from the walls, or getting drookit swimming – I am ower auld and lacking appendages for such derring-do.

Cunning, Batty thought. Both to get in and get out – he had people he yet counted friends in and around Norham. The biggest trick of it would be avoiding Sabin. He will have worked out matters, too and though he has trackers and will ken where I am by and by.

The thought shivered him and then he was comforted, just as suddenly, by the appearance of Bella's face in his head, bright as sunlight. Yet her words were chill as haar.

I will kill him in the worst way possible.

Akeld, at the same time...

Charity was a lady, wore a dress of green-blue brocade which might once have belonged to a whore or a rich gudewife. She carried it off well, for all that it was too short and showed her stick ankles, for it was also too tight and her ample curves – those La Tormenta curves – were all displayed. It laced up the front in a coquettish way and Sister Faith knew that it was chosen by a man.

She came with fruit and meat, climbing the steps to the bare, charred upper floor of Akeld and let through by guards who knew her as Maramaldo's woman. The news she brought was more sustaining than the food to Sister Faith.

Twa Corbies held still and Musgrave was furious, the Ogles fretted and all the men were growing bored and wet waiting for Maramaldo's guns.

'Which have been fixed for a day,' Charity confided, 'though he keeps the fact of it secret in the hope that Batty Coalhouse can stop this affair.'

There was more – Charity had persuaded Maramaldo to at least remove the corpses of the treacherous captains from where they hung, swinging and blackened and crow-picked. Cornelius was gone and good riddance to him. The treacherous Sabin, too, was gone from Musgrave's army and Maramaldo was sure he pursued Batty. He did not want to send men after Sabin and it was not because he did not want to aid Master Coalhouse but because he could not trust any enough for such a task.

'There is no word of Master Coalhouse,' she ended, picking up the licked platters and preparing to leave.

No word. Life hangs by a Coalhouse thread and six days remain before it is severed, Sister Faith thought as she watched Charity leave, her dress iridescent as a blow-fly.

Yet it was something that Maramaldo held his hand from them and Sister Faith had no doubt God was responsible for that, touching the Captain General with a scorch of shame and redemption. Though even she had to admit that Maramaldo's own reasons were all to do with advantage; for all that, she offered prayers.

I believe in God the Father Almighty, Creator of Heaven and earth and in Jesus Christ, His only son, our Lord...

Later, in the long dark, she heard him grunt up the steps and started to breathe shallow, pretending sleep and wondering why he was here, fearful for the children though she did not really think he was as fell cruel as to murder them in their sleep.

She smelled him close to her, a mix of leather and sweat, brandywine and Hungary Water. And heard him speak, soft and low and urgent, realising that he did not care whether she was asleep or awake and that the words were not for her. Himself perhaps – or even God.

I think you may be a witch because after everything I have been it is my heart that is touched as I watch you and wonder if you are one who licks the backs of toads and sucks emeralds to preserve their beauty, even though you are hardly that, yet your soul is young Sister Faith and I have burned your likeness many times before now and I could reach out my hand now and snuff the life from you like the blowing of a candle but I won't and want instead to set you free like the bird you are and your chicks with you for the salving of my own soul and yet we have only a one-armed angel at our command, an angel I made with blood and blade and anger...

It rolled on and on, a soft muttering unholy prayer, a rill like a stream reaching spate. Then it stopped as suddenly as it began, there was a shifting and a thump and he was gone.

Conceived by the Holy Spirit, she continued as if never interrupted, born of the Virgin Mary, suffered under Pontius Pilate, was crucified, died and was buried...

And rose again to glory.

Chapter Fifteen

Next day, on the moor road to Norham…

He sat on Fiskie and contemplated the parapet of the hill, brackened and turfed and studded with black boulders and wet sheep. Green Hill, they called it, which was a friendly name for something most remembered their old kin calling 'Faerie'.

It had stones on it older than God, Batty had heard, placed there by the Silent-Moving Folk and, behind it, a loop of the Tweed rolled sullen and slow. At the foot of it, directly in front of him, was a huddle of cruck and daub houses calling itself Horncliffe. Beyond that was Norham, its towers straining to be seen.

Between the two sat a rider, no more than a wavered shape and Batty sighed. It had been too good a hope that he had evaded Sabin, but here was proof of the death of that – a man set to watch this way to Norham. There would be at least another close by, probably in a shelter by a fire, for they would not go in less than pairs, taking turns to watch. There would be others further out and when the signals went up, the whole pack, Sabin probably at their head, would come riding and that would be the end for Batty.

He had ridden north from Alnwick, as close to Berwick as he dared before turning west, following the rain-dark ribbon of the old Wall, then branching off, closer to the Tweed. He'd hoped to come up on Norham all unnoticed, but had not relied on it.

Stucley will be furious, Batty thought, when he finds his good doublet and gauntlets missing – my auld jack of plates will be poor compensation but he hoped to get it back in time; he missed the weight of it and the doublet had taken him a long time of awkward fastening to get into. He remembered the Elbe and getting out of that jack in less time that it took to curse the ambushers; he would never get out of this doublet in a day, even with help.

It was a fine affair, green plush with gold wire, all padded and embroidered and went well with the cloak Batty had reluctantly taken from Maramaldo. Tucked under the cloak was his hat, with the panache of plume on it only slightly crushed; underneath that was his old, stained sark, still damp. His boots were old friends which leaked and creaked, all were still damp and he felt the insidious chill, the leach of sweat at odds with the shiver he felt. He coughed and spat a gob of something thick and noxious.

He knew he looked like a lump of dung half-eaten by a papingo, but that was what he wanted – the look of a threadbare money-sojer of learning and skill, with an armoury of weapons that warned ne'er-do-wells that he was hard beneath the plumage.

Better still, the doublet had an arm on the left, stuffed now with grass and covered with one of Stucley Taylor's fine gauntlets at the end, the fingers of it stuck in Batty's belt in a casual gesture.

Now he was no longer one-armed, though he excited as much attention as he rode up to Horncliffe's green, which was thronged with too many folk for such a wee place.

The tootling and drums and raucous laughter gave it away in the end; there was a wedding feast, with a hog roasting on coals and barrels of ale. The noise grew subdued when Batty rode in, replaced by sullen and suspicious looks, which was no strange thing in a vill sitting just across the Tweed from folk they were at war with.

A man stepped forward, hitching up his furred robe and trying to puff up for importance, his cinder and ash beard horse-brushed to make it lie against throat and chest.

'Squire Paxton,' he announced and Batty gave him a neck bow.

'Balthazar Kohlhase,' he answered, knowing the name was no lie and yet not all the truth, either. 'On my way to Norham and my lord Richard Lee.'

The Squire relaxed a little, thinking he had the measure of this stranger now. One of Lee's masons or surveyors from the Germanies, an expert in building and fortifications – there was a deal of work going on at Norham, putting it back in order as a bulwark against the Scotch. Which was all to the good as far as Squire Paxton was concerned, so he beamed and bid Batty welcome.

The bridegroom was a wheyfaced Weatherburn boy in uncomfortable finery, his lips like roses in a face made brosy because the impatient drunks who had been his friends had tried to get the garter off the bride, with much lewd comments besides.

The bride was an Adair in a lace dress so old and passed down that the white of it had turned yellow as old bone, but she curtseyed neatly and was glad of the interruption which had saved her new husband from having to strike out. She had crumbs on her shoulders from having had a round cake crushed on her head for luck and clutched her half of a split coin; the groom had the other.

Batty eyed the chaplet she wore and blinked away the hiss of slow match and Klett ghosts as he drank a stoup to her good health, for politeness sake and trying out the effect of his disguise a little. He would have to face the rider with it and it did no harm to let that man see him, as if known in this place.

He asked, casually, who the man might be and the Adairs and Hobkirks, Weatherburns and Paxtons thronging the place all professed ignorance, though none liked the cut of the strange rider, who kept his distance even when approached. There was another, for sure, tending a fire close by.

'Nae good,' a red-cheeked Adair declared between belching. 'Twa' chiels, up to nae good.'

The Squire was an old hand, who squinted milk-blue eyes, one at a time like the moon with wind on it; it was an old Border reiver's trick for staring at the dangerous dark and Batty recognised it at once, knew it did not miss much.

'Been here two days,' the Squire said darkly. 'A brace of them, watching and waiting and well-armed besides, with swords and pistols.'

'Well that's strange,' Batty said jovially as the fiddlers struck up a tune. 'I hear there is trouble to the south a little – perhaps they are from there. Or Scotch spies from across the river.'

'Aye,' the Squire replied, blinking one eye after another like an owl. 'I heerd o' that trouble also. He might well be Scotch – he is not a local man, for certes and we shall ride out to him by and by.'

When more drink had been taken and boldness grew as a result, Batty thought.

'I am heading that way – do you wish me to mention this visit? Or will I invite him to your wedding feast?'

The Squire stroked his beard, the colour of old burned fields and then nodded. Batty offered the bride a wave and rode on, feeling the tension creep into his belly.

'Easy, easy' he murmured, though Fiskie was not the skittish one. 'Ride up all perjink and polite, invite them to feasting and ale as you pass, a two-armed man of note headed for Norham and not the one they seek…'

He rode slowly, softly and kept his eyes fixed ahead, though he was aware, with an intensity sharp as an edge, of the smell of ransom, the wild garlic that grew on the fringes of the path and the slow slide of the stream, the moorhens high-stepping through the mast of beech and hazel and oak.

A bowl of enchantment, that was the Border lands. Gentle hills and loamed sweeps no matter which side of the divide you lived on. Batty knew it well and would have loved it even if it hadn't once cradled his mother in it.

'Ho.'

The voice stripped him of glaured memories and he turned, spreading smile that cracked his face like dried mud. The man was easy on his mount, one hand resting on the pommel, the other on the butt of a big horse pistol, a wheeled dagg already wound and ready.

'Ho yourself.'

'Who are you and where are you going?'

The voice had a lilt to it; Ragusan, Batty thought. A mercenary or my name is not Balthazar Kohlhase and that can only mean he is a man of Maramaldo – or more likely Sabin.

'Who asks?'

'A man who is want to know. You will tell, pretty quvick.'

Batty eyed the rider up and down, as he would if he were what he pretended to be and let his bluster sag and his crest droop a little.

'I am headed for Norham and the Lord Dacre,' he answered. 'As if it is any business of your concern.'

He saw the man look him over. Take it all in, he thought triumphantly, and come to the part where two arms are no use to you.

There was a burst of music, faint on the wind and the rider flicked his eyes towards it. Batty widened his smile and shifted in the saddle a little, as if his arse pained him; it let him slide his good hand nearer to his own horse-pistol.

'A wedding,' he said and nodded. 'They issue invite to anyone passing. Good ale and better food, not to mention the lassies who will be relieved to find a man with finery and less dung smearing him.'

The man opened his mouth and Batty knew he was about to order him to ride on. Then a second voice cut the words from the air with a slash of wicked tongue.

'Batty. Now there's a miracle, for I know the face, but the face belongs to a man with only one working wing.'

The owner stepped out from where he had been watching, from where the thin blue reek of a carefully tempered fire barely hazed a presence. He wore mud clothing with bits of iron filched from little raids all over Europe and a draggle of baldric and pistol holders and apostle bandoliers. His face was a wasteland of scars and age shrouded by a frosted beard long enough to work into two plaits; Batty recalled the man wove in the fingerbones of dead enemies – once he had removed their rings. He wore earrings and amulets and a gap-toothed black of grin.

An *askouret*, Batty recalled with a sickening plunge of bowels to boots, a mercenary from Greece he had once shared bread and wine with. He fought for a name and came up with Epifadi Laskaris, but that wasn't what most people knew him as. He found it, even as he cursed it.

'Phaedra,' Batty said. 'Bright by name if not by wit.'

The man's grin was lopsided because of the scar that ran from the left corner of it all the way to the ear. I gave him that, Batty recalled miserably, when he came at me with a knife for winning at Primero. Sister Faith and Trottie were tenfold liars; neither God nor Satan seemed to be looking after Batty Coalhouse this day.

'Clever enough to catch you,' Phaedra answered, grinning. The other man scowled back and forth.

'He has two arms,' he insisted and Phaedra's brows lowered.

'It is Batty. I know him well enough.'

'You said that about the last one – he was a wearing a cloak that covered one side of his body and you said...'

'*Gamato hristo soo! Waa fagri, koos...*'

There was Greek and possibly Mussulman in the stream of curses that spewed darkly from Phaedra. The other man jerked his horse's head round and urged it up to Phaedra, as if to run him down; he was waving both hands and shouting something in his own tongue, which was just as ugly and dark.

Knock or draw, Batty thought. And drew.

The big wheeled dagg hissed out of its holster and Phaedra screamed when he saw it. Batty checked the dog with its pyrite was positioned and triggered the engine. The rider half-turned as the pan cover clicked open, the wheel spun and flicked, the sparks flew. There was a slight hiss and pause and then the world blew too bright for Phaedra.

Batty did not see what an ounce of lead ball did to Phaedra at close range because the great plume of smoke, the crashing thunder of it and the dazzling gout of flame blew away sight and sense.

Fiskie shied from it, collided with the other horse which was rearing; it gave a scream and staggered sideways, caught a leg and fell, spilling the rider to the ground.

Batty did not wait. 'Ride, my bonny,' he yelled and dug in his heels, knowing even as he did so that he was galloping the wrong way, away from Norham. Knowing also, by that old itch that had never betrayed him, that he was followed, that the pack was closing.

He went a long way in a daze, oblivious to peewits and the curl of breeze, the lowering clouds and even the rain that left him drookit. He came to the bit when the thump of himself in the saddle, riding like baggage instead of a Borderer slowed and stopped entirely. He looked back and thought he saw two riders, but couldn't be sure. He kicked Fiskie on anyway and they went away at a stumbling run.

He was barely aware of anything much until Fiskie came to a shambling halt, at which point Batty woke up and stared around. Fiskie was blowing and backing nervously while Batty sat like a half-empty sack of grain, the big gun hanging down, staring at a Barbary ape while the Cheviot day went down to a ripe of rain and curlews.

The Ape came out and made Fiskie throw up his head and whicker back another half step of two; the act of it finally shook the dagg out of Batty's hand and he heard it thump to the sod. That sharpened him and he shook himself like a dog out of a pool, became aware that he had lost his fantoosh hat – and that he was staring at an ape.

'How now, Master Coalhouse,' said the Ape from behind the trees. 'At least, I says it is you, though I misremember the other arm.'

Batty blinked again and cursed his luck, then cursed it again. He had had dealings with the Ape before and the Ape's master; he wondered how he stood in the regard of the King of the Egyptiani after the business of the stolen babe.

'How now, Ape,' he answered carefully, then forced smile into his voice. 'You are frightening the horse with that – it's a gelding, but never could match you even when it was whole.'

The Ape was a half-sized man completely naked save for a small cloak, long-armed, hunchbacked and wild with long, ginger-brown hair which shrouded part of his stunted body, though his hands and feet were normal. From underneath the curtain of hair round his face and head, eyes peered like small independent beasts and he growled, stroking the chubby curve of a considerable penis.

'Well met, Batty. Or whatever you call yourself… it seems you always come to the king when you are foxed and pursued by hounds. He is expecting you.'

'Batty will do,' he answered, wondering about how he had been expected. The Ape's hairy face parted in a grimace masquerading as a grin – his teeth had been filed sharp for effect, which spoiled the sweetness of the smile. He came forward while Batty stilled the nervous Fiskie, smiled and handed up the dropped pistol.

'Follow on. It is not far.'

He turned and lolloped off in the twisted gait he had, swinging his short legs and long arms from the shoulders and so much like the beast he was named for that it took little artifice to complete the picture for those willing to pay. Some clawed, haired gloves for his hands, similar little boots for his feet and he made the ladies 'ooh' and 'aah' at every Fair. Later, discerning clients – male and female – who paid considerably more would see Beauty reduce the Beast to her power; the Ape was stroked to cross-eyed panting by red-haired Merrilee Meg for the price of a beefsteak dinner.

A bawbee or two for a larking cull? The Ape would have done it twice the three times a day and for nothing. He was just one of the King's many enterprises.

The King was called John the Wanne, though no one knew why but his da, Johnnie Faa, who had been Lord of the Egyptiani for years and given the title of 'Earl' by no less than then the ill-fated fourth James, who fell at Flodden.

Johnnie Faa promptly elevated himself to king and had died only recently so that his son, John the Wanne, had his writ renewed by the fifth James – who died, they say of a broken heart, after the defeat at Solway Moss.

There were those who cried that the Egyptiani had put a curse on the kings who granted them Royal writ of authority over all the Travelling Folk of the Scotch, up to and including hanging malefactors. Others just didn't trust or like the mysterious folk who spread like a rash from Carlisle to Shetland, travelling where they pleased, staying where they willed and never for long in the one place.

Johnnie Faa had been elevated to even greater heights, if rumour was right, when the Earl of Cassilis hung him from a dule tree in front of his castle for running off with his wife. The Countess, it was said, had to watch from an upstairs window.

Johnnie's son was cut from the same rough cloth, a robber, a horse-dealer – thief, if you listened to some – and maker of hornware, which crafts he did with equal skill and counted them all as honourable. When Batty had first met him, a fierce bare-knuckle fighter surrounded by a strange moving fair of the bizarre, he had been relying on the King of the Randies, the Earl of Cipre, Lord of all the Egyptiani to get him safely through Galloway at the time. That and provide some information on the Egyptiani who had stolen a babe.

He was hunted then as now and in a freezing November frost which had all but laid him low with blinding snotters and a cough. It came to Batty that nothing much had changed, save for a lack of snow.

John the Wanne had been irritated by the business of his own folk stealing a royal babe and not fazed in the slightest by the fearsome tally of men hunting Batty. He simply counted the coin Batty gave him, winked and went off, calling out to people in the hazed woodsmoke dark. Later, he had kicked Batty awake and signalled him to follow into the snow-whirling dawn.

Batty remembered the smell at first, like a forge where hot iron has been just quenched. He had smelled it before, but not as strong and did not need John's warning hand to stop, crouch and fetch out his sword. It was blood, lots of it and not yet so frozen it would not reek.

The blood belonged to eight Armstrongs, throat cut and belly slit in a grue of their own entrails. The snow

273

whirled, and Batty, squinting, saw a woman on her hunkers, dress carelessly ruched back to her thighs and the dark mystery of her naked fork all exposed.

He had not felt a twitch at it. Not the way she was gralloching a man, to make sure he had not swallowed his wealth before dying. She was singing, soft and dreamy while the flakes swirled and it was as if she did nothing more than stir the makings of a blood pudding in a bowl.

> *There was a maid this other day and she would*
> *needs go forth to play; and as she walked she sighed*
> *and said, I am afraid to die a maid.*

And she sliced and cut and Batty became aware of other women, heard their added sibilance of sinister chorus.

> *For I will, without fail, maiden, give you Watkins*
> *ale; Watkins ale, good sir, quoth she, what is that*
> *I pray tell me? Tis sweeter far then sugar fine and*
> *pleasanter than muscadine.*

'Aye, aye,' a voice had said in Batty's ear and the grinning horror of King John the Wanne slid to his shoulder, all admiring. 'Don't they sing nice? They do, though, don't they? I thought you'd like to know that them lads will be no trouble to your sleep now.'

Them lads were not, for them lads were all dead. It had done little for Batty's sleep, all the same, for he heard the soft voices all night and was not sure if they were in his dreams or just beyond the canvas he slept under.

> *He took this maiden then aside and led her where*
> *she was not spyde and told her many a pretty tale*
> *and gave her well of Watkins ale.*

He thought of it all now, wavering like a whitened dandelion waiting for the wind to puff. He was not right still and the hard run with Fiskie had left him dulled and dazed, with the arrow-wound in his calf still offering up a stab or two to remind him what had happened – but he was woken to the bit at last when he arrived in the King's camp.

It was a the same Fair Batty had marvelled at before, so it came as no surprise to find a man with the skin of a serpent leading a bear on a rope, herald of the wonders yet to come.

The Serpent Man was called Nino and was afflicted with a disease – not transmittable – which made his skin appear scaled in a half-light. With the addition of paint and a fake fish-like tail, he joined the Two-Headed Man and Lucia the Sybil, who told fortunes with cards.

Nino was bear-keeper when he was not serpent, looking after three or four beasts the size of large dogs, all chained to a cartwheel and seemingly contented with their lot, even when they held paws and danced in a ring like bairns.

There were sixteen or seventeen such carts, surrounded by a mushroom cluster of curve-pole tents where folk worked at various tasks from making baskets out of wet withy to hornware, the burned-hair reek fighting woodsmoke for possession of the place.

The children, half-naked ragarses, all begged from the 'kind gentleman' until scattered by cursing women dark as Moors and clinking with cheap brass and silver ornaments. There were ponies, panniers full of babies, cabbages, empty strawberry baskets, horn cups and spoons and, when Batty climbed off Fiskie, he tied it up next to a ring of cheering, betting men watching two others who were stripped to the waist and trading bare-knuckled blows with bloody intensity.

John the Wanne wore a Turkish turban and a *kaftan* a Turk would scorn, embroidered all over with plants and flowers. He was naked to the waist underneath it and wore only linen underdrawers below that, while he stuck his fists in alternate bowls of pungent liquid.

'Vinegar,' he explained, grinning from out of the stubble of his face. It was a battlefield that face, with a nose broken so many times it had lost even the memory of bone and ears little more than lumps of gristle; it made it timeless like some ruin that might have been Roman or a recent folly.

'For the toughening. You took your time getting here, Batty.'

'Good to see you, too, King John,' Batty replied laconically and sat where the King waved, a long seat round the pit fire. A hand thrust a horn cup at him and he followed it up past the brass and copper bracelets to the heart-shaped face framed with red hair; one of the brilliant blue eyes winked lewdly at him and Batty took the cup gingerly from Merrilee Meg. Same hand she uses on the Ape, he thought and lost the thought by burying his nose in the pungent smokiness of *uisge beatha*, the 'lively water' – illegally made, of course, like almost everything in the Randie King's Court of Wonders.

'You have grown a new arm,' the King said matter-of-factly and then laughed and nodded to Meg. 'That's a spell you must teach.'

'A confection,' Batty replied, 'to fool watchers. It should have been the face I altered.'

'Aye, well, we can do that, too,' the King answered mildly, 'though it will cost you and not only in coin.'

'No, you are not needed there,' Batty said, feeling as if he stood on a steep edge and was sliding. 'I am fine as the sun on shiny watter with the one I have, thanks all the same.'

The King nodded. 'I had a dream you were on your way,' he said casually, wiping his hands clean – the knuckles needed no vinegar, Batty knew, for he had seen the man casually smack bark off a tree with the hugely calloused affairs. 'You were in a wee bastel house out on the far moors, surrounded by a wheen of armed men. Are they the ones on your trail?'

Batty stared, feeling the flesh creeping on his good arm and the back of his neck. 'John Wallis of Twa Corbies,' he said dully. 'He is not the one chasing me, but he is swaddled up in it.'

The King nodded, took a cup from Meg and grinned more gap than teeth back at her.

'Aye, well, there it is. I set Meg to finding out more and guiding you and here you are.'

Batty looked at him, then at the smiling Meg; he felt a shiver take him and put it down to the ague not being completely shifted.

'Guiding me?'

The King waved one hand, slopping drink on his knuckles. 'Aye, aye, we'll come to that. Who are the chiels efter you? I saw men armed like Landsknechts and dressed like hoors.'

'Where?' Batty demanded and the King soothed him.

'In the smoke, Batty. In the smoke Meg makes in water.'

'You were with nuns,' Meg said in her soft flute of voice, which repelled and ripped lust through Batty in equal measure; he glanced sourly at them both, trying to quell the rise of panic and unease.

'Your smokey watter tells a rare tale.'

The King waved one dismissive hand, trailing vinegar reek behind it.

'Och, well – you are safe enow here. There are all sorts stravaigin' across the Cheviot, but they are more feared of the Cheviot than it is of them. Some horse bought a keg from us a few days since.'

'Horse?'

'Dinna fash. They number thirty or so, dress like the worst Mahomet houris I have seen and call themselves Men of the Sable Rose – ah, I see by your look that those are the ones who want you. Dinna seem much to me. Never seen a battle that didn't involve drink and a meat-pie and a hoor.'

Batty shook his head, feeling the fire of the drink and lifted by it. 'You should not dismiss them so lightly. They are well tempered in vicious across many lands.'

'As well we smoked them from you and brought you here, then,' the King said, smiling. Batty scowled. Here we are again, he thought savagely. If it is not nuns with God it is the Egyptiani with Satan, or worse if such exists.

'I was not brought. I came.'

Meg appeared, smiled knowingly at Batty and handed the King a small box; Batty eyed it suspiciously as John the Wanne handed it to him.

'As you say, Batty Coalhouse,' he said. 'Of course, if you dinna believe in it, then this is of no concern.'

He leaned forward. 'But you spent time at Powrieburn and those Faerie speak well of you. Those Silent-Moving Folk and we Cipre have a pact.'

Batty opened the box and drew back at the pungent reek from it. A man-shaped doll lay within, carved from a root. There was hair in it and Batty's hackles rose.

'Mandrake, your hair and seed,' the King explained. 'A simple Calling, which is why you are here. Now you place it in the flames and destroy it, so no one else can harm you. If someone else drops it in the fire, you will suffer, but if cast from your own hand it will simply burn to ash and nothing.'

Batty looked from one to the other. He wanted to ask how they had come by the seed, but thought he knew from the knowing curve of Meg's smile; it had been months since he had lain with her and he made a vow not to go there again if this was what she was up to. Then he dropped the box in the fire and shivered as it caught and burned, trying not to believe that the sudden flush of heat, like a flare of sunlight on his skin, was anything other than coincidence.

'I was not called,' he said sullenly. 'I came here of my own will.'

'Aye, aye, so you say,' the King replied and sipped drink. 'Have ye ever thought, Master Coalhouse, why it is that the woman is credited as the weaker sex, when ye can nivver pull the blanket back to your side of the bed? Now that's Faerie, sure.'

He laughed lightly. 'You need me,' he added.

Batty blinked a bit at that. 'I need to get in to Norham. I need to see the Dacre without getting myself seized for it.'

'I saw some of it,' the King answered, pursing his lips with thinking. 'I saw a man with a rare cote. He is coming from Berwick and will be at the River Howf tomorrow's morn.'

Batty glowered at him, though the hackles on him were up and bristling. 'Dinna cozen me with your magickals, king or no king…'

King John The Wanne simply smiled and called out to Meg, who came swaying into the tent, smile bright and red hair brighter still.

'Master Coalhouse needs rest and then we will talk matters out,' he said.

Batty followed Meg into a tent which, for all he did not wish it, was as comfortable a nest as any he had seen; he thought he vaguely remembered it. She helped him with the doublet and, when it was off, laid one soft hand on his stump and laughed.

'Now you are the Batty I recall.'

'Nice to be remembranced – is that a truckle? I will try it.'

'These cushions are better.'

Batty did not want to know the cushions, but her smile was big and sweet and her hair was red and fine.

–

He came awake with the kick on his foot and mumbled up into the grin of the King.

'Up and away,' he said and Meg pouted her way out, wrapped in a blanket that failed to cover her ample rear. The King watched her and shook his head admiringly.

'A fine wummin,' he admitted, 'though her bun is no doubt a little too buttered at present.'

Batty had no answer to it and was struggling with the doublet until the King lashed him into it.

'You are keeping that, then?' he said, slapping the straw arm. 'Next you will have a fa'se heid o' hair.'

'I have reasons,' Batty growled back truculently. The King shrugged.

'Then you will go to the Howff with Meg and a couple of good men and find the one you seek.'

'With a rare cote,' Batty answered. The King nodded, grinning and flourishing his *kaftan*. 'I fancied it more than this,' he said, 'but the owner will cling to it for dear life.'

He paused, then smiled that crinkled smile that never went further north than his lips.

'I wouldna carp and hang on the edge of the ring,' he said. 'Riders are coming and you will need to dance or die.'

Batty thought of the strangeness, the circling unseen magicks, the madness gibbering at the fringes. Witches and war, he thought, are both best avoided. And nuns.

Then he did what always did when he'd been badly dealt and his purse was out for rent – he bent his card in the middle to show he was doubling his wager and went for broke.

'Lead on,' he said and, in that moment, had a flash of her as he had first seen her, a face peering out of the tower. He felt a sick lurch at the thought of it being some sort of omen, that Sister Faith had just died.

The ride drove that anxiety away in a long streak of wet misery. Fiskie stumbled as often as he walked while Meg seemed unaffected, riding solid as a meal-sack on the back of a spavined mare. Two men came with them, loping like hunting dogs on foot and armed with bollock knives and long matchlock muskets slung across their backs.

'This is Michael and this is Baptiste,' the King said. 'They will make sure no harm comes to you.'

They looked the part, too, being grim as dark reefs against the bright flame of Meg, but nothing but weather crowded them all the way to the Howff, which was a spit from the Tweed; on the other side of that was Scotland.

It was night before they halted, dragged to a stop by Baptiste appearing from the dim like a wraith. He spoke soft and in a tongue Batty knew was the Egyptiani's own, he and Meg sibilating softly while the last of the rain fell to drips.

'The Howff is just ahead,' Meg said. 'Packman ponies in the garth and one finer mount, shod and well accoutred – that will be your man.'

Batty thought about it. The man would have got here at dusk and for all it was a short push – an hour, maybe two – on to Norham Castle, he had not dared the dark. That revealed much, but he kept it to himself.

'How will I ken this man to look at?' he demanded. 'Did your smokey vision show you that?'

'You will know him,' she said and then kissed his cheek. 'We will be gone now. Three Egyptianis appearing in the place will excite more interest than yourself alone.'

Folk would almanac the day over it, Batty thought – and, besides, the Egyptianis would not be welcome.

'Tell the King he has my thanks,' Batty said and Meg laughed.

'There is a price to be paid, Batty Coalhouse. Not now – but the King has your note for it, be sure.'

Aye, Batty thought bitterly, watching the figures fade into the dark, leaving only a last memory of Meg's flame head, I did not think Johnnie the Wanne would forget a bill.

He rode Fiskie into the garth, where the mewl of goat and sheep gave him as much guidance as the wriggling, pallid worm of light from the lantern. He had to thump on the outbuilding door like a ram before it was opened by a tousle-haired boy, all plooks and sleep-eye.

'Rub him down, feed him,' Batty commanded and if the boy had a smart reply he kept it behind his teeth; Batty gave Fiskie a wet slap and plootered into the tavern proper.

There was a moment when the place paused, all heads turned to the door and the newcomer bringing in the rain-wind and the night. Then Batty was in on the plank floor, shaking his cloak free of drip and the inn's customers turned back to their talk and drink.

There weren't many of them and all were packmen, working their way from coast to coast; this was a night that kept local folk in their own homes, but this was home to Batty and the smell of beer, the vinegar staleness of sweat and the savoury of food reeled him in like a gaffed salmon. He tasted the warm fug, saw the bright fire – and heard the rough voice of the innkeep.

'What want ye?'

'Food and lodging. A mug of something wet.'

'All available – if you have coin.'

Batty brought out his purse with a one-handed flourish, which allowed him to shrug off the wet cloak; the doublet sparkled, its tawdry gilt made true gold by firelight and dim. The innkeep was a big man with a doughy face and a beard badly barbered, but he had eyes that missed little.

He counted the coin scrupulously, asked a question with his sheep-dropping eyes and had the nod from Batty, who swept the purse and its remnants back into the doublet.

'Pie, a good mutton in it,' the innkeep said. 'All rooms are taken, but you can have a place on the bench near the fire if you dinna mind the packmen's feet.'

'I have had worse,' Batty said, which was no lie. The innkeep turned to go and Batty stopped him with a quiet hand.

'There is a gentleman here,' he said, making it a statement. The innkeep frowned.

'There is.'

'Point me at him.'

The innkeep shook his head. 'The gentleman is in his own chamber, paid for it too. Has eaten there and clearly does not wish disturbed.'

'Send him a message, then,' Batty said and the innkeep's face brightened.

'You must be the one he is expecting, then. From Norham, is it?'

Batty said nothing and the innkeep nodded furiously. 'Aye, aye, he said to keep an eye open for ye.'

'Upstairs, is he?'

The innkeep nodded and pointed to the solid slab of stairway leading to the only room besides his own. A gallery ran all round but the doors in it were painted fakes, to make the place look grander than it was.

'Bring my pie and a decent jack to the room,' Batty said, feeling less confident than he sounded. He hitched his doublet and went up the stair, stood for a moment, then rapped on the door once, hard.

'Who's there?'

The voice was suspicious; Batty backed a little and took a step sideways, for he had an idea that the voice came from over a hand full of readied dagg.

'A friend.'

'That remains to be discovered.'

'From Norham.'

He heard the door unlatch and it creaked a little way, so he pushed and ducked inside to a room glowed with tallow; he smelled the pungent reek of it and was looking round when he felt the hard stab of something in his side.

'I sent word an hour since that I needed no guide from Norham,' the voice said, 'so you have be thinking of how to answer that – you have as long as it takes for you to detach from the wheen of weapons I can see and those I cannot.'

There was something about the voice. There was something about the glitter of the cote hung carefully on the back of the only fine chair in the Howff and Batty came to it almost at the same moment as he saw the fancy heraldry and the motto.

'Diligent and secret,' he said and turned into the fleshed, wary face he had last seen muddied and bloodied and pale with fear, huddled on Ancrum Moor. 'By Christ's Bones,' he said, feeling like a falling man waking up.

'Harry Ree, the wee herald from Berwick.'

Chapter Sixteen

'Harry Ree.'

'So you keep saying. It is a good name and needs no
whetting to a nub with your tongue.'

Henry Rae, Berwick Pursuivant of Arms in Ordinary
did not look like someone who should be scowling at a
man freshly unloaded of fearsome ironmongery which still
lay too close.

He was short and slight and paunched a little, his head
drooped like a Spring daffodil and the entire appearance
was of a pox doctor's clerk. He wore a fine lawn shirt and
heavy leather riding breeches as if he had stolen them from
his too-large da.

Yet here was a man who carried secrets between
courts. Two years earlier, he had left Edinburgh with
the Somerset Herald, Thomas Trahern and the Dingwall
Pursuivant, Davey Lindsay. Two miles from Dunbar, two
dafties still clinging to the Pilgrimage of Grace shot down
Trahern; the other two had a wild ride to escape.

So there was iron in the man, though it had to be said,
Batty thought as he caught sight of himself in a water-
waver of mirror-glass, that he was not himself entirely the
image of a fierce Borderer.

The food had arrived and now his beard was crumbed
and drooped with wet from the jack of ale. He was damp

and Stucley Taylor's doublet had never been clean to start with, nor fitted well; it fitted less now.

'What want you here?' demanded Rae. 'I remembrance that you were the boasted architect of English ruin at Ancrum, so you are on the wrong side of the divide. You had one arm before, so the one you have is a fakery – I can see straw at the cuff – and I am thinking there is espiery here, probably directed at Norham and its new defences. Get you gone back across the Tweed man; I will stay silent, since I owe you some small debt for Ancrum.'

'Some small debt, is it?' Batty said, wiping his greased fingers down the doublet and frowning at the added ruin. 'Man – you were up to your hurdies in mud and tremble and they lads around you were fired for more of the horrors they had already visited.'

It was a lie, of course; anyone of the College of Arms was safe enough if recognised as such. Save for dafties and the sort of stray shot God reserved for vicious humour, Batty added to himself.

But he swallowed the last of the drink and looked ruefully into the leather mug. 'I need your help,' he said, when it became clear that Henry Rae was not about to unveil a decent bottle and offer some up.

'In what? If you need across the Tweed, I suggest you ride hard at first light.'

Batty shook his head. 'I need to see Bull Dacre.'

There was a moment when Rae opened and closed his mouth; Batty had seen the look before, on a salmon he had guddled out of a pool one time.

'I... you,' Rae began, then stopped spluttering and gathered a breath. 'You want into Norham is the truth – I am as likely to escort you as I am to wed you.'

'I ask for *a* hand, not *the* hand. There are matters the Baron needs to know,' Batty went on, 'which touch upon his rights to the Warden of the Marches.'

Rae looked and frowned. His face had a suspicious brow on it now and Batty knew what he would ask next. He took a breath.

'There is a man called Horner, a greedy man,' he began and then laid the whole tale of it, talking low and fast and stopping only when Rae demanded answer to a question; they were good, sharp questions, too and Batty was surprised and admiring of the man's acumen and then wondered why he should be – here was someone who negotiated the reefs of Courts which made a Border ride on a moonlit night resemble a wee *pavane*. Who was an agent in the pay of Ralph Sadler, ambassador to Scotland and spymaster to Fat Henry.

'You have proof of this nun's Glastonbury pie?' he demanded at the end of it and Batty grinned a savage and bitter grin. Aye, aye, there's the way of it. I can show Bull Dacre that his wayward bastard brother is putting the Name at risk, that Musgrave and Maramaldo and the Wallis Riders are all spoiling the country and looking for a fight with someone and that wee innocents are at risk of death. I can even wave the Musgrave name at him, one that he hates above all.

But it comes to the shine in the end. He said as much and Rae shrugged.

'The Bull Dacre is a Border man.'

It was all he needed to say and Batty acknowledged that with a flap of a hand; Dacre knew the ways of blackmeal and righteous confiscations. He showed the contents of the leather case.

Rae flicked through them, lips pursed then thought about it for a long minute, pacing a little. At one point he put the muzzle of his pistol to his head and scratched before he became aware of what he was doing and hastily set the engine down on a table.

'I will help you,' he said slowly. 'If only to stop Mad Jack and the Wallis having at yin anither – that greed of Lanercost for Wallis lands is at the root of this. Also, I owe you a debt for my freedom. Lastly because I am a loyal servant of His Majesty who will only see rebellion in it and call out the whole of the north. It will spoil many plans already in train.'

France being the biggest one, Batty thought. Yet, there was also Maramaldo, who had given him a constraint of time, otherwise Sister Faith and the rest would suffer his wrath.

Rae nodded when Batty spilled this out and then wagged a stern finger.

'Dinna fash Dacre with that,' he warned. 'Saving a parcel of wee Catholics getting hung or flayed or burned is a danger to him with the views he holds. These are less Reformed lands up here, but the Baron Gilsland is known to favour a Latin Mass.'

'I gave my word,' Batty said and Rae sighed.

'Aye, I heard you are soft on wee wummin – was it not one who got you in that morass at Hollows? Away wi' you. I take it you have a place downstairs, so go to it. I dinna want you snoring near me at any time, but we will look thief-thick if we do it here. Word may get out that I am conspiring with a known Scotch agent.'

'Agent is it?' Batty said, nonplussed by being flung out. 'There's fancy for you.'

He tramped down the stairs and found a place as near to the fire as he could get without irritating packmen. He sat on the bench he would sleep on once he had rolled a packman off it and thought on matters and how God seemed, this time at least, to be smiling.

Thought, too, on Merrilee Meg and her magickals which had brought him here – if they were magickals. He shivered a little and made a warding sign older than the Cross.

No one noticed; they were all snoring or drooling, or whimpering like pups so that the thunderous hammering on the door sprang them all awake.

The innkeeper had put a quine across the barred door to prevent folk leaving without paying; she was a plump woman, either daughter, doxy or wife, who slept on a pallet bolstered against draughts and now rolled away, scrambling to her hands and knees and keening with shock.

The packmen woke in panic; there were more thunderous hammers, enough to rattle the bar in the locks and the innkeeper appeared, tousled and annoyed, with a big blackthorn cudgel in one hand.

'We are shut – wha's that there?'

'A giant, a dwarf, a warrior and a witch,' said a voice and Batty's head came up because he knew it.

'Awa' wi' ye,' the innkeeper growled. 'Japes is it? I will set the dugs oan ye.'

'It's a foul night,' Batty said into the whimpers and panting. 'You have not the custom to be turning payers away. Nor the dugs, I might add.'

'Is Batty Coalhouse there?' demanded the muffled, sweet voice. 'He kens us.'

An apparition appeared on the stairs and Batty almost laughed aloud; Henry Rae had had no time for breeks, but had pulled on his cote, which was as good as armour. He stood, truculent as a routed boar with his pale shanks sticking out below his shirt and the richly embroidered cote; one hand held a long basket-hilted backsword, forty inches of bright steel.

'Whit's a' this?'

There was another thundering hammer and Henry Rae waved at the innkeep.

'Let them in, man, else we will get little sleep this night.'

The innkeep looked at Henry Rae and his sword, then at Batty, who had taken his axe-handled dagg and laid the fearsome-looking weapon on the bench top. Then he nodded to the luckless woman who had to creep back to the door and lift the bar. As soon as she did, she dropped it to clatter on the floor and scurried away screaming.

Everyone waited, breath bated. The door swung inwards and in strode… a giant, a dwarf, a warrior and a witch.

'How now, Batty?' said the witch and shook free her red hair; the rain from her hood sparkled like diamonds in it. Behind her, Abie stood dripping and the Ape, mercifully clothed against the weather, made sure Abie was between him and harm.

'Whit the Devil…?' demanded the innkeeper and Henry Rae balked on the stairwell, the sword up. Merillee Meg looked him up and down, cocked a brow and laughed; Rae blushed to the roots of his sparse hair and tried to pull his shirt down further on his thighs.

'I see a giant, a dwarf and a witch,' Batty said with a wry chuckle. 'I see nae warrior, all the same.'

Meg grunted and came forward; the packmen all shrank back. 'That was maybe a Faerie's tale,' she growled. 'Warrior is a stretch for him now – but he's the reason we are come.'

She stood back and Abie moved to one side. The man hidden behind him swayed a little, then stumbled two steps forward, shrouded in a wet, hooded cloak. One hand, ragged lace at the cuff, reached up and brought his face out. Batty stared.

'Indeed,' Maramaldo declared. 'It is I.'

Then he bowed, though it nearly tipped him forward to the floor.

'Captain General Maramaldo, at your service – is that drink I see?'

'Captain General of bugger all,' Meg added with a trill of laughter. 'They have thrown him out on his ear. The King told Abie and the Ape to bring him to you if only before he swallows every last drop of decent drink. We met on the road – Michael and Baptiste keep watch.'

Batty's head roared with the bad cess of it. Maramaldo staggered to the bench and sat, then reached a hand for Batty's little bowl, still with drink in it.

'I widnae,' Batty managed and Maramado frowned.

'How else am I to drink it, man?'

Batty fought for sense and found just enough to lean forward and take Maramaldo by the front of his stained torn shirt. The act of pulling brought the stale of the man out in a puff that stung Batty's eyes. Maramaldo blinked from his wobbling head and then gave a lopsided grin.

'Batty,' he said, then frowned. 'Ye have grown a miracle of arm – does this mean I am forgave for it by God? Yon wee nun said it might happen...'

'The nuns,' Batty growled, shaking him like a terrier with a rat. 'What of the wee nuns?'

–

Sister Charity wore hodden grey and had changed into it by bartering the finery Maramaldo had given to her with a slattern from the camp. It was verminous and stained – she had an idea what some of them were but did not care; it was closer to the nun than she had been for some time. Now that Maramaldo had gone, she dared it and did not think the new commander would care.

She feared him all the same and knew she could not hide forever, sitting side by side with Sister Faith in the dark dim of the charred bastel house, her eyes lifting from the dark shadows now and then to concentrate on the square of light from the doorway.

'I pray he is all right,' Sister Faith said in a low voice, for others were in the undercroft dim, snoring or muttering quietly to each other. Probably as afeared as us, she thought, at the turn of events.

'I ken how much you believed in him,' Sister Charity said softly. 'I am not hourly expecting his return – he is a man for the practical is Master Coalhouse.'

There was no victory in her voice, but Sister Faith reached out and took her hand, which made Sister Charity start to tremble; her skin was cold, even allowing for the poor pit fire and the weather.

They sat for a moment in silence; outside were shouts and strange noises that might have been chains or shackles or the accoutrements of carts.

'I wonder what it is like to die the way our Sisters did,' Sister Charity said staring off into the embers of the pit fire. 'Why would Our Lord allow them to die like that?'

Sister Faith squeezed her hand a little tighter, knowing Sister Charity was birling with confusion, as much at events as at having been plucked from her nun's habit by Maramaldo. Now the man was gone, probably dead.

'The only difference between saints and ourselves,' she said, half to herself, 'is that saints have relived the suffering and passion of Christ. Used it as a guide on how to die in agony, even that they might live.'

She felt Sister Charity nod.

'The Lord will help us,' she went on, 'if not through Master Coalhouse who is yet with us, I believe, then in letting us accept the pain and welcoming us into glory when the time comes.'

She felt Sister Charity move closer and reached out; they hugged and pulled apart; Sister Faith saw tears in her friend's eyes.

'I still believe in Batty Coalhouse,' she said. 'He was sent to save the children and us and save them he will.'

Sister Charity glanced to the sleeping forms and dashed a tear away. 'He will have some trouble with Daniel,' she said and Sister Faith was forced to agree; Daniel had a pearl drop in one fresh-blooded ear and was swaggering with a gifted dagger in his belt, the new darling of the roughs who had helped string up Sabin's conspirators – and then flayed the Captains who ordered it.

She sat and listened to the moaning of Horner, prised free of Maramaldo's chair, his hands swaddled in fat wrappings that still leaked watery blood. She tried hard to find Christian sympathy and felt herself so lacking in it for the man that she concentrated on spooning pap into the baby and tried to pray for forgiveness. But it was all about Batty.

'Was I wrong about him, Lord? Was he not from You?'

There was a burst of wild shouting and cackled laughter from outside and the thought came to her that perhaps she had been so wrong, so seduced, that he was the Antichrist come to weaken their faith in this, their hour of need and testing.

The possibility of that was numbing and stoppered the prayer in her mouth with thoughts of how, all her life, she had fought her own nature, the headstrong, headlong gallop of her will and tried to humble herself before God.

Had she failed the Lord at this, the end? Had the Prince of Darkness preyed on her frailities and vanities and love for the children to drive a dagger wedge between her and God?

Would Satan come at the last to offer salvation at a price – and would she take it?

The light from the door vanished.

–

The light in the room was poor, served up by a guttering crusie that reeked. It was the best room in the castle, which had never been much more than a grim fortress at its best. Its best had been ruined out of it by the Scots thirty-and-some years ago and, though recovered after Flodden, the place had stayed grim and cold as a whore's heart.

The room had no wood-panelled comfort and was warmed by a mean affair of sticks – but there was some excuse for that, it being an hour before dawn. Still, it did not make improvements to the mood of Sir William Dacre, Baron Gilsland and, even if the castle was not his and he was a guest, he had cause for complaints.

The witch, the giant and the dwarf had taken their leave after an hour's warmth – neither the Howff nor the environs of Norham suited them. They also, as Maramaldo said often, had taken his fine horse and left him a spavined nag.

'You drank the weight of that beast,' Meg replied sourly. 'You get nothing for free with the King.'

'I asked for nothing at all,' Maramaldo replied owlishly and Meg had laughed.

'Away, man – you were wandering in circles, drookit and afraid. You would have died.'

Batty knew they were fortunate to be in Norham at all and only thanks to Henry Rae. He and Maramaldo were now considered under a black gaze and it was a wonder Dacre had stayed silent for long enough for them to spill the sorry tale out.

'I know you both by reputation and description,' Dacre said eventually. 'As bad a brace of lawless ne'erdowells as any I have hemped as Warden.'

'That was a time since,' Maramaldo said mildly, 'for you have not been Warden or anything like for a period. Is that drink there?'

'You will not wash away Sabin with it,' Batty growled and Maramaldo spread his hands, scowling.

'That bastard moudiewart,' he said and then seemed to grow fascinated by his knobbly fingers. 'Once I could bring down a bird at twenty paces with a bow. Now I can scarce see twenty paces on a fine day.'

He stopped and looked wet-eyed misery at them all. 'I have had many betrayals and picked myself up from them all – but that is the worst one, the betrayal by your own trusted men.'

'Aye,' Batty agreed morosely, 'if ye live long enow, you see everything fall to ruin.'

'Like a stone tower and powder mill in the Debatable,' Dacre growled. He was wrapped in a great affair of fur collar and wool, a man whose forty-plus years had sailed after one another and made a landfall on his face, where they colonised chins. He had a florid nightcap under which the remains of his hair clung desperately to a scalp.

'I widnae have thought you cared much,' Batty replied levelly, 'considering it was Armstrongs and the ones from Hollows. I remembrance a Dacre kin of yours burned out the timber version of yon tower a few years back.'

Dacre had the grace to acknowledge it, but with a dismissive wave of one hand.

'This is fascinating,' Henry Rae declared firmly, 'but scarcely moot. My lord Dacre – I have confidence in the tale Captain General Maramaldo and Batty Coalhouse bring and so you must. Jack Musgrave has stirred up a slorach of bad cess out there on the Border and your name is being dragged into the mire of it since folk know Mad Jack as the Bastard's Buzzard.'

Dacre hunched himself a little, bringing the fur collar up round his ears. 'What my bastard brother at Lanercost does is neither here nor there to me.'

'Not true,' Rae persisted, 'with respect. Besides – your bastard brother may have no hand in it, but he is bound by reputation to the Musgrave running riot with fire and sword. Folk will talk. They will talk all the way back to the ears of the King and one of the words that will be said will be "rebellion".'

He lowered his voice a little. 'There is Catholic in it, too.'

Dacre winced. Aye, there it is, Batty thought. Henry Rae was coming here with folded, sealed packets, no doubt plans and plots about getting a Wardenship again.

That will float off into the mists and a Musgrave would be the cause of it – twenty years before, a Musgrave had born witness to 'cross-border transgressions' that put Dacre in the Tower and a trial in Westminster Hall.

He got off with that, Batty remembered, but the name Musgrave must itch him. As must the fact that his base-born brother is staunchly Catholic when the rest of his family is not.

The kinch of it, though, Batty thought, will be an armful of persuasions…

'I am to be persuaded by a murderous burner of cruck houses and an auld *ingeniateur* who ruined our forces at Ancrum Moor?'

'God moves in mysterious ways,' Henry Rae intoned piously. Maramaldo laughed but there was too much rheum in it and he fell to coughing.

'A Levantine houri with seven veils is mysterious, sirs,' he managed at last. 'God simply seems… mad as a stone-sinking cat.'

'Less of your blasphemies,' Dacre snapped, then slapped the table loudly enough for them all to wince. 'Andra. Andra – get in here.'

Andra appeared, a worn-thin man needing more sleep.

'Take this one to Soor-Faced Tam,' Dacre ordered, indicating Maramaldo. 'Tell him to accommodate the Captain General here in the Upper Ward, with all comfort, but that he is not to go anywhere.'

Maramaldo straightened a little and offered a little neck bow, managing to make it dignified for all that his hair was a plastered memory of greatness, his finery stained and torn and a chancre on his lip wept as much as his liquid eyes.

'I have been here before,' he said, 'and each time I ask myself "how did it go so wrong?" So many disappointments, so many opportunities, so much hard work, all squandered.'

'Save it for the hemping,' Dacre growled. 'Broomhoose will gie you that on its own.'

'To be fair,' Batty said softly, 'that wisnae him, it was his treacherer lieutenant, Sabin.'

'Now commander of the Company of the Sable Rose,' Maramaldo added bitterly.

'How did that happen exactly?' Dacre asked, ignoring Andra's impatient foot-hopping. Maramaldo sighed.

'Musgrave came. He was the one who issued the contract, after all, so he came and spread vicious rumours about what was negotiated. The sums involved were… at variance.'

'You lied to your men about what was being paid out?' Dacre interrupted incredulously and Maramaldo spread his hands.

'Expenses. Overheads. The differences between florins, guilders and thalars, kreuzers, groschen – and what the fuck are testoons in the name of God?'

'A coinage as debased as the man whose head is on it,' Batty growled and Dacre wagged a finger at him.

'Have regard for your lip,' he answered sharply, 'else you will find it drooping on a hemp loop.'

Then he turned back to Maramaldo and shook his head with with amusement.

'Aye, doing them out of coin would dae it. Men who fight for money need salted with the full price.'

That and Maramaldo's illness would do it. That and the vicious he expelled to show he was still a power – the captains of his Company ill-used and dangling.

Maramaldo's worst betrayal, Batty thought, was to betray what he knew of the governance of a mercenary band.

Dacre indicated Andra should take the man away. Batty watched Maramaldo shuffle out of the door and could not equate the walking corpse of him with the monstrous chimera he had pursued most of his life.

Then Maramaldo stopped and turned back, his face a rank pool of strange misery and loathing. 'She is in my head, Balthie.'

Charity or Faith. Aye, Batty thought as Andra huckled the man away, either of them will do that – and for a man so steeped in sin any drop of purity polluting his black cess would ravage him. Or mayhap it was the pox crawling through his brain.

Henry Rae was frowning. 'He came under my protection.'

'Protected they are,' Dacre declared grimly. 'Nae harm will come to them until the trial.'

'Them?' Batty demanded. 'You include me in this?'

'Ye are a Scotch gunner caught fairly on the wrong side of the divide,' Dacre declared. Batty made a sound that made Dacre's eyes narrow.

'Ye growl at me, sir?'

'I came in the hope of saving your good name – and the nuns still held by a band of mercenaries now controlled by a savage hand.'

'Musgrave will not slay nuns,' Dacre muttered.

'Musgrave is called Mad Jack for a reason,' Batty spat back. 'He has already had his own sister slain and she was the nun I was supposedly sent to save – did you listen to any of this tale?'

Dacre's face darkened and Henry Rae was swift to step in to the coiling tension.

'Maramaldo is one who will not be missed in this enterprise,' he said, 'but Master Coalhouse is another matter. He has secrets which will assist me if I am to deliver your writ to cease and desist to Musgrave.'

Dacre hitched his collared gown a little. 'The only secret I see about him is how he grew a new arm – I had been told he was single winged.'

Henry Rae looked expectantly at Batty, who grinned at them both with a cemetery of teeth.

'Help me out of this confection,' he said.

Chapter Seventeen

The Cheviots, not long after

Fat grey-bellies sagged in a dull sky and spat rain that was danced across clinging grass. A lone pie started from cover and whirred away. No sign of a mate, Batty said eyeing the bird morosely, which is a bad cess. How be, Captain General – how's the wife?

He growled the old spell against the curse of magpie, feeling as peevish as the rain and fretted about the nuns; he wanted the business done with and was aware that this was the hardest part of it – sticking his neb back into the man-trap round Twa Corbies.

'A man should avoid three things,' Henry Rae had advised. 'War, women and witchcraft – you have courted all of them out in the Cheviots Master Coalhouse.'

Batty needed no telling on it and said that much, too, tugging at the doublet which he now thought was sent from the Earl of Hell to torment him. The sleeve was empty and fastened to his chest by a bone pin borrowed from Norham – all the contents of it, nine neat scrolls worth a king's ransom, had been passed to Dacre who had read and stared and read and stared until Batty thought the man would stay pop-eyed forever.

Instead, he had called for ink and quill and parchment and given Henry Rae the writ to stay the hand of his bastard brother and the Buzzard of Bewcastle. He had not, however, had the grace to present Batty with a replacement jack and so he had been left with the doublet, tight to start with and not helped by what he still had stuffed inside it – a wee rickle of wool and needle as well as the bowl and its snug of pottery vials.

Henry Rae was unimpressed by Batty's mood. 'Wind your neck in. Remember what good friends we should all be today – Musgrave will not be best pleased at the writ I carry from Bull Dacre and the ones he has dragged into this affair on the promise of advancement or riches that will not now materialise will be well facered.'

'Sabin is the yin to watch,' Batty said and Henry nodded.

'Which is why we go to Twa Corbies. Musgrave and his rickle of men will be there, but Sabin and the Sable Rose will be yet around Windylaws. He'll have to make sure of those men before he moves – but if he has any sense, he has guns and nuns both, so that Musgrave will have to honour his contract to the full.'

'Sabin hates you more even than he hates Maramaldo and that's saying a wheen,' Henry Rae went on. 'None of them will pick a fight with me – but you are the notorious Batty Coalhouse, who cut the left arms off a slew of Armstrongs, blew up the tower in Hollows and a powder mill with it and who ruined English hopes and lives at Ancrum. None in this place will have any good humour towards you.'

'I am not planning to invite them to a roast goose dinner,' Batty answered sullenly.

'I am not asking you to like them, just keep from annoying them.'

Henry Rae shifted in the saddle; his arse swellings were bothering him and he hated the wet, hated the chafing and, above all, hated the place he was going to – all such camps were thick with swirling diseases, from the Death to the Sweats and everything in between.

As if all that was not purgatory, he had Batty Coalhouse, with his beak nose and his bearded chin rising to meet it, fat-bellied, one-armed, dressed like a ravaged papingo and dangerous as a canker. There are people, he thought, who are born to rub others up the wrong way; Batty Coalhouse was born to rub the whole world up the wrong way.

They came up over the lip of another rise of Cheviot, expecting yet more of the same – a treeless sea of sere grass rolling in breakers to a pewter horizon. Instead, Batty reined in and squinted at the funeral-feather of smoke. He needed to say nothing to Henry Rae, who knew well enough what it meant.

'Whose hand did that?' he asked and Batty peered, rising up a little in the stirrups; Fiskie blew out distaste from his nostrils as a waft of char tendrilled round them. Then Batty lowered himself slowly down.

'Lobsters,' he said and tried not to let the relief show that it wasn't the whore-dressed killers of the Sable Rose.

'King's Men?' Rae demanded. 'Are you certain?'

Certain enough to ride on, Batty thought – then thought better of it and slowed so that Henry Rae could take the lead and wave his fancy Berwick Pursuivant coat at them.

It was a wee cruck house with a muddy garth and a feed-store whose thatch smouldered. There was blood in the garth, churned up to a froth by running feet. There was blood on the broken cart and on the bodies coiled round their wounds.

Heads looked up and hands went for weapons; they were all in the new-style red that seemed to be replacing white as the preferred colour of Trained Bands. These were not from London, all the same, but looked the part, with metal helms and pikes and longbows.

They had started that way at least, but now were festooned with dead poultry and the plunder stripped from the place. A packman's beast lay dead, all four hooves sticking up like Northumberland pipes; the owner was simply a pair of feet poking from under it and the commander of this troop – or so Batty presumed because he had a horse – had a bolt of blue perse slung over his shoulder and a list in the saddle. He looked them over owlishly, belched, then had the grace to look embarrassed when he spotted Henry Rae's herald coat.

Rae went to him and Batty heard him speak, soft and firm while the other nodded and let the perse slip from his shoulder to the bow of his saddle, hoping no one had seen it.

Twenty men, Batty thought, counting them. None of them looked ashamed and were happily plootering through the scattered debris of someone else's lives; Batty saw the ravens circle the smoke. It is always ravens, he thought. Them and the pies, that ill-omened bird marked by its failure to weep for Christ on the Cross.

He saw the sheepfold and the tree and the slow, sick realisation curdled in him that he knew the place, had lain in that cruck house while Trottie moved round him and John Wallis spoke. Had been dunted to oblivion by Mickle Jock under that tree – he wondered what had become of the ram and feared the worst.

He urged his horse a little way towards the bodies, whose feet alone were revealed, blue-white and marbling. They were bare and not an old woman. A man, then, maybe one of the Wallis chiels set to watch and guard.

A red coat burst from behind the cruck, chasing a chicken with whoops of merriment and no skill; others laughed and a cloud of memories rose up like fallen leaves, whirling Batty into their midst for a dance he did not want.

'Are you all there, Master Coalhouse?'

Henry Rae's voice came with a solicitous face, though there was an irritated cast to it. A man who disnae care to be ignored, Batty thought, shaking the last of old memories from him.

'This is Ventenar Jonas Appleby,' Rae went on, indicating the mounted soldier, who nodded and smiled slackly. 'His men are at our disposal and will escort us to Twa Corbies. It seems Musgrave is not there, but others he has dragged in are and the man himself is hourly expected back.'

'He'll be at Windylaws,' Batty answered, working it out, 'trying to get Sabin to shift his engines to where they can knock the stones out of Twa Corbies.'

'Heaven forfend,' Rae declared. 'I suggest we get there before that happens.'

Batty did not think it would ever happen. The weather that had sluiced the war between Wallis and the Sable Rose, had softened the ground too much to move heavy engines and Batty had seen the powder for them reduced to slurry.

He smiled at the thought. At least that place is secure. All I need now is to have the nuns and bairns safe and my task is done. The idea warmed him, a feeling so strange that he almost laughed. He felt good, his bones didn't ache as much and he put that down to his own resilience. His wounded leg no longer pained him either and he put that down to God or the Devil, since three women had worked on it and two were Satan's own, while Sister Faith was firmly on the side of the Lord.

Henry Rae saw what appeared to be the astonishment of a smile on Batty's cragged face and almost fell off his horse. He was doubly facered when he heard the man intoning.

> *Na! tho' I gang thro' the dead-mirk-dail; e'en*
> *thar, sal I dread nae skaithin.*

--

The good feeling lasted until Sext, which is when the Wallis men fell on them. Batty had been half-ready for it, fretted with that old feeling that had crept on him at puberty and never left. When the itch and scratch of it finally erupted from the head of a beck his hand was already hauling out the dagg from its horse-holster.

Appleby was no fool, but the scouts he had out were archers on foot – the only horses belonged to himself, Rae and Batty – so they had little time to react before the mounted prickers came bursting up over the rise and descended on them, howling 'Tarset and Tyne' and a clamour of grayne Names.

Appleby was bawling out for his men to form, halberds up to allow the archers to nock and draw. The Border horsemen knew the trick of it and relied on speed and shock to shatter that idea, so that the one who rode down on Batty had his latchbow in one hand, lance in the other and reins in his snarling yellow-toothed mouth.

Batty did not wait; Fiskie was starting in to dance, so he prayed for dry powder and a working pyrite and triggered the engine. The wheel spun, the pan flashed and the affair went off with its usual fearsome noise and kick; there was flame and a great deal of smoke.

The man vanished out of the saddle and his horse veered off, squealing at the noise. Fiskie, well used to it, stood his ground – good for you, auld freen, Batty thought and had no time for more; a second rider was closing out of the white smoke of the pistol, this one with a basket-hilt and a good three feet of steel whose edges were the only bright part of it.

He cut, Batty ducked it – the horses slammed together and Fiskie grunted and went sideways, tangled his feet and fell. Batty felt him go and kicked free from the stirrups, then hurled himself away so he would not be trapped.

There was a thumping whirl of muddy bracken and sky then Batty was on his hands and knees, whooping in fresh wind. He still had the axe head dagg and saw the rider, savage with triumph, kicking his mount closer and leaning down a little to get a good cut.

Batty flipped the dagg, dodged the blow and slashed ruin into the horse's muzzle with the axe head; it shrieked and leaped away, trailing blood from its open mouth while the man, off balance, gave a hoarse cry and fell, rolling to Batty's feet.

He had no chance, scarcely even time to throw up a useless warding arm before Batty rained blows on him in a frenzy of fear. When he came to his sense again, he was sitting on the wet grass with a fistful of clotted gore, staring at the ruin of the man's face. His ma would not know him, Batty thought and then glanced at the hand clutching the muddy grass so hard it had squeezed between the knuckles. One finger was missing, an older wound but still raw. But I ken him, Batty thought. Chilman. Ah Christ... I took his finger, now I have taken his very face and his life.

He heard Fiskie whicker and turned to see the horse on its feet, trembling slightly but standing patient as a dog. There were shouts, but fading and he heard the thrum and wheep of arrows; the Wallis Riders wouldn't stand for that and were off, shooting wee latchbow bolts back as they went.

'Are ye hurt?' demanded Rae, riding up; his blade was bloody but his face was grim. Good for you, wee herald, Batty thought, levering himself to his feet.

'Were they them money-fighters from the Germanies?' demanded Appleby, red-faced and wild-eyed.

'Wallis men,' Batty declared and Rae agreed. Batty indicated the bloody fretwork of face.

'This yin is called Chilman,' he said dully. Rae did not ask how he knew, simply nodded. Appleby went off, calling for 'lists'.

Batty heaved himself back into the saddle and looked ruefully at the blood slathering his dagg; it would take a wheen of cleaning. It came to him, suddenly, that he was not bruised, or aching and that he had sprung free from Fiskie with an ease that had previously only been a memory. He felt a thrill of fear at that – the hand of God or Satan?

'War, wummin and witchcraft,' he muttered. 'Sooner I am done with them all the better.'

There was one dead from the Trained Band and three with wounds, all from pricker lances. Two of the attackers lay in the mud and the other, Batty saw, had been shot through the eye by a long arrow which had burst out the back of his skull.

'Leave them,' he advised Appleby. 'They will retrieve them for their families to kist up and mourn.'

They plodded on until Evensong carrying the dead and half-carrying the wounded as well as ducks and chickens and everything else they had plundered. Batty was aware of a dull ache in the stump of his arm that grew to a vicious nag and made him worry a little – but he put it to the back of the fire when Twa Corbies stuck defiantly up into the growing dark.

'Well, at least it is not reduced,' Henry Rae said with some relief, then squinted. 'Whit's that up there on the roof? Do they have some wee beast?'

Batty did not need to squint. Up there on the gabled slates, dancing between the merlons and hurling curses at the mushroom foulness of makeshift shelters and cookfires surrounding the tower, was Trottie. Batty almost laughed – then his eyes robbed him of humour.

'Aye, aye,' he said softly, 'we are graced.'

Rae followed the gaze and stiffened in the saddle when he caught side of a panoplied tent and the blanket-sized banner, a great red affair with three yellow scallop shells.

Dacre, Batty thought, but no Red Bull is displaying it, so it is not the man himself but his wee kin from Lanercost, come to witness the triumph of his suit against the Wallis.

This will make it interesting…

–

'What say you, Coalhouse?'

Batty blinked out of his sloe-eyed reverie to a tent fetid with leprous heat and old fears, at a table littered with

310

discarded war gear, wooden platters of half-eaten food, bread mouldering quietly and plans gone the same way. Not that much different from the one he'd left in his dreams – it was the stump, he thought, which had been banged hard in the fight and was aching.

'Utter folly. Ill-advised, ill-thought and ill-judged,' the voice said again and Batty focused on the speaker while sleep shredded away like blue reek. The man raised his head from the paper he was reading. 'My brother does not stint himself.'

Nor would he, Batty thought, for the writ Rae had handed the Dacre of Lanercost was full measure for the nine neat Rolls, each with a fortune in Glastonbury see lands. Some would have to find a way to Fat Henry, but enough remained to slake Bull Dacre's greed.

'Are you done with the sleeping?' demanded Cuthbert Ogle testily, then turned round all the others at the table. 'Why is this notorious brigand and Scotchman here at all?'

'Be quiet,' Dacre said softly and Batty heard Cuthbert's teeth click; the look he shot back was one of outrage and then barely-concealed annoyance that he was not to be supported. The boy Ogle already kens the dance of this, Batty thought.

'You have attempted to use these good people for your own ends,' Henry Rae said looking at Dacre of Lanercost and the good people stared at him, then one another and saw a way out. 'They are not yet so mired in it, though – your quarrel with the Wallis of Twa Corbies over their lands has dragged you here with a pretence of putting down a rebellion that did not exist until you made it.'

'God's Legs, herald, you go too far...'

Musgrave's face was a bag of blood. Next to him was an Oswin or another Cuthbert and on the other side sat

Luke Ogle, Captain of the Trained Band out of Berwick and the wee lord of Eglingham in his own right. Next to him sat a pallid, wasted-faced figure, his hands bound with fat wrappings and his eyes bruised – but Tom Horner, architect of the entire business, was thin-lipped silent and the reason for that was a manor Roll snugged up inside his doublet. He would stay silent, to his Commission and anyone else who asked how he came to have the mark of Christ's crucifixion on both palms. Mayhap they'll think it a wee miracle, Batty thought.

'I go as far as the Bull Dacre commands,' Henry Rae answered levelly. 'And he commands that you cease and desist and return you to tranquillity lest he has to make a report to Wharton and the King himself, whose ear he has.'

'Aye, aye,' Dacre of Lanercost agreed mildly. He was of ages and size with Musgrave, but his face was pinched and narrow. Too much fret, Batty thought, about being in the backyard of his legitimate brother and not having the station or coin to be much more than a wee lord.

'Is that what you have to say?' demanded Musgrave, rounding on Dacre. 'Aye aye? You set this this Ride out…'

'And now the Ride is done,' Dacre interrupted and Musgrave glowered. He kens the writing here, as do I and I cannae even read, Batty thought. But Musgrave is even lower in station than the Dacre of Lanercost and his stewardship of Bewcastle hangs on a shaky peg – he is only Deputy there, appointed by his da. And his da is the very Musgrave who had both the Dacres, father and bastard of Lanercost, thrown into the Tower and put to a treason trial.

They'd got off with it, but a dozen years had not mellowed their hate much.

'What has been promised here?' demanded Musgrave, eyes narrowing; Batty saw the Ogles and assorted relations shift surreptitiously away from him. Henry Rae's stare was glass and old ice.

'Whatever it was,' Batty said, his voice startling all the faces to stare at him, 'you are not included in it. That should tell you much.'

In fact, Dacre of Lanercost held another one of the parchment Rolls – Batty was sure it was not the best of the holdings, but it was enough to make him relinquish his wee war with John Wallis. Musgrave had been promised nothing and would have to thole it, but the way he looked made Batty think he had made an enemy there.

Hey-ho, he thought, let him join the throng…

The young Lord Ogle cleared his throat, which brought Musgrave's scowl round to scour him; the boy was blissed as a sleeping bairn under it, Batty saw.

'I know this much about fishing,' he said to Musgrave, smiling sweetly. 'I know when to drag in my line and go home from an empty pool.'

A few of his relations laughed softly and rose with him.

'So, my lords,' Henry Rae declared, gathering up his gloves. 'We are done with the business here.'

'I have my orders,' Luke Ogle said sullenly, 'to recover a brace of guns from Captain General Maramaldo.'

'Good luck with that,' Musgrave declared, ripping himself from the table in a fury. 'Maramaldo is no longer commander of anything, not even his own fate…'.

'You have the right of it there,' Batty said easily. 'His fate is in the hands of Dacre. God and the Bull knows what he is saying to forestall it. Nuns will be part of it.'

The Ogles hurried to gather up and leave, not wanting to hear anything they might have to ignore at their peril.

Musgrave went pale and blinked, but he was Border bred and came back from it, though he must have been seeing hemp and flames, Batty thought.

'You had a writ from me to save my sister,' he said, 'which you failed. That is the all of it.'

'I recall it. I recall also telling you your carrot was poor and your stick wormy and now both have broken,' Batty said and the ember in his voice made others draw back, as if he might combust on the spot.

'There are two other sisters you need to hand over to me,' he added and Musgrave's smile was vicious as wolves.

'Good luck with that,' he replied. 'You and Captain Ogle here have the same problem with recovery it appears. Ask the new Captain General of the Sable Rose.'

The tent emptied like a burst water barrel, a flood of wee desperate men heading for cover like disturbed crows. All except Luke Ogle and Henry Rae and Batty.

'It seems you have need, one for the other,' Henry Rae declared. 'As yon moudiewart Musgrave might say – good luck with that. My task is done here. I will ride to find John Wallis and appraise him of the situation – it would be an obligement on me if you would assure the occupants of Twa Corbies that they are now safe.'

'As safe as anyone in these lawless lands,' Batty agreed and Henry Rae shot him a sharp look.

'We part, all obligations discharged then,' he said and Batty saw that was important to the herald, so he inclined his head in agreement. Rae took a breath, blew it out, nodded to them both.

'Assure the safety of those inside Twa Corbies,' he said and left.

Ogle looked at Batty. 'Well – it seems we are left with the harrigles of this poor feast. Have you any suggestions as to how we might encompass our mutual desires?'

'Short of forming up and taking on a brace-hundred and more hardened fighters from the Germanies, you mean?' Batty said and Ogle blanched. Batty knew his own command was scarce a hundred and, red coats and Trained Band name apart, they had little resemblance to fighting men.

He felt crushed by it. All this from a rickle of nuns in an auld fortalice…

'Aye, well – thanks for your thoughts, empty though they are,' Ogle said bitterly.

'It appears to me,' Batty said, 'that John Wallis of Twa Corbies might be persuaded to help, if not out of gratitude for the ending of his feud with Bewcastle, but for something the Borders kens well enough.'

Luke Ogle's face was uncomprehending, so Batty told him what Henry Rae carried in his scrip – one more Roll that would sweeten the Wallis. No matter that it was for lands far to the south and never to be seen by Wallis – Henry Rae would help broker the sale of them, take his due and pass the bulk to John Wallis.

'Blackmeal,' Ogle said, sitting down and starting to see the possibility. Batty frowned as he hitched the uncomfortable doublet, rising wearily to his feet.

'The other matter that will bring him galloping here,' he said, 'lies in yon tower.'

'The mad old woman?'

Batty chuckled. 'In part – but the most of it is the boy she has been protecting, a lad with the worst name in the Border lands.'

Ogle blinked and then Batty told him why he had hopes for the aid of Wallis. Ogle's face grew bright with admiration.

'His son is in there? Ye can strop your wits sharp talking with you, Batty Coalhouse,' he said, then cocked his head to one side like a suspicious crow. 'What is in this for yersel'?'

Ever the Border lord, Batty thought and felt the crease and twist of the doublet.

'God be thankit if you have a front-buckle jack to spare I would consider it a blissing from Heaven itself.'

Ogle took a moment to realise the man was serious, then shook his head with mock amazement and agreed to it.

'You will need it,' he said, 'if you are to face the Wallis Cheviots. You might not even make it to where you can speak with the heidman himself.'

Batty leaned back. The ache was back in his knee, the stump throbbed, he had a touch of lime in one foot, felt like a Border pony that had been ridden hard and left wet and was more tired than he had ever been; he had never felt better about his life.

E'en sae, sal gude-guidin an' gude-gree gang wi'
me, ilk day o' my livin; an' evir mair syne, i' the
Lord's ain howff, at lang last, sal I mak bydan.

Chapter Eighteen

Windylaws, not long after

Woodsmoke swirled sullenly on the damp air like a mourn to the last rays of a dying sun. It had never been more than puling weak, but it had made an appearance like a Henry Rae for better weather, then sank gratefully below the horizon.

There was still rain on the wind and the grass under his belly was leaching chill wet into him, but the vantage was a good one and Batty would not move from it.

A man whistled his way from the horse lines, his mind empty of anything but broth and joining his gauded friends round the fires. There was good cheer and a tendril of music – Sabin must have paid them something, at least in part, Batty thought.

The camp was a leprous sprawl of mushroom tents and fires. It had been here too long and was already starting to stink; there would be sicknesses soon and folk would die.

But the ground was wet. Those big German wagons were heavy beasts, Batty thought and heavier still was the brace of guns. You couldn't move them without a decent road and this part of the Cheviot, even allowing for Windylaws, was a stranger to roads.

Batty looked at the buildings. The broken-toothed tower where he had galloped up to, following the trailing flames of a dead, burning nun. Where Sister Faith had told him he was chosen by God.

The bastel was still blind-egg empty and streaked with char. Maramaldo's big tent sat close to it and that, Batty was sure, now had Sabin squatting in it. The toad.

There was a lad at the broken door of the bastel, leaning on a pike and yawning-bored. There is no point to a guard if there is nothing to guard, Batty thought – so at least one nun remains.

He looked at the sky. It would be a long night and he had laid out the plan carefully – he would locate and petard the last of the powder for the guns. Then he would locate and free nuns and children. At dawn, regardless, the Trained Band would start in with noise and arrows and, when the Sable Rose spilled out to form up and laugh at them, the Wallis Riders would sweep down.

'Simple,' he had ended. John Wallis, one hand on the shoulder of his returned boy, Will, had nodded.

'You take much on yourself, Master Coalhouse. Why is that, I wonder?'

Trottie cackled and Batty eyed her sourly. God or the Devil, he thought, neither of them having much regard for my auld bones. He said nothing all the same and, in the morning, had ridden Fiskie out with a wave and a nod to Captain Ogle and trying to avoid the hard stares of folk he knew were Chilman's relations.

Join the bliddy throng, he thought savagely.

The wind shifted like a fine lady wafting through a hall; Batty tasted it like a horse, curling his top lip back from his yellowed teeth; the memories crowded on him.

—

You need to proof that against weather, Ned Yelland told Batty.
Else it will get iron rot and fall to ruin.

Batty, proud of his new burgonet, had listened carefully, as he
did to all the mysteries Ned Yelland passed on regarding engines
large and small.

Orkney Butter, Ned told him. A mix of oil of olives, wax
and sheep tallow. It stinks like a dead hoor's armpits, but if you
keep rubbing it into the metal regular like, it will keep the rain
off.

Then he laughed and added: 'keep everyone off.' And he
slapped the brown-black gleam of his big gun, beaming while
Bella stirred something over a fire and turned to him with a
smile that even managed to honey the putrid in the pot…

–

He tasted it now on the wind, a wee treacherer of Orkney
butter reek that let him know where the guns were laired.
All he had to do was get to them, find the powder store
and hope it was not too close – the guns were not to be
damaged – take the slow match he had made from under
his buttered burgonet, set it, fire it and hope the winking
red eye would not be noticed until it was too late, yet time
it perfectly for the rise of dawn.

After that, he would find a way to save the nuns and
bairns.

Ach, a wee stroll, he said grimly. And God or the Devil
is on my side, if you listen to wummin with witchcraft.

He waited, eyeing the wind on the moon, watching
the camp, hearing the murmur and remembering, with
an ache as sharp as the one in his stump, all the times he
had sat round that fire with men such as these, listening to
them talk. Of women and war and plunder. And women.
And food. And women.

These were not Landsknechts but tried to dress like them, the best of them doing it the way those big German fellows had fallen into – plundering the fallen and making the ill-fitting fit. They looked as if they dressed in gaudy rags and the nobility had aped them with stylishly tailored versions.

But these were not big Germans, whose day was passing anyway. These were *stradioti*, Albanians and Greeks, Saxons and French though they were steeped in sin and war, Batty thought. There were even men from the Italies – Maramaldo had liked to think himself a fine *condottiere*, but he was just an Italian bandit with aspirations to station. Batty wondered how the man fared, then wondered why he cared.

Sabin, on the other hand, was a blood-dyed belly-slitter with no aspirations to anything other than murder. I have, Batty admitted to himself, mayhap been blinded by my own arm into hunting the wrong man in the Sable Rose.

There was a moment when Batty knew it was time and he moved back to where Fiskie stood, patient in the dark. Batty patted him with soothings, collected what he needed and gave a last hitch to the new jack; it was not yet comfortable, but a balm after Stucley Taylor's ill-fitting doublet. Then he took a breath and moved, soft as Faerie.

All things that breathe must light on the world, must turn it, must slide, scart or scuff some trail, move mulched leaves with a wingbeat, drip sweat in dusty hollows, scar bark or just scour silence.

Batty had a lifetime of silent moving, a cold cunning that had kept him alive, a one-winged hawk in a land of two-winged buzzards. He moved like a whisper of breath, softly pounding heart and rushing blood.

He paused – no sign nor gesture, not in the wind like blood in the water to a shark. No ripple on his neck warned him and the grinding wheel of music and raucous song was a balm in the dark.

The ground trembled a little, a smell touched him – oxen, big beasts shifting with hunger for their forage was running out and they were being fed too little. Too little, Batty thought, to heave big engines over the sort of ground that sank under his boots.

He stopped and raised his head like a dog nosing air. Somewhere, now out of sight, was the bastel of Windy-laws and a nun and mayhap even bairns, waiting in the dark. If it was Sister Faith that well-named quine would be clinging still to her belief that he would come.

I am not bliddy Saint Michael with flaming sword, he thought bitterly. Yet, demanding and patient, he felt her waiting for his enlightenment.

–

The first thing Sister Faith registered was the heat. Wearily, she cracked her eyes open, lifting her head from where it had been lulling against her chest. Light flickered an open brazier on her left, dancing lurid shadows on the walls of a tent.

She was fastened to a chair and she was naked, which fact made her panic until she realised that it was simply a means to an end, to make her less of God's bride and more the whore who could be so treated.

There was a table, littered with maps and plans, old food and ugly weapons; the tent smelled of leather and grease, oil and wickedness.

Her breasts hung loose, a strange feeling and even here she thought to herself – not so withered for an old woman and then was ashamed of it. Her hair had grown out from under the removed kerchief and was sticking to her temples with sweat, even as she felt the cold ruck her to gooseflesh.

She worked at the fastenings, pulling as hard as she could until the skin of her wrists was raw-red and aching.

'They won't come loose,' said a voice and a shadow made a shape out of shadows. 'I had Cornelius incant them with fastening spells.'

Sabin was black in the black, his shirt dark, his fat breeks midnight and his pale face stamped with pits for eyes. The silvered streaks of his wings of hair seemed painted on and stirred in the heat of the brazier as he passed it.

In behind him was the hesitant lurk of Cornelius, betrayed by the arcane symbols of his stained, torn robes; his face was stretched with fear and Sister Faith's bowels twisted at the sight.

'Stout rope will do,' Sister Faith managed, realising that she had to step carefully here. 'But if the Lord wishes me free, I will be free.'

'I am lord here,' Sabin said, turning a chair backwards and mounting it as you would a horse. He leaned on the back and raised a hand, summoning Cornelius forward. The robed man did so, stumbling a little; his face was pinched with terror.

'There is a King in Heaven who would tell you differently,' she said.

'He is not here. Nor is Maramaldo, who was soft on your Spanish doxie. Maramaldo, I am thinking, is already swinging in the wind – he was the old way. I am the new.'

'New?'

She shifted, feeling the chair on her buttocks, feeling the heat down one side of her skin and the cold down the other. Watching Cornelius and the iron thrust into the brazier.

'There is nothing new here,' she said. 'Guns and larger engines. Fear. Hate. Pain. Why can't you people stick to hunting and cards?'

'Fine pursuits for fops in fancy doublets,' Sabin said. 'Maramaldo loved such things.'

'Love is not a word I would use in the same breath as Maramaldo,' she answered. 'He thinks of power and little else. You think of vengeance and little else. Even this, here, now, is no more than vengeance. Who did it to you, Sabin, that you hate so much?'

His eyes flickered a little. 'God, if I thought such existed.'

She eased her wrists from chafing, watched Cornelius, standing hunched round his own trembling fear. He had come back, she realised, because he had nowhere else to go.

'If you do not believe He exists, Master Sabin, why do you spend so much time fighting him? Do you think on your immortal soul? I believe Captain General Maramaldo did, seeing as how he was close to facing his Maker.'

'You should pray to your god,' Sabin said, standing up. 'And I am Captain General now.'

'God and I have an arrangement,' she answered. 'I put my trust in Him and he never fails me.'

The truth was that and sometimes less. She was not sure, sometimes, that God really cared and suffered agonies of remorse for thinking it. But He left folk to get on with it, to make a mess as they chose. Folk were good at that, so widows and bairns went hungry, ending their short, squalid lives in want and fear and pain.

'Your chest,' Sabin said, 'is very fine.'

For a moment, she wondered and felt herself blush at having done so. He meant the one with the accoutrements of Mass, of course and he smiled at her mistake, a twist that never went further north than his lip.

'It is richly made and Cornelius has been through it, in it, over it and broken it to pieces. There is no treasure,' he said.

'If you follow the Lord our God and Jesus, our Saviour,' Sister Faith said, trying to keep the tremble from her voice, 'then there are riches within.'

'Some baubles for canting priests out of Glastonbury. Not what was promised.'

'There is no other treasure,' she said wearily, knowing what would come. 'I am as naked as I can get. Where would I hide it?'

He laughed, soft and vicious. 'You think that is naked? I have guddled in cunny before this, woman and found coin and jewels. I have slit bellies and found wee fortunes. You are not nearly naked. Even flayed is not naked enough.'

She said nothing.

'What are they saying, Jew?' he demanded and Cornelius jerked at being addressed, as if he had been speared.

'The men say we should leave this place,' Cornelius answered waveringly.

'And what else?'

Cornelius fought for a moment until Sabin turned his head and then it seemed to Sister Faith that he was seared by the look, flinching away; she held her breath.

'They look for more coin, lord,' he said, near to weeping. 'All that was promised by Maramaldo from the *condotta*.'

Sabin nodded and turned back to Sister Faith.

'You see? Coin. You will tell me where it is. I am not foolish enough to believe that pain and suffering will be anything but martyrdom to you, woman. You are innocent but strong. There is another, even more innocent and not strong at all.'

He nodded to Cornelius, who whimpered a little and put a length of cold iron in the embered coals of the brazier, working it deep; the flames flared.

'While it turns white,' Sabin said, 'I will go and bring yon babe. Then you will tell me everything. If not, you can watch Cornelius at work. He is not a man for children, this *marano*.'

Sister Faith had confirmed what she already knew and tried not to rave as two men came in, took the chair and carted her out into the chill night, back to the dark char of the bastel house.

'There is no treasure. There is no treasure. Hail Mary, full of Grace...'

–

Good hempen cord, soaked in limewater and saltpetre for the nitre, washed in a lye of water and wood ash. The raw hemp burned with a lot of ash, so it had to be bucked – boiled. Bucked rope was boiled in ash to rid it of ash. You did not want ash when a slow match burned, for it could drop in the priming pan when you were aiming.

Always blow off your ash before opening the pan was good advice, Batty remembered. That and how even a bucked rope yields some ash. Tranquilo had taught him that, among other things.

A good slow match was laid flat all of a piece, for if you hung it up soaked the nitre collected at either end and got sucked out of the centre, so that all you got from that piece was a few seconds of dangerous flare and spit before it fizzled out.

No match with a slow match, that was Batty Coalhouse. Everyone said so, so it must be the truth – but, Christ's Wounds, it makes for a hard life, he thought. I am never done blowing matters up. On behalf of wummin. Wi' wee bairns involved. The sudden realisation of it, of the resemblance to Mintie and the wee Royal babe and the powder mill at Hollows made him pause.

Christ and all His Saints, he thought. I just wish I was the Archangel Michael, for a flaming sword would be of use now if only to light the slow matches when the time comes.

He worked by feel and the fleeting light of the moon when the wind on it blew clear and shining. Each time it did, old Tranquilo looked accusingly back at him, killed by Brother Curved and left with a smile beneath his lips. Batty had a Brotherhood of knives about him – there was Edge and Point, the three Throw brothers and Brother Curved, who was hungry for throats. And the cousin in his boot, Old Bollock.

Tranquilo had been named Zuann by his ma back in the Italies, but that had been a long time ago. He had been with Maramaldo and the others since the beginning. When Batty was young with both arms, it had been old Tranquilo who had taught him the ways of camp life and the slow match.

Age takes everyone differently, like knives. It sharpens some, blunts others, hardens them, to a point. But, in the end, it weakens and ruins and rots them with the fear, the knowledge that is always fear, of how they are birds forever flying south, or fish that are never done swimming upstream. An old money-soldier such as Tranquilo gains the knowledge that he will never be done with it, that there are no peaceful still pools or warm wind beneath his wings, or roosting tree at the end of a hard day.

Tranquilo had been put to the task of sleeping in the powder store because it was always dark and always cold and always lonely – who would risk light, or fire or even his person in such a place? You needed someone who would not be missed and that itself was a measure of how low you had sunk – and added to the fear.

Batty had known there would be one, but not that it would be Old Tranquilo. He had died swift and easy, like a blown-out wick. Mayhap it was for the best, Batty thought, before he was finally stripped of all he had been by the fear.

He worked, swift and assured until the thought struck him. He looked at Tranquilo's dead eyes.

If I was still with this company, he thought, I would be the new Tranquilo. He was frozen by it, fastened to the world as if nailed – then someone called for a new tune and the *vielle* ground out anew, snapping him back.

'I am not done yet,' he said fiercely, then snapped his lips shut on having said it aloud. It is those wummin, he added to himself, working faster now. War, wummin and witchcraft…

–

She knew Daniel looked at her, even though he tried to make out that he wasn't. In the dim of the bastel house, with the stale of the beasts and the old char wafting up from the undercroft, it wasn't hard to pretend, but he wasn't good at it.

The others didn't look, genuinely uncaring. The tall, lanky Spaniard they called Marillo had shot a few glances at Sister Charity, still in stained homespun and unfettered because they used her to fetch and carry. He might, once, have raped the nun who had been called La Tormenta before her cloistering, but everyone knew she was poxed.

The blond Portuguese albino they called Nevar and the Fleming known as Witt played endless cards and never shot Sister Charity a second glance. She was, she realised, not attractive yet. More drink would do it, but the real reason they hadn't already was Juup, their leader.

He sat fixing a leather strap by the wavering light of a poor crusie. Now and then he looked up as Daniel made an excuse to move, to get closer to her. The simple act of moving his head was enough; Sabin had decreed they kept away.

Daniel is lost to us, she thought. No, no – I must not believe that. God will find a way, despite him wearing the old finery of a dead man, a pearl drop in one new-blooded ear, a knife at his belt. Despite the way he growled and spat and laughed at the filthy jests the others trotted out – half the time it was to get Daniel to join in, for they knew the boy had never indulged in anything like they described.

Now and then Juup would root about in his beard or hair and come up with something which he cracked between the frayed nails of thumb and forefinger. Then he would grin.

'Louse,' he would say in his thick accent. 'Even Eden had problem of snake.'

And Daniel would dutifully laugh.

The other children huddled like mice round Sister Charity, clinging to her homespun and watching, big-eyed and afraid. They had been afraid for a long time – too long, Sister Charity thought.

She felt for them and started to weep, though she made no sign other than wet on her cheeks.

But Daniel saw it. And laughed.

–

Sister Faith wondered, dully, how long it took for an iron to grow white hot. She saw it in her head, a ball glowing balefully.

–

Batty watched the moon. He had the Nuremberg but even putting it right up to his nose he could only make out that the hour hand might have been at four or five. Anyway, he thought moodily, the bliddy thing is another wee alchemikal worn more for the look of it than the practical; they were expensive, too. King Johnnie the Wanne had given it as a gift, which should have been an expensive statement save that he took it from a box crammed with them.

Batty did not need it – no match with a slow match, that was the boast and the most of that was in timing, making and cutting it to burn to the last second. He glanced at Tranquilo, still accusing though his face was stiff and moon-blued, death-darkened. No one had even come to find out how the old lad was, stuffed into the powder store with the musty smell of it drying out.

It had been grained, but the wet had caked it again, for all they had spread it out. If it wasn't combed carefully it would sputter and fizz and not much more – but that was in the pan. In this confined space...

He waited, watching the moon get dressed and undressed by clouds. An owl shrieked and the *vielle* finally faltered, the *trompette* and *mouche* and *chanterelle* of it winding down, dying in the dark.

At some point Batty moved and could not tell why he was shoved into it. He slid silently out of the low powder store, following the thin white fade of his match back to where they met like mating snakes.

Crouching, he took a breath, for this was the Devil in the detail; his wheel-lock dagg felt right, all wound and primed and empty of ball. When he squeezed it to life, the great cartwheels of sparks made him almost shriek aloud with the blasting hole they made in the dark. A blind man could see it, he whimpered to himself. A bliddy blind man...

The match stayed stubbornly unlit, so he had to do it again, the rasp now as loud to him as the light. At the end of it, when his scarred eyes stopped blurring everything, he saw the match glow faintly on one side and, with more gasp than puff, he blew life into it. It winked conspiratorially back at him with its red eye and began to creep away.

I am never done with this, he said, remembering last year and the powder mill at Hollows – but, bigod, this will be the last time I creep about in the dark blowing petards.

He left the match to run and slithered away, out towards the silhouette of the old tower, the broken tooth of it stark against a lightening sky. Up there was Trumpet, probably still hanging off the top by his rope – he had deserved better. And inside was the old nun with the eyes as blue as a Virgin's robe. *Ah kin coup ma lundies.*

Somewhere, a baby wailed. On his other side, Batty heard the grunt-squeal of a couple in the final throes; when the light comes, he thought sadly, all these wee lives will be put to the hazard.

Including my own.

Chapter Nineteen

Her moved up to the big panoply, because he knew that was Maramaldo's – or Sabin's now. It was where the other Captains had lounged, playing cards or dice, listening to the plans for the next day.

There were other bits of canvas and hurdle dotted around, some pallid with wormy lights, scattering music and small voices, but Batty saw the dull red glow he knew to be the Big Tent's brazier and the shadow that seemed to flit back and forth.

He was sure he had seen Sabin scuttling off, hunched and almost running towards the bastel, but he could not be sure. So he ducked under the flap, Old Bollock in his one good hand; he wanted Sabin at the end of some sharp steel.

He had expected Captains, though he did not know who they might be after Sabin's purge. He expected the fusty smell of wet leather and food gone off and he wasn't' disappointed there. What he hadn't expected was a naked woman tied to a chair.

He hadn't expected it to be Sister Faith.

'Don't gawp,' she snapped. 'Cut me loose – and 'ware Cornelius.'

Batty swung round, dagger up but saw only a shadow, like a rat scrabbling in a grain store. He moved to Sister Faith and cut her free.

'Sabin has gone to the house to fetch Baby Stephen,' she said. 'He was about to let that little imp of Satan, may God forgive me, loose on him with a hot iron unless I told where the treasure was.'

She tried to stand, failed and sank back with a gasp. Batty, glowering with it all, moved to the table, put Old Bollock back in his boot and seized a corner of the damask table covering. He had seen a mountebank do this at a Truce Day meet, but then the cloth flew free and everything else stayed where it was.

When he did it, everything went in the air – plates, platters, plots and plans, whirling in a frantic dance. A blizzard of paper drifted in a snowstorm that made Cornelius look up and focus from his blind hunt for his book. He saw Batty and whimpered.

Sister Faith took the stained damask and wrapped her nakedness in it. 'Give me the ability to see good things in unexpected places and talents in surprising people,' she muttered hoarsely. 'Give me, O Lord, the grace to tell them so.'

'Aye, aye,' Batty echoed, feeling the itch on his palms, where he had rolled his fuses. 'Thank me later – but move quick for now. Hell is coming.'

He shoved her to the entrance, just as Cornelius found some courage – and remembrance of what was stuck in the brazier fire. He grabbed the black handle and gave a hoarse cry of triumph which brought Batty whirling round to face him.

What he saw was the mountebank magister screaming and dancing like he was moonstruck, sticking his scorched hand under his armpit; the white-hot iron sizzled on the plank floor, the deceptive black of the handle smouldering the wood.

Serve ye right, ye poor-tin Nostradamus, Batty thought triumphantly, then turned to where Sister Faith stood aghast, both hands clutching her damask tight round her.

He bundled her out of the panoply, felt the fuse burn down, heard the deep-throat crack and saw the bastel light up like a sick dawn. There was a moment, an eyeblink where he flung Sister Faith to the ground and fell on her, hearing the air oof out. He had time to wonder if she thought he had been overcome with lust after seeing her naked – then the huge roaring pressure crashed on them like a wave.

He was shifted by it, heard something slam into the bastel roof, scattering tiles. His ears buzzed and he knew it was the same for her; their mouths moved, wet and silent and he could not even hear his own voice let alone hers.

He forced himself upright, staggering, half-turned to see the panoply collapsed and on fire – yon wee brazier, he thought dully. In the middle of the flames something struggled in a shroud of burning canvas and he knew it was Cornelius. Magic yourself oot o' that, he thought viciously.

He heard her voice then, thin and far away and urgent. He stood for a moment, trying to understand, watching the tent burn, watching the rain of embers sift like falling stars. Stood in a blaze of burning, hearing the faint cries, the screams, growing louder, feeling the world turn under his feet, knowing what babies know when they wake crying in the night.

'God save us,' said a buzzed voice he knew as Sister Faith. 'What have you done?'

What I always do. Unleash Hell into the world with powder and slow match. He turned and looked at her

334

through smoke heavy with human fat, looking for God and seeing only her in her winding sheet, pale face horrified. I am forever blowing things up, he thought dully, then was pinked with anger at her.

'The Archangel Michael with flaming sword,' he said, hearing the words now as if from far off down a wynd. 'That's what you wanted, Sister. Beware of what you pray for.'

Behind her, he saw a figure lurch unsteadily out of the bastel doorway and now the screams and shrieks were everywhere. Batty and Juup saw each other at the same time and Juup got to his blade first, drew it, brandished it and roared a challenge.

Something dark slithered down the tiles of the roof, teetered on the edge and fell on him with a wet slap; Batty watched the dark descent of it, a boulder-sized chunk of what had been an ox, landing with an ugly sound. From under it's splayed back legs and spattered entrails, Juup's arm twitched once, twice and then was still.

Batty stared, vaguely aware of the noise behind him, including the blare of a trumpet. How low did you need to be in the estimation of God, he thought, to die ingloriously under the back-end of a deid ox?

'The children,' Sister Faith said, made the sign of the cross over Juup and tugged Batty by the wrist. He followed her into the dark of the bastel.

The door had long been burned and torn away, so there was no barrier there, but beasts shifted nervously and squealed in old stalls – Maramaldo's finer mounts, kept drier and safer. Above, the trap to the next level was open and a voice echoed hoarsely down it.

'Juup? Is that you? Juup? Where is Sabin? What is going on?'

Not 'Captain General'. Just Sabin. There is the full measure of Rafael's standing with Maramaldo's old guard, he thought.

The ladder shifted and a figure came down, awkwardly fast. At the bottom, he froze to stillness at the cold touch of steel on his neck.

'Holy Cross,' Batty said, seeing the scars. 'Who is above? Itemise them all or I will open your thoughts to the light of day.'

Holy Cross thought he might get from under the barrel before the whirr made the spark that ignited the powder in the pan. The thought lasted a heartbeat and no more.

'The *kinder*,' he said, resigned and bitter, 'Babe and all.'

'No one set to watch?'

'Me.'

Sister Faith was already on the ladder, the damask cloth flung over one shoulder because she could not climb with it wrapped round her. For a moment Holy Cross stared at her naked rear before a hard poke with the barrel changed his view.

The trumpet blared again; Sabin was out there, trying to bring order to the chaos and realising now who had done it. Realising all his powder store had gone.

Batty jerked his head to where the lurid blood-glow flared and dipped as the Big Tent burned away to nothing and Cornelius with it.

'Get gone,' he said to Holy Cross, giving him a shove. The man looked warily at Batty, expecting to be shot in the back as a cruel jest just as he reached the door. It was what Maramaldo might have done and Batty saw his look and curled a lip.

'Run or die.'

Holy Cross ran. Batty stuffed the dagg into his belt and climbed the ladder to the upper croft, wary as a dog fox in a farmyard.

He saw Sister Faith, naked and sliding into a dress provided by Sister Charity, who scowled at him and told him to turn his back. Sister Faith laughed.

'He has seen more of me than even Christ himself,' she said and Charity signed the cross by reflex – then laughed.

'Aye – we are far from the convent now, Sister.'

'Is any other here?' Batty demanded, looking round suspiciously.

'None but childer,' Sister Charity replied and they came out of the shadows, as if summoned – Batty struggled to remember their names, but they announced them to save him the trouble, each one accompanied by a curtsey, as if they were dressed in their finest instead of char-smeared rags. Joan, Margaret and Alice. Sister Charity, now that Sister Faith was decent in homespun, plucked the baby up and cooed him to quiet with his name – Stephen.

'Daniel you know,' Sister Faith said and there he was, gangling and hunched, with his glower and pearl-drop earring and a knife in his belt that he wanted in his hand. Batty nodded to him.

'Understand me, boy,' he said. 'Men will be coming for us. If you look to me to be aiding them in any way, I will…'

'What did you do to Juup?' Daniel demanded in a voice that wanted to be broken but wasn't yet. Batty blinked and realised that, of all Maramaldo's men, the boy had fastened on to Juup. Maybe he saw him as a father because that was long-lost from him – if he ever had one at all. Batty recalled his own and the lessons dinted into him, done with love and harshness both. He had no milk of human kindness left.

'Dead,' he answered blankly. 'Just outside the door.'

'Did you kill him?' the boy demanded, trembling hard enough to vibrate.

'In single combat? Blade against blade, all glorious like you imagined?' Batty responded hoarsely, then laughed, shaking his head.

'Half a coo fell on him,' he declared. 'He is lying under it covered in shite. That's how paid sojers end up, boy, that or something kin to it There is little glory in war.'

'You killed him.'

'Aye, aye – I threw the hind-end of an ox at him with my single mighty arm.'

'You blew up the camp.'

Batty saw the boy was wide-eyed and angry; he threw off the comfort of Sister Charity's arm and moved into the shadows. Batty watched him go and then turned quietly to Sister Faith.

'Watch that Daniel,' he said. 'Best if he does not get near a serious weapon. We have to hunker in here for a while until the weight of Wallis and the Trained Bands of Ogle come down on a Sable Rose with no powder nor shot for their fancy guns.'

'He's a boy,' Sister Faith answered. 'Afraid and having been put through a deal in the last few days.'

'So have your girls,' Batty pointed out. 'So have you and Charity. None of you look to the likes of Juup and Holy Cross to soothe their tremble.'

She had more to say but he moved away from it to a slit window, trying to see if any of the shouting and horn-blowing was making anything better out of the chaos. He did not want better, but Sabin was good. He was no

Maramaldo, but he was good enough to shuffle them into shape.

There was a sour smear of milk-light heralding dawn; with luck Ogle's men were already approaching and with even more, Wallis would appear with his lances and riders.

He heard the trapdoor open and turned in time to see Daniel vanish down it like a stoat down a hole.

'Christ – was no one watching him?'

He scrambled down the ladder in time to see the heels vanish out the door and cursed him to the ninth circle of Hell, then followed – only to come to a skidding halt at the sight of the boy held in the cradling circle of an arm. Behind it was a face and another arm with a dagg in it; it looked like the tunnel drop into a dungeon pit.

Sabin grinned. 'You will call off those dog-riding prickers and the Trained Band. Else I will kill the boy here and then start on those cursed nuns and their childer.'

Batty felt the cold haar of morning settle on him, all the way to the bone and the depth of his belly; his arm and hand did not feel like it was his own, but he raised it anyway, the axe-handled dagg fat and heavy.

'You should know,' he said levelly, 'that as soon as yon lad goes down, I will blow the inside of your head so far away you couldnae find it with maps and almanacs.'

'I was coming to you…' Daniel said hoarsely and had it cut off by Sabin's hand on his neck.

'You will not risk this stupid boy,' he said. 'I know you Barthelmy. You are soft on kits.'

There were shouts and more trumpet blasts, making Sabin jerk his head round, then back again; Batty knew that the Sable Rose had spotted the enemy.

'Your bairns are calling you, Rafael. No' easy to be the leader, is it?'

'Do what I ask, Barty – else you are of no use to me.'

Batty saw the boy get his hand on the hilt of his knife and wanted to cry out for him to stop, but knew that would spark everything up. Instead, he did a foolish thing – he lurched towards Sabin, who reared back and fired.

There was an instant of smashing pain on Batty's chest; he felt the impact of it throw the legs out from under him and propel him backwards so that he fell and skidded in a mist of dirty smoke. He lay, gasping for breath and unable to get any in or out; something trickled on his skin.

Shot through, he thought bitterly, mouth sucking like a landed fish. Bloody stupid way to die. Heard screams but they seemed far away and he finally managed a breath just as the whirlpool void sucked him in to oblivion.

Twa Corbies Tower
A week later

Four he hurt, an' five he slew, till down it fell
himsell O; there stood a fause lord him behind,
who thrust his body through…

'Yer back I see. The De'il still needs you loose in the land.'

He blinked and swam for a bit before everything settled on Satan's own imp in the person of a hag with a face like scorched leather flap. He knew the face, fought for voice and eventually managed a croak.

'Where…?'

'No' Heaven – the Wallis tower at Twa Corbies.' The voice pinched him like thumb and forefinger, slapping some recognition into his fog.

'Trottie.'

'The same. You should be deid.'

'He is not, clearly. I will thank you not to slather him with whatever cow-piss remedies you used last time you met.'

Trottie drew back and squinted at Sister Faith. 'I spent most of my time wiping the contents of yer own wee potions, blood and some noxious grease – they vials he had tucked up under his doublet, which broke. There was some pottery bits as well.'

She paused and glared from one to the other, then made the horn-sign to Sister Faith's signed cross. 'I said last time I saw them. I said then so I did – that's no poison or love potion you had in them wee jugs. Yet there was power there. I wiped away a deal of blood and found no wound, only a great bruise like the hoof of a horse.'

'Probably the pale rider,' Sister Faith threw in tartly. 'Looking for you.'

'Ha – he can look…'

'He will find you in iron chains at the stake,' chimed a new voice and Sister Charity thrust her face into the debate. 'If ever you leave this moss, besom.'

Trottie hissed like a cat, then scuttled for the door, trailing a cracked bell of a laugh.

God, thought Batty. I instantly knew I had not made it through the Gates when I saw her face… but he could not work out why he was still on God's good earth at all…

'Sabin?' he croaked and Sister Faith nodded as if she had expected it.

'Daniel stabbed him in the cods,' she said, 'but that was after he shot you.'

'I felt it,' he managed. He felt it shoot him through the backbone. Straight through his heart – how was he not dead?

'This,' Sister Faith said and presented the wooden bowl, cradled in her hands like a loving cup; Sister Charity crossed herself and muttered prayers.

It was inside my jack, Batty remembered. Coddling yon wee vials.

'Mair uses then just to drink broth from,' he croaked and Sister Faith smiled softly and Charity clapped her hands with seeming exultant joy.

'Is that what you did with it? Well, there it is. Not turned to dust nor ash. Thought worthy. The Archangel Michael right enough…'

Sister Faith held up the rough-carved bowl and turned it this way and that, reverently, gently. There wasn't a mark on it, as she pointed out.

'Yet this is where Rafael Sabin's shot struck. I suspect the shot struck a little more off-centre of the bottom – the resultant mark from the rim is the horseshoe bruise Trottie saw. The blood she wiped from you was Christ's own, taken from the Cross, vialed up and sealed with the provenance of the Templar knights. Likewise His last dying sweat. The force of the ball broke the pottery.'

'She burned the cloths,' Sister Charity said bitterly. 'So there is no more of it. Besom…'

Sister Faith smiled. 'The true treasures of Glastonbury, Batty – the blood and sweat of our Lord's last moments and the Holy Grail he drank from at the Last Supper. You have been anointed with one and blessed to sup from the other. God be praised.'

Rafael Sabin was led, hunched over and shuffling from the wound in his groin, to the gibbet in Carlisle and it must have come as a greater shock for him to see Maramaldo there, smiling benignly at him as Sabin danced in the air.

Yet Maramaldo was under his own sentence of hemping, waiting only on the scrawl of King Henry on a writ for it – but Fat Hal was away raising men for France and he already had the core of a new unit, mainly a grumble of foreign mercenaries called the Sable Rose. That Company was led by a new Captain General known as Holy Cross, who had petitioned to be carried across in the King's own flagship, the Mary Rose.

Batty learned all this sitting in the Auld Unicorn, a tavern halfway up the steepest climb of Edinburgh's West Bow. He listened closely, because no one knew more about what was going on with mercenaries or politics than Leone Strozzi, brother of Piero. Piero Strozzi had fought in Florence – against the Medici for all that he was married to one – and was coming to Scotland, fresh from being soundly thrashed by the Imperials and Spanish in a fight in the Italian mountains and looking for new pastures.

There were matters Batty knew that Leone didn't, some of which he exchanged and most of which he kept to himself.

He did not tell the big bluff man stuffing meat and ale in his beard that two nuns, now homespun good-wives of impeccable character had headed south to the last holding from the Glastonbury pie – a small manor in Kent. Accompanied by some children and a hard-eyed man-boy who would not be put off by any resistance from servants who thought the place forgotten and that they could live as they pleased.

He did tell Strozzi that the Sable Rose, Holy Cross proudly at their head, had marched on the Mary Rose to be taken to France. Since the King's flagship had sunk in the Solent north of the Isle of Wight only a month since, Strozzi's mouth forgot the pie and ale and dropped open for a long time.

Then he took off his hat and scrubbed his kiss-curl.

'All dead?'

'Unless God raised them up,' Batty replied curtly, not wanting to think on faces he'd known bloating in that salty deep.

'God's Wounds,' Strozzi breathed, then drank a long swallow and squinted at Batty.

'What of yourself?' he demanded. 'I hear you were shot – but you look hale to me.'

'Sabin was never good with a pistol,' Batty replied curtly, feeling the slow, strangely comforting, ache of the horseshow bruise, glorious as a sunset beneath shirt and jack. He did not miss the bowl, tried not to think of being covered in the blood and sweat of Christ… it would not be real, he thought. Those Templars swore to everything holy because their provenance raised the price of pig's blood and labourer's grease.

But still – it was possible, just possible, that the Lord's last leakings had transmuted the centuries to anoint me, Batty thought and shivered at the idea. If my lost arm grows back I will be on my knees all the same…

'Brother Piero will be looking for good men when he comes.'

'Not Maramaldo,' Batty muttered sourly. 'He will hang if God has the right and Fat Henry finds the time.'

Yet, even as he said it, he felt... regret. For all he denied it, Batty had been forced to admit that Maramaldo had been right – we are the same, you and I.

Leone laughed. 'I would not touch that one with gloves on,' he said, then signalled for more ale. 'What say you Batty? You are a good gun-layer and you know how to site and set defences besides. No match with a slow match either I hear...'

Batty thought about it in the whirl and noise and fug, the smells of ale and farts and old sweat. Someone cranked up a *vielle* and he raised his head at the tune. It would be Sister Faith, he thought, sending me the Lord's thoughts on matters.

O I hae dreamed a drearie dream,
ayont the isle of Skye.
I saw a dead man win a fight
and I thocht that man was I...

Author's Note

Most of this is fiction, set against a true tale – the Rough Wooing (a later term) was the period where an ailing Henry VIII tried to assert his power to ensure the union of England and Scotland with a marriage between his young son Edward and Mary Queen of Scots. The more violence he used, the more violence he met from Scots who would not be forced.

Ancrum Moor was a real battle, the latest in a sad list of them, and the victory was won in part by the big guns which I have Batty leading – the determined Scots foot faked a withdrawal that brought the English army – mainly German and Spanish mercenaries – in exultant pursuit right into the mouths of those cannon. What really won it, all the same, was the Border horse who had taken English money to fight the Scots – and who suddenly changed sides.

The Wallis of Twa Corbies is an invention, though the Wallis Clan was certainly extant in the 16th century, notably in South Yorkshire. The main clans of the English side of the Border were the Charltons, Dodds and Robsons among others.

The Egyptiani – Gypsies – were a feature of life on both sides of the Border and Johnny Faa, self-styled king, was indeed chartered by King James V in 1540 establishing his lordship over all the Gypsies in Scotland.

Fabrizio Maramaldo is all-too real. An illiterate from Naples or Calabria or perhaps somewhere in Spain, he was always listed as an 'Italian condottiere'. He fled Naples after murdering his wife, fought the Ottomans in Hungary and the French in Piedmont and his reverse at the siege of Asti – where Batty lost his arm – made him notorious until the incident with Ferruci, his arch-enemy.

Maramaldo attacked the wounded, dying and disabled Ferruci in full view of everyone, stabbing him to death and kicking the corpse while cursing him, an act which gained him a reservoir of disgust among the great and the good. So much so that today in the Italian language, he substantive *maramaldo* and the adjective *maramaldesco* means 'ruthless' or 'villainous'. There is also a verb *maramaldeggiare* in the sense of 'treat someone badly by ruthless mockery'. He died in 1552.

Lastly – Little Jack Horner. Always popularly thought to be a satirical rhyme on the misuse of power, in the 19th century a story began to gain currency that the rhyme is actually about Thomas Horner, who was steward to Richard Whiting, the last abbot of Glastonbury under the dissolution of monasteries ordered by Henry VIII.

It is asserted that, prior to the abbey's destruction, the abbot sent Horner to London with a huge Christmas pie which had the deeds to a dozen manors hidden within it as a gift to try to convince the King not to nationalise Church lands. During the journey Horner opened the pie and extracted the deeds of the manor Mells in Somerset which he kept for himself. It is further suggested that, since the manor properties included lead mines in the Mendip Hills, the plum is a pun on the Latin *plumbum*, for lead. While records do indicate that Thomas Horner became the owner of the manor, both his descendants and subsequent owners of Mells Manor have asserted that the legend is untrue and that Wells purchased the deed from the abbey.

I hope I have done them all some sort of justice. If not – crank up the *vielle* and play a different tune.

Glossary

APOSTLES – A collection of wooden, stoppered flasks filled with an exact amount of powder and ball for a single pistol or caliver shot, which made for quicker and more reliable loading. They were suspended by a cord from a leather bandolier worn by arquebusiers, seven flasks in front and five in back, for a total of twelve, hence the name.

BARMKIN – A defensive wall built round a castle or keep, usually with a walkway for sentries.

BIRL – To spin round.

BILL – An official warrant, issued by a March Warden or the like, demanding that a suspected miscreant present himself for judgement. If ignored – fouled – then someone appointed by the Wardens would go and bring him to justice. This was Batty's job until the war stopped all Warden activity.

BLACKMEAL – A payment made, in coin or bartered goods (grain or meal), to the more powerful family who could do you harm. In essence, the 16th century Borders were run like Mafia bosses and paying to keep them away was sometimes the only recourse. Origin of the word 'blackmail'.

CALIVER – An improved version of the arquebus, in that it had standard bore, making loading faster and firing more accurate.

CRUCK HOUSE – A building made of a frame of curved timbers set in pairs. Used to build small huts up to large barns, it was the simplest cheapest building method of the medieval age.

CRUSIE – A simple container with a wick that provided light.

DAGG – A pistol as opposed to an a long-barrel musket.

DEBATABLE LAND – An area ten miles long and four wide created by edicts from both countries about settling it or raising any permanent structures. The area's people ignored this and powerful clans moved in, notably the Armstrongs. For three hundred years they effectively controlled the land, daring Scotland or England to interfere. It became a haven for outlaws of all sides.

GRAYNE – Borders word for 'clan'. 'Name' is another version of it.

HEMP – Hanging, from the material used to make the rope.

HIRPLE – Limp.

HOT TROD – The formalities of pursuing reivers, usually by the forces of the Wardens. Up to six days after the seizure of any cattle by thieves taking them across the other side of the Border, the forces attempting to recover them and apprehend the guilty were permitted to also cross the Border freely in pursuit. They had to do it with 'hue and cry, with horn and hound' and were also obliged to carry a smouldering peat on the point of a lance to signify the task they were on.

JACK – The ubiquitous garment of the Border warrior – the jack of plates. Most ordinary Border fighters had a jack, a sleeveless jerkin with either iron or the cheaper horn plates sewn between two layers of felt or canvas.

JALOUSE – To surmise or suspect.

KERTCH – A kerchief, usually used by married women to cover their hair.

KISTING – Funeral. A kist is a chest or a box.

LATCHBOW – A cheap crossbow, light enough to be used from horseback, with a firing mechanism as simple as a door latch. The power was light but at close range it would wound or kill an unprotected man and knock the wind out of a one wearing a jack.

PERJINK – Proper, neat.

PRIMERO – 16th century poker where you attempt to bluff your competitors out of betting against you. Players *vie* or *vye* by stating how high a hand they are claiming to have and can flat-out lie to overstate it. It was played using a 40-card deck, but there are no surviving written rules, only descriptions.

RAMSTAMPIT – Blustering loud boaster.

RIDE/RIDING – The raids mounted by one reiver family, or Name, against another, either for robbery or revenge. Depending on how many family members and affiliated Names you could get to join you, these were brief affairs of one night or ones involving several thousand men who could lay waste to entire villages and towns on either side of the Border. The usual Riding times lasted from Lammas (August 1) to Candlemas (February 2).

SCUMFISH – How raiders got people out of their bastel houses – the modern definition is 'to disgust or stifle' which is what raiders did, by getting on the roof and throwing damp burning bracken down the chimney, essentially smoking out the inhabitants. The defenders kept covered wooden buckets handy, forked the burning bracken into them and closed the lid until the contents could be thrown back outside.

SKLIMMING – Moving fast. Can also mean throwing stones across a pond.

SLORACH – Any bog or morass or filthy mess you might step in.

SLOW MATCH – Early firearms were called 'matchlocks' because they were ignited by a smouldering fuse, called a slow match, brought down into the pan. Keeping a slow match smouldering required constant vigilance, a good manufacturer – and no rain. By the middle of the 16th century, pistols with a wheel-lock mechanism were being made, which utilised an iron pyrite to create sparks and was more reliable.

SNELL – Cold, icy.

STRAVAIGIN – Wandering or scattered.

TESTOON – Coin minted during the last days of Henry VIII, with more copper than silver in it, so that the portrait of Henry on one side wore down to the copper on his embossed nose becoming known as 'coppernoses' as a result. They transmuted, eventually into the English shilling.